TRAVELER OF HEART

ELLE KISH

EK

Copyright © 2024 Elle Kish.

All rights reserved. No part of this publication may be reproduced, distributed, or transmitted in any form or by any means, including photocopying, recording, or other electronic or mechanical methods, without the prior written permission of the publisher, except in the case of brief quotations embodied in critical reviews and certain other noncommercial uses permitted by copyright law.

ISBN: 9798339216018

Library of Congress Control Number: 2024912138

Any references to historical events, real people, or real places are used fictitiously. Names, characters, and places are products of the author's imagination.

Front cover image by Ronny Varela and Shelby Mandernack.

First printing edition 2024.

ElleKish.com

For every twenty- or thirty-something that fell back in love with fantasy novels after a ten-year hiatus and now they're your whole personality: this one's for you.

Also, to my husband. Sorry I straight up ignored you for months to write this.

PRONOUNCIATION GUIDE

Dorolan: Door-o-lan
Fracilonia: Fra-ci-loan-eya
Pateko: Pa-tee-ko
Roladif: Roll-a-dif
Schasumetsats: Sch-az-oom-ets-ats
Skaans: Sk-ah-ns
Sol Salnege: Sol Saln-ege
Stobon: Sto-bone
Tswangohin: Swa-go-heen
Tesalte: Teh-salt

PROLOGUE

September 22, 2006

The air smells of last night's rain, still pooled on the edges of the pavement. Consulting my phone's GPS, I turn right, out of the gleam of the streetlight, and walk up to the freshly painted red facade of The Coffee Bean. Today is my first day as their newest barista. Yesterday, I went over all of the recipe cards, looked up online how to use an espresso machine, and prayed to God that I didn't burn the place down.

My watch reads 5:45 a.m. "Early is on time and on time is late," I whisper aloud, recalling one of the few mantras my mother instilled in me as I question my arrival time. Paul, the owner, said my shift starts precisely at 6 a.m. and that I'll meet another barista named Gabriella to start my training. Leaning against the wall under the white overhang, I wait anxiously for her arrival.

Cool morning wind hits the back of my neck, sending a chill down my spine. My heels bounce nervously up and down as I look down the street, realizing how dark it still is. Mount Dora is a safe, quiet enough town. At least, it's quieter than Orlando, but something about being alone in the dark makes me uneasy. Distracting myself, I take a deep breath and look at the cute shops that line the strip and the massive oak trees in the park across the street. Hopefully the morning shifts will be less daunting once the Christmas lights are up in a few months.

Footsteps come from my left. Am I about to be murdered? Right as my life is beginning to feel like my own? After all, I'm an eighteen-year-old girl, alone, outside before the sun has risen. The perfect target.

Ready to face the threat, I pivot quickly. Thankfully, instead of a man in a ski mask holding a sledgehammer, it's a short, curvy young woman. Her curly blonde hair bounces as she jiggles a set of keys from the jean skirt she wears over black leggings. She unlocks the door of The Coffee Bean. This must be Gabriella.

"Good morning!" I say with as much enthusiasm as I can muster before 6 a.m.

The girl looks up from the lock, startled, revealing dark circles and smudged mascara under bright blue eyes. "Sorry hun, we don't open for another thirty minutes. We have to get everything ready. But if you come—"

"Oh, no! I'm not a customer. My name is Daphne." I point to my name tag and stick out my hand. "Usually, I go by Daph. Paul hired me a few days ago. Today's my first day. You must be Gabriella!"

Giving me a puzzled look, she reaches out her hand to meet mine. "You can call me Gabby. Sorry, Paul didn't mention that you were starting today. Let's get on inside." The slightest hint of a southern twang develops the more she speaks. We walk inside and Gabby makes herself a cup of coffee. Once she takes a few sips, her eyes brighten. She glances down at the new employee paperwork I handed her and smiles brightly. "Your birthday was yesterday? Mine was last week. I turned twenty-one. It says here you're only eighteen. You're a baby! What did you do for your birthday?"

Pushing a lock of hair behind my ear, I remind myself not to overshare. There's no need to unload the reasons why I needed to move out of my mom's house as fast as I could. "I moved into my first apartment as a birthday present to myself. So I spent yesterday unpacking."

Last year, I worked my ass off to graduate high school a year early. The second I could sign for my own place, I did.

My mom had me when she was nineteen. She couldn't tell me who my father is, but she always said I must look like him, because I got none of her likeness. She's a tall, tan, blonde bombshell with big blue eyes. I'm an average-height brunette with boring brown eyes on a plain round face. My pale skin burns the moment I go outside without sunscreen. If she told me I was dropped off by the stork, I'd believe her.

She married Richard when I was ten. My four half-siblings are all under the age of six. To say that the house is chaotic is an understatement. Since meeting my stepdad, she never paid me much attention. She isn't a bad mom; I just got lost in the crowd. When I told her I was moving out, she seemed relieved. Seven of us living in a four bedroom house was getting pretty cramped, especially as my siblings got older.

Someone told me about quaint, quiet Mount Dora and I took the forty-five minute drive from my mom and Richard's to visit. The cute town had a magical vibe and I felt a tug that I was supposed to move here. I'd dreamed of living in a small town since I was a young girl. After considering my options, I decided it was close enough to be a safe test run of adulthood.

Shoot, did I space out? When I look up, Gabby is staring at me with concern. Great, what an excellent first impression: the young, spacey new girl.

"I did the same thing. Congratulations and happy birthday, girl." She shuffles the papers into a neat pile. "I'll take you out sometime when we're not working to show you around the town."

With a calming breath, I let a small smile creep onto my face. I think I've made my first friend here. Hopefully we have more in common than The Coffee Bean; I don't want to end up being her clingy new co-worker.

Gabby gives me a black apron with The Coffee Bean logo on it—a white bean with "Coffee" written in cursive script across it. I pull it over my head. Over the next thirty minutes, Gabby teaches me how to work the cash register and the correct way to write orders on the cups. L for latte, M for macchiato, A for Americano.

"Usually, there's one person on the register and one person making the drinks. But lately, it's been just me in the morning since the school year started. Most of the girls have morning classes at the community college." The smell of fresh ground coffee fills the air as she grinds beans and turns on the machines to prepare for the day. "I swear it's not all taking names. After we survive the morning rush I'll teach you how to use the machines," she promises apologetically.

"No, no, this is important. I don't need to be making enemies because I messed up someone's name or order." We both laugh at my bad attempt at a joke. She doesn't know I'm only half kidding. Mount Dora is so small, everyone probably knows everyone. I want to make sure I'm liked here.

As soon as the clock hits 6:30, customers stagger through the door. Slow bodies move like zombies to the counter, searching for their life elixir. I ring them up while Gabby makes the drinks. It amazes me how quickly she makes each order, and what's more impressive is that she doesn't mess up a single one. *Focus, smile, remember their names.* It'll come naturally... eventually.

After we get orders out for the last of the customers in line, Gabby gives me a high five. "You killed it! We're going to make a great team." A smile pushes her round cheeks to her eyes. We get to work cleaning the machines and a relieved smile crosses my face. I did it.

Gabby pulls her phone out of her apron pocket. "Fuck. It's my kid's daycare." She answers the phone, "Hello, yes this is Logan's mom. He does?" She unties her apron. "Well, have you tried calling his dad?" She lifts her apron over her head. "Of course he didn't pick up. Okay, I'll be right there." She grabs her worn tote bag from under the counter.

I raise an eyebrow. "Everything okay?"

"Yeah, my baby is sick at daycare. I need to go get him and bring him to his dad's. Do you think you can hold down the fort by yourself for thirty minutes? It's just up the road, I swear. I'll owe you one." She hangs up her apron on a hook behind the counter.

My heart begins to race as the panic sets in. "Gabby, I'm not sure... I don't even know how to make a drink yet."

"You'll be fine. No one ever comes in at this time. The whole town is at work by now. We won't have another customer until lunch," she calls over her shoulder and walks out the door before giving me the chance to respond.

Oh god, please don't let anyone walk in.

Glancing at the machines, I try deciphering which buttons do what. These are way fancier than the Mr. Coffee my mom has. Why do these things need so many buttons? The videos I found online did not prepare me well enough. There can't possibly be this many different ways to make a cup of coffee.

No one's going to come. *It's just thirty minutes*, I repeat to myself over and over until fifteen minutes pass and I start to believe it. Figuring now is a good time, I grab my bag from under the counter and reach for the orange plastic bottle that holds the ADHD medication I've been on since middle school. I fill a cup from the water spigot against the back wall.

As I pop the blue pill in my mouth and swallow, the door creaks open. Shoving the bottle in my bag, I throw it back under the counter and spin around to face the door. Looking at me through stunning jade-green eyes is the most beautiful man I have ever seen. He has tan skin, short blond hair, and looks a few years older than I am. A charming butterfly-inducing smile pulls at the corners of his perfect lips as he walks up to me. My heartbeat quickens. Why is he walking toward me? Oh right, because I'm at work at my new job and he probably wants to order a coffee that I don't know how to make.

Remembering I'm indeed working, I smile and give him my most chipper "Good morning!"

Close up, his features are more alluring: big round eyes, clean thick brows and sharp cheekbones. Smiling curiously, he looks me up and down. If my heart beats any faster, it is going to jump right out of my chest.

"Good morning. I haven't seen you here before. You must be new." Intrigue and amusement play through his low voice.

Is it that obvious? With shaking hands, I pick up a cup and marker from the counter. "Yep! Just started today! What can I get for ya?"

"An Americano, please." He pulls a thin black wallet out of the back pocket of his well-fitting Levi's. He smiles at me again, stealing my breath. Surely it isn't legal to be that good looking.

"Coming right up. Can I get your name?"

His face scrunches slightly and his eyes shift to the side in confusion, as if to say 'How do you not know my name?' Then his perfect smile returns. "It's Wyatt."

In cursive, I write his name and the letter A on the cup and turn to face my enemy: the coffee machines. Which one is an Americano again? Digging into my brain, I beg it to recall how to make one from the hours of coffee recipe videos I watched over the last few days. Americano. Espresso and water. I can do that. The machines taunt me as I stare at them. His eyes don't leave me as I continue to stare blankly, trying to decipher which machine will make the correct drink.

"It's the one on the left," he calls playfully from the opposite side of the counter.

"Uh, yeah, I know that," I say defensively, approaching the machine, no less confused about how to proceed than a few seconds ago. The door opens again. Another customer. Great.

When I look up, Wyatt is behind the counter. I must have spaced out again. He takes his leather jacket off, revealing muscular forearms, and puts Gabby's apron over his white t-shirt. "Here, let me help." He takes the cup from my hand. Somehow, he gets the machine to make four shots of espresso and adds hot water from the second spigot.

All I can do is blink. This man, this gorgeous man, probably thinks I'm the dumbest woman to ever walk this Earth. He's probably going to tell all his hot friends in town about the dumb new girl at the coffee shop. There goes not ruining everything on my first day.

"I am so sorry," I mutter. "I just started a few hours ago and I haven't learned how to make the drinks yet. Gabby had an emergency. She told me no one would come in." My face sinks into my hands.

"Don't worry, I've got some time. I can help you until she gets back. My parents are friends with Paul, he won't mind. Promise." He winks and I notice how thick his dark lashes are.

This is either a blessing or a curse. Hopefully, he takes pity on me and doesn't tell Paul that he hired a girl who can't figure out how to run the espresso machine. Taking the lifeline he's throwing me, I take the next couple of orders from the growing line of customers Gabby promised wouldn't come in. Wyatt makes their coffee. All of the customers seem to know him. He exchanges friendly conversation with all of them, most of them asking him how his parents are doing. Small-town things, I guess.

Wyatt hands the last man in line his drink. "Here you are, Teddy. See you for Sunday football."

The tall, handsome older gentleman with light brown cropped hair smiles at me as he grabs his coffee. "Good luck with this one." He winks at Wyatt, who's hanging up Gabby's apron and putting his jacket back on.

With a sigh, I rest my hands on the counter. "Thank you so much. You didn't have to do that. How can I repay you?"

Pretending he's thinking incredibly hard about how I'll return the favor, Wyatt puts his hand to his chin. He leans onto the opposite side of the counter and brings his face inches from mine. "You can thank me by learning how to use this contraption by the time I'm back here tomorrow morning so that I don't have to make my own coffee."

Laughing, I step back from the counter. "Alright, I think I can make that happen," I say cautiously, unsure if I'll be able to fulfill my promise. But he's coming back tomorrow. The thought of seeing him again sends my heart fluttering.

"Great, I'll see you in the morning." Grabbing his lukewarm Americano off the counter, he walks out the door, tipping his head at Gabby as she walks back in.

Throwing her apron back over her head, she stares at me and back over her shoulder at Wyatt as he walks down the street. "What was Wyatt Silver doing here?" Man, this guy really does know everyone. Or at least everyone knows him.

"He was getting a cup of coffee." I pause. "But... When I couldn't figure out how to use the espresso machine, he stayed and helped me make other people's drinks. He said he knew Paul, so I figured this time it was fine. I'm sorry, I panicked. I didn't know what else to do."

Why can't I lie? Surely I won't have this job for much longer.

She looks surprised, but not angry. "Weird. Yeah, I won't say anything as long as you don't say anything about me leaving to go grab Logan."

A too-loud laugh of relief escapes me and she laughs too. "I pinky swear." Linking pinkies, we giggle like old friends.

We get to work cleaning the dishes Wyatt and I created. "So, what can you tell me about him?"

"Who, Wyatt?" Gabby puts on a fresh pot of coffee.

"Yeah, what's his deal? It seems like everyone knows him here." Straightening up the counter, I try to sound as casual as I can while I try to figure out where the coffee stirrers are supposed to go.

"Well, he's super hot. The town's resident perfect all-American boy. So, I know that." Her lips pull into a tight, knowing smile. "How do you take your coffee?"

I roll my eyes. "Obviously. I mean, do you know anything else about him? And lots of cream and sugar. Basically milk with coffee. And ice."

She pours coffee and adds cream and sugar into two cups, handing me the almost white one. "He's a couple years older than me. He played football in high school before he went off to some fancy college up north. No one's heard from him in years. He's twenty-three now if I'm doing my math right. He just moved back to town after taking time off from school to travel and do this antiquing thing that his family is into. He and his twin sister, Whitney, are getting masters degrees at one of the schools in Orlando."

"Impressive," I say, taking a sip of the perfectly sweet coffee to hide my uncontainable smirk.

"Everyone knows them because their parents are these really rich, eccentric people. They have the biggest house in town. Despite all their money, they're all incredibly nice. Plus they're great tippers." She pulls a delicately folded twenty-dollar bill from the tip jar. "They're a little weird, though. Why do you want to know so badly anyway?" The look she gives me tells me she knows exactly why I want to know more about my Prince Charming.

A blush rises in my cheeks. "Just curious."

She takes a long sip of coffee and grins mischievously as she pulls the cup away from her lips. "Well, I won't discourage it... but going after the hottest guy in town? That'll ruffle some feathers, my friend."

CHAPTER ONE

October 2, 2024

"All right guys! Are you all packed? It's time to head to the shop to meet everyone!" I shout down the hallway. The sound of suitcase wheels and three sets of little footsteps echoing off the hardwood floor tells me they heard me.

My in-laws, Mel and Gina Silver, have an obsession with antiques. Mel, Gina, and Mel's best friend, Teddy, are taking the kids on the annual family antiquing trip in Europe. Usually I go with them, but I can't endure this year.

This trip will be the first time I've been away from the kids since they started homeschool last year. I've spent every waking moment since the accident filling our days with distractions and outings, creating happy memories for them. It's unbearable thinking about not being with them. They've hardly left my sight in the past year. At night, I even let them sleep with me in my otherwise too empty bed.

"Move faster!" Ariella shouts, irritated, at her brothers, Ronan and Ryan, as they tumble into the living room.

At thirteen, Ariella is sassier and bossier than ever. She was born right after our fourth wedding anniversary. She's a replica of her dad in both looks and personality, utterly brilliant, strong-willed, and opinionated. Four years and a few rounds of failed IVF later, we had the twins. They both look more like me, with round faces, light brown hair, and big dark eyes. Luckily for them, they inherited their dad's thick lashes and good eyebrows. They're brave, mischievous, and are always getting into trouble together.

"Do you guys have everything? Are you excited?"

"I can't wait! Grandma says we can visit Galileo's museum when we're in Italy." Ariella smiles wide, giddy joy filling her features. She's been really into astronomy lately—the stars, the planets, all of it. Her Aunt Whitney got her a book on stargazing and a telescope for her birthday two months ago. It's turned into quite the obsession.

I'm happy she's so excited. She hasn't been very enthusiastic about anything lately. "That's good, baby. You guys are going to have so much fun. You'll have to take lots of pictures for me."

"I will." She looks up at me with her big green eyes—her father's eyes. Eyes that hold wisdom and understanding beyond her age. "You're going to have fun on your trip too, Mom." She gives me a big hug.

It takes everything in me to hold back the tears I feel trying to surface. As I grab a few of their things, a glimmer on the wall catches my eye. Light dances off the pile of Wyatt's birthday balloons that sit deflated on the floor.

I'll clean them up when I get back.

Grabbing my Americano off the entry table, I walk over the wine-stained carpet. I really need to replace it when I get back so I don't have to live with the memory of how that stain got there. When I reach the front door, I pause. Even as we approach the first anniversary of the accident, sometimes I still think Wyatt will walk back through the door with an iced coffee for me, an Americano for him, and donuts for the kids. How will my heart ever heal from this kind of pain?

I've been trying my best for my kids. While they're with their grandparents, I'll be on a grief retreat that Gina set up for me.

We load up the van and once everyone is settled, we start the daunting ten minute drive from our house to our shop on the downtown strip.

Driving to work is always the worst part of my day. I have to pass every restaurant we used to eat at, the shops we frequented, and The Coffee Bean. That one is the hardest. My chest tightens and I hold my breath as we pass the long faded red exterior. They say time heals all wounds, but how can it when everything around me keeps ripping it wide open?

I wish we could leave this town. Move across the world and have a fresh start in a city that didn't hold so many memories.

Pulling the van in my usual parking spot, I look up at the faded sign above our shop. When Wyatt graduated from business school his parents gifted him an antique store, combining his degrees with the family hobby. His mom very creatively named the store Silver's Antiques, which Wyatt quickly amended to Silver's Antiques and Books, gifting me a whole part of the store to run. I quit my job at The Coffee Bean and worked with him to build one of the most popular shops in town.

Wyatt's twin sister, Whitney, graduated with her masters in folklore and started working with us soon after. The flexibility of working for her brother allowed her to continue her research at the same time. Not many jobs would have allowed her to travel as frequently as she did. Part of me envied her; funded mostly by her parents, she got to travel all over the world studying myths and fairytales. Gina's only condition was that she brought back antiques to sell from each trip.

The kids run inside, leaving me to lug in all their crap. My eyes drift across the street to *that* spot. The scorch marks washed away this summer from the heavy rain, they're still burned in my mind. Images of Wyatt's car in that spot, or what was left of it when I arrived, haunt me constantly. With a shake of my head, I clear my mind and take the luggage inside.

Whitney and Gabby have already opened up the shop for the day. Last year, Gabby agreed to leave the stay-at-home mom life to help us out and has been working for us since. She and Whitney don't necessarily see eye to eye on a lot of things but I'm happy I get to work with my best friend again.

"Alright kids, go hang out on the couch while we wait for Grandma, Grandpa, and Teddy. And remember, don't touch anything." Getting myself and their suitcases over the uneven threshold is a struggle. Whitney walks the kids over and tells Ariella she'll braid her hair. Seeing Whitney is hard; she looks just like Wyatt. She has the same thick blonde hair—which she always has in some sort of intricate braid—sharp features, muscular build, and heartbreakingly similar jade-green eyes.

"Hey." I smile at Gabby as she grabs one of the overpacked suitcases from me and puts it behind the counter. She looks almost exactly the same as she did when we met. Expensive facials and botox, paid for by her new husband, keep her skin youthful and bright. I'm jealous, but Wyatt didn't agree with those kinds of things. He always told me he preferred my natural beauty.

"Hey, how are you holding up today?" she asks, looking at me carefully, assessing my mood. Just like everyone else in town, her face is always full of pity. I know I went through something horrible that no one should ever go through, but I wish my best friend would stop treating me like I'm so fragile. "I'm good. Same old, same old. How's the store been today?"

"It's been fine. You know Saturdays, always busy. Hell, every day is busy. Are you ready for your retreat? I still can't believe you, of all people, agreed to go on a retreat without access to your phone."

"Yep, I'm all packed and as ready as I can be." I shrug. The retreat's website says it's an extremely unique experience. It's two weeks in the woods and the entire campground is tech-free. They advertise healing the heart through meditation, finding yourself, and allowing yourself to feel happiness again.

I'm skeptical of how well it's going to go; there probably isn't another thirty-six-year-old widow attending. Personally, I'm not sure how happy a bunch of sad people in the woods are going to be able to get. But, the pictures of the mountains and lake look like a good enough getaway, so I'm willing to give it a shot.

After the year I've had, I need a break. Whitney keeps telling me it's going to be good for me, and good for the kids to get a little sense of normalcy with the antiquing trip. I'm trying to convince myself of that.

"And it can't hurt," I add. "I heard going off the grid can be empowering. I don't think I could go on a family trip without Wyatt yet anyway. Maybe next year."

She gives me a warm, sympathetic smile. "It will be. You're so lucky to have Mel and Gina. You won the in-law lottery there, girl."

A few years after I met Wyatt, Gabby started dating her now husband, Tommy. They got pregnant with her second son, Isaac, and at the same time we got pregnant with the twins. The bonds of motherhood and our shared ADHD personalities are what really sealed our friendship into place. Tommy is fine enough, but his parents literally crawled out of the pits of hell. They expect Gabby to wait on Tommy hand and foot because he's the "provider." Luckily, they live in Alabama so she doesn't have to see them very often.

The door chimes and my kids squeal excitedly for Grandma and Grandpa. "Are you guys all ready to head to the airport?" Mel asks the kids, picking up the boys and swinging them in the air. He looks like an older version of Wyatt. *Genetics.* For someone in his seventies, Mel sure doesn't act like it. He has a muscular frame and youthful face. Once, he told me that no one ever believed his age. He and Gina are constantly traveling and doing things in the community. That's probably what keeps them both so young.

Gina takes off her oversized Versace sunglasses and places them on top of her freshly highlighted blonde bob. Her blue hooded eyes have the smallest amount of neutral eyeshadow on the lids. "Can Grandma have hugs?" The kids surround her, giving her a big group hug. Ariella comes almost to her shoulder already. "Where are your jackets? You guys can't go to the airport without your jackets. It's going to be freezing on the plane."

"Don't worry Gina, they all have one in their carry-ons. But it's still ninety degrees outside," I point out.

"Mel dear, why don't you start loading up all the stuff into the car," Gina says sweetly. The kids hurry outside with their grandpa. Gina plays with the stack of silver bangles that sit on her dainty wrist. "Daphne, I wish you were coming with us, but I think the retreat is going to be good for you. You know one of my girlfriends, Deb, went on this retreat a few years ago when her husband Marvin passed away. She came back feeling so much better. I know it's been really hard. Wyatt was the most special boy." Gina wipes a tear from her eye and gives me a tight hug.

With a heavy sigh, I bury my face in the shoulder of her pink top. She's wearing the perfume Wyatt gifted her on her birthday. He picked it out during a trip to Norway and bought it for her. He brought her something back from everywhere we went, whether it was a day trip to a theme park or somewhere across the world. I'm sure she misses his thoughtful little gifts. I'll have to remember to pick her up something while I'm on my trip.

She's grieving too, I know that. Her strength is admirable. Wyatt is the second son she's lost. They lost Wyatt's brother when he was just a child. They don't talk about him much, but they don't talk much about Wyatt anymore either. Everyone grieves differently, I suppose. Wyatt was the love of my life, but I can only imagine the pain his mother hides beneath her perfectly composed exterior.

A sad smile tugs at my lips. "I know he was. Thank you, Gina, for everything." I hug her back, blinking away any sign of sadness from my face. Leaving my hands on her shoulders, I pull back. "Are you sure you guys will be okay with all three of them by yourselves?"

I'm nervous for them to go without me, but Gina and Mel are

amazing grandparents. And Teddy has always been like a third grandparent for the kids. Plus, I couldn't handle the kids' disappointment if I didn't let them go. The trip has been an annual tradition since Wyatt and I started dating.

Running a hand down the pressed white linen pants that hang perfectly on her petite frame, she laughs. "Even if we weren't, I think they'd kill us if we cancel on them now. But trust me, if we could handle that one." She points at Whitney, who's dusting something on the other side of the store. "We can handle a dozen civilized children."

"You know, I can hear you!" Whitney calls, annoyed, from across the shop.

"Honey, it's nothing I haven't told you before." Pulling a tissue out of her Hermes bag, she blots her eyes. "Listen, when we get back, why don't you all come over for a game?"

The Silvers are known for hosting lavish events in their massive lake house. One of the first times I met them was at their house for a football party. Gina had it decorated in red and gold with plates upon plates of catered food. To impress them, I learned the name of every single player on the team and how the game worked. That won them over. From that day on, I was always invited for weekend football. Over the past year, the once huge parties dwindled down to Mel and Gina, Whitney, Teddy, the kids, and me. The eight of us are all we have.

"That'd be nice." Remembering how excited Wyatt and Mel used to get cheering for touchdowns, I smile.

"Don't worry, Daph, there are three of us and three of them. We're equally matched." Teddy laughs, his smile crinkling the skin around his brown eyes. He wraps his arm around my shoulder and gives me a quick squeeze.

After Wyatt passed away, Teddy stepped up and helped me out more than I could ever have imagined. Taking the kids to sports practices, dropping off dinner, and just being there when we needed him to be. He doesn't have a family of his own and was adopted into the Silver family long before I was around. Since I don't have a relationship with my parents, I've started to think of him as my honorary dad, too.

The kids run back inside saying, "We're ready!" in sing-song unison.

"Don't you dare leave without saying goodbye!" I hug and kiss each of them.

The twins wiggle free. "You're crushing us!" they complain as they run off to hug their aunt.

Giving Ariella one more tight squeeze, I whisper to her, "Take care of your brothers for me, okay? You're the biggest. Make sure you're watching over them."

She rolls her eyes dramatically. "I always am."

"Don't forget to have fun, though. Love you, baby." I kiss the top of her head before she runs to join her brothers.

More goodbyes are exchanged and they file out the door. They load into the Uber and drive away. As the car turns the corner out of sight, tears start streaming down my cheeks.

This is going to be a lot harder than I thought.

"Aw, Daph!" Gabby hugs me tightly and wipes my tears. "They'll be back! It's just a vacation!"

"I know, I know." I wipe the tears off my nose. "I'm just going to miss them."

It's only going to be two weeks and hopefully, I'll come back refreshed and with some new perspective. That way, I'll be able to get back to being a better mom for them. That's what this is all about for me—they deserve the best mom, and right now? I'm not that.

"Hey, when you get back into town, when you're feelin' up for it, Tommy has this friend. He's cute, rich, and single!" Gabby grins.

"Can you not talk about her dating anyone? She's clearly not ready. It's barely been a year." Putting her frustration into the rag she's dusting with, Whitney rolls her big green eyes. "Seriously Gabby, what's wrong with you?"

"Hey, she's gotta get back on the horse sometime. Us ladies don't stay young forever," she retorts, sticking her tongue out when Whitney turns her back to return to the shelves. Knocking Gabby on the shoulder, I silently tell her to knock it off. Whitney has never been someone whose bad side you want to be on, but since Wyatt died, she's been more testy. Like whatever kindness she had left with him.

"Thanks, Gabby, but Whitney's right. I'm not ready for that." I reach up to grab the snapdragon pendant I wear around my neck. I don't know if I ever will be either. Wyatt, he was… he was my soulmate. We were made for one another, I firmly believe that. I've thought that since the second he walked through the door of The Coffee Bean. No one could replace that kind of love. I haven't looked at another man or thought about dating since I met Wyatt. We were young, and he was my first serious boyfriend, but he was my everything.

And now he's gone. The idea of trying to let anyone else fill that spot in my life makes me want to puke.

The change in Gabby's demeanor makes it obvious that she can tell I'm uncomfortable with the idea. "It's okay, hun. You can take your time." She looks away and pretends to clean the counter.

A few grandfather clocks ring at the strike of noon. "Would you look at that, my shift is over, and I have to go grab Logan from his dad's. See you when you get back, Daph! Bye Whit!" Dropping the rag she had in her hand, Gabby grabs her keys, hugs me, and heads out the door.

Leaning on the counter, I wipe a finger through the dust Gabby didn't actually clean, then look over at Whitney. "You hate it when she calls you that, don't you?" Whitney has never been a fan of nicknames. She insists on using my full name 100 percent of the time.

She sighs. "Correct."

I run the damp rag through dust. "Well, why don't you tell her?"

"It's not worth it. She won't stop. I've already begged her." She slumps onto the counter.

Looking at one of the singing grandfather clocks and back at Whitney, I smile sympathetically. "It's lunchtime. Why don't you go get something to eat and take the rest of the day off?"

Relieved that I gave her an out, her eyes soften. "Are you sure?"

"Yes, Whitney. You've barely taken a day off since the shop opened. Go rest. I'll see you when I get back from the retreat. I'm going to get an Uber to the airport in a few hours and leave the van here for you to use. The keys will be in the cash register."

With a quick awkward hug, she's out the door. Whitney isn't the most touchy-feely person. As long as I've known her, she's always preferred to be alone. I don't think she's ever dated anyone either, or if she did, she didn't tell me. Other than Wyatt, she's never really had any friends.

Whitney's car drives past the window. Flipping the sign from "open" to "closed," I lock the door and head to the vintage, jade-green velvet couch that Wyatt and I spent months looking for to specifically fit this nook. We went to a dozen different estate sales until we found the perfect one. The now worn fabric is still soft beneath my hand as I run my fingers over it, pulling memories of how it used to feel when we first bought it. Late nights after work, Wyatt and I would usually end up here with glasses of wine, laughing and talking about our day. Releasing a deep sigh, I sink into the cushions and allow the tears to fall.

CHAPTER TWO

It takes me a few deep breaths to gather myself. My therapist told me that this is a part of the grieving process.

This is normal. Everyone grieves differently. Going on this retreat and letting the kids go to Europe are steps I need to take to get back to normal.

Getting up off of the couch, I gather some misplaced books, reorganizing for the first time in months. Running my finger along the edge of the shelf carves a deep line in the dust. The book nook, as we call it, is my area of the store.

Wyatt gave me this part of the store so I could quit my job at The Coffee Bean. I liked working there well enough, but it didn't pay very much. And Wyatt thought it would be more fun working together. Our little shop has really grown in the years since it opened. The once quaint town has become busy as people moved further out of Orlando and into the surrounding areas. The traffic isn't fun, but it definitely helps our business.

The book nook was once a trove of pre-loved books dutifully tended and displayed. The rare vintage ones are lovingly tucked behind a locked display case that Wyatt built. Now it's disheveled. The only sign of life is the occasional line a regular leaves in the layer of dust that coats the shelves while browsing.

Getting lost in a good book has always been one of my favorite things to do. It was my way of escaping my mom's crazy house growing up. Later, I read romance novels and stared over my pages at Wyatt while he studied at The Coffee Bean. As a mom, I started a book club with the moms from school drop-off in an attempt to make friends. We call ourselves "The Hot Moms Book Club." We meet every Wednesday morning—or at least we did.

The members still stop by every once in a while to visit, but not nearly as frequently.

This area needs to get back in shape. Maybe I can get the book club back up and running. Gabby tried to help me clean up and organize a few times, but I always got frustrated with her. She didn't understand my system and she can't tell a three dollar book from a 300 dollar book.

Maybe this trip will motivate me to pick up the pieces of my life. Might as well start a list of things I need to get done once I'm back. Lists are the only way I remember to get anything done. Pulling out my phone, I title a note "Shit that's gotta get done."

I add my first task: Clean and organize the book nook.

While putting the books back in their correct places, a faint humming sound comes from somewhere in the shop. My phone has no notifications. The humming continues, growing louder. Someone must have left a phone around here somewhere.

Time to investigate. With a tissue from the counter, I wipe my face, still damp from tears and snot. Whoever left the phone here will probably be back soon to claim it. No need to look like the world's most unstable antique store owner—even though that's exactly who I am right now.

I start searching high and low. No sign of it by the book nook or in any of the usual spots where people leave things. Nothing on top of the side tables or under the display cabinets. Crouching down to get a better look, I notice how dusty and honestly gross they are underneath. We've really gotten behind on our cleaning.

One more thing to add to my to-do list: move all of the display cases and deep clean.

The humming intensifies as I walk past Whitney's office door. The phone has to be in there. Whitney probably found it earlier and put it away in her desk. I try the handle, but the door is locked. I wish she had told me that she found a phone. What if the owner came while she was away and I told them we didn't have it?

With two bobby pins I pulled from my hair, I try to pick the lock. Just like how Wyatt taught me to do on old antique pieces we bought that didn't come with their keys. I smile wistfully at the memory of the devious look he gave me when I finally got it.

One... two... and on the third click the door springs open. The sound abruptly stops as I step into Whitney's office, turning a triumphant smile into a feeling of frustration.

Great. How am I supposed to find it now?

There's a distinct change in the air around me as I take a few more steps into the office. The room feels like it is full of static energy, like the summer air after a lightning storm. It must be my nerves. Did I remember my medicine this morning? I check the many drawers of Whitney's weathered walnut desk but find nothing. This place is a mess. Papers and stacks of books litter every surface. Now I remember why I haven't been in here since Wyatt died. It's a pigsty. There are store items, receipts, McDonald's wrappers, and god knows what else covering every square inch of this place. This room looks like it's straight out of an episode of Hoarders. The clutter fuels my anxiety.

When I get back, I'll help her get this place organized like Wyatt used to. Another item for the list.

I quickly add: Help Whitney get her life together.

Rummaging through the office, I look under the piles of books and papers strewn about the office. She has some interesting titles here, mostly fantasy novels and a few antique-looking ones in a language I don't recognize. One is a very old leather-bound book with a silver dragon on the cover. It's gorgeous. I'll have to ask her about it. Maybe I'll pick up reading again when I get back.

Where is this damn phone?

In the corner of the room, I notice something under a tarp. I don't remember us getting any new art. Art, we've learned, is a way riskier investment than furniture, so we usually discuss any big purchases beforehand. It takes all of my strength to tug the heavy piece out of the corner. Under the white dust cover is a tall, arched, floor-length mirror.

It's stunning. Taking a step back, I take in its full beauty. The mirror looks like it's made of real silver. The frame was forged to resemble tree branches, and at the top rests a small silver dragon. The bent prongs under the dragon tell me it used to hold some sort of stone that is now missing. I can't believe Whitney hasn't shown me this. It's probably worth a ton. My eyes meet my reflection and I look at myself for what seems like the first time in ages.

I look tired. I push the tendrils of what used to be curtain bangs behind my ears. The caramel highlights I used to pay a fortune for have grown out, my baggy sweatshirt is faded and torn at the edges of my sleeves, and the two-day-old leggings I'm wearing have seen better days.

A frown appears on my face as I notice the small lines that have taken up residence on my forehead and the corners of my large brown eyes.

I lost myself this past year, didn't I? When I get back, I'm making hair, facial, and botox appointments. I add: Spa Day.

Exhaling a sharp, annoyed breath at my growing list, I lean onto the mirror to pop a pesky pimple. The mirror starts humming at my touch.

There isn't a lost phone. It's the mirror making that sound.

Suddenly, it feels like liquid beneath my palm. Before I can pull it back, my hand starts sinking into the glass. Panic surges through me. No, no, no, what is going on? I try pulling with all of my strength, but I can't get my hand out. "Help!" I scream. My horrified expression stares back at me. One more pull—too hard, my balance falters and I tumble forward. A final scream echoes through the shop as the rest of my body is tugged through the liquid glass.

CHAPTER THREE

The nothingness around me swallows the sound of my petrified screams. My body feels weightless and sinkingly heavy all at once as I continue to fall through empty space—empty, except for a blinding light. A pulse of energy rushes through my body. Suddenly, the blinding light turns to darkness and my body hits the ground with a thud, knocking the wind out of me. Shock overtakes me as I lay on the hard, uneven surface, taking deep labored breaths. The hot, dry air smells similar to a petting zoo, and inhaling it leaves me feeling nauseated. With effort, I push myself up to look around.

Where am I?

This isn't our shop. What is happening? My heart races and chest tightens—the beginning stages of a panic attack. I try to breathe myself through it. I need to figure out where I am. Whatever this place is, it's definitely not in Florida.

Taking out my phone, I turn my flashlight on and try to call for help. No signal. The orange and red clay walls indicate that I'm, somehow, in a cave. Behind me, there are seemingly endless caverns and small puddles of water along the floor. Okay, definitely a cave. The air is full of the same static I felt in Whitney's office.

How did I get into a cave? Did I hit my head in Whitney's office?

This must be an insanely vivid dream. Crap! If I'm lying unconscious in the shop, no one is going to find me until tomorrow and I'll miss the whole retreat. I have to wake myself up. Grabbing the skin under my arm, I pinch myself as hard as I can—it hurts.

Golden sunlight illuminates the area in front of me. If light can get in, there must be an opening—and a way out of here. I just have to follow the light.

My body feels... different when I stand. When I try to walk, I stumble like I'm wearing a new pair of heels. I adjust myself as I walk a few steps and, eventually, the awkwardness levels out. Putting weight on my right leg causes a sharp pain up my hip. I must've landed on it weird. What happened to not feeling pain in your dreams?

I rub my hip, trying to relieve some of the pain. It doesn't feel broken or sprained. Probably just bruised. The pain subsides as I keep walking around the dimly lit cave, the only light coming from my flashlight and the entrance that must be hidden behind the pillars of rock.

Several yards in front of me, something on the ground catches the light from my phone and gleams a shining silver. Taking a few more steps toward it, the oval-shaped object nestled in a pile of tan rocks becomes clear. Is that a—

A loud screech comes from the front of the cave. What the hell was that? The panic returns, instantly flooding my senses. Searching for a place to hide, I run and duck behind a large boulder as quickly and quietly as I possibly can. Footsteps shake the ground I'm standing on. Trying to stifle my ragged breathing, I cover my mouth with my trembling hand.

Peering out from the side of the boulder, I let my flashlight illuminate the cave. Standing in front of me is a towering form—the height of at least three men—covered in shimmering deep blue scales that ripple across its massive body as it spreads its wings, letting out a low snarl. Flattening my body against the boulder, I hold my breath and freeze in terror.

A fucking dragon? This has to be a dream. I turn my flashlight off and power down my phone. God forbid it rings and give away my hiding place. Maybe if I don't move, it won't see me? That's what the twins told me to do if I ever ran into a dinosaur, so hopefully dragons operate under the same mechanics.

The dragon lowers its long neck over the single silver egg in its nest. A mother dragon protecting an egg. It can't get much scarier than this. With a deep inhale, she swings her head to face the boulder, and a fierce roar pierces the air. She definitely sees me. More ground-shaking steps and her head lowers over the boulder directly above my head, snake-like golden eyes looking into mine. Hot breath encompasses my body. Screaming, I back up to the cave wall, abandoning the protection of my boulder. There are tunnels behind me, but I have no way of knowing if they lead to an exit or more danger.

Wake up. Wake up. Wake up. This is just a dream. This is just a dream. This is just a dream—right?!

The dragon stalks toward me, smiling mockingly in a way that seems to say she knows I've got nowhere to go. Tears of fear stream down my face. Bending down, I pick up the closest rock and with all of my strength hurl it at the dragon. The rock hits her leg but it doesn't faze her. She looks... annoyed. Good job, Daph, annoying the dragon that already wants to eat you.

The dragon's eyes meet mine again and she bares her razor-sharp teeth, inches from my face. Her mouth is so big, she could easily swallow me in a single bite. I take what will probably be my last breath when she whips her head to look behind her and snarls deeply. She leaves me cowering and charges protectively toward her nest and the silver egg that lies in it.

My ears finally pick up what must have made her momentarily forget about me: approaching light, quick footsteps. From the corner of my eye, I see a golden arrow fly through the air and land a direct hit on the dragon's neck. A gut-wrenching cry echoes off the cave's walls. The dragon takes one more look at her egg and falls, rattling the ground beneath her.

Where did that arrow come from? No time for questions. Grabbing another rock off the floor, I get ready to defend myself against whoever or whatever is approaching. Three shadowy figures appear at the entrance to the cave, illuminated from behind. Two of the figures walk up to the dragon's egg. They look human, but taller and more beautiful. One of them has longer dark black hair and the other cropped brown hair. Making out more of their features in the dark is difficult; all I can tell is that they're vaguely handsome. Then the light shifts, brightening the cave. That's when I notice *the ears*. They all have pointed and elongated ears.

I must be going into shock. I pinch myself again. Why aren't I waking up? I've never failed to wake up from a bad dream before the bad thing actually happened.

The two who approached the egg move it onto some sort of sling that's hung between two wooden poles. Each of them puts one side on their shoulders to lift the massive egg, which is easily half their size. The third of the trio slings a bow around his body and walks toward me.

The man has dark hair that's short on the sides and a bit longer on top, tan skin, and a strong jawline under short, well-kept facial hair, all of which add to his ruggedly handsome appearance. But his clothes... and the ears. I can't stop staring at his ears. Who, or what, is he? Is he an elf? A fae?

"Well, this is unexpected. Who are you?" He smiles and raises a curious brow, his voice deep and with a slight accent I can't identify.

Gripping my rock tighter, I shout at him, "Stay back!"

He lets out a soft chuckle. "No 'thank you' for saving your life?" He steps closer, making his way over the rocks between us. Pushing his hair out of his face with one hand, he stares at me quizzically. It's probably safe to assume that when they went into this dragon's den they didn't expect to find a woman armed with a rock. Oh god, what if they think I was also trying to take the egg, and that I'm some sort of sorry competition? The last thing I need is for these people who are capable of taking down a full dragon with a single bow to think I'm after their prize. My heart hammers like it's about to beat right out of my chest.

"I mean it!" I shout and raise the hand that holds the rock defensively.

"What are you going to do with that?" Gesturing to my hand, he chuckles, revealing the tips of sharp canines within his lingering smile.

As I stare at him, unable to say anything, my nails dig deeper into the rock. This is all too much to register. It would be stupid of me to try to fight my way out of this. He probably has a foot on me in height and looks very muscular under his fitted leather armor. Too bad I'm stupid. I toss the rock at him. He swiftly dodges it and I scramble to get another from the ground.

Casting a side-long glare, he takes another step forward. "I do want to point out that we saved your life. I think you can put the rock down."

I don't. What am I supposed to do?

He stops and cocks his head. "Suit yourself then." He shrugs and turns away, calling over his shoulder, "You can either come with us or wait around for when that dragon wakes up to an empty nest. Undoubtedly you'll become her dinner. The choice is yours."

Realistically, either of my current choices can end with me dead. Going with the handsome stranger who saved me probably has slightly better odds. Or, he could murder me. No. Why would he save me if he was going to murder me? Hesitantly, I drop the rock and follow him out of the cave. "Who are you?" His ears capture my attention again and I can't help but think he look like a dark-haired actor women would swoon over if he was cast in a fantasy movie. "And *what* are you, some kind of elf?"

"Elf? No," he scoffs and raises an eyebrow. "I do believe I am the one who should be asking you those questions. I will admit that I am quite impressed that a lone female was able to get into a dragon's den nearly unscathed. Where are your weapons? You can't tell me you made it this far with just a rock."

Narrowing my eyes, I purse my lips. I'm not sure if I can trust him yet. I'm still not sure if this is even real. "What did you do to the dragon? She's not dead?"

He takes the lead and I follow his footing over the rocks. "Many questions for the male who saved your life. The dragon is asleep. The arrow has an enchantment to render her unconscious so we could retrieve her egg."

Why do they want the egg? Now isn't the time to ask. Survive first, question his morals later. I do need to figure out what is going on though, starting with what he is.

"So if you're not an elf, what or who are you?" I balance delicately on my injured leg as I climb over the next pile of rocks. Turning back and finding me struggling, he offers me a steadying hand to help me get to the next patch of flat ground.

"Those are two very different questions. You can call me Silas. I am fae. As are my friends over there, Ajax and Knox," he says, gesturing to the other two figures, several yards ahead of us. "Admittedly, I'm embarrassed to say I don't recognize your clothing from any of our kingdoms. Are you not also fae?" I glance up and take in the leather armor they all wear over tunics and linen pants. Feeling suddenly self-conscious and under-dressed in my oversized sweatshirt and leggings, I cross my arms over my chest.

"What are you talking about? I'm just a regular person." Reaching a hand up, I push the hair that had fallen in my face behind my ear. My fingers are met with a slight point.

CHAPTER FOUR

Looking at this man—not man. Fae. Fae-man? He said male before I think. That's what they call them in romantasy books. But are they using accurate terms? Whatever. Looking at Silas in disbelief, I grab my other ear, my other pointed ear, and run my tongue along my teeth until they reach sharp canines. My hand covers my mouth as it drops open. My eyes widen as I put my hand in front of me and stare at the longer, more dainty-looking, fingers at the ends of my somehow smoother skin.

Silas narrows his brows. "I take it, those are new?" He's looking at me like I'm a total crazy person.

"Uh yeah. They weren't there before..." I pause. Can I trust him? He did save me from the dragon, and we made it out of the cave alive. We're now in a vast canyon surrounded by a mountain range and crisp fresh air, his companions still ahead of us with the dragon's egg. The vibrant orange and red rocks seem endless around us.

There's no other option but to trust him. It's not like any other fae person is going to come save me.

"Before what? How exactly did you end up in that dragon's den?"

He continues forward along the path, effortlessly moving over rocks as I struggle to navigate the uneven terrain.

Something within me tells me I can trust him. A gut feeling has never let me down before. My best chance at getting home is telling him. If he wanted to hurt me, he would have let the dragon roast me. "I was looking into a mirror. I touched it and I just... fell through," I whisper, looking down at my hands, not sure if I believe myself. "I'm pretty sure I'm dreaming and I'll wake up any minute. But why are my ears different? My world doesn't have any of this." I gesture to the strange world around me. "We don't have dragons, we don't have fae. There is no magic there." Pausing, I glance down at my legs and arms. They seem longer.. The sleeves of my sweatshirt don't quite reach the ends of my wrists anymore. Is anything else about me different?

Silas turns around to face me, the sun hitting his handsome tan face. Stopping in my tracks, my heart skips when I realize how attractive he is. Stop that. Worry flashes in his eyes. Am I coming off unhinged? Have I shared too much? I tend to do that.

"Well, I can assure you, this is real. From the look and smell of you, you are indeed fae. If what you are saying is true and there is no magic in your land..." Casually, he looks up in thought. His face scrunches as if he's trying to solve a difficult riddle. "Then maybe there is a glamour or something of the sort hiding the fae that are there. Since I don't know where you are from, though, I can only speculate."

What does he mean by the smell of me?

Before I can ask, he continues, "As far as how you got here, I am not sure about that either. A few fae were gifted with traveling abilities by the gods, but as far as I know, they can only travel through this world and to places they have been before. Not many are gifted with this ability, though, and they are quite secretive about the workings of their magic. Falling through a mirror from another world by accident is not something I have heard of before." He studies me for a brief moment and his lips quirk in a half smile. "I'll tell you what, how you ended up in our world fascinates me. So my friends and I will help you."

My stomach clenches. If he's never heard of this happening, he might not actually be able to help me get home. "So you don't know how I can get home? You don't know anything? Surely I can't be the only person this has happened to." I bite my nails, dreading the answer. He turns back to the path and continues forward without answering. I'm not sure if my question somehow offended him or if he's thinking. "Please, I have to get back to my kids," I whisper.

The wooded areas we pass look strikingly similar to pictures of mountains in national parks I'd seen. Wyatt wanted to visit them, but my fear of heights and utter un-athleticism made them low-priority destinations for me. As the stunning scenery unfolds around me, I regret that I let my fear hold us back. He would've loved this view.

After walking for a few minutes in silence, Silas says, "I am afraid I do not know with certainty, but I believe there are people in my kingdom who may have some answers for us. Once we arrive we can send for their aid."

As we approach a cliff ledge along the side of the clay mountain that's just wide enough to sidestep along, I spot the other two males. Their backs are skillfully pressed against the mountain wall, walking along on the cliff ledge with the dragon egg balanced delicately between them.

He's going to make me walk on that to follow him? Absolutely not.

He's insane. I'm not nearly coordinated enough to not fall right off and plummet to my death. Not glancing back to see if I'm following him, Silas takes a step onto the ledge.

Gaping at them, I look over the ledge. It drops straight down the side of the mountain, into a rushing river. One wrong step would lead to a quick demise. "There is no way I am walking on that!"

"Why not? Are you afraid?" he teases as he continues walking, following his friends.

"Yes."

"Of what?" he laughs.

"Death, mostly," I respond through shaking breaths. "Death and heights. Both are big no's from me."

His face softens when he realizes that I'm serious. "You will be fine. I will not let anything happen. I promise it is only like this for a short distance." The attempt to reassure me fails. Taking a step back in my direction, he reaches out his hand. "Remember, it is come with me or stay here with the dragon."

Good point. Guess it's time to face my fear of heights and pray that I can do this. Turning to the side so my back is firmly pressed to the side of the orange and red canyon walls, I grab Silas's hand. His large hand nearly swallows mine. With a deep breath, I step onto the ledge.

One step.

Two steps.

I'm really doing this. Silas and his companions make it look so easy, so effortless. As if they know they won't fall. Like they've done this a million times before. Are the fae automatically skilled at such things, or did they train for this? So many questions. If I keep my thoughts going, I'll keep my body moving.

"Talk to me. Maybe it will distract me." I say, more aggressively than intended. Silas pauses and looks back at me, clearly taken aback by my tone. My anxiety grows worse the farther away from the start of the ledge we get.

Three steps.

"Sorry. When I'm anxious, sometimes I come off as rude, but I can't help it. Tell me, where am I anyway? And where is this kingdom you're taking me to?" I ask.

Four steps.

Five steps.

"Do you want specifics?"

"Whatever keeps you talking the longest. The more you talk, the less anxious I'll be."

Continuing forward, he begins, "Our world is called Threa. You are on the continent of Carimea. We are traveling to our home in Sol Salnege, the capital city of the Kingdom of Fracilonia. Right now, we are in the western half of the southern region, which is where the dragon breeding grounds are."

Six steps.

Seven steps.

"Fae and dragons alike guard these areas well. They are nearly impossible to get in. So, finding a random beautiful female in a dragon's den was quite shocking for us. Especially when we learn she does not know she is fae and that she just fell into our world. Now, you tell me, where are you from?"

"Why do you keep calling me that?" I snap.

"What? Beautiful? I think that is the first time I have said that." He flashes an almost impish smile.

I lower my brows. "Female. It's offensive."

"You called me an elf earlier!" he retorts.

My eyes widen with embarrassment. "Well, I didn't know it was offensive."

"What would you like me to call you then?"

"A woman. I am a woman."

"That term implies you are a human. Which" —he points to my ears and I cover them— "you are not."

"Well, I was human until I fell into this world." I roll my eyes.

"Well, not anymore." He shrugs.

"Fine. I guess female is fine," I mutter. *Don't look down.* "What exactly is a fae anyway?"

Eight steps.

"It is simply a term for certain powerful magical beings. Long ago we used terms like elf or fairy, but over tens of thousands of years, our people moved from secluded forest communities into unified cities. It became difficult to keep track of everyone's exact species as pure bloodlines of nearly every subgroup and species intermingled."

Nine steps.

Ten steps.

"So everyone on this world is fae then?"

"Not exactly. Some beings still use labels, like the witches and vampires, who tend to marry their own kind. I would like to hear more about your world."

Eleven steps.

Twelve steps.

"My world is called Earth." The ground beneath my right foot starts to crumble as my foot comes down for what I hoped would be step thirteen. I panic as stones fall over the edge of the cliff and my foot slips.

"Fuck." Quickly and instinctively, in one swiping motion, Silas catches me by the arm with one hand and pulls me against him. He stretches his other free arm out away from us as a strong gust of wind pulses from his hand, pushing us back against the mountain wall.

"What was that?!" I gasp.

"My magic. One of my gifts is air," he says as if that's a totally normal thing. Using every ounce of strength left in my body, I clutch onto this stranger for dear life.

Don't look down. Don't look down. Don't look... down. Holy crap, we are up so high. My heart starts thudding rapidly. Tumbling to my death and splashing into the roaring river below isn't how I imagined today going. The faint cry of a dragon echoing through the canyon interrupts my panic. My eyes jolt to the horizon. In the golden glow of the sunset, not one, but two flying shadows emerge high above the mountaintops, sweeping up and down through the clouds. My first thought is the dragons are hunting us, but they glide peacefully, dancing mesmerizingly in the sky.

"They are beautiful, aren't they?" A faint smile crosses Silas's face. "Deadly, but beautiful."

This snaps me back to reality; the panic returns and my grip on his chest tightens. Beads of sweat form along my hairline. Sensing my crippling fear, Silas wraps his arm around me and pulls me tighter to him.

"It's okay. You're safe with me. I'm not going to let you fall. But we have to keep moving." He places me down on the ledge next to him. "We're almost at the end of the ledge and we'll be at the camp shortly after." Staring into his bright blue-hazel eyes, I try to convince myself that this handsome stranger won't let me die here. My eyes widen with embarrassment as I realize how close I am to him and release my grip. Pushing my back against the canyon wall, I try to pick up my foot, but I can't.

Another, louder roar reverberates through the canyon and a look of fear crosses Silas's face. Is the dragon coming for us?

"We need to go. Now." His tone is harsh and commanding. It's an order. Still, I don't move. Apparently noticing I'm not budging anytime soon, he grabs me and picks me up like I weigh nothing.

"Put me down!" I scream.

"I am not leaving you on this ledge." His voice grows impatient.

"Why not?" I squirm in his arms.

"Stop moving. You're going to make us both fall over the edge." He stiffens, tightening his hold on me so I can't break away.

"No. Put me down."

His grip around me grows tighter the more I try to free myself. "You didn't have any problem with me holding you a few moments ago."

"That was different."

"How? I'm still saving your life. Look, the dragons are out and the sunlight is almost gone. Dragons hunt at dusk and I'm not letting us fall. We don't have time for this. Sorry." He runs a hand over my face and the world goes black.

CHAPTER FIVE

Stretching out my arms, feeling incredibly refreshed, I lay under the covers. When was the last night I got a full night's rest? The kids are on their trip and I'm... The smell of my lavender and lemon fabric softener is absent when I inhale. Where am I? My eyes fly open. The blanket covering me isn't my fluffy white comforter. Instead, a thin green blanket that smells of pine is draped over me haphazardly.

Sitting up and looking around, I find myself on a camping bedroll in what appears to be a tent. I go to push a stray hair out of my face and my hand hits a pointed ear. Small glimpses of what got me here flood my mind. The memories aren't entirely clear, but quick flashes of the mirror, the dragon, the fae, the cliff, and Silas knocking me out all come back to me. He didn't hurt me. Did he drug me? Was there something on his hand or did he use some sort of magic on me? Either way, not cool.

This is actually happening. I'm not just dreaming. I stand up and look at myself. I seem fine; I don't have any new cuts or bruises. My fingers instinctively reach for my silver snapdragon pendant. It hasn't left my neck since Wyatt gave it to me a month after we met, when he cheesily asked me to "be his boo" at Gabby's Halloween party.

My phone is still in my pocket. My wedding ring is still on my finger. Everything is accounted for and I'm in one piece. Aside from Silas knocking me out, we'll call my overall survival thus far a win. But what did he do to me?

I take out my phone and turn it on. Still no signal, but it doesn't hurt to try. Pulling up Gabby's contact, I dial. Nothing but screeching comes through. I hang up. The battery is at 80 percent. The screen turns black as I hold the side button. Realization floods in. No one will try to reach me for two weeks. No one will look for me. Everyone will assume I'm on the retreat. This is bad—or, I guess it's actually good. There's time to figure out how to get back before my family starts to worry. I have two weeks to find a way home.

Pacing around the small, square tent, I think through my next move. There has to be a way to get home. A mirror got me here; maybe a mirror in this world can send me back. Queasiness settles in my stomach at the thought of having to return to the dragon's nest to get home. That's assuming these people—these fae, whatever they are—agree to help me. They wouldn't have saved me twice just to leave me here, would they? Only one way to find out.

I push open the canvas flap enough to peek my head out. The smell of smoke fills my lungs and I can hear people talking and laughing. I just have to be direct, walk right up to Silas, ask what he did to make me pass out, and then make him figure out how to send me home.

Trying desperately to hold onto my conviction, I follow the smell and rising laughter until I find Silas and four others eating around a fire. Two of the fae I recognize from the dragon's den. Another male cooks over the fire and next to him, a female sits on a cushion reading a thick leather bound book. Behind them, several more canvas tents stand in front of a dense treeline.

"Look who woke up!" a deep, light-hearted voice calls. My eyes flicker to the handsome male Silas called Knox earlier. He has warm olive skin, short and clean-cut dark brown hair, and the stubbled shadow of a beard. He's the kind of guy whose broad shoulders Gabby would ogle at the gym before I reminded her she was married. But the kindness radiating from the smile he flashes me seems authentic.

With all eyes on me, I clear my throat, stand tall, and look pointedly at Silas. "I need to talk to you, now," I say as authoritatively as I can.

The laughter vanishes. Silence grows in its place so thick you can physically feel the shift in the atmosphere.

The other male from the cave, Ajax, stands from his seat beside Silas. His pale skin heats with anger as he pushes a lock of shoulder-length, wavy, jet-black hair away from his deep blue eyes. He tilts his clean-shaven, square jaw down threateningly as his deep-set eyes become ice-cold daggers above his sharp nose. Preemptively, he places a hand on the hilt of his sword.

Okay, wrong approach, Daphne.

Swallowing, I scramble to fix my offense. "Please. I need to talk to you now, please."

"It's alright, Ajax. Remember she tried to arm herself with a rock earlier. I am certain she is harmless." Brushing dirt from his pants, Silas gets up and walks over to me. Those gathered around the fire chuckle at the jab as if they've already been informed of my weapon of choice. Ajax removes his hand from his sword and takes his place back around the fire without dropping his cool stare.

"Join us, you must be starving," Silas says. "Everyone would love to figure out who you are and where you came from."

My plan to tell him off for putting me to sleep and demanding he send me back crumbles. My whole body becomes overwhelmed with emotions; I'm not good at hiding them. I can only imagine the distress that's written all over my face. This fear is confirmed when Silas's expression softens with concern and he leads me away from the fire, behind one of the larger tents. At least I won't start crying in front of all of those people.

"Are you okay?" There's apprehension in his tone.

"No, I'm not okay." A lump forms in my throat and tears cloud my eyes. I blink them away, trying to hold my composure. "One minute I'm about to leave on a retreat that's supposed to help me mourn my dead husband. The next I land in another world with fae and dragons and knights in shining armor ready to save you when you almost get swallowed by said dragons. Then I'm knocked unconscious. What was that? Did you hit me? Did you drug me? Or, or was it your... your... magic? Apparently, there is magic here, which is definitely not a thing where I am from. And I'm fae now? Or I have always been? What does that even mean?" My cheeks are wet with tears. I take a deep breath.

"First of all, not a knight. Second of all, I'm sorry I had to put that enchantment over you. The magic I used can make you a little groggy when you wake up, but you should remember everything in a few hours. Usually, I reserve magic like that for extreme circumstances, as it takes quite a bit of my power reserve. But with a dragon nearing and you paralyzed with fear, I deemed it necessary for our survival."

The memory of the moment before Silas put me to sleep becomes clear. I remember my body frozen on the ledge, not willing to move. I cross my arms over my chest. Whatever. He did what he had to do, but that doesn't mean I have to be happy about it. "Okay. Fine."

Looking more intently into my eyes, he says, "I am truly sorry I did that to you. I will not do it again unless a life depends on it. And I'm not sure how you can be fae if you're from a world without magic, but we can teach you about what that means, if you'd like. Or we can pretend you're not and just try to get you home, and you can go back to your normal."

Nodding in acceptance of his apology, I try to relax. "I do want to know what this all means—what it means that here I have this body. At least I think I do. I'm not sure. All I really know is I need to get back to my world, to Earth. My kids are there." I bite the inside of my cheek to stop more tears from falling.

I swear there's a small tinge of sadness in his eyes. "None of us have ever met or heard of someone from another world before. If you come back to our kingdom, we can request aid from the oracles and priestesses. They are your best hope at finding the answers you seek."

As I wipe my tears with the arm of my sweatshirt, Silas pulls out a white silk handkerchief from his pocket. Gently lifting it to my cheek, he wipes my face. "We will do what we can to get you home."

"Are you sure they'll help me?" I sniffle.

He nods with certainty. "While I cannot guarantee they will be able to get you home, I do know that if I send word to the oracle and priestess in my city they will respond."

It's not the answer I was hoping for, but I have no other option. I take a deep breath. "We'll figure out how I got here and we'll figure out a way to send me back. I have two weeks before anyone notices that I'm gone. I need to be back by then."

He raises a questioning brow. "No one is going to notice you're gone for two weeks?"

"It's a long story." I laugh. What a ridiculously convenient time it is to go missing.

He smiles and his eyes light up as if accepting a challenge. "Two weeks it is. We plan to start our journey home in the morning. Why don't you come sit and have some food with us? I'll introduce you to the others." Silas makes a large gesture motioning forward and leads me back to the fire and circle of fae. Ajax rises defensively as we return. *What is this guy's problem?*

"Everyone, this is Daphne," Silas says.

Glancing up at Silas and then toward the group, I wave awkwardly. "Hi, most people call me Daph. You guys can call me that if you'd like." Trying to appear friendly, I smile and hope my face isn't red and puffy from crying. Some sort of objection to a stranger joining them would've been completely understandable. But, no one argues.

Grabbing a bowl of soup, Silas takes his seat. "As expected, Daphne will be traveling with us back to Sol Salnege." They all nod, like they're accepting an order. It gives me the distinct impression that Silas is their leader.

"You've already met Ajax. He is my second." Once we take our seats, Ajax sits down, glaring at me from Silas's other side. "Knox over there is my third." He gestures to the male on Ajax's right. He gives me a slight wave and a nod as he eats his meal.

Are they his first and second as in an army, or are they some band of thieves? It's probably better not to ask for clarification until we get to their city, where there will be other people around.

"Next to you is Syrrus. He takes care of the camp. He sets up the tents, cooks the food, and sharpens our weapons. Anything we need. He's the silent type, so don't be offended." The male is the largest of the four before me, at least a foot taller than I am, and a large body swallowed by oversized clothing. The burly male offers me a kind smile through his long thick beard, pushing his round cheeks near his brown eyes.

"And last we have Syrrus's mate, the lovely Brynne. She is our healer and potions master. Her half witch lineage makes her the strongest healer in the five kingdoms." The female, like all four males, is undeniably stunning. She's tall and lean with long blonde hair pulled into a thick braid. Small pieces of wavy hair have fallen out of place and hang by her slightly up-turned bright green eyes, brushing the sides of her round face. Her full pink lips smile softly at me.

There are so many words Silas just used to describe these people that I don't understand or know the meaning of, but one word stands out. "What do you mean that she's his mate?"

Silas's brows lower and he cocks his head. "You don't have mates on your Earth?"

"No... uh... we don't. Are they married?" I ask, confused.

"Yes, they are married, but a mate is much more than that. They are destined by the gods to be together."

"Oh, so they're like soulmates?"

"Kind of, but more than that still. Their souls and minds are intertwined with one another through a bond."

Accepting I won't fully understand what that means, I give up for now. My brain is still too foggy. In a nervous effort to keep the conversation off of me, I turn to face Brynne. "So how did you two meet? I love love stories."

A faint blush and wistful smile appear on Brynne's face. "Syrrus was a soldier during the war. He was badly injured and brought into my tent unconscious, on the brink of death, to be healed. I didn't know why, but I had an urge to save his life at any cost. It was an overwhelming sensation and need. I'd never felt it before for any other person I was helping. I worked nonstop for days healing him. I think he had broken about every single bone."

She rubs Syrrus's leg as he smiles down at her. "Once my work was done, I sat by his bed until he woke. When he opened his eyes and met mine for the first time, I knew in my heart and soul that he was my mate." Her smile grows, revealing dimples on her cheeks as she glances up to Syrrus.

"And she's been fixing him ever since." Knox laughs before chugging back something from a wooden stein.

The towering man sitting beside Brynne looks perfectly fine. Strong and healthy. I can't believe there was a point that his whole body was as badly broken as Brynne described. "That's..." I look for the right word, "impressive."

"She can probably fix that leg of yours if you'd like," Silas suggests.

I almost completely forgot about landing on it when I got here. Have I been limping? My body must be in survival mode, because I haven't noticed.

"Allow me." Brynne places her bowl on the ground and leans over Syrrus, placing a gentle hand on my thigh. She locks her eyes with mine and closes them. Five delicate inked stars dance on her collarbone. A slight pulse of energy courses from her hand and just like that, pain lifts from not only my leg, but the rest of my body. The constant ache in my shoulder and back from holding kids is... gone. The pain I normally feel in my knees and feet from years of standing for long hours at the shop has also disappeared.

My eyes widen as I stare at her in disbelief. "You just took away every drop of pain I had. With a single touch. That is amazing. Thank you."

She blushes and laughs softly. "Oh, that was nothing. You should see how these three come back sometimes." She lifts her hand from my leg. "You had those ailments for a long time, didn't you?"

I nod in response.

"They're quite easily dealt with, but I imagine the discomfort must have been rather annoying. Do they not have healers where you are from?"

Nervously pushing my hair back, my fingers once again meet that pointed ear, sending a shudder rippling down my back. I let out a small, anxious laugh. "No, we don't have healers. We have doctors, but they rarely listen or take aches seriously. We don't have any sort of magic there at all. This is all very new. So forgive me if I seem a bit shocked by all of this." All heads turn to me.

Brynne furrows her brows. "Interesting. Yes, I believe it would be quite a shock to come here, to a world so abundant in magic, if you've never experienced it before. If you have any questions about this world, feel free to ask any of us. We've all been around a few centuries; we should have any answers you need."

My mouth drops and I almost choke on my saliva. "You can't be serious. Centuries? How old are you?" The group of fae around me all look to be in their mid-twenties, early thirties at most, not centuries old. Not that I have any reference to what a centuries-old person would look like.

"That's right... Silas mentioned you thought you were human before you found this world. Well, fae don't age quite like a human would."

She knows how humans age. Does that mean... "Are there humans in this world?" I blurt out.

Nodding, she says, "There are, but not many anymore. Most married fae or witches and have reared demi-fae or half-blood children. Over many generations, most beings with human blood are now only a fraction human."

I look down at my long fingers. "I thought I was human."

"It doesn't look like you know your whole story then." Knox winks and takes another swig from his stein.

Syrrus gets up from his seat and pours a bowl of soup from the pot above the fire. He hands it to me with a piece of bread.

"Thank you very much," I tell him. He smiles and nods in a way that tells me he's saying 'You're welcome.'

"You'll have to forgive my mate. He is a male of few words. I promise you, though, he makes an amazing meal." Brynne rubs her hand lovingly over Syrrus's chest as he returns to his place next to her.

Taking a spoonful of the warm soup to my mouth, I smile and sip. It's divine. The rich savory flavors dance in my mouth. I have never once had anything with so many delicious components. The bread is incredibly soft with the most wonderful buttery flavor. Realizing how hungry I am, I scarf down the food. "This is delicious." Syrrus smiles at my compliment.

"Do they not have soup in your world either?" Knox asks.

I laugh. "They do, it just doesn't taste quite as good."

"Syrrus uses his flora magic to grow the most delectable herbs and vegetables to use in his cooking," Brynne remarks.

"He has... flora magic? And I think Silas... earlier you told me you have air magic when you saved us from falling off the cliff. Do you all have magic or is it just some of you?" Is this too invasive of a question? Brynne did say I could ask them anything.

Silas looks to me. "All fae here have a main element or two, if they're powerful, that they're able to wield. Each fae's magic is unique. My gifts are air and water, Syrrus and Brynne both have flora magic, Knox is able to control fire, and Ajax has both light and water magic. He can manipulate the light around the campsite, making us invisible to anyone or anything around us. It's quite brilliant."

Ajax nods at the compliment.

"Some individuals possess greater power and more diverse gifts, such as Brynne's gift of healing. Others have gifts of intuition, travel, and things of that nature."

Curiosity gets the best of me and I ask, "What about when you knocked me out? What kind of magic was that?"

Pausing, Silas looks me over, as if deciding if I had asked him a trick question. I smile, letting him know it wasn't. He smiles back warily before continuing cautiously, "That would be lesser magic. Almost all can do that type of magic in addition to their elemental magics. They're smaller spells, similar to enchantments."

Luckily, my last book kick had been fantasy and it seems to have prepared me well. The magic seems simple enough to understand: regular everyday magic, elemental magic, and sometimes fancy magic. "That's all there is to it then?"

Knox interjects, "Our senses are also superior to those of humans. That's how we could tell that you were not a threat the moment we found you scared shitless in the dragon's den."

Glaring at him over the insult, I touch the tip of my ear. "You said all fae?" Does that mean I may have magic too?

"Yes." Silas's eyes land on my hand and figures out my next question before I can ask it. "We can all feel your power. There is definitely something within you waiting to be unlocked. We don't know how much of you is fae—perhaps only a distant ancestor was fae, and there is not much magic... Only you can discover what power lies within yourself."

"Ah well, with that little bit of inspiration, I think we should call it a night, yeah? Long ride in the morning and all." Stretching his arms over his head, Knox gets off his cushion. With a swish of his wrist the fire dims and vanishes into smoke and ash.

Silas is next to stand. "Right, Ajax, can you show Daph back to her tent? I have to talk to Brynne."

Ajax, who hadn't participated in any conversation the whole evening, stares with his dagger-like eyes. "Yes, sir." He sounds slightly irritated by the order. I get a strong feeling—maybe it's those fae senses kicking in—that this guy doesn't like me. The others disperse to their tents. I stand up and follow Ajax over to my tent, which is a bit further from the rest of the camp. Did they set up my tent so far away because they don't trust me?

"Well, thank you for walking me to my tent." Smiling anxiously, I turn to let myself in.

Ajax grabs me by the shoulder, leans in, and whispers threateningly in my ear, "I do not know where you came from, but unlike the others, I do not trust you. My sworn duty is to protect Silas's life. I will be watching you. If I so much as suspect a threat on Silas, I will personally end you."

He releases his grip on me and chills run down my back. Freezing in place, my stomach turns and my heart pounds. I'm going to throw up. He's already gone when I turn around to tell him that I would never.

CHAPTER SIX

My breathing turns ragged as I push my way into the tent. Ajax's voice echoes in my mind, sending waves of nausea through my body. He has no reason to trust me, I know that. To him, I'm just a stray his friend—no, his leader he's sworn to protect—saved and decided to bring home. Ajax doesn't seem like the kind of person whose bad side I want to be on. Trying to calm myself, I run my hands over my sweatshirt and down my legs.

New clothes and an ornate metal hairbrush on the bedroll catch my eye. Brynne or someone must have placed them there while I was talking to Silas. The soft, long nightgown clings to my body when I put it on. I plop down on the bedroll to start brushing out my hair, hoping the familiar motion will ease my nerves. My brain goes over everything that's happened today as I get to work detangling the long, thick strands, so full of knots. I only come up with more questions, no answers.

What was that mirror doing in the shop? Did Whitney know what it was? Or was it a random find that she wanted to sell? Maybe I could activate the mirror because I'm fae. Perhaps I'm one of those fae that Silas mentioned—the ones who can "travel." At least, I think that's what he called it… it's all speculation. But how could I be fae? I'm just Daphne.

Then my thoughts drift to my kids. I need to get back to my kids. Back to Ariella, back to Ronan and Ryan. They can't think they lost me too. I refuse to let them grow up as orphans when I'm very much alive. What happens if I don't figure out how to get home? My jaw clenches. They have Gina, Mel, and Whitney to take care of them if anything ever happens to me. And Gabby and Teddy are there, and they would damn well make sure they got everything they need… No. I will get home. Raking a tight knot from the back of my head, I stop holding back the tears and let them fall down my face.

I am so tired, but my body feels the best it has in years, thanks to Brynne. All that's happened today has left me emotionally and mentally drained. Finally finished combing out all of the tangles from my hair, I lay down and tuck myself under the thin blanket to try and get some sleep.

My body is restless, tossing and turning. Theories and questions pop into my mind each time I nearly fall asleep. Never has so much happened to me in a single day. It's too much to process and compartmentalize into neat little boxes like I usually do. I don't even know who I am. How am I fae? That question repeats itself, driving me crazy. Does anyone in my family know? My mom doesn't know who my dad is… Is this from him? Or is it from her? Are my siblings also fae? Are my kids fae?

Sighing of frustration at my inability to lie still, I pull the blanket over my head. A rustling noise comes from behind my tent. What was that? Is Ajax back to end me before I can become a problem? My fingers grip the blanket tighter as if it can shield me from magic and weapons.

After a few minutes, against my better judgment, I toss the blanket to the side, get up, and peek outside the door of the tent. It doesn't look like anyone else had heard whatever it was; they must have all been able to fall asleep easier than I could. I shimmy my feet into my boots and decide to investigate. It's not like I'm going to be able to sleep until I find out if Ajax has come back to kill me or not anyway.

The rustling sound grows louder as I make my way around the tent. Gripped with the intense feeling of defenselessness, I scan my surroundings for something, anything, to protect myself. Finding only a brick-sized rock, I bend and pick it up. I really need to figure out a better way to protect myself. A faint glow comes from a few feet into the wooded area behind my tent. Doesn't Ajax have light magic? Crap. This is it, isn't it? Ajax came back to kill me. Maybe if I beg, he'll spare me.

Prepared to grovel for my life, I take a few steps closer to the light. A small-statured figure with long, perfectly-straight onyx hair and wide feminine hips becomes clear. Whoever or whatever this is, they're female. Definitely not Ajax. A twig cracks beneath my boot, startling the figure and making her turn around. She's transparent, like what I imagine a ghost would look like. Oh, crap. Did I disturb a ghost in the middle of the woods? What good is this stupid rock going to do against a ghost?

Cocking her head, she stares at me and smiles. "I've found you." Her hushed sing-song voice makes my skin prickle.

My brows lower apprehensively, but I say nothing.

"We sensed your power when you entered this world. I am so happy we found you."

What is she going on about? "Who are you? What are you talking about?" I whisper, matching her volume. Movement comes from the campsite and I glance over my shoulder, but don't see anyone.

She follows my gaze and worry fills her face. "There isn't time to explain. Just stay alive. We will find you again. Do not tell anyone that you saw me here. They will kill you if they find out about this."

"Who is we? Why would—" I try, but as quickly as she appeared, she's gone. All that's left of her is a small lingering glow that fades in seconds.

There's already been one threat on my life today, so the idea of another is enough to keep me from mentioning this interaction to my new companions. I haven't been here long enough to know who I can trust.

A heavy hand lands on my shoulder. I quickly turn around and raise my rock. "Calm down. It's me." Silas steps back and raises his palms to show he's unarmed. He looks at my raised hand. "What is it with you and these damn rocks? What are you doing out here all alone?"

Lowering my arm, I take a deep breath. I've never been a good liar, so I come up with the best excuse I can think of to explain myself. "I, uh, thought I heard something."

Silas seems to accept my reason. "I assure you there's nothing out here. Syrrus makes sure any camp we set up has the strongest wards. No being can enter. You're safe here," he says reassuringly.

I toss the rock to the ground. "You're right. This whole world is so different. I don't remember the last time I went camping... I'm sorry for waking you. I'll head back in and try to get some sleep."

"It's okay. I can only imagine how much this has been to accept. But since we are both awake, let me show you something." Silas heads away from the campsite. "Follow me." I follow close behind him, throwing glances back over my shoulder in search of any signs of glowing. I'm not sure if I'm more afraid of Ajax or the ghost lady. If Ajax finds out about whoever she was... that would definitely add reason for him not to trust me.

"Just remain quiet," he whispers. "Ajax and Knox would never let me hear the end of it if they found out I didn't wake them for this." We make it to a cliff and Silas lies right on the hard bare ground. "This is the best view."

I lie next to him and look up. The view is breathtaking. The sky is dancing with more stars than I've ever seen before. It looks like an entire bottle of silver glitter was splashed into the heavens. The stars I've seen from Earth never shone quite as brightly. This sky is untainted by human light, and it's utterly and completely mesmerizing. Two brilliant crescent moons sit on either side of my view of the night sky. Struck for words, all I can muster is, "Oh wow."

"I figured you'd like this view of the moons."

Breaking my wonderstruck gaze, I turn my head in time to glimpse his triumphant smile. "How did you know I liked the moon?"

"Who doesn't like the night sky?"

"Oh..."

Pointing at my right arm, he says, "I noticed your tattoo and was confused as to why there is only one."

Smiling, I look down at the small crescent moon tattoo on my wrist. Gabby and I got matching ones for our birthdays one year. It's my one and only tattoo. The pain of the needle hurt so much that I swore I'd never get another. "We only have one moon on Earth."

"Really, only one? It must get lonely." He turns his head to face me.

"I don't think so." Did it though? There's the sun and there are eclipses. Ariella got incredibly excited about the amount of eclipses we had this year. Whitney promised to take her to see one at an observatory in Orlando, but our trips clashed with that plan. "The sun and moon cross paths during an eclipse. Maybe they keep each other company."

Silas looks back to the sky. "Hmm... That's one way to think of it. The sun and the moons, complete opposites, friends. Quick, look up. The show is about to start."

A few stars twinkle as they begin to move. They move faster, more joining, until dozens, then hundreds of stars shoot through and light up the inky sky. Gleaming meteors dart between Threa's two moons, twirling and dancing in a celestial symphony. Static fills the air, just as it did on Earth before the mirror started humming. Bathing in the starlight, Silas is smiling with his eyes closed. Is this feeling magic?

"This is the most beautiful thing I've ever seen," I whisper.

"Isn't it? It's like you can feel the energy of the stars radiating down to us."

Turning my head to the side, I look at him, really look at him, for the first time. This male, this strong protective leader of a male, is lying on the ground, looking up at the stars with the joy and amazement of a child. My heart aches. It's the same look Wyatt had when he looked at the stars. Smiling to myself at the memory, I look back up. Wyatt and I loved stargazing when we were younger. He'd point out constellations and planets. And now, Whitney has gotten Ariella into the stars, too. Oh, what Ariella would do if she were here with me. She'd be blown away. A tear slides down my cheek and hits the ground beside me.

"Is everything okay?" Concern lingers in Silas's voice.

His face is illuminated by starlight when I face him. One corner of my mouth pulls in a sad half smile. "My husband, when he was alive, really loved the stars. And my daughter, she loves them too. I was thinking about how much she would love to see them like this."

"You can tell her all about it when you get back." A sympathetic smile crosses Silas's face. "You know, the moonlight suits you."

"You think I look better in the dark?" Knowing he meant it as a compliment, I laugh. After having multiple panic attacks in front of him in the less than twelve hours since we met, I'm sure he's just trying to be nice.

Not catching the sarcasm, his eyes widen apologetically. "No that isn't—"

"What are you doing Silas?!" Ajax's low, irritated voice comes from behind us. "Do you have any idea how worried I was when I woke and I didn't sense you in the tent next to mine?"

Silas gets up quickly and offers me a hand, helping me to my feet. "It's alright, Ajax. I wanted to show Daphne the meteor shower. Did you know that her world only has one moon?"

"Always with your head in the stars, Silas. Both of you, let's go. You need your rest for tomorrow," Ajax grumbles before throwing a quick appreciative glance toward the sky.

I dust off the dirt from my nightgown and follow Silas and Ajax back to the tents. Ajax goes back into his tent and Silas walks me over to mine. "Thank you for showing me the stars. I'll tell Ariella all about them."

Silas smiles as he opens the tent door for me. "Good night, Daphne."

"Good night, Silas." Smiling at him, I duck under his arm into the tent. I lay back on my bedroll and finally, my mind lets me drift to sleep.

CHAPTER SEVEN

Day One

The sounds of nearby horses whinnying and hooves shuffling startles me awake. A fraction of golden light makes its way into the tent, telling me it's barely daybreak. Not ready to wake up, I pull the pine-scented blanket up, covering my head. Staying up with Silas was a mistake. I'm groggy and not ready for any kind of travel. And by the sound of the horses, it will be a bit more physical than the plane ride I was supposed to take yesterday.

Knox's voice carries from wherever he is. "Time to rise and shine, everybody! We leave in five minutes."

Five minutes? Quickly getting to my feet, I strip off my nightgown, which is partially covered in dirt from lying outside. "Good morning," Silas's voice chimes. He walks right into my tent before I can tell him to wait.

Scrambling for the blanket, I try to cover myself. Heat rises to my cheeks. My face is probably bright red with embarrassment. "Good morning," I say, trying to play it cool, as if I'm not nearly naked beneath the thin blanket I'd barely been able to wrap around myself.

"I didn't know you were changing. I can come back in a few minutes," he says, turning to leave.

"Uh, no, no it's okay." Adjusting the blanket to try to cover more of my body, I ask, "Did you need me for something?"

"When you are ready, I want to introduce you to Lucy before we get into the sky," he answers, still facing politely away from me.

Did he say get into the sky? I must have misheard him. "I'm sorry, what did you say?"

"I thought you would ride with me. We don't have an extra pegasus with us. Lucy doesn't have extra cargo like the others. I thought it would be the most fair for everyone," Silas says nonchalantly. Like riding a pegasus is no big deal.

"I'm sorry... Did you say pegasus? Like a horse with wings?" I ask in disbelief.

Silas turns his head halfway over his shoulder. "Yes, precisely. You have them on your Earth, then? Are you familiar with flying?"

I can't help the laugh from slipping out of my mouth. "Of course not. I don't think I've ever ridden a regular horse before, either. Don't you remember what happened yesterday with the cliff? Me and heights? We don't mix. I have to take medication just to step on a plane."

Silas turns his body, fully facing me now. "A what?"

Oh, right. If I had no idea that any of this world existed, how would he know what a plane is? "It's a huge machine. It flies you from one place to another. But you're in a seat, and you have a seat belt. You can have a glass of wine or two while you're on it. And you don't feel like you're really above the ground, for the most part."

Pursing his lips, Silas raises an eyebrow. "That sounds like an awfully boring way of traveling." He shrugs. "I will leave you to put your clothes on. Syrrus will come to take your tent down. Then you can come meet Lucy and decide if you really do not want to fly with us."

And with that, he's gone. If I don't want to fly with them, what am I going to do? Will they leave me behind? If I'm left to my own devices—which in this case would be no devices—I won't survive. I better figure out a way to get over my lifelong fear of heights real quick.

Breathing through the building nerves, I pull my leggings and sweatshirt back on. God, do they stink. They don't fit the right way, either. My boots are slightly too tight and my sleeves and pant legs rest a little higher on my arms and legs than usual. The waistband of my leggings feels a little looser, too.

I probably got more steps in yesterday than in the last year. Thankfully, this fae body or whatever seems to have much more stamina than my human one.

I hope they have mirrors in Sol Salnege, because I have no idea what I look like right now. Detangling my hair is rough. The brush snags on knots and a few pieces of grass fall to the floor before I give up and toss it into a messy bun.

I grab my phone and hold the power button until my lock screen glows to life: a photo of all five of us on the beach the summer before Wyatt died. Wyatt is smiling at the camera, all three kids are bent over laughing at something he said, and I'm looking up at Wyatt. The battery has dwindled to 75 percent. Sucking in a frustrated breath, I shut my phone off and leave my tent.

Syrrus is waiting outside; all of the other tents are already down. He smiles at me through his long beard and waves his arm in front of my tent. It folds in on itself over and over again until it's no bigger than a business card. He walks over, picks up the now minuscule tent, and places it in the leather satchel hanging across his body.

A grin of pure astonishment pushes at my cheeks. "That's amazing!" I'll never get used to this world and all its magic.

Syrrus chuckles lightly at my bewilderment. He's probably as used to these tasks as I am to folding towels. My utter amazement at things they find mundane must be entertaining to watch. He hands me a muffin from the bag—which seems to have an infinite capacity

—and walks off. I like Syrrus, I decide. He may not talk, but he's sweet and makes sure everyone is taken care of. He's kind of like the dad of the group.

I eat the delightfully buttery, perfectly sweet blueberry muffin and follow Syrrus. We find the others gathered at a clearing near a gently flowing stream. The darkness must have concealed this area, because I can't remember seeing it last night. A pegasus stands with each of the fae. All of the pegasuses—pegasi? I wish I had cell service so I could Google it—bask in the morning light, sipping from the stream.

They're enormous, larger than any horse I've ever seen. Their pure white coats shimmer softly beneath silver manes. How I didn't notice such massive animals last night is beyond me—another thing I'll blame on yesterday's traumatic events. They could probably crush me if they decide I'm an annoyance. I try not to come off as intimidated as I approach them.

Ajax's eyes immediately land on me like daggers. What is this guy's problem? I'm the least threatening person on this planet. On any planet, really.

"Good morning everyone," I say as chipperly as I can to prove I'm indeed friendly.

"I hope you slept well." Brynne pets the braided mane of her pegasus.

"Yeah, how did you sleep?" Knox teases and Silas nudges him with his elbow.

"I slept very well. Thank you for healing me, again. I'll never be able to thank you enough, truly," I tell Brynne.

Brynne smiles and climbs into her saddle.

"Have you ever flown before?" Ajax asks dryly, giving me a skeptical look. He knows the answer.

"No, we don't have, uh, pegasuses in my world." My anxiety kicks in. I reach for my necklace and twist the pendant between my fingers. Everyone except Knox and Silas has mounted their pegasus. "How do you get on one of these?"

Silas strokes the nose of the largest pegasus, whose mane is braided neatly down the side of her neck. "It's easy, do not worry. I will help you up. This is Lucillia, but you can call her Lucy. My mother named her."

Lucy dips her massive head toward me as I approach her. I reach my hand out and place it on her forehead. Her coat is cashmere-soft beneath my palm. She lifts her head and gives Silas a nod. "She says she likes you," he tells me.

"You can talk to her?!" I gasp. Everyone around me chuckles and my cheeks flush.

"No, no." He laughs. "Just a feeling. When you are around an animal long enough, you form a relationship and can tell what they are thinking. But trust me, if she did not like you, everyone would know. This one is very opinionated." Silas gives Lucy an affectionate pat on her side and she snorts as if offended.

Protesting isn't an option. It's this or be stranded. Silas grabs me by the waist and lifts me effortlessly onto Lucy's back. I swing my leg over and steady myself on the saddle, grasping the pommel with all of my strength. Silas climbs on and sits behind me, wrapping one strong arm around my waist and grabbing Lucy's reins with the other.

His solid torso behind me gives me a strange combination of feelings. Being so close to a man who isn't my husband is weird. But it's also... comforting? I'm not sure that's exactly what I'm feeling, but the sensation is somewhere in that realm. This is the only way we can get to the city, a means to an end, nothing more, I remind myself. The confusing feeling slips away, replaced by fear as I realize how far off the ground I am.

Peering down over the edge of Lucy's long, feathered wing spikes my anxiety. We haven't lifted off yet, but even this is too high for me. My heart accelerates and I try to steady my breathing.

"We head right for Sol Salnege, quickly through the mountains. No stops. We want to beat the weather." Silas's voice is strong and commanding. Each of them nods in acceptance of the order. He leans over my shoulder and whispers, "I will not let anything happen to you. Just hold on and do not let go."

Thanks for that oh-so-helpful advice.

With a running start and a few flaps of his pegasus's enormous wings, Ajax is in the sky. The dragon's egg is attached to the side of his pegasus in an intricate metal cage. Knox climbs onto his pegasus and I can't help but notice the glimmering black weapons strapped to his every limb. A quick glance confirms all of my new companions are fully armed. Are they armed for protection from the dragons, or is there another threat I don't know about yet?

Knox's pegasus follows Ajax's lead, shooting into the sky. Silas pulls on Lucy's reins, but she doesn't move. He tries again and she shakes her head.

Brynne looks knowingly at Lucy, then at me, her gaze finally landing on Silas. "She will not fly because Daphne is not ready. She can sense her heartbeat. She knows she does not know how to stay in the saddle while in the sky."

Wait a second, falling is a possibility? My heart accelerates uncontrollably.

"You will have to take the journey by land," Brynne states. Syrrus and his pegasus trot over to us. Syrrus gives Silas the satchel with the tents..

"You cannot be serious. Why are you just saying something now?" Silas protests.

"Because Ajax and Knox would not have left you. The dragon egg needs to get back to Sol Salnege before it hatches, which could be as soon as this evening. Now that they are in the air, they will have no choice but to keep going," Brynne states very matter of factly.

"Brynne, you cannot make these kinds of calls. We should all go by land together, then." Sharp bitterness edges Silas's voice.

"Silas, you know these lands better than anyone. You have made the journey alone before numerous times. Syrrus and I must get back to tend to the egg. Everything will be ready for you when you arrive home. If you have a problem, talk to Lucy about it." She shrugs, no room for further argument in her tone. With a few strides, she and Syrrus are in the air.

Though I know I've caused a rather large issue, my nervous system calms down, knowing I won't be flying. Silently thanking her for saving me from the trauma of flying, I stroke the side of Lucy's neck.

"Fuck," Silas mutters under his breath. Lucy starts trotting westward.

CHAPTER EIGHT

"You know, it is quite messed up. My own damn pegasus listens to you over me," Silas says in a tone that I can't tell is amused or really pissed off.

"I'm sorry, I didn't ask her to not fly... I was ready to die internally the whole time," I reply.

Lucy snorts again, as if saying she wouldn't have let that happen.

"It is fine. But, so you know, this slows us down and you are the one on restricted time." Okay, he definitely sounds annoyed now.

My heart drops into the pit of my stomach. "How much longer does not flying take?"

"Well, it's only a few hours flight. Pegasuses can fly incredibly fast. But it'll be about a day and a half by land."

So much time is going to be wasted. Every drop of time I have to figure out how to get home is important. Frantically, I look back over my shoulder at Silas. "I only have fourteen days to get home. Tell her to fly. It's okay, Lucy. You can fly. I'll be okay."

The external signs of my panic cause Silas's attitude to shift from annoyed to empathetic. "Daphne, there is no changing her mind. She is quite the stubborn ass once she has decided on something. Like I said, she is opinionated. This is the way we will have to get there. It is longer, but at least it is a scenic journey."

"Are you sure there's no way we can make her fly? What about treats? Does she like treats?"

"No, Daph. She's a pegasus, not an obedient dog. It'll be okay. The others will be there shortly and send out the messages to the oracle and high priestess."

"When will we meet them?"

"I have some business I must attend to when we arrive, but hopefully, they will be ready to meet soon after I have finished."

I chew the inside of my cheek in an effort to keep tears of frustration from forming. Lucy's gallop turns into a high-speed run, but I still feel stable in the saddle. It's similar to riding in a car; I know I'm going fast, but only because of how quickly the world around me changes and the deafening wind around us. We ride in silence for what feels like hours. Trying to relax, I stare off into the trees. Silas was right. It's beautiful here. The mountains, the greenery, the magical fauna and regular forest animals we pass—none of which act startled by our presence—all of it is gorgeous.

Drops of water fall on the top of my head. Looking up, I notice how dark the sky has turned. Great, now we're going to get soaked. If Silas wasn't annoyed before, it's only a matter of time before he is.

"The rain is nothing to worry about." Silas says, as if reading my mind. He moves his arms, surrounding us in a ball of swirling air. The air shield protects us from the rain and stifles the sound of the wind. Could he have done that the whole time? Lucy keeps trotting and the air shield moves along with us.

Enthusiastically, I ask, "How did you learn how to do that?"

"The shield? My magic." The obvious answer.

"Yes, but how?" I press.

He contemplates for a moment before responding. "When a fae's magic manifests, we receive lessons on how to control it. Over time, it becomes second nature. Magic is an energy you can feel running through you, to your very core, wherever it lies. It is part of you."

I stare at my hands, turning them over a few times. Will I be able to wield magic like Silas and the others? "When I was falling through the mirror, I felt a pulse of energy through my body. But I haven't felt it since."

Silas stiffens behind me. "Interesting. When we make camp for the night, I can give you a short lesson on how to center yourself and feel for your magic. I'm no teacher, but we can try a few things."

I look back at my hands, not wanting to wait. "Why can't I try it now?"

He laughs softly. "You are not serious, are you? It is not safe to attempt magic for the first time while riding a pegasus. Especially since we don't know what form your gift will take."

I nod in understanding. What will my magic, if I actually have any, be? All the powers I pretended to have growing up come to mind. When I was a kid, I wanted to be invisible to hide from my perfect younger siblings. Since I'm the only one who isn't Richard's, I just never felt as important as my siblings. My mom tried with me, she really tried. But she was always happier with my siblings. They're all incredibly talented, and always got good grades in school, and could follow instructions and I was... well I was just Daphne. Too much energy, always with her head in the clouds, and couldn't do anything without asking a million questions Daphne. Until I left home, I felt like a burden on her new family. She didn't do anything to make me feel that way... I just did.

I haven't talked to my family much since I moved out seventeen years ago. There's the occasional call from my mom on my birthday and sometimes my siblings will react to my social posts, but that's about it. I don't mind it, though. Wyatt and I built so much together. The life I wanted.

What powers do the others possess again? It's hard to keep it straight. Water and fire both seem like fun. Ajax controls light and he could make a shield around the camp so we wouldn't be seen. Maybe I'll have light magic and be able to bend the light around me to be invisible. Learning the lesser magics will be just as amazing.

Thinking of loads of laundry magically folded and put away, dishes done, my task list completing itself makes me laugh quietly to myself. In reality, I guess it doesn't really matter. Once I get home, I'll be back to just Daphne.

The sound of pelting rain hitting the air shield harder jostles me from my thoughts. "How much longer do we have to go?" I shout to Silas.

"To make it in time, we have to ride until sunset. I am hoping that Lucy can keep going through the mud."

"Is the rain here always this bad?"

"No, this storm is unusual so late in the season. By now, it is normally just sun showers, not full-on downpours." Lucy is putting in noticeable effort to keep from slipping on the slick ground. Howling winds cause the trees to sway violently back and forth.

"Are you sure this is safe?" The heavy rain and strong wind pushes back off the edges of the shield, making it shutter. Anxiety fills my body.

A bolt of lightning crashes into a massive pine tree in front of us before Silas has a chance to respond. The tree glows with the energy of the bolt, illuminating the clearing as it catches on fire. It snaps at its base and its heavy trunk collides with the forest floor, shaking the ground around us.

Silas tightens his grip around me as Lucy rears, kicking up her front legs and crying out in distress. A scream escapes my lungs as my body falls back against Silas's chest. Grasping the pommel, I squeeze my legs, desperate to keep my seat.

"Whoa, girl!" Silas shouts, attempting to calm Lucy. She backs away from the fire as it begins spreading to the nearby trees.

"Over there!" I scream, pointing to the shadow of a nearby cave. Silas pulls Lucy's reins and kicks his legs to urge her toward the opening in the rocks.

The fire behind us grows rapidly as we approach the cave. Silas dismounts and unsheaths his sword. "Stay here. I have to make sure it's uninhabited before we enter."

I don't argue. Silas keeps the air shield around Lucy and I as he walks deeper into the cave. My fingers run through Lucy's mane and I rub her neck to calm her—and myself.

Silas returns a few moments later. "It's a small cave, but it's empty and will keep us safe from the rain and fire." He grabs hold of Lucy's reins and leads her inside, sealing the mouth of the cave with an air shield to keep the elements out. "Throw your legs over. I'll catch you."

He has no short-term memory. Does he not remember the reason we're here is because my fear of heights is so crippling that his own pegasus could sense my terror and refused to fly us?

A look of realization crosses his face and he adds, "It's not that far. You're not jumping to the ground. You just need to slide into my arms. Unless you have any other suggestions on how to get down?" He smirks.

I roll my eyes and carefully reposition my legs over Lucy's feathered wings in a side-saddle position. I glance from the ground to Silas, my heart racing at the idea of him not catching me and me hitting the hard ground of the cave. Then, Lucy kneels, bringing her chest nearly to the floor. The look of surprise on Silas's face tells me this is not a common occurrence.

Dropping the short remaining distance to the ground, I smile victoriously. "Looks like she does like me more than she likes you."

Silas scoffs. "Unlikely." He glares at Lucy. "She's just being uncharacteristically polite."

I survey the tan walls of the cave. It's indeed small. There's just enough room for us all to fit inside comfortably.

Silas strokes the side of Lucy's face and feeds her some carrots from Syrrus's satchel. "As soon as the storm passes, we will keep moving."

My stomach tightens. We only made it a few hours before we got stuck here; we really do need to keep moving. Silas puts his hand in the satchel and hands me an apple and some bread before sitting against the wall to eat something from a leather pouch. "Sit, eat, rest a bit. You didn't get much sleep last night."

The shiny apple is bigger than any I'd seen before. From the first bite, I can tell it's perfectly ripe and sweet. Lucy eyes it from the other side of the cave, so I give her the rest. "You can teach me about my magic now. It looks like we have the time." The sounds of the storm raging outside echo off the cave walls around us.

Silas stops mid-bite and looks up at me from his seat on the ground. A spark of excitement glows in his eyes. "Alright then, time to see what you've got."

CHAPTER NINE

Silas pushes off the ground and dusts off his pants with his free hand. Still holding his piece of bread in the other, he explains, "Magic comes from your soul. It is connected to who you truly are at your core. It feels like an energy within the center of your being. You said you felt energy when you fell through the mirror. Have you felt it since?"

Trying to remember if I'd felt it again, I bite my lip. "I'm not sure. Maybe, but with everything happening… I don't know. There's been a lot on my mind and a lot of new information in the last twenty-four hours. But no. I don't think so."

He breaks off a piece of the bread and puts it in his mouth. "That's okay. You can try to feel for it. Close your eyes, try to silence your thoughts, and focus on your physical being. When you become aware of every single part of your body, you should start to feel your magic."

Doing as he says, I close my eyes and take a deep breath. It's like what they teach in yoga: centering yourself. Trying to empty my mind proves to be incredibly difficult. My brain is accustomed to multitasking and doing as many things at once as possible. Instead of clearing my thoughts, my mind is flooded with every possible thing I should be thinking about. My kids. The mirror. Threa. Earth. Who am I? Did I remember to lock the front door?

My eyes fly open. "I'm sorry. I know this was my idea, but I don't think I can do this right now. I can't make my mind stop. Maybe we should try again later."

He finishes the bread and pulls a water skin out of the satchel. "Yes, you can. I know you can." He takes a swig of water before offering it to me. I take a few sips and hand it back to him.

"Go on, try again," he says encouragingly.

I wiggle my shoulders to loosen up my body and close my eyes again. *Focus Daphne, focus.* This time, I successfully clear my mind. Focusing on becoming aware of my body, I start with my toes and work my way up. When I get to my chest, I feel it. My magic. A warm energy radiates from my heart. Finding it sends emotions of joy and excitement through me.

My voice comes out as barely a whisper. "I can feel it." I open my eyes.

He looks as excited as I feel. "Where do you feel it?"

I smile, placing my hand over my chest. "My heart. Why? Does it mean something?"

He looks me up and down and grins. "The source of your power is said to be where the core of your soul lies. It is how one is guided through life. Generally, it is found in one of three places: the gut, the head, or the heart." He points to each one on my body, before gently landing his hand over mine. My breath catches at the contact.

His large hand encompasses mine. When I look back up, his blue eyes meet mine and I notice the flecks of gold and green that live in them. He clears his throat and pulls his hand away from its precarious position over mine. "It is something they tell us when we are children in our magic lessons. But I have found that particular tale to always have some truth behind it." His smiles turns wistful as he runs the same hand through the dark tendrils of his hair.

"If it reveals so much, I feel it's only fair you tell me where yours is."

"My magic stems from my head."

I chuckle to myself, and without thinking, I blurt out, "Which one?"

He stiffens and looks at me in complete shock. I'm an idiot. Why did I say that? Why do I always have to say something weird? What if the females here don't crack dick jokes? Oh god, what is wrong with me? I got too comfortable too fast. That has always been my worst character flaw. Once the shock settles, he starts full-on cackling. My embarrassment fades and I laugh too.

"I'm sorry, I didn't expect that from you." Silas wipes a tear from his eye.

I take a breath of relief. "You're just getting to know me. Trust me, once I warm up, I'm full of bad jokes."

"Well, I cannot wait to hear more." Silas takes a sip of water to calm his laughter.

"Okay, so what do I do now that I can feel where my power lives?"

"Right, back to your lesson. Face your body toward the opening of the cave, just in case your power is something that can kill us if you misfire. Cup your palms in front of you, close your eyes, feel your power again, and will it through your arms and into your hands." Silas demonstrates by spinning a very tiny tornado in the palm of his hands. I study it in wonder before he sends it off, disappearing beyond the cave's opening. "If it feels too strong, drop your hands and release the energy."

"Will I have to close my eyes every time?" I ask, half joking.

Silas lets out a small chuckle. "You are a funny one, aren't you? No, this is only for training purposes. Once you are fully connected to your magic, it will feel as natural as anything else. You will barely have to think about it."

Silas presses his back against the wall. Rolling my eyes, I turn to face the cave opening. Obviously, he doesn't trust me not to kill us by accident. *Okay Daph, let's do this. You got this.* I repeat the mental mantra several times to hype myself up. With my hands out in front of me, I take a deep inhale and close my eyes. Searching for my power again, I find it a fraction faster this time, and do exactly what Silas told me to do. I visualize the energy moving from my heart through my arms, down into my hands, and out my fingertips.

"Daphne, open your eyes," Silas says, his voice closer now, like he's standing right behind me. One eye flutters open, then both. My mouth drops at what's levitating in my hand. I can't believe that I'm doing this. My reflection stares back at me in the sphere I manifested. It's beautiful.

Crystal clear liquid swirls in my hands as I bring it closer to my face. "I did it! I can't believe I did this!" My body trembles with excitement—apparently too much excitement, because the ball plummets to the ground seconds later. Before it can crash, Silas picks up his hand and the water ball glides through the air to him. He holds it in his palm and gazes into it. That's right; he mentioned he also possesses water magic. I'd almost forgotten. Half turning to face him, I whisper in near disbelief, "I have water magic."

Silas walks over to me, now juggling the ball, tossing it up in the air with one hand and catching it with the other. "You have water magic," he parrots happily. "Here, put your hands back out."

I lift my hands back from their fallen position and Silas places the ball back into them. I concentrate on not dropping it again. I don't know what else to do besides stare in wonder at my creation.

"If you keep practicing, you'll eventually be able to freeze it, boil it, defend yourself with it, use it in any way your mind can think of. I don't think you'll be here that long, but some people catch on rather quickly, so..." he trails off.

"It's okay. I want to learn what I can while I'm here. I'll never have this opportunity again. It's a once-in-a-lifetime chance."

Outside, the sounds of wind and rain disappear. Dropping my hands, I let the water fall to the floor as Silas leaves the cave. Lucy and I follow closely behind him, surveying the area. The rain clouds are gone and the fire is no longer raging. Despite the pouring rain, the fire from the lightning strike caused significant damage to the forest. The struck tree is burnt to a crisp pile of black ash and the ground lies scorched beneath it. The sight triggers unpleasant memories of the car accident.

Silas tilts his head and his pointed ear twitches. He seems to be listening to something. His sudden alertness makes me freeze. I can't hear anything. Maybe my hearing isn't as good as his? Before I can ask Silas what he's looking for, he grabs me and hoists me into the saddle.

"We need to get out of here. Now," he whispers urgently as he climbs behind me. He securely grabs me by the waist, presses my back firmly against his chest, and picks up the reins. Lucy breaks into a run. Her movements are far less smooth and more frantic than earlier. She seems to understand what's happening more than I do.

"What's going on?"

"We need to go. Before they realize we are here."

"Who is they?" I press, grabbing hold of the pommel with both hands to keep myself steady.

"Let's say they're not our friends."

With that, I know I'm not getting any more information for now. I turn, giving one the burnt trees one last glance. As I'm about to face forward, a glowing figure appears in the ashes and I freeze. Silas looks back, following my gaze, but she's gone. It's just my mind playing tricks on me.

"Did you see something?"

The cryptic words the female whispered last night echo back to me. I shake my head and whisper, "No."

CHAPTER TEN

Once we get several miles away from the cave, Lucy's stride finally levels out. Silas loosens his grip on me slightly. The muscles in my abdomen ache from how firmly he held me. "You probably bruised my whole stomach," I inform him.

"Sorry. You will survive the bruise, but you would not have survived them," he answers gruffly, not offering anything further on why we fled so aggressively. Whatever it was left him shaken up. I decide not to push him further on "them"—not yet, anyway. I'll try again once we settle somewhere for the night, assuming he's returned to himself.

Who am I to say what his "normal" self is? I've only known him a little over a day. If he's so fearful of what I assume is an enemy, is this really someone I should be trusting? The logical me says no. But for some reason, I do.

I put my hand to my neck to feel for the comfort of my pendant, but it's gone. Frantically, I check down my shirt and in my bra, but nothing. "Silas, my necklace. It's gone. It must have snapped off. We need to go back." Panicking, I look behind us, as if it would jump out at me from the piles of leaves that litter the ground.

"Not happening. It's too dangerous," he says sternly.

"We have to. My husband gave it to me," I plead.

"That necklace, no matter how much sentiment it may carry, is not as valuable as your life." There's no room for argument in his tone.

A single tear slides down my face and I bite my lip. That necklace was one of the few things that made me feel connected to Wyatt. Now it's gone. *It's just a necklace*, I tell myself, but I can't help the ache that builds in my chest.

Lucy slows her pace as we approach an overlook on the mountain. An absolutely breathtaking view comes into focus when Lucy halts. The sunlight shifts to gold over the mountain peaks, turning trees into shadows. The sky is full of swirled clouds against painted hues of orange, purple, and pink.

Silas jumps from Lucy's back. "The sun is setting. It's not safe to travel the desert past this mountain at night. We will set up camp here." Lucy kneels and I slide off of her after Silas. His broad shoulders are still tense and he is barely speaking. He pulls out a pocket-sized tent from the satchel and lays the square on the ground. The tent unfolds magically, much larger than the one I stayed in last night. I run my fingers along the edge of the tent door flap. The fabric is a higher quality, too.

One of the things I learned while antiquing with Gina is how to tell whether an item is made with quality materials, an extremely important skill for gauging the resale value of items for the shop. Gina was insistent that we only ever bring back high-quality items.

I stretch my legs as I wait for Silas to pull out my tent. It took all of my arm, leg, and core strength to keep stable on top of Lucy. My whole body is sore from riding for so long. Who knew it took so much energy to stay seated in a saddle? All I want to do is lie down. Silas pulls things out of the bag to set up a fire. A ring of scorched stones indicates previous use of the campsite. "Have you been here before?"

"Once or twice." His tone is still less than friendly. Clearly, there's more to what happened earlier than he's ready to tell me. To hide my discomfort from how little he's sharing, I cross my arms over my stomach. The touch reminds me of his tight grasp on me as we fled. Despite not knowing if I can trust him yet, it seems like he at least has an interest in keeping me alive.

"I thought you would only fly places. Why travel by land?" Maybe if I can lighten his mood and get him talking, he'll eventually explain what happened back there.

"Well," he starts, still setting logs for the fire, "when you're not in a rush, it's sometimes more relaxing to take your time and see the world. Living for centuries, you have a lot more time on your hands than a mortal." He bends over the fire pit with a flint, trying to spark the logs. He tries several times, unsuccessfully. "Fuck, I wish Knox were here." Knox's fire magic probably could've had that fire up instantly. Silas continues trying to light the logs.

"That reminds me, how old are you, anyway?" He looks up at me with wide eyes. "Oh shit, sorry, is that rude? You don't have to tell me." Damn it Daph, where are your manners? How would you feel if some stranger asked your age?

"Oh no, it's no problem. Age isn't really important to the fae. It's just been a while since anyone has asked me that. I'm 193 years old. Quite young by fae standards, honestly. My friends are all in their 300s or so. Brynne is a little younger, only around 250," he replies.

Raising my hand to my chin, I cock my head and tease, "In my world, you'd be absolutely ancient."

He smiles at my jab, giving the flint one more try. An ember finally ignites the logs. The fire sparks to life, dancing in front of us. Silas stands. "How old are you?" he asks.

My eyes widen. Indeed, I do not like it when people ask me my age. I tuck a loose strand of hair behind my ear. "How old do you think I am?"

He raises his eyebrow and purses his lips. "Come on now, I told you. Now you tell me." He has a point. I'm not nearly as old as he is and he didn't have a problem telling me.

"I turned thirty-six a few weeks ago," I answer reluctantly.

"Aw, you're a baby," he teases. I haven't been called a baby by anyone since I worked at The Coffee Bean. Gabby always called me the baby since I was the youngest one there.

My smile tightens and I narrow my eyes at him. "I guess I am in this world, aren't I? So how does that work here? Aging, that is. You all look so young."

"When we are in our late twenties or early thirties, whenever our body decides it is at its peak, we stop aging physically."

Exactly like all of the books about fae and fairies. How did all the stories get it right?

Silas pulls out some cushions from the infinite satchel and tosses them down for us to sit by the fire. Silas gets onto his with ease, but I struggle to get low enough to the ground, thanks to my burning thighs. I wish Brynne were here to lend me another healing thigh squeeze. I get low enough to plop the rest of the way down and let out a heavy sigh from the relief of sitting on solid ground.

"Maybe you're the ancient one after all." Silas chuckles, tossing me a small pouch containing nuts and dried fruit and taking another one from the satchel for himself.

"How does that thing fit so much stuff?" I point at the satchel.

Silas stops rummaging for whatever he was looking for. "It's enchanted. It can hold basically everything we need."

"How do you find anything in it?" I could barely locate my lipstick in my not-endless bag back home.

"You stick your hand inside and think about what you are looking for, then it comes to you." He demonstrates by pulling out two sandwiches wrapped in parchment paper. "Those assholes."

"Come again?" Confused, I look at the sandwiches.

"Syrrus packed us food, which means he and Brynne knew that Lucy was not going to fly with you." He shakes his head and laughs in annoyance at his friends' kindness. "I wish they clued me in so I did not make such a scene this morning when Lucy threw her tantrum." Silas sighs and hands me one of the sandwiches. "At least we don't have to hunt for dinner tonight."

Silas unwraps his sandwich, sparks reflecting in his eyes as he stares into the fire. I unwrap the one he handed me. I should be hungry. My body is too exhausted to eat, but I try taking a few bites anyway.

Silas seems calm enough now; it's as good of a time as any to ask him about earlier. "So, what happened back there? What did we run from?"

Silas stiffens. Okay, maybe I didn't wait long enough and this isn't a good time. But I need to know what dangers I'm facing if I'm traveling with him.

"I have some enemies…" He starts. "Well, my kingdom has some enemies. Some magical beings in this world are stuck in the old ways. They disagree with how we use the dragon eggs. One group in particular wishes for the previous ruler to take back the throne of my kingdom. This group calls themselves the Reclaimers. That is who I sensed near the cave."

My eyes narrow at the weight of all that he is saying. They're going to do something with the dragon egg. That's how he found me, isn't it? They found me in the dragon's den, and they took the dragon egg with them. What exactly are they going to do with it, if some people disagree with it enough to consider them enemies?

CHAPTER ELEVEN

"And how is it that you use them?" Knowing he can probably sense my nerves, I try to sound casual. Are they poachers? Am I casually traveling with the leader of a group of poachers? The boys made me spend hours watching animal documentaries. They explained in detail the importance of conservation and the threats animals face from humans. Anger fills me, thinking that could be happening to the dragons here on Threa.

"It is a complicated history," he says avoidantly.

Likely story. My anger grows stronger. He took that dragon's baby. What am I doing with him?

"What are you going to do with the dragon egg?" I press.

Silas runs his hand through his dark hair and pulls at the edge of his tunic. "It's a long story, Daphne. It's been a long day. I'm tired."

"I've got time." My temper rises with my impatience. Why won't he tell me?

His eyelids lower, scrutinizing me, deciding if I'm trustworthy. "We siphon power from the eggs."

They *are* poaching the eggs. My stomach churns; I feel like I am going to be sick. I have no connection to this world and didn't know that dragons were real until yesterday, but stealing their eggs still feels messed up.

"So, you take the egg from its mother and steal its power?" I bite the inside of my cheek, anger making my magic rise through my body. What am I doing? He's the only hope I have of getting home. My reaction is uncontrollable, though, as emotions overwhelm me. There's a baby dragon in that egg and they took that egg from its mother. What if I were the mother dragon?

Silas frowns, raising his hands. "No no, it's not like that. Let me explain."

"Go ahead. I'm listening." Grinding my teeth, I clench my hands at my sides, trying with every fiber of my being to control myself. I don't know what my plan is here. What am I going to do if I don't like what he says? It's not like I have any control over my magic, unless I want to throw a ball of water at him. It probably wouldn't hit him anyway. I don't know how far we are from any other fae who may be willing to help me. I'm stuck with him no matter his answer.

"Long version or short version?" He wipes a bead of sweat from his brow.

I roll my eyes. Why doesn't he spit it out? "Dealer's choice."

Silas nods. "We have time. I believe you will understand better if you have all the details. Long version it is."

Biting my tongue, I gesture for him to continue.

"When I was about seven, my mother was pregnant with my youngest brother, River, when she fell very ill. My father brought in every healer who tried every potion and every remedy they could concoct. But nothing worked and she continued to fade.

"The high healer, the best in all five kingdoms, came to visit her. Even she could not help. She told my father there was no cure for her ailment. Despite the potions and remedies, her body deteriorated. The high healer said both my mother and her unborn child would die. She said we needed to say our goodbyes.

"My father was inconsolable. He had three other children, but my mother is his mate, the love of his life. If she left this world, his heart would soon follow. My father, Hearst, was a dragon rider. He and his dragon, Onixya, could communicate through their bond and she felt his anguish. She told him how to save my mom and brother."

For a split second, the reflection of a teardrop forms in Silas's eye, but he turns his face before I can see it clearly. He pauses, as if deciding whether or not he should continue. "What did she tell him?" I ask softly.

"She told him some dragon eggs are too powerful for this world. That when these hatchlings are born, they barely survive a few weeks, because they burn out from their overwhelming power. Some dragons, like Onixya, and our oracles, can sense this power emanating from the egg over vast distances.

"That is where we come in. Those with healing abilities, like Brynne, can take the power from the baby dragon while still in its egg. We bottle the energy to use as a cure for the sickest of our people. The baby dragon is spared because we have taken just enough of the power so they don't burn out."

My hands shift uncomfortably at my sides. Did I push too hard? To reveal such intimate details of his life to a stranger must have been difficult. On Earth, differing opinions often spark controversy, but this use of dragon eggs doesn't seem like the kind of thing that should create enemies.

Everyone wins here: the sick get a cure and the baby dragons live. I shouldn't have gotten angry at him for not telling me. After all, he only found me yesterday and he's already saved my life more than once. I should have been more understanding and minded my own business. He's doing me a favor and trying to get me home. He owes me no explanations, yet I acted like a complete ass, thinking that he did. "I'm sorry that you went through that... Why are there people who disagree?"

"The Reclaimers believe the previous ruler of Carimea—a strict enforcer of the old ways, and a dragon rider—should be still seated on the throne. They think we should let the sick die and the too-powerful hatchlings burn out. Those fae believe we are cheating death and the gods' wills. But I strongly believe we are doing the right thing."

Guilt settles in my stomach. I was so quick to judge him, which is probably exactly what the people we fled from did. I would do the same thing if I had to make that choice. "I don't know much about this world, but I believe you're doing the right thing. How anyone could think saving people and dragons is a bad thing is beyond me. Why didn't the dragon want you to save her baby?" If I were the dragon, I would have willingly handed my baby over if it meant saving their life.

"I agree, but unfortunately it's been this way for a long time now. As far as the mother dragon, the baby dragons, well... There are flaws. Once the process is done, they never grow to full size; they rarely grow larger than an average dog. The bond these dragons have with their caretakers is more like that of a pet than equals. Other dragons think less of them for it and reject them from the den. Some dragons believe death to be a better fate."

My face scrunches as I digest the information. "What about the dragons you save? Do they have any feelings about it?"

"They cannot communicate with their caretakers the way a full-sized dragon does with their rider, but all of the dragons we have helped seem perfectly happy. They all choose someone to bond with and live good lives under their care. My dragons don't have any complaints." He smiles.

If one of these dragons chose him, he must be trustworthy. I don't know much about dragons, but I assume they're picky about who they bond to. "You have dragons?"

His smile widens. "Three, actually. You will get to meet them when we arrive."

Imagining him with three dog-sized dragons is both adorable and amusing. The image I've created in my mind settles my power, allowing my body to calm. Silas taking the egg isn't something I can be upset about. He's doing what's best. He's saving the sick and saving the dragons... sure, it's not a perfect system, but it's better than the other option. "I'm sorry I came off so harsh. In my world, there are people who poach, and hunt, and take from the world until the damage they do is irreversible... my mind went there first."

"It is okay. I understand why you would think that. Our world has terrible people too." His smile softens and he earnestly adds, "If you have any other questions, I'll answer them."

Going over what he told me, a small detail sticks out. "What happened to your father's dragon?"

His eyes dart to the side and back at me, like he's trying to figure out if he misheard me. "What?"

"You said your father was a dragon rider. Did something happen to Onixya?"

"Ah... yes, I did mention that, didn't I? A Reclaimer's dragon took her life. Though several full-size dragons who supported him using the power from the eggs have offered, he hasn't bonded to another since."

"I'm sorry that happened. She was trying to help."

He takes a relieved breath. "I am glad you share our mindset. I am not sure what I would have done with you if you turned out to be one of them." He laughs.

The blood drains from my face and my heartbeat picks up. What would he have done? Would he have killed me? I need to be more careful about what I do and say. "I don't know, try to kill me?" My voice fails to keep steady enough for the joke to land.

Silas's face hardens. "Of course not. Why do you think I would do that? Have I not spent the last day and a half saving you? Killing you now would be a little counterproductive, don't you think?"

I inhale sharply and exhale, realizing I'd fumbled and insulted him yet again. I'm safe with him. "I'm sorry, I don't know how this world works. I need to learn to keep my mouth shut."

Silas rolls his eyes. "We are not the savage ones. We are allowed to have differing opinions in my kingdom. There are some who disagree more aggressively than having a lively argument about ethics in the tavern after they have had too much to drink. Those are the ones we have to be afraid of—the ones trying to take the kingdom.

"I assume since you are not from this world, you do not have any interest in doing that. In all honesty, I probably would have had somebody else help you find your way home..." He pauses, tilts his chin, and raises a brow in thought. "Are you not allowed to have different opinions in your world?"

Silas probably thinks I'm an ignorant, naive girl. It's a wonder he hasn't decided that helping me is a mistake and left me here to defend myself... yet.

"We are. I'm sorry." There's nothing else for me to say, because he's right and I'm an idiot. I awkwardly pick crumbs off of my sandwich, looking for something, anything, to do that doesn't involve talking.

Silas returns to his sandwich. "I am sorry I was so defensive."

I choke on my bite of food and cover my face to stifle the coughing. "No, no. I should have more tact. You've done so much for me and I'm just a stranger. Where I'm from, we're pretty open and talk about whatever. I didn't even stop to think about what I was asking, and I should have."

Silas hands me the water skin and I take a long sip. "Really, it is fine. You know it is a good thing to ask questions and push for answers. It means you've got a good mind, and in my opinion, that's one of the most important qualities someone can have." He puts his hands behind his back, leaning his head toward the sky. "We told you that you could ask questions. I just did not expect you to get so straight to the point so quickly. I am not used to people being so blunt around me. Hopefully, you still want to continue this journey with me now that you know. I am enjoying getting to know you."

"Of course." A blush reddens my cheeks and I follow his gaze to the sky of countless stars and its two moons. Am I nervous that I'm traveling with someone who has enemies scary enough to make him flee? Absolutely. If other fae aren't compassionate about saving the sick and baby dragons, I can only imagine what other horrible ways of thinking they possess. But if Silas can trust me with this history, I can trust him to keep me safe.

I tilt my head to look over at him. He looks incredibly attractive under the starlight. Maybe that's what he meant when he said that to me yesterday. I cannot be thinking that right now.

His gaze drops from the sky to me, starlight reflecting in his gorgeous blue-hazel eyes. "It has been a long day. We should get to bed." Silas says, pushing himself off the ground.

Shoving the last bit of sandwich in my mouth, I get up to follow him. My legs are weak with soreness and buckle out from under me. Before I hit the ground, Silas is at my side, arm under mine, supporting me. My breath catches. "Thank you." Silas only smiles as he pulls back the door to his tent, holding it open.

"Uh..." I stammer nervously. "Where's my tent?"

"What? You think I would have you in a separate tent after being so close to a group of Reclaimers that I could taste them on the winds?"

Could he really taste them on the winds? Is that part of his air magic? Or is it just a figure of speech? My eyes dart nervously from the door to Silas, to the single bedroll on the floor. While larger than the one I slept on last night, it's still sharing a bed. I haven't slept next to anyone besides my kids in almost a year now, and before that, there was only Wyatt. Now I'm going to sleep next to this gorgeous fae male? What is going on right now?

My first instinct is to refuse, but after so many offenses, I can't risk another strike out of his favor. My body does not cooperate as I attempt a single step forward.

"Come on now. I already told you I am not going to kill you." Silas uses his free hand to gesture me into the tent. I enter reluctantly.

Standing awkwardly in the corner of the tent, I watch as Silas unlaces his thick leather boots and tosses them to the side. He sits down on the bedroll and pulls off his shirt, revealing his muscular body. My face flushes with embarrassment, but I can't look away. His back and arms are inked with lines of tattoos I couldn't see beneath his long sleeves. The silhouette of a dragon wraps around his left arm. It's too dark in the tent to figure out exactly what shapes the other lines make. Luckily, he isn't paying attention to me as he lies down and pulls the blanket over himself.

"I will sleep on this far side and you can sleep on the other. I do not bite." He smirks. "Unless you ask me to."

Forcing a small chuckle, I walk over to the bedroll to take off my boots. Silas rolls over and closes his eyes. Where are the night clothes Brynne gave me? I guess changing isn't an option. I take my hair down from its place on the top of my head and put it in a braid down the side.

Was that flirting? Or am I delusional? I'm most definitely imagining it. There's no way he would find anything attractive about a widowed mom of three—with both the physical and emotional battle scars to prove it. Especially one who has irritated him constantly since she arrived. I'm just sleep deprived. I lay my head down and tuck myself under the other side of Silas's thick plush blanket.

"Get some sleep, Daphne. Tomorrow's journey will be more treacherous," Silas mutters as he drifts asleep. How can it get more treacherous than today? He's right, though. I need sleep, so I close my eyes.

"Good night, Silas," I whisper.

"Good night." He yawns.

Body heat radiates off of him through the sheets and I can't help my mind as it begins to wonder. He is definitely not my type. Normally I fall for the clean-cut, "all-American" type, like Wyatt. Silas is... none of those things. I'm only having these feelings because he saved my life. Nothing can ever happen between us. Sure, he's handsome, but in a dark and mysterious sort of way.

I roll my body closer to the edge of the bedroll, putting as much distance between us as I can, and pull the blanket tightly around me. There's absolutely no way I can be attracted to him. There's no point. There's no world in which it would ever work. I hold in a sigh as I scoot my body to the very last inch of the mattress.

Then again, two days ago I never would've thought I'd fall through a mirror and end up in a magical world, but here I am.

CHAPTER TWELVE

Day Two

The combination of loud snoring and sunlight that enters through the crack in the tent, right onto my face, wakes me. I try stretching my body out as I fight the lingering exhaustion, but find myself unable to move, trapped beneath a heavy, tattooed arm. Turning my head to the right, I find that some time in the night Silas rolled from his edge of the bedroll to mine and draped his arm over my waist. The sunlight casts shadows on his handsome face, mere inches from mine.

My eyes widen as I try to wiggle free. "What are you doing?!"

Silas yawns and slowly opens his tired eyes. Realization of what he's doing sweeps across his face. He removes his arm from my waist and shoots out of bed. He clears his throat and swallows as the slightest tint of red burns under his tanned cheeks. "I, uh," he stutters. "I am sorry, I did not realize that I..." He runs a hand through his hair as his voice trails off.

Pushing myself into a seated position, I stare up at Silas. His embarrassment is rather endearing. "Um, yeah, it's fine, you were asleep. Obviously neither of us woke up. We must have been tired from riding all day. I'm okay. It was just a little shocking to wake up to you cuddling me. I haven't ever slept next to anyone besides my husband." I laugh and play nervously with the tangled end of my braid.

"Oh, I am sorry about that."

If I were to wake up being cuddled by someone, I guess there are worse options. In an attempt to laugh it off, I let out a small giggle. "It's okay. Hopefully I can get my own bed once we get to Sol Salnege, though."

He straightens, seemingly unsure if I'm joking or still upset. "Yes, of course, you can have whichever bed you would like." His eyes search the tent for anything but me to settle on.

My stomach rumbles. "Do we have breakfast?" I ask, trying to change the subject.

Silas's face relaxes, relieved at the suggestion. "I will go make us something right now." He takes the satchel with him as he leaves the tent.

With a deep breath, my lips curve up slightly.

No, no. I can't become attracted to him. Wyatt hasn't even been gone for a full year. I'm an adult; I can control myself. You can't fall for someone you just met. I'm not staying in this world. Is he attractive? Obviously.

But no.

The painful process of unraveling my braid helps push those thoughts from my brain. We should get to Sol Salnege today. The rain, fire, and fleeing only added a few hours to our trip. I stand up, expecting to barely be able to stand, but instead, I feel relatively fine. I'm a bit achy from laying on the ground, but my legs should feel like I spent the entire day at the gym. Is this part of my fae body, or is Brynne's healing magic lingering and helping me recover faster?

I pull on my boots, dust off my clothes, and exit the tent. The sun still hasn't risen, and the air feels damp and cool from yesterday's rain. Silas squats over the fire. The embers are nearly extinguished after burning through the night. He's bent over attempting to cook... something.

"Whatcha making?" I take a seat on one of the cushions.

"I was attempting to make some eggs I found," he sighs, "but I regret to inform you, I am a lousy cook."

The still-runny eggs look pathetic in the pan, which is unable to reach a high enough temperature with the sad excuse of flames it sits over. "What else do you have in there?" I point to the bag, open on the other cushion.

Silas scrambles to the bag. "Looks like we have potatoes, jerky, dried fruit, and some more bread. Usually, when I am traveling by myself I hunt or fish for protein... but those things take time, which we do not have. And I am not leaving you alone out here, either." He looks up at me, appearing rather frazzled.

"Jerky and fruit are fine. Can't be too picky, can I?" I answer.

Silas pulls two small pouches out of the bag and hands them to me.

"You don't have any coffee in there, do you?" I yawn.

"Any what?" The look he gives me tells me they definitely don't have coffee in this world.

"It's a drink. It's warm and made with coffee beans. You add cream and sugar, sometimes flavors. It has caffeine to give you energy."

"A drink made with beans? I have never heard of it before, but it sounds awful."

I laugh. "It's really quite delicious. I have to have a cup every day or I get headaches." I haven't developed one in the past two days, though.

"So, it is medicine?"

"No, not exactly." Coffee isn't a medicine, but my ADHD prescription is. And I haven't needed that since arriving here, either. Strange. My usual symptoms haven't reared their ugly heads like when I forget to take my medicine at home. Excess energy isn't causing me to bounce and fidget. My thoughts have been clear and focused—for the most part, anyway. I log that thought as something to think about later.

Silas raises an eyebrow. "So, it is a drug?"

A laugh bursts out of me. "No, no. Not really." I mean, he isn't *wrong*, but I'm not going to let him think I'm a drug addict over my caffeine intake.

Lucy captures my attention with a stir as she wakes up. Silas tied her reins to a tree overnight. Getting back in the saddle today is not something I'm looking forward to. "How much farther do we have to go today?"

"If we leave shortly, we can be there by lunch and hopefully have some real food."

"Oh, good." I bite into the chewy, flavorless jerky.

"I do have to warn you: the ground path is more dangerous than flying. We have to go through a valley to get to Sol Salnege. The mountains on either side are where the fae and others who left Sol Salnege after the war are said to have fled to. They have not been seen in decades… but that does not mean they are not there lurking in the shadows. We will have to be silent as we pass through and move quickly."

My heart races. I've been in more danger in the past two and a half days than I have in my entire life. I suck my teeth and bite the inside of my cheek. The other times, I didn't know I'd be putting myself in danger in advance. There wasn't time to process the danger. But now, I'll be thinking about all of the horrible possibilities until we get to Sol Salnege.

The suction in my mouth releases with a clicking sound. "Alright, then. When do we leave?"

Silas waves his wrist, folding the tent, and places it back into the satchel. "As soon as you are ready."

I finish up my last bit of dried apricot and stand up, dusting the dirt off my leggings. "We can leave now."

Silas forms a bucket's worth of water from thin air, splashing it over the fire. Smoke fills the air, encompassing us with its thick scent. "Alright, we leave now," he agrees.

Standing next to Lucy, I mentally prepare to be hoisted into the saddle, but instead, she kneels for me, like she did so I could get down. Smirking at Silas, I climb into the saddle and pat Lucy's side in gratitude.

Silas rolls his eyes and follows, wrapping his arm around me—this time cautiously. He must remember my comment on how tight he held onto me yesterday when we fled. I nearly forgot myself. "You're okay. It doesn't hurt anymore," I say softly and run my right hand over the spot that felt bruised yesterday, finding it's no longer sensitive. "That's so strange. I've never had a bruise fade so quickly."

"That's your magic. Part of being fae is that we heal very fast," he tells me.

Interesting. I close my eyes, feeling for my magic. The warming presence within my heart brings a smile to my face.

CHAPTER THIRTEEN

We begin our journey just as the sun begins to rise over the mountain range, creating a brilliant purple sky. The wind is cool and crisp on my skin as we ride to the bottom of the mountain we camped on. Lucy trots into a desert, a sea of seemingly endless cream sand dunes.

I attempt to make pleasant conversation with Silas to avoid a repeat of yesterday's blunders. I never would have thought I'd be talking to a 193-year-old fae. I'm pleasantly surprised by how easily conversation flows between us. We chat about mundane things, like the weather and our surroundings. As time passes, the conversation turns to more serious topics.

He tells me about Carimea's five kingdoms: Skaans, Fracilonia, Roladif, Schasumetsats, and Tswangohin. He talks about his three siblings and his overbearing parents. I tell him more about my life on Earth: the shop, my kids, Gabby. I avoid talking about Wyatt, though. I didn't want to start crying, like I often do when I bring him up.

Silas clears his throat. "So, have you thought of any possibilities for your heritage?"

His question startles me. I gave it some thought, but... "I'm not sure. My mother doesn't know who my father is. She conceived me on one of her many drunken nights."

"Hmm." Silas clicks his tongue.

"I was thinking... You said there are some humans here. Maybe there are other fae on Earth, but they just don't know it. My mom could be fae, too. Would that make my siblings fae?"

"Yes, it would," he says, processing my idea. "How many siblings do you have?"

"Four. I have four half-siblings. My mother married her husband when I was ten. The oldest is twenty-six and the baby is twenty-one. I left home at eighteen, though. My mom basically forgot about me when she met her new husband. I don't really speak with them anymore."

"Oh, I'm sorry to hear that. Well, then it's unlikely your fae blood comes from your mother," he says with a hint of sadness in his voice.

My inability to not overshare makes me cringe. I'm not sure why I got so personal. Generally, I don't share anything about my family. I'm an open book about most things, but I keep everything about my past, before I left home, private. The only people I've talked to about my family are Wyatt and Gabby. Maybe I shared it with Silas so freely because his opinion of me doesn't matter. Once I leave this world, I'll never see him again. What difference does my past make to him?

"Why is that? How could you know?" I object.

"Having that many children so close together is nearly impossible for a fae. Not completely unheard of, but rare. So, it makes more sense that your fae blood comes from your father. You said you were conceived on a random night of passion, so it is quite likely your father doesn't know you exist."

My face scrunches in both anger and relief. What he said possibly answers so many questions about myself. Could the reason it took so long to get pregnant with the twins be my fae heritage? I've always thought my father was such an asshole for not being around. If he doesn't know I exist—that somehow makes me feel a little better about growing up without him.

"Interesting," I say under my breath. "What about my kids? Would they be fae too?"

"Well, you are at most half-fae."

"So they'd be a quarter fae? Would they have magic?" I look at my hands, remembering the water they wielded yesterday.

"Yes, they would only be one-quarter fae—that is if you are fully half-fae. But I am sure they would have some magic. The smaller the percentage, generally the less powerful the magical abilities. When non-magical blood mixes with the magical blood, the power is diluted. Here, we have many different mixed bloodlines, all with varying levels of magic," Silas explains.

I let out a "Hmm..." in response, thinking about what this means for my kids. When I get back home, do I tell them? Or do I not tell them? It'd break their hearts knowing they could never come to this place or access their magic. And god forbid they tell someone at school—that would definitely get me reported to CPS for being an unfit parent. I'll probably have to keep this whole ordeal to myself.

"How many children did you say you have again?"

"Three. A girl and twin boys."

"What are their names? What are they like?"

I smile as I picture their faces and my heart grows heavy with longing to be back with them. "Ariella just turned thirteen. She's brilliant and kind. She reminds me the most of my husband. My twins, Ronan and Ryan, are nine and as mischievous and clever as little boys can get. What about you?"

"What about me?" Silas says confused.

"Do you have any kids? A wife?" I clarify. He didn't wear a wedding ring, but that may not mean anything in this world.

"Oh, no. Not yet. I only want to have children when I find my mate, whenever that happens. It's unfair to have children with another only to be torn away when you find your mate. That happened to Brynne's parents. Her older sister still holds it against them."

"Are you meaning to tell me you're a 193-year-old virgin?" I joke, laughing to myself at the idea that that statement could ever be true. He's far too handsome for that to be the case.

He throws his head back, laughing. "Oh gods, no. We have tonics for such things. At a young age, I decided I want what my parents have, what Brynne and Syrrus have, and what all of my siblings have."

The sweet confession brings a smile to my face just as Lucy comes to an abrupt halt. I grab onto the pommel to stop myself from lurching forward. I lost track of the time. The desert behind us seemed to disappear as quickly as we entered it. In front of us stand two incredibly tall mountains, between which an eerie valley of shadows awaits us. A strange energy radiates from the valley, sending alarm bells ringing in my head. *Do not go in there.*

Shadows encompass the valley, making it dark as night, despite the glowing mid-morning sun rising in the east. "We're going through that?" I shriek before remembering Silas's previous warning about the mountain's possible inhabitants.

"Unless you suddenly get over your fear of heights, then yes. It is the quickest way. Remember we need to be completely silent."

"How will we be able to see in there?" I whisper through a shaking breath.

"Fae sight." I feel him shrug behind me.

Great. That's a comforting explanation.

I inhale deeply, attempting to swallow my growing fear. Lucy slowly makes her way into the dark valley until the only light comes from each end of the passage. This new body didn't come with any sort of enhanced night vision like Silas implied he had.

Lucy walks the path like she's done it a dozen times, carefully placing each hoof before the next. Her every step echoes back at us off the mountain walls. The sounds of owls and animals moving around us raises the hair on the back of my neck. The passage is incredibly tight. Claustrophobia makes my chest tighten and palms sweat at the narrow path before us. There's no turning back now.

The sound of rustling leaves behind us breaks the silence. Lucy's ears twitch with warning as she turns her neck to face the sound. Following her gaze, squinting through the darkness, my human vision barely makes out the massive panther stalking us in the shadows. Its black fur blends easily into the darkness. The beast is easily twice the size of a normal panther; its paws alone look as big as my head.

"Fuck. Hold on, Daphne." Silas pulls the reins tightly and Lucy faces forward again and runs with unparalleled speed. The sun creeps into position, right above the gap in the mountains, illuminating the valley floor. Pitch black nothingness is replaced with a hoard of various predatory animals of extreme size, making their way toward us on all sides.

Lucy halts. Frozen, with nowhere to go.

"Silas, what are these things?" I whisper.

"Shifters," he responds under his breath as his grip tightens around me.

Lucy's head whips in every direction, looking for an opening. The sounds of roars and howls echo off the mountain walls as the shifters close in on us. My chest fills with a building scream I refuse to release. Silent tears drip down onto the brown leather saddle. This is it.

Silas sends a powerful burst of air around us, pushing the shifters back just far enough away from us to buy us a few more seconds.

"Daphne, close your eyes and hold on," Silas instructs. I do as he says, forcing my eyes shut. I hold my breath and brace for the pain of the beasts ripping me to shreds. But it doesn't come.

All I feel is the cool rush of wind.

CHAPTER FOURTEEN

The shifter's cries grow distant and are replaced by the whooshing sounds of fast winds.

Don't open your eyes.

Do *not* open your eyes.

You do not need to know what is happening right now, Daphne. Silas's grip around me is secure; he won't let me fall. Just breathe and keep your eyes closed.

I can't do it. My eyes shoot open. Lucy is flying high above the mountains, her wings fully extended and gliding effortlessly through the sky. My scream fills the open air. Silas creates an air shield around us, quieting the surrounding winds.

"It is okay, Daph. I will not let anything happen to you." Silas says soothingly in an attempt to calm my panic.

My heart sinks into my stomach. I'm going to vomit right over the side of Lucy's wing. My knuckles turn white as my fingers dig into the saddle. We're flying. I'm flying. On top of a pegasus.

Well, this is one version of exposure therapy.

"What the hell were those things?" I shout. My anxiety makes me unable to control the volume of my voice.

"Shifters," he answers, as if I hadn't heard him earlier.

"I know. You said that. But what does that mean? Remember there aren't any magical anythings in my world."

"Unlike fae, witches or vampires, who only have one form, shifters have a human-like form and a beast form. Some shifters second form is fae. It comes down to where we get our magic from. Fae get their magic from the gods, witches get their magic from Threa itself, vampires get their magic from the blood they drink, and shifters get their magic from the one they bond to."

"What do you mean bond to? Like Syrrus and Brynne's mating bond?"

"Sort of, but shifters' bonds are platonic in nature. Full-blooded shifters need to bond to another magical being when their abilities appear as they reach adulthood. The shifters use a small portion of their bonded's magic and in exchange offer their counterpart protection and unbreakable loyalty."

"Who are those shifters down there loyal to, then?" I ask.

"The Reclaimers. During the previous high king's rule, shifters promised their children to the high king at birth to secure a bond to one of his soldiers. Without a bond, a full blooded shifter becomes mortal, with nothing else to power their magic. That is why a large majority of shifters ally with the Reclaimers. They never had a choice."

"That's awful." How can a mother sign away her child's life like that? But I understand; I would do anything to make sure my children survive. Anything to ensure they have a future.

"It is. That's why all the kingdoms made it illegal for parents to swear their child's bond away. Shifter bonds must now be consented to by both parties." He pauses, looking out into the distance. "Look, beyond the mountains there. That is Sol Salnege. We will only have to fly a few minutes more. I need you to hang in there, Daph," Silas whispers over my shoulder, pointing at a breathtaking view of a city built on the side of a mountain.

From this angle alone, the architecture exudes a charming

magical essence, like it's not a real place at all, but one built from pure imagination. Carved stone buildings—shops and homes I assume—are surrounded by an impressively tall wall. At the back of the kingdom and closest to the top of the mountain stands a stone palace with four distinct towers overlooking the entire city. To the west of the awe-inspiring city is a sparkling, deep blue ocean.

We're almost there. This is happening. Once again, I've been saved by a magical and handsome fae male and now we're flying on a magical pegasus into a beautiful kingdom. What in the romantasy novel is going on right now? Adrenaline and wonder rush through my body and my screams turn to uncontrollable laughter.

"Are you okay?" Concern coats Silas's voice. He probably thinks I've completely lost my mind. Maybe I have a little—just enough to enjoy my time in this world.

"Hold onto me," I instruct him.

Without any hesitation, he grabs my waist firmly. "What are you going to do?"

I lift my right arm out to mimic Lucy's wings. Silas understands where I'm going with this; his grasp around me becomes unbreakable. My left arm follows and I turn my head back at him. "Silas, I'm flying." I look forward and lean my head back against him, smiling wildly.

"Yes, you are. Like a bird."

"No, like a Pegasus," I correct him.

"Like a pegasus." He laughs softly, probably relieved that I'm no longer panicking.

Lucy soars gracefully through the sky, before gliding over the high city wall that surrounds Sol Salnege.

The intricate architecture of the city reminds me of the stone castles and streets of the cities I visited in Italy on our antiquing trips. We fly over a market where people smile and wave at us—or at Silas, rather—from the ground. The delicious aromas of savory spices and food being cooked fill the air as we soar over the market square. The city below us is full of charming cottage homes and small apartment style buildings that line the street. Which of these buildings is Silas's home?

"Brace yourself," Silas warns as Lucy lowers toward the ground.

I grasp the pommel, tighten my legs, and close my eyes, readying for impact. Lucy lands on the cobblestone path more smoothly than I anticipated.

When I look up, the imposing stone palace wall stands before me. "What are we doing here?"

Silas is grinning widely over my shoulder. Before he can answer me, Ajax, Knox, Brynne, and Syrrus exit through the black metal gate to greet us. They're no longer wearing leather armor, but are dressed in fine clothes. The males wear fine tunics and vests. Brynne is in a gorgeous royal blue gown with delicately woven golden embroidery.

"You're earlier than expected. And you flew in?" Brynne gives Silas a sharp, disapproving glare.

"Brynne, it was either we fly or be torn apart by shifters in the valley. Lucy and I agreed we would rather live, thank you very much. After that flight, I do not think Daph minds flying too much." He shrugs and jumps off of Lucy, landing on the cobblestones with a thud.

"Hi, everyone." I give a small, shy wave as I try to piece together what is going on right now. Lucy leans down and I slide off onto the ground. I stroke her velvety soft nose until someone comes from beyond the palace gate and grabs her reins, bringing her past the gate toward a wooden stable to the right of the palace.

"Would you look at that, Silas? Lucy really does like her more than she likes you," Knox says, embracing Silas in a bear hug. "Good to have you back."

Three colorful flashes of scales the size of large dogs charge toward Silas. They pounce, knocking him to the ground, flapping their wings and wagging their tails as they lick his face. Silas laughs as he pushes the tiny dragons off of him. "Alright, Ash, Kaida, Hurik down. Down!" He sits up and rubs their bellies as they continue jumping on him. "Daphne, these are my dragons."

"They're adorable!" I squeal, bending down and scratching the scaly chin of the yellow dragon sniffing around my ankles. She has big golden eyes and a curious face. Her demeanor reminds me of a golden retriever. I've never seen anything so cute.

"That is Kaida. The black one is Ash and Hurik is the red one."

Hurik, sniffs me and licks the side of my face, leaving a trail of warm slobber on my cheek. "I can't believe these baby dragons are real."

"Oh, they're not babies," Ajax says cooly from his position leaning against the wall that surrounds the palace.

That's right. Silas told me that dragons who have their magic siphoned when they're in their eggs don't grow to full size. The three dog-sized dragons in front of me seem perfectly healthy and happy. I can't imagine what Wyatt would've done if I came home with a dragon. He wouldn't even let the kids have a hamster. The closest thing we ever had to an animal in our house was the stuffed busts of deer Wyatt hunted.

"Oh, well they're a lot less scary this way. They're like puppy dragons." I laugh.

Knox chuckles. "Puppy dragons. I like that."

Ash, the black dragon, remains stationed guardingly near Silas. I reach my hand out for him, telling him I'm safe. He furrows the ridge of his brow and makes his way cautiously over to me. He lifts his snout in the air, sniffing repeatedly. This dragon's face is nearly as expressive as a human's. He creeps closer to me, his eyes raise, and his nose twitches as if he's deciding if I can be trusted. He freezes just out of reach. His nostrils flare as he takes a long, final sniff of the air.

He lurches forward, putting his paws on my shoulders, the tips of claws making their presence known as he knocks me to the ground. My eyes shut tightly as he presses his snout against my face. He exhales a warm breath over me. Slowly, I open my eyes to find crystal blue irises staring contemplatively into mine.

Oh my god, he's going to eat me.

Ash huffs another steamy breath over me. My eyes close once

more and I press the back of my head to the stone ground. He's going to bite my head off. Suddenly, he collapses his body onto mine, snuggling me to the ground. I open one eye and lift one hand to run down the back of Ash's scales.

"See, she's fine. She's not here to kill us all. That dragon doesn't like anyone." Knox announces, cutting a sidelong glare toward Ajax.

Silas stands, dusting sand off of his clothes. Ajax, Brynne, and Syrrus offer him embraces and greetings. "Come, I will show you to your room," Brynne says, putting her hand on my shoulder to lead me through the gate.

Silas is catching up with his friends when I glance back over my shoulder. This all feels like a dream. The fae, the dragons, the pegasuses, and now Brynne walking me up to the most gorgeous palace I've ever seen. To them, this is just another normal day.

At the front of the glimmering palace, a staircase leads up to a heavy wooden door. Brynne starts up the stairs. I pause, gaping up in confusion at the impressive structure before me. Its architecture is similar to Renaissance-style castles with intricate masonry details in the bricks, rows of arched windows, and a light and airy presence.

"What are we doing here?" My brows furrow as I follow quickly behind Brynne. Two guards in chainmail and metal helmets open the heavy, wooden double doors for us.

"What do you mean?" she counters avoidantly as we enter the palace.

The sparkling floor and walls are made of large slabs of marble. In the center of the foyer, a grand, dark, wooden staircase leads to the next floor. Above us, delicately carved metal railings line the second floor. There's a hall or doorway in every direction. This is easily the largest palace I've ever been in. Gina has an affinity for palaces and castles, so they're a frequent stop on our family vacations.

I admire the palace for a moment before responding, "I mean what are we doing here, in the palace? Do you guys work for the royal family?"

Brynne laughs politely and something like amusement twinkles in her eyes. "Something like that, yes."

My thighs scream like they are on fire as we head up the staircase to the second floor. Stairs should be illegal after spending several hours on horseback.

"To the right in the east wing is where you will find the guest rooms," Brynne chirps. She leads me down a hall until we reach a dark, wood door embellished with a silver dragon's egg. Brynne waves a hand to unlock and open the door for me. "Here you are, dear. Amaleana will be here shortly to get a bath running for you. She will help get you into some more appropriate clothes for lunch. I have to go prepare for the high priestess and the oracle to arrive, but I will see you later." She twirls and leaves me, closing the door behind her.

Bright daylight filters into the room through the large windows. In the center of the room is a four-poster bed with a white linen canopy and draping. The mattress looks as fluffy as a cloud. Without hesitation, I drop my body onto the mattress and let myself sink in. It feels as heavenly as it looks. I could fall asleep right here, right now. My eyelids flutter closed and I almost do until I remember where I am.

I'm in a palace in a magical kingdom in another world.

I prop my body up on my elbows to look around the room. There's an open door that I presume leads to a bathroom, a door that may be a closet, and a large wooden floor mirror in the corner, near one of the windows.

I shoot out of the bed and rush toward it. I can finally look at myself. A knock at the door catches me before I have the chance to get a glimpse. "Come in." Looking back at the mirror, I sigh.

The door creaks open. "Hello, ma'am." A petite female with a bob of copper hair and large, friendly green eyes enters the room. Freckles dance across her sun-kissed skin. Her pointed ears seem slightly smaller and protrude less than the other fae I've met. "My name is Amaleana. His majesty sent me to take care of you and make sure you were ready for lunch. I can draw a bath for you."

I look down at myself, still coated in the last three days' filth, "Hi, Amaleana. My name is Daphne. You can call me Daph, though. A bath would be great. Thank you very much."

She dips her head and scurries down the hall that I assume leads to the bathing chamber. Once the sound of water filling the tub trickles out, I approach the mirror. The reflection is of myself, but not the one I know. When I looked into the mirror I knew I'd see my now-pointed ears—which are smaller, closer to Amaleana's than Silas's or Brynne's—but I wasn't expecting such a difference.

My limbs look longer, more elegant. My skin seems smoother. My body is slimmer. I look beautiful. I don't think I've ever thought that about myself before. Not without following it with one form of judgment or another. I've never thought I was ugly. Just plain looking. Average. Nothing special. But in this body... It feels like I'm looking at myself through an Instagram beauty filter. My hand reaches out to touch the mirror, to see if this is real. My arm freezes, leaving my hand lingering midair, remembering the last time I touched a mirror. I take an apprehensive step back.

The sound of Amaleana's footsteps make their way back toward the bedroom. I turn around to face her before she catches me staring at myself. I'm not sure if it's known to everyone who I am and where I came from yet. If it's not, the way I was gawking at myself would certainly give it away.

"Follow me, please," Amaleana says, her soft voice almost a whisper. She leads me down the hall into the bathroom suite. Steam seeps over the edge of a bathtub, which is carved from a massive piece of crystal quartz. It sits pressed against a window overlooking the woods beyond the palace walls. Light filters through the window onto orchid petals floating atop water that reaches the brim of the tub. The smell of fresh-scented soap and lavender essential oil emanates from the bath. I note the faucet as a sign that there's running water in this world. This has to be the most luxurious bath

I've ever seen. Why is the king being so hospitable to a woman—a female—he's never met?

"Thank you, Amaleana." I smile, dismissing her.

"I will be waiting in the main room to help you get into your clothes for lunch." She gives another nod of her head and exits.

What is going on? My head can't wrap around all of this. I strip out of my dirty clothes, placing them carefully on the floor, afraid to get dirt on any inch of the pristine bathroom. Testing the water, I dip my toes in to find it perfectly warm. I need this bath. I slide into the tub and scrub the last three days' grime off of my body with a loofah before falling beneath the surface, holding my breath for a moment before resurfacing.

What are we doing in the palace? Am I going to meet the king? Or queen, I suppose... Silas didn't mention that we'd be coming here. How am I supposed to act around royalty? What kind of fork should I use at lunch? I stop scrubbing. What if Silas brought me here to turn me in as some kind of reward? No, he wouldn't do that.

Pushing the thought out of my head, I grab the only bottle from the ledge of the tub. I pour some of the rose-scented soap into my palm and lather my body and hair. Once I finally feel clean, I step from the bath and wrap myself in the plush towel that Amaleana left for me on a stool near the tub.

Amaleana is sitting stiffly on the bench that runs along the end of the bed, waiting for me, just as she said she would be, when I re-enter the bedroom. Laid neatly across her lap is a dress.

"That was the best bath I've ever had," I tell her as she hands me the pale blue linen dress, small white flowers sewn throughout the full-length skirt. The top half is a lace-up corset bodice. I wait for her to leave, but she does not.

My face scrunches uncomfortably. "Would you mind if I change privately?"

Her held tilts and her mouth moves to the side, like my request is very odd. At first, her response confuses me, until I remember that people on Earth used to have people dress them all the time. That's probably what Amaleana is used to.

"I'm shy. You don't have to leave. You can just turn around," I say.

She doesn't respond, but does as I ask and faces the other way. The dress looks way too small as I hold it to my body. I'm not sure how they would know my size anyway. But I try it on. And it fits. Perfectly, in fact. "Okay, you can turn back around."

Amaleana goes behind me and ties the laces up the back of the dress. "If you sit, I'll dry and braid your hair for you." She gestures to the long bench at the end of the bed. I take a seat and let her detangle my dripping hair. Without warning, a rush of air magic wraps around my head. Grabbing one of the loose, now dry, strands by my face, I look at Amaleana in surprise. She looks bored; she's just doing her job.

This is normal here. I'm the weird one for not knowing you can dry your hair in seconds with a touch of air magic. She continues working fast, braiding half of my hair up and letting the rest fall down my back.

"Magic can be strange to someone who has never seen it before."

She does know at least a few things about me, then. "I'm getting used to it."

"They say you came from a world with only humans. Is that true?"

"It is." I respond, running a hand over the soft fabric of the dress.

"My great-grandmother was a human. She worked for the old high king in Skaans City. She fled during the war and my family has worked for the new royal family in all parts of the continent ever since."

Amaleana being part human gives me hope that I can make a friend in this world, but it also brings an unsettled feeling to the pit of my stomach. My heart speeds and my hands tighten on the skirt. Do fae keep humans as slaves? Is that what I'm actually doing here? I need to know if this is going to be my fate. "So they keep humans as slaves?"

She looks startled at the accusation. "No. Being part human has nothing to do with my position here. It is an honor to work for the royal family. Everyone who works in the palace is very well taken care of. You have no need to worry about us. We are all happy here."

My hands relax and my heart slows. That's one less thing to worry about. But who are these people? "Amaleana, what's the royal family like? Do you know if I'll meet the king today?" I turn to face her again. Her eyebrows raise in confusion and her mouth parts in answer when there's a knock at the door.

Amaleana hurries to answer it, but it opens before she can reach the handle. Silas stands in the doorway, now dressed in a white button down and fitted tan linen pants. "Amaleana, thank you for taking care of Daphne."

"Of course." Amaleana sets down the brush she was using, bobs a small curtsy, and quickly and carefully squeezes past Silas as she leaves.

Silas leans on the frame of the open door. "Well, you look better now."

"What is that supposed to mean?" I snap.

The corners of his lips quirk in a teasing smile. "Before you were covered in dirt and, well, I'm not sure what you were wearing. So, you look better." He laughs.

I roll my eyes and relax. "You look the same, just less smelly."

He laughs. "I'm sorry, I didn't know my smell was offensive before."

I look up at him for a moment, enjoying the sense of normalcy our banter brings me before I ruin it. "Silas, are you going to tell me what's going on? What are we doing here? When are we going to figure out how to get me back home?"

He folds up his sleeves, revealing the dragon inked around his forearm, ignoring my questions like everyone else. "Come with me. I'll show you around before we have to meet Novalora and Embryanna."

CHAPTER FIFTEEN

Silas shows me the upstairs wings of the palace as we make our way downstairs. "The east wing is where the guest rooms are. The west wing is where the king's rooms and meeting rooms are."

"The king? Will I meet him today?" I ask curiously as I stare longingly down the bright hallway of the west wing. What could the king of a magical kingdom look like?

He sighs. "It's safe to say he will be at lunch later today."

I cock my head at the annoyance in his tone, but decide not to ask about it further as I follow him down the staircase.

The first floor holds a grand dining hall, which is being set with plates and floral centerpieces, as well as a more intimate dining area, likely meant for the royal family's private meals.

Beyond the dining areas is a busy kitchen with dark wooden cabinets and a sparkling marble countertop, full of trays upon trays of lavish foods. The warm savory smells of the meal make my mouth water, reminding me how hungry I am.

On the opposite side of the palace is a ballroom. The amount of servants rushing through as we pass suggest it's being prepared for some sort of celebration. White flowers wrap around the pillars through the ballroom, and intricate mother of pearl and marble mosaic floors glisten under the open skylight. It looks too beautiful to be real.

Our next stop is the library.

Olive-green shelves to the ceiling line the walls of each floor of the vast, multi-leveled room. Rolling ladders lay against the shelves of endless leather-bound books. A skylight illuminates the room and small particles of dust float through the air. The smell of old paper and glue brings me a welcome sense of familiarity.

"Do you like to read?" Silas asks.

"I do. I run a bookstore on Earth." I glance up and down the aisles of bookshelves before my eyes settle on the nearest one and I step toward it.

"I thought you said you have an antique shop?"

"It's both, actually. What about you? Do you read at all?" I turn my head over my shoulder.

He picks up a thick black leather-bound book, rifling through the pages before setting it back in its place. "Of course. They keep our histories and all of our knowledge. Plus, when you have an immortal life span, you find you have a lot of time on your hands."

His answer surprises me. Maybe it's because Wyatt never had any interest in reading. He supported my love of books, but across the eighteen years we were together, he never read one that wasn't required in school. He'd rather be out riding his bike or fishing with Mel and Teddy than cozy at home with a book. Before we had kids and ran around with them all the time, we spent many nights separately doing our preferred activities. The all-too familiar feeling of regret over not spending enough time with him while he was still alive creeps over me. We were both doing things that made us happy, so I try not to let my mind dwell in that place too often.

A fond smile makes its way across my face as I run my hand down the spines of some of the most beautifully bound books I've ever seen and picture Silas with his nose in a book. Some of the books are in English and some are in languages I've never seen before. "What languages are these in?" I ask, holding onto a green leather-bound book, beginning to skim the pages.

Silas takes the book from me, looks at the title, and places it back in my hands. "Those are in the old language. It hasn't been spoken in centuries. The priestesses and oracles keep them alive. But the common tongue is much simpler."

How are we speaking to each other? "Silas, how do we speak the same language?" Overwhelming realization sweeps his face as well. We've been so busy trying to get back here that this little tidbit just slipped right past us. Is there anything else we missed?

"I'm not sure." He raises his hand to rub his bearded jaw. "If there is time this afternoon we will ask Embryanna and Novalora. Come on, there is one last place I would like to show you before we are expected for lunch." I take one last glance at the book before I return it to its spot on the shelf.

Silas leads me back up the grand staircase and out onto a large terrace overlooking a garden. The smell of blooming flowers wafts up to us. Near the garden is another building that reminds me of a stable, but is made of metal rather than wood. Beyond the walls of the palace, you can see the city.

"This is one of my favorite spots in the entire palace. There's nothing quite like the view of the stars and moons shining down on the city at night. And when the gardenias bloom in the summer, they fill the air with the most intoxicating smell." He leans onto the railing, the warm sun kissing his face.

"You say that like you come here often." I join him to get a better view of the gardens and city.

A light breeze blows around us. The skirt of my dress billows around my ankles. Silas's gaze flickers over to me; maybe he's finally ready to tell me why we're here. I tilt my head up to meet his blue eyes to ask him when the breeze pushes the unbound portion of my hair over my face. He laughs, then reaches out to gently push the hair behind my ears. A playful smile settles on his face. My lips pull in a tight embarrassed smile and a slight heat prickles my cheeks. Staring back at him, I notice things I didn't before. Like the perfectly symmetrical strong angles of his jawline. The way his tan skin glows in the sun, and how his smile lights up his entire face when he's amused. His entire handsome face. And his gorgeous eyes, blue with flecks of gold and green, bright with energy and kindness.

"You have the most beautiful eyes," he says, interrupting my own admiration.

I blink in surprise. "Me? My eyes are just brown. Your eyes are beautiful. I was just thinking that. Blue-hazel. They're so unique. I've always thought people with blue-hazel eyes look like they have the world in their eyes."

"Your eyes aren't *just* brown. They're golden. Like pools of warm honey that glow in sunlight." My heart skips. No one has ever told me that my eyes are beautiful before.

The terrace doors open and Ajax strides up behind us with a small silver dragon at his heels. "I hate to interrupt whatever *this* is. But it's time to eat." I suddenly remember how late in the afternoon it must be and how empty my stomach is as it growls in response to the mention of food. I'm looking forward to a hot meal. The food must be as good or better than the soup Syrrus made. I look up at Silas and bite my lip, wishing that we hadn't been interrupted.

Silas rolls his eyes at Ajax and flashes me a quick, apologetic smile. "Alright, Ajax. I will be right there. Can you and Arian escort Daphne?"

Ajax glances from Silas to me, looking annoyed. His dragon, presumably Arian, echoes his expression. My chest tightens at the thought of being alone with Ajax and his dragon, but I follow without argument. I glance back over my shoulder at Silas, who's returned to his perch over the railing. Ajax takes me downstairs, remaining quiet the whole way to the dining hall. He has no reason not to like me, but I suspect he'll keep good on the threat he made my first night here, so I keep a few paces behind them.

We're greeted with the scents of savory roasted meat and cooked vegetables as we enter the grand dining hall. A long wooden table, overflowing with various foods plated on silver trays, sits in the center of the room. Five small dragons lay curled near the fireplace. There are two green ones, an orange one, a pale blue one, and one a deeper shade of red than Hurik. Knox, Brynne, Syrrus, and two others I haven't met yet are already seated around the table. Is one of them the King of Sol Salnege? Ajax pulls out the cushioned chair between Knox and a beautiful, heavily tattooed male with white-blonde hair, a sharp nose, and hollow cheeks. Brynne gestures for me to take the seat next to her. Two other seats are set at the far end of the table that haven't been filled yet.

"Where is Silas?" Brynne whispers to me, frantically glancing at the head of the table. A fireplace casts a warm glow behind an empty chair.

"He was right behind us," I reply.

"Gods damn it, he better make it back before Novalora and Embryanna arrive." Her hand fists the royal blue fabric of her gown.

A burst of flames draws our attention to the front of the room. It vanishes under... snowflakes? The room fills with cool smoke as the fire extinguishes, the air warm and freezing all at once. Are we being attacked? No one is rushing or panicking, so I try to remain calm. The smoke dissipates, revealing two gorgeous women in flowing red and blue gowns at the end of the table. Brynne and the others stand, bowing slightly at the hips. Copying what Brynne did—to the best of my ability, anyway—I bob at my hips and tilt my head down.

"Daphne, this is Novalora, the Oracle of Sol Salnege." Brynne gestures to the shorter of the two. Navlora's hair is cut into a sleek white-blonde bob that makes a sharp line right below her jaw, perfectly framing her heart-shaped face. Ice-blue eyes pop against her pale complexion. "And Embryanna, our high priestess." Embryanna has warm chestnut skin and dark brown hair gathered at the side of her head in rows of small, tight braids. Golden cat-like eyes sit at the top of her high cheekbones.

"Pleasure to meet you." I clumsily bow again, unsure of what else to do or what formalities are expected. I stumble to regain my balance as I straighten my body. My palms feel damp with sweat. If this is how I react to an oracle and a priestess, I'm even more anxious about how my nerves will behave in the presence of a king. Novalora lifts a dainty manicured hand over her mouth to stifle a giggle.

"Where is he?" Embryanna asks, her voice strong and demanding. "Can't that damn king ever be on time to his own meetings?" An annoyed hand lands on her hip. "We put a lot of effort into our entrances. The least he could do is be here on time. We are doing him a favor today." She rolls her eyes before she and Novalora take the seats at the far end of the table. Once they're seated, everyone returns to their chairs.

"Are you not the oracle, Novalora? Should you not know when he is going to be late?" Knox jabs. Novalora gives a delicate flip of her wrist, sending water splashing into Knox's face before they both laugh.

"Stop annoying me before I tell you what I see in your future, Knox," Novalora says, her voice high pitched and airy. I look at Brynne, my eyes asking for confirmation if this is normal behavior. She shrugs, taking a sip of the berry-colored wine from the full crystal glass in front of her.

The doors swing open and Kaida, Ash, and Hurik fly into the dining hall, followed by Silas in an equally dramatic fashion. "Good to see you, Novalora, Embryanna." He leans down, giving each of the females a kiss on the cheek. His three dragons land and curl on the floor near the fireplace and the other dragons. There's only one chair left at the table.

"Wish we could say the same, but you did miss our entrance. It was quite grand." Embryanna replies, irritation coating the edge of her voice.

"She wanted to do fire and ice again," Novalora adds, sounding bored as she examines her nails.

"Sorry. I promise I will not miss it next time." He strides confidently to the only open seat. The smile on his stupid handsome face is smug. He winks at me from the opposite side of the table as he passes.

My eyes widen under furrowed brows as I watch Silas. My heart falls into my stomach as what's already unfolded in my mind plays out in front of me. Coolly pulling out his chair, he stretches back in his seat and throws his feet up on the table.

Turning to Brynne for answers, I find her covering her mouth to keep a laugh contained. Across from me, Ajax and Knox are waiting for Silas, their king, to address them.

What the actual fuck.

Am I really that oblivious? I thought he and his friends worked for the king, bringing him dragon eggs for their kingdom. But no. He *is* the king. And his friends... are his inner circle? His court? Whatever they call it here. My anxiety and anger grow as I go through the events of the past three days. Why did a king save me? Why did a king's friends make him take a different path with a random female they found stranded in a dragon's den? Why did this king continue to save me or have any interest in trying to help me? Why didn't he tell me? What else is he keeping from me? What other lies has he spun? If there's one thing that I can't stand, it's liars.

Fae, I remember from all of the books I've read over the years, are tricksters. Manipulators. Why didn't I see this coming? Why was I so desperate to trust them? Had I been so taken away by their beauty and kindness that I let my guard fall too freely?

"Daphne, are you okay?" Silas interrupts my thoughts.

No, I'm not. I'm probably visibly squirming in my seat. My eyes narrow on him. "Yes, your majesty," I bite out.

Knox lets out a loud laugh before Ajax jabs him in the ribs, silencing him.

Ash flies over and lands next to Silas, who strokes the top of his head. "Right. Now that that's been taken care of."

My jaw clenches. It most certainly has not been taken care of. The next moment we have alone—if we have another moment alone

—I'll let him know exactly how I feel. Could I though? If he is a king... oh god.

"Embryanna, Novalora, have you been caught up to speed on how Daphne got here?" he asks. They both nod. "Great. Have you found anything yet?"

"Not yet. I have my priestesses searching the temple's library for any record of traveling occurring between worlds. So far, there is nothing. But we have only been searching for a day now. I've met over the astral plane with the high priestesses of all five kingdoms to ask them to aid in our search. We will be having nightly meetings to discuss findings," Embryanna answers.

"I have been waiting to see her in person." Novalora's icy eyes scan me. "I think she and I must do a full reading together, in private, once lunch is over. Then I can use what we see to find a direction to look in the universe."

"A full reading? Really? It's been a while since you've done one of those." Silas tips his head to the side.

"You did not tell me that was your plan," Embryanna snaps as she glares at Novalora.

"It's the only way I can think of to begin to figure this out," Novalora responds.

Tension builds between Embryanna and Novalora as unsaid words linger in the air.

Silas glances between the two females and places his napkin over his lap. "If it is the only way, it is the only way. Let's eat."

CHAPTER SIXTEEN

Knox and Ajax argue over portions of thick-sliced ham. Syrrus dotingly makes Brynne's plate. The others politely place food on their own plates. My eyes turn into daggers as I watch Silas from my seat. He chats with the two males whose names I still haven't gotten nonchalantly, about what seems to be idle gossip and the dragons, who sit curled beneath Silas's feet, purring. I can't believe he kept this from me. Lied to me the whole time I've been in this world. To think that I thought we were having some kind of moment earlier on the terrace. That makes me angrier.

"Daphne, you need to eat," Brynne whispers to me. "I know you must be confused, but you need to trust that he had his reasons for not revealing who he is."

Obviously, they knew who he is and no one clued me in. Why would they? He's their king. And I'm... an idiot. My fingers instinctively reach for the pendant that no longer hangs from my neck, longing for its comfort.

Reluctantly, I serve myself some meat and vegetables from the platters within my reach, then angrily cut my food and eat it. I imagine stabbing Silas in his muscled arm—the stupid muscled arm that held me on that pegasus—with my fork.

"Daphne, this is Stone," Silas finally introduces one of the striking males he was chatting with. He has an athletic build, deep brown skin, shoulder-length black dreadlocks, and trimmed, clean facial hair along his square jaw.

His full lips pull into a kind smile as his deep amber eyes meet mine. "Nice to meet you, Daphne."

I finish chewing my bite of food and smile back at him. "Nice to meet you as well." Looking back at my food, I go back to eating.

Silas scratches his head before continuing cautiously, "Right, well Daphne, Stone has trained all of us since we were children in physical fitness and combat. He says he has no students right now and he will be able to train you." If he's trained all of them... how old does that make him? Doesn't matter.

"Why would I need to do that? I won't be here very long." I answer quickly between bites.

Embryanna's head snaps toward me. "Make no mistake, we make no promises to get you home. The priestesses of the five kingdoms are doing their best to find answers for you, but we've never seen this before. You'd best take the generous offer. If you end up not being able to leave, it's better to start training as soon as you can. You are so far behind where you should be for an adult fae."

Tears build in my eyes and my chest tightens. In the back of my mind, I knew it was a possibility... but no one else was so direct. I could be stuck here and forced to figure out how to survive in this world, whether I like it or not.

"Embryanna," Silas growls a low warning.

Novalora's airy voice chimes in, "She needs to know, Silas. Clearly, she is not a female who likes things being kept from her, based on her reaction to finding out you are not who she thought you were." She tilts her head almost mockingly.

Silas's cheeks flush in rage or embarrassment, I can't tell which.

The thought of never seeing my children again twists the

growing knot in my stomach. "She's right." I blink away the single tear that escaped. Stone gives me a kind, empathetic smile when I face him. "When can we start?" My voice comes out shakier than I expected it to be.

"Let's start the day after tomorrow. Your body needs a day of rest, especially after tonight's festivities. Right, Silas?" His smile widens to a grin. My eyes dart to Silas as he rubs at his temple and glares at Stone, knowing very well there's something else he forgot to mention to me.

Knox glances from me to Silas. "Silas, you didn't tell her about the party yet?"

"It would have been hard to explain without first explaining who I was." Silas shoots a glare at Knox, telling him to shut up.

Knox ignores him. "We are celebrating our good ol' king here returning from such a treacherous adventure, alive and well. But mostly it is a reason to drink on his dime." Knox raises his wine glass and winks at Silas, who is growing more visibly irritated.

"A party? How will we find a way for me to get home if we don't start looking?" I ask.

"We can't do anything tonight. Embryanna needs to find more information before we can even begin to look. I promise tomorrow we will start," he answers with a half smile that pleads for forgiveness. As if! I am not going to just forget he lied about who he is. "Besides, you need to have a little fun while you're here. I would not be a very good host if I did not make an effort to show you a good time."

Wait—he doesn't expect me to go to this party, does he? Parties are one thing I absolutely do not enjoy. "I hope you all have fun."

He looks at me with confusion. "You will have fun as well. You are my guest, after all."

I need to figure a way out of this thing. "Oh—I don't have anything to wear to such an occasion."

"I'll have something brought up to you."

Arrogant piece of—what does he mean he'll have something sent to me? "Is it like a ball? I don't know how to dance."

"Do not worry about that." He smiles as he swirls the red wine in his glass and takes a long sip.

As lunch ends, everyone starts to take their leave so Novalora and I can do the reading. Whatever that means.

Ajax leaves hand in hand with the last unintroduced guest, who only spoke briefly to Silas throughout lunch. The shorter, slim male has straight, white-blonde hair, the same color as Novalora's, that's shaved on the right side and long on the left. The tan skin of his arms contrasts Ajax's pale complexion. I lean over to Brynne. "Who's that with Ajax?"

"That's Finch, Novalora's protective older brother and Ajax's husband."

"Husband? Not—"

"No," Brynne whispers back sharply. It's clear there is something more behind that response, but she quickly changes the subject. "He is quiet at first, but once you get to know him, he is a great time to be around. Wait until you see him at the party." She and Syrrus make their way from the table, Syrrus guiding her by the waist, leaving only Novalora, Embryanna, Silas, and I in the dining hall.

Novalora scans me up and down, as if assessing my whole being. She looks pointedly at Silas and purses her lips. "This will not work when she is so mad."

Silas cocks his head at me. "Are you really that angry with me?"

I shift my gaze from Silas to Novalora, to Embryanna, who raises her hands to avoid involvement, then back to Silas. "Well, yeah. You lied to me about who you are and then you ignored me when I asked why we were at the palace."

Silas tightens his jaw, runs his tongue along the front of his teeth, and takes a deep breath. "I did not lie. I simply withheld information."

"Same thing."

"We will be back when you two sort this out." Embryanna says, linking arms with Novalora and exiting the room, leaving Silas and me. Crossing my arms in front of me, I stare at him, waiting for an explanation.

Silas runs his hand through his wavy dark hair. "I never lied," he repeats.

So this is how this is going to go. "No, but you didn't tell me you were the king, either."

He rolls his eyes. "Semantics. Why does it matter? You know now and it does not change anything. The only thing I forgot to mention was my title."

"Because, Silas, you're the king. You're not a random person who saved me. You're a king." I sigh heavily as I try to put into words why I'm so angry—with both him and myself. "I wouldn't have acted so... so like myself had I known. I could have tried to save my dignity at least a little bit and attempted to have some better etiquette around you and your friends. Are they even your friends? Or are they your court or your inner circle? What do you call them?" I throw my hands on my head in frustration, as if it will keep me from exploding. "There are so many things I don't understand about this world. I look like an idiot. Is that what they all think I am? What do you think I am?"

"No, Daphne let me—"

"You've had so many chances to tell me. We were alone for a day and a half. Hell, we slept on the same bed. You could have told me when we got here, but instead, I got to find out in front of everyone that you're their king. And what am I then? Some charity project that will make you look good? Your damsel in distress? *King Silas saves female who fell into our world.*" I exhale sharply.

With a single step toward me, his blue-hazel eyes lock on mine and narrow. I will the tears not to come. I've always been an angry crier. Lately, I've become just a crier, and I'm tired of it. I'm stronger than that.

He takes one more step, leaving barely an inch between us. He looks down at me, our foreheads nearly brushing. In a hushed tone he says, "Do you not understand that is exactly why I did not tell you? Everyone on this whole continent knows who I am the moment they lay eyes on me. You are the first person I have ever met who has looked at me and did not immediately recognize me as the King of Fracilonia. You are the first female who has ever treated me like I was normal. Everyone, outside of those who just left this room, treats me like I'm, well, a king. I am sorry I didn't tell you sooner. I should have. I wanted to hold onto whatever bit of realness you gave me for as long as I could. It was selfish. I realize that now."

Not saying anything, I look away. What do I even say to that? It was so intimate. So honest. But it doesn't excuse anything.

Silas continues, "Ajax, Knox, Brynne, and Syrrus—they are my friends. I told them before you woke up at the camp that I wanted to wait to tell you who I am."

"You mean when you knocked me out?" If they agreed to go along with this fabricated truth, what else did they discuss or plan while I lay there unconscious?

"Did we not already move past that? As I was saying, they are also my inner circle, my most trusted advisors, and an elite task force. They are better known in this land as the Azurite Force. I did not lie about that. I told you Ajax is my second and Knox my third, and Brynne really is the best healer in the kingdom.

"They all know exactly why I did not tell you any of our titles. No one thinks you are a fool. And you are definitely not some charity case. For some reason, the universe placed you in my path, and who would I be to ignore her? That is why Novalora is waiting outside this door. To tell us what you are doing here."

I take a deep, steadying breath, understanding starting to diffuse my rage. I exhale slowly through my mouth. "Fine."

Silas raises a brow. "Fine?"

I nod. "Fine." That is all he is getting from me right now. That is all I can manage to muster without crying.

Novalora's airy voice comes from behind us. "You can go now, your majesty." She reappeared so quietly I didn't notice her. Silas turns to leave, glancing over his shoulder at me in confusion. His dragons take notice and fly to join him.

Novalora and I stand alone in the empty dining hall.

"This way." Novalora heads toward the smaller dining room behind the grand dining hall. We take seats across from each other at the small, round table. She claps her hands and various items appear on the table: parchment paper with black drawing charcoals, a few different colored crystal vials, two empty glasses, and a golden incense holder shaped like a dragon.

She lights the stem of an incense from a nearby candle. "I assume this is all a bit unsettling and new to you, coming from a world without magic. So, before we start, I will tell you what I do as the oracle." She places the incense in the small hole in the dragon's mouth, small ashes landing on the table. "Usually, the stars show me large-scale events—turning of times, things that affect our society as a whole. But in some cases, they urge me to look at the smaller scale. When I do these smaller readings on an individual, they are not always certain and can be altered.

"You see, when the gods created our world, they gave us free will over our fates. What we see today may be different from what we would have seen yesterday or what we would see tomorrow. A lot of this reading is based on the choices you or those around you make that have led you here, to this very moment in the universe and time. Every choice affects your path slightly, adding up to your final destiny."

That's pretty heavy to spring on someone. I nod in understanding.

She takes my hands in hers, her skin soft and as cool as ice to the touch. "I do have a confession." Her large doe-like eyes meet mine through her thick, coal-lined lashes. "I have decided to make it now, since I believe it can help us see more during the reading we are about to do."

Confused, I try to pull my hands away from her, but she has a firm grip on me. "What is it?" How can she have something to confess to someone she just met? A chill runs up my spine and I swallow nervously.

"I sent Silas to save you."

More new information that leaves me unsettled. Disbelief, anger, and confusion fill me as I scrutinize her. "What do you mean? Silas knew I would be there? That's why he saved me?" I was set up. No one told me. Are they all in on this? Is this a trap? My eyes dart around the room, looking for an escape. How would I escape? Where would I go? My chest feels like it's being crushed by rising panic.

Her eyes plead with me. "No, it's not like that. I only told Silas that what he seeks lies in this cave. He probably thought I was talking about the dragon egg. That is, until he saw you."

Holding my breath, I anxiously chew the side of my cheek, waiting for her to say more.

"Daphne, I had a vision. I saw you in that cave with Silas. And like I told you, the stars only show me significant events. My job as the oracle is to guide whomever I see to their fate, if that is what the stars decide. Silas and the others did not know you would be there. I am not allowed to give direct instruction, only guidance. Once they found you, I knew they would know you are important and do the right thing and try to help you get home. King Silas does not ever leave people who are in need of help. I knew, inevitably, he would bring you here."

"You trapped me?" I try to pull my hands away again, but she still holds them tightly. She is much stronger than she looks.

"No, this is not a trap. You are free to leave if that is what you wish. What I am saying is that you are supposed to be here. I do not know exactly why yet, but either you or something about the way you got here is going to have a significant impact on this world." With one more tug, she finally releases my hands.

"Why would I have a significant impact on anything?" I ask. "I'm only going to be here until we find a way to send me home."

She shrugs. "I do not control what I am shown. And I cannot tell you everything. The stars do not allow it. That is why it is so important we do this reading. It will allow me to see your past, your future, and possibly your connection to Threa."

How should I feel about this? I guess I should be grateful she didn't let me become a snack for that dragon, but I can't wrap my head around why she would see me. I'm just Daphne, no one special. Maybe it's about the magic that got me here. There's really only one way to find out. Reaching my hands back out across the table, I let her grab them again. "Okay, let's do it."

The corners of her pink-stained lips pull up slightly. "Thank you, Daphne. Now, this is what we have to do. There is one vial for each of us. They contain two ends of a connecting potion. We will each drink one half, allowing me to temporarily access your mind to see your past. Then, we will be able to search for your future. It is my hope that this will help us figure out where Embryanna should start her research on getting you home and maybe give me an inkling of why you were brought here." She pops the lids off of the two crystal vials, pours the glittering yellow liquid into the glasses, and hands me one. "Cheers." She clinks her glass to mine.

My head shakes at the disbelief that I am really doing this. "Bottoms up." I tilt my head back and drink.

CHAPTER SEVENTEEN

The thick, herbal, metallic liquid sends a burning sensation down my throat as I finish every last drop. My face scrunches from the lingering sting on my tongue.

Novalora's icy eyes glow as she whispers, "Per mentem, fenestram invenimus animae." The world around us fades away into pure darkness. The room, table, and chairs we were sitting on are all gone. Novalora and I are the only things illuminated by small circles of light around our feet as we stand in a void of complete darkness. She reaches out her hand and leads me to a small, white stone sculpture. It resembles an ornate bird bath with a vessel on top that holds a rippling silver liquid.

"What is this place?" I whisper in near-terrified awe.

"This, Daphne, is your mind. This, right here, is your memory reservoir," she says, gesturing to the silver liquid. "It's how I will look into your past and see the moment you fell into this world."

Our eyes meet as we stand across from each other on either side of the memory reservoir. What will she be able to see? Worry must fill my face, because Novalora gently places her hand on top of mine, resting on the edge of the bowl. "I will not look farther than I need."

She removes her hand and dips a single finger into the liquid, causing it to still. "Now, you need to concentrate very hard on your memory and find the moment you were pulled from your world. I will turn away until you find it. Be prepared—memory reservoirs gravitate toward moments with high emotions."

Novalora turns her back to me and I stare into the stilled liquid. Small memories play back to me: my wedding day, Ariella's birth, and then the twins. My surroundings change suddenly, as if I'm sucked into the memory reservoir. I'm on my couch in my living room. Except, not really; I'm seeing through my eyes, but my actions and thoughts are not my own. Well, they are mine, but they're not my current ones. It's as if I'm back right at that moment.

Ariella and the twins snuggled into my arms as I told them a bedtime story. "We built the life that I dreamed about having when I was a little girl. It's all I ever hoped for and wanted. Our little family is my entire world. I wouldn't change it for anything."

The crowd favorite the weeks before Wyatt died had been the story of how Mommy met Daddy, of which I'd perfected the SparkNotes version. I kissed each of their foreheads. I yawned and stretched my arms in front of me. The clock on the mantel read nearly 8 p.m. "Now, time for bed!"

No. Not this moment. Not this memory. I can't do anything except watch it play out.

"It's a good thing Auntie Gabby left you alone in the coffee shop, otherwise who knows if you would've ever married Daddy?" Ronan pointed out smartly.

"I love that story, Mommy. It's like a real-life fairy tale." Ariella stretched her arms high above her head and rubbed her eyes. She grabbed her stuffed iridescent white dragon and made her way off the couch and to her bed.

The twins, as usual, put up more of a fight. "I want Daddy to tell us a story too," Ryan complained.

"Yeah! We want to wait for Daddy," Ronan chimed in with puppy dog eyes for dramatic effect.

"Daddy loves you both, but he had to work late with Aunt Whitney, like he does every Tuesday. It's already well past your bedtime. C'mon, let's go," I told them.

"We want to sleep in your bed," Ryan begged.

"Not tonight." I stood and ushered them to their rooms. Wyatt hated it when the kids ended up in our bed. The twins kicked so much in their sleep. "You've got school tomorrow. No more arguing."

A few more whimpers and complaints and they finally gave in. They walked hand in hand to their room. Since the school year had started, Tuesdays had become incredibly hectic. It was cleaning and inventory day at the shop; then, after school, Ariella had gymnastics lessons and the twins had karate. I didn't know why I hadn't considered timing when I signed them up for lessons.

Before leaving work that day, I had done as much cleaning as I could. The antiques were dusted and I had made sure all of the books were in the right places. Wyatt had been busy all day taking stock of all of our inventory and taking photos of new arrivals to post online. I'd barely even spoken to him. The lack of my help that year meant Wyatt and Whitney's Tuesday nights had grown increasingly late. I took the kids to their respective activities, brought them home, made dinner, and got the kids fed and ready for bed. So, we didn't get to see each other much on Tuesdays.

My body ached badly with exhaustion after such a long day. I threw a bag of popcorn in the microwave, poured myself a healthy-sized glass of red wine, and plopped back on the couch. In the corner, birthday balloons from Wyatt's forty-first birthday party still hung, half deflated; at the time, I had thought I'd throw them out the next day. Netflix was on in the background while I sat aimlessly scrolling through social media, decompressing from the day. A video of some recipe I would never have time to make was playing when Whitney's photo flashed across my screen.

Expecting a mock apology for keeping my husband so late, as she normally called me with on her Tuesday night drive home, I grabbed my glass of wine, took a long sip, and picked up the phone. "Hey!

What—" All that came through the line were sobs. Whitney was hysterical. "Whitney, what's going on? I need you to calm down and tell me what's happening." Horrific realization and dread seeped in.

"It's Wyatt," she sobbed. "He had just left. I was finishing locking up and I heard a loud crash. I went outside and…" Struggling to continue between labored breaths, she finally got out, "Daph, his car is in flames. The fire department is here now. The car and everything… everything inside is gone." Her cry grew deeper, the sound desperate and gut-wrenching.

The gravity of what she was telling me hits me like the first time I heard it, all over again. My heart drops into my stomach and tears swell in my eyes. My hands tremble, the wine glass I held shattering to the floor. Bright red wine seeps into the plush white carpet as I raise my hand over my mouth in a useless attempt to muffle the cry that escapes from a place painfully deep inside my soul.

I blink and I'm back standing in front of the memory reservoir with Novalora. My chest tightens and the world around me stills. Tears drip down my face onto the still liquid and my body trembles.

Breathe, Daphne. Breathe.

My hands grip tighter around the stone of the memory reservoir. Nothing could have prepared me to relive that. I need to get home. I need to get back to my kids. They can't lose me too. Taking a moment to compose myself, I lean closer to the bowl. The memory of the day I landed in this world replays like a movie shot through my eyes on top of the silver surface.

"Here, I found it." I get out with a shaky breath.

Novalora puts a hand on my shoulder. "I am sorry about whatever you just saw." We look down on the silver surface at the memory, which starts right after I sent Whitney away. There's the store, me crying, cleaning, then the buzzing, uncovering the mirror, falling through the mirror, the dragon's den, Silas. Everything is in crystal clear detail. She places her finger back on top of the still liquid, making it ripple once again.

"Interesting," she mutters.

"Did you see anything that can help?" Removing my hands, I take a step back from the memory reservoir.

"I am not sure. Now, we have to look around for your future." She walks away into the nothingness.

Looking up, I find a glowing, golden thread floating across the top of my mind. Novalora notices I've stopped and follows my stare, her glowing eyes tilting up. "Hmm... very interesting."

My gaze drops to her and then back up, as if the thread is drawing me to it, calling to me. "Why, what is it?"

"That is a tether. We have them when our soul is or was bonded to another, or has the potential to be. It is not complete, so either it is looking for its match, or it was severed."

My emotions rise again. "Can't you tell which it is?"

"Yours is... different from ones I have seen before. The end is frayed, like something affected it, but it is still growing, searching. Maybe it is because you are not from our world. I am not sure."

I hold back a frustrated sigh. Novalora's evasive responses are getting on my nerves. What good is an oracle if she can't tell me anything?

Seeming to know what she's looking for, she starts walking again. I wish she would tell me what exactly we're looking for so I can be of some help.

Breathe, Daphne. You don't know enough about the people of this world to keep pushing, so just follow behind her and keep your questions to yourself for now. A faint light comes into view in the distance. Novalora must also notice it, because she picks up her pace, nearly sprinting toward the light. I struggle to keep pace with her.

We arrive at two doorways made of pure light in the darkness. I have to stop a few feet behind her to catch my breath. How am I out of breath in my own mind? This doesn't seem fair. Novalora turns her glowing gaze at me in astonishment as a tight smile quirks on her lips. She takes a step closer to the doorways and the ground under us begins to shake.

Panic spikes across Novalora's face. She lunges back toward me and grabs both of my hands in hers. "We need to wake up, now." She glances back at the doors one last time, then bows her head and mutters under her breath, "Expergiscimini somno. Corporalia receptus."

The shaking intensifies and an energy pulses, bringing us back to the dining room with a burst that shatters the vials and glasses on the table. Making sure I've actually woken up, I run my hands over my face and then my body. Novalora's nails dig into the wood of the table as she struggles to support the weight of her own body. Silas, Embryanna, and Finch burst into the room.

"What happened?" Embryanna demands.

"Novalora! Are you okay?" Finch goes to Novalora, lowering her into a chair. He rubs her back and glares at me through piercing blue eyes. It'd come as no surprise if Ajax told him how he distrusts me. I'm sure being found with his sister in this state won't win me any favor with him, either.

Silas rushes to me, placing unwelcome hands on my shoulders, crouching down to me, his eyes moving up and down, checking me for physical damage. "Are you all right?" The worry in his tone softens my annoyance with him.

Despite this, I instinctively glare at him and shrug off his hands. My forgiveness is not easily won. "I'm fine. We saw these two doors, then there was a burst of energy and we woke up back here." I look to Novalora so she can give them more information, as I don't really understand what happened. But she's already moved on to drawing feverishly on the scraps of paper, smudging bits of charcoal dust on the table.

Embryanna and Finch peer over Novalora's shoulder at the papers. "Is that what you saw?" Finch's brows lower, scrutinizing the image Novalora is drawing.

Embryanna glances at me with a tilt of her head and narrowed eyes, without saying anything. Then, she returns to watching Novalora, who continues to make swift, precise marks on the paper.

This is my mind they're talking about. I deserve to know what's warranting such responses. I won't allow them to leave me in the dark any longer. "Are you going to tell me what just happened to us?" My voice comes out sharper than I had anticipated.

Novalora pauses, her charcoal-coated hand still hovering above her paper, as if I broke her out of whatever trance she was in. She places the piece of worn charcoal cooly on the table. "There are two doors in your mind—two futures. In all my years, never have I seen more than one door. Many firsts are happening with you. I must consult the stars." She sounds out of breath and exhausted. She and Embryanna both study me like they don't quite know what to make of me. Novalora makes a few more quick lines on her page with her charcoal before standing up.

"We must go now. We will let you know what we find." Embryanna answers, continuing her vagueness.

"Do not worry, I have got you." Finch puts his arm around Novalora to support her as she stands. Her body has grown incredibly weak. Is that normal for a private reading, or is that yet another thing unique to me? Novalora leans most of her weight on Finch as they exit slowly through the door.

"Are you sure you are okay?" Silas asks again, looking down at my hands, which are clutching the blue fabric of my dress.

I relax my hands and smooth the skirt over my lap. "I think so. Is that what usually happens to her? Being so drained?"

"More or less. It is one of the reasons she does not do private readings very often. They require a lot of energy from both parties. I am surprised you are not in the same state." He cocks his head and looks me over.

"I feel... fine. I wish she would say more. I feel like no one is telling me everything I need to know." I huff a sigh.

When I look up, something like shame briefly flickers in his eyes. "I am sorry again for misleading you."

He really does feel bad, doesn't he? I've never received such a genuine apology. "I didn't mean you. I understand now why you didn't tell me. I was talking about Novalora and Embryanna."

The small smile he gives me tells me he doesn't quite believe me, but my words were true. As annoyed as I was earlier, it's easier than I thought to forgive him. "That is how all the oracles are. They are bound by the stars not to affect the free will given by the gods, so they have to be careful," he says.

"Well, that's annoying."

He laughs. "It can be, yes."

Scanning the room for a change in subject, I notice we're completely alone. "Where did all of the dragons go?"

"They're off in the dragon barn with Brynne and Syrrus. They spend most of their time there or flying around the castle grounds." His face softens with concern. "I have to run into the city to pick something up. Will you be okay here?"

After my oracle experience, being alone doesn't sound appealing. "Can I go with you, actually? I'd love to see what the city looks like." A rush of light-headedness makes the room spin for a second as I stand. The feeling fades quickly and I shake it off—must be the adrenaline wearing off.

CHAPTER EIGHTEEN

Walking the city is euphoric. Magic radiates from the ground out into the streets, the buildings, and people walking. Rays of sunshine beam down on us as we walk the wide main street of Sol Salnege. A light breeze pushes through the perfectly warm pine and sea salt air. Magical beings of all kinds pop in and out of white stone shops and homes. Most of the females wear airy long skirts and dresses with corset bodices. The males wear tunics and trousers. The fashion looks just like what I'd imagine of a fairy tale kingdom, but a bit more modern.

Turning to peer into the shops across the street, I catch Silas watching me, a glimmer of joy in his eyes at my awe-struck smile. I look away shyly as we continue past the shops, into the crowd of people. Every friendly face we pass smiles at Silas. A few even stop him to congratulate him on returning home with a dragon's egg. The myriad of different races all living here in harmony is surprising. This is all so new to me, so it takes a conscious effort to not gape at them. Some are taller, some smaller, some have wings, and some don't look human-like at all.

I'll have to remember to ask someone later about the different beings and creatures of this world. I wish I had my phone to add that to a checklist. However, I haven't had too much trouble remembering things the past few days.

Gorgeous ball gowns decorate the windows of a few clothing shops we pass. One boutique looks a bit more modern, with legging style pants and flowy tunics hanging on a rack outside. A candle store emanates a fragrant smell of wax and citrus through its open doors. Weapons shops boast long glimmering metal blades and intricately carved bows with sets of sharpened arrows.

Outside of a tea shop, a large fae male with red hair, tan skin, and golden membranous wings sits reading a newspaper and drinking from a cup of tea. Both the gorgeous wings and the small orange dragon snoozing at his feet are mind-boggling.

"How many of these tiny dragons are there?" I ask.

Silas glances over at the male. "In Sol Salnege? A few hundred. At the palace alone there are ten. My three, and then each member of the Azurite Force has been chosen, then Finch and two of the palace workers. But in the continent? I'm not entirely sure. Probably thousands by this point."

"How do the dragons choose who will take care of them?"

"When the dragon sees the person, they know."

That's what Brynne said about Syrrus, isn't it? She just knew. "Like the mating bond?"

He looks up in thought and scratches his head. "Not exactly. Dragons choose who they bond to. The bond is more intense with full-sized dragons. They can communicate mind-to-mind with their chosen rider, and the rider can harness their dragon's power to enhance their own. With our dragons, it's more like the bond of a parent and a child. Except the child is deadly. But it is still a powerful connection. That is what some of these marks are." He offers his forearm. The tattooed dragon wrapped around it looks like Ash. "The other two are on my legs. Maybe I'll show them to you another time."

Unable to tell if he's joking, I force a small laugh. "Probably best if you keep your pants on."

A soft startled chuckle escapes his mouth. "I can just roll up the leg." He smirks at me and an embarrassed blush crosses my face. We continue walking and he picks up where he left off: "With the mating bond, there is shared power and a single line marked around the left index finger. So, in that regard, it is similar to the dragon bond. But your mate is a fate decided for you by the gods."

"When Novalora and I were in my mind, we saw a floating thread. She called it a mating tether."

His head snaps toward me in quick surprise. "Did you now?"

I shrug. "But she said it wasn't complete, or that it was severed. I wonder if we have the same thing on Earth that we just don't know about. I always called my husband my soulmate. Maybe my tether is like that because he died."

Something shifts in his face, but I can't quite make out the emotion behind it. "This is us." The blue door he opens has "Farver's Emporium: Potions, Spells, & Enchantments for all Occasions" painted on its oval window.

The dark dusty shop is lined with shelves of vials of all colors and sizes. A slender male with onyx hair and pale white skin stands behind the counter. With a smile, he motions for Silas to follow him through another door.

"You can look around if you'd like. This will not take very long." Silas offers me an apologetic smile and follows the male through the back door.

In the corner of the shop, a silver-haired male sits hunched over behind a jewelry case, pliers in his hands and jewels arranged on a cloth beside him. He wears tinted goggles with a jeweler's loupe on one eye, which make his large pointed ears more pronounced.

He's so heavily immersed in the task of assembling an intricate pair of dangling sapphire earrings that he doesn't look up from his work when he addresses me. "Thanks for stopping by. All the jewelry is handmade by me with the finest metals available in all of Carimea.

The stones you see are all sourced ethically from the cave fairies. None of that crap the pirates down south try selling off as genuine," he mutters under his breath as his eyes narrow on the gold he's using to solder a small stone in place.

"Thank you." Did he say cave fairies and pirates?

"Feel free to look as much as you'd like."

The delicate pieces are all stunning. Some have rough gems, some have polished stones. Any of the bracelets would make a great gift to bring back for Gina. But even if I had my wallet, I don't think my money would be any good here.

A dainty necklace dangling on a small metal display tree catches my eye. Hanging on a delicate silver chain is a silver pendant shaped like a dragon wrapped around an egg-shaped opal. I pick the necklace up off the display to get a better look at the fine craftsmanship. We have a very particular way of inspecting antique pieces we're interested in for the shop, and I now apply it to any purchase.

"Excellent eye, lady." The scrawny male looks up at me from his chair, the skin around his blue eyes wrinkled from hours spent squinting while making jewelry. "That, there, is a genuine dragon shell opal from the dragons' dens in the Izon. It is said that particular gem carries protection to whoever carries it. It's got a hefty price tag though. And I don't do refunds."

"I'm just browsing while I wait for my friend." I place the necklace back on its stand.

He snickers. "Friend? You are friends with the King of Fracilonia?"

A heavy hand lands on my shoulder. "All set. Are you ready to go?" Silas asks.

"Yes. I'm ready." I glance back at the male, who's already back to work on his earrings.

"It has gotten late. We have to go change for the party. The guests will be arriving shortly. I think you will like what I picked out for you to wear." What he picked out for me? No one's ever done that for me before.

When we get back to the palace, Silas takes me to my room in the east wing of the palace. "Amaleana is waiting for you inside. She will help you get ready. I will be back to escort you once I change."

I hate parties. My mom's behavior when I was younger kind of ruined them for me. I saw how she acted before she met Richard and settled down. I knew, from way too young of an age, that I never wanted to be that person. "Silas, so you know, I'm not really a party person. I'm not sure how much fun I will be."

His full lips curve into a smirk. "Perhaps, it is because you have not been going to the right parties." He opens the door for me. I step inside and watch him walk down the hall to his wing of the palace. Maybe a fae ball is different from the parties on Earth. I'll at least try to not act completely miserable.

Amaleana waits for me in my room. "How was lunch, ma'am?" She stands hurriedly from her spot on the bench as if she had been caught doing something she wasn't supposed to be doing.

Now understanding the formalities—I am a guest to her king—I look at her cautiously. She probably thinks every interaction we have will be reported back to him. Gross. I take a seat on the bench. "It was fine. Please, call me Daphne or even Daph. No more 'ma'am.' There's no need for you to treat me special. You can sit on this bench as much as you'd like."

Her nose and mouth twitch slightly. "With all due respect, ma'am. You are definitely special. King Silas has not had any nonpolitical guests outside of court members or family the entire time I have been here."

She undoes the braids in my hair, replacing them with curling rollers. This is something I could get used to; doing my hair is my least favorite part of getting ready. The thick, long blanket of hair that grows from my head takes forever to do. I don't possess the time or patience for it. I used to try to do things so I would look nicer for Wyatt, but that was before we had kids. Now it's always up in a mom bun or ponytail. On multiple occasions I was tempted to chop it off, but Wyatt preferred it long. For some reason, I still feel like I can't cut it and risk feeling like I lost one of the things my husband always loved about me.

A blast of warm air wraps the top of my head. "Those have to set for a bit. Let me go fetch your dress." She walks into the closet and returns with a long sage-green evening gown that has small gems sewn into the bodice.

It, like the dress I'm currently wearing, looks like it's going to be way too small. Maybe if it doesn't fit, I will have found an out to this party. Amaleana turns around and I undress and pull the velvet gown over my head. It fits like it was made for me. "How do all of these clothes fit me?"

"The fabric is enchanted, ma'am. All of the clothes in the guest closet are. Most of the clothes in this world are. They are made to fit any body exactly how they should. Whoever should stay here and require clothing would be able to wear anything from the closet."

This world is incredible. "That must make shopping a lot easier."

"Indeed it does, ma'am." She chuckles, buttoning up the back of the gown.

I walk over to the mirror to look at myself. The dress has long pointed gauntlet sleeves that end in loops around my fingers, a sweetheart neckline, and fabric that clings to every dip and curve of my body before brushing the floor in a slight flare. As I turn, I notice the back plunging to below my waist right, above the small of my back. For a full-length dress, it's... revealing.

I face Amaleana. "I can't wear this."

"What do you mean? Why not? You look stunning, ma'am."

I stare back at my reflection. I do look good, I can't deny that. It just makes me feel so... exposed. I usually prefer dresses that cover my body, hiding all of the parts I don't like about myself. This dress showcases and hugs my new figure, which I'm admittedly not used to yet. "I don't know... You don't think it's too much? Too sexy?" I run my hands down the fabric over my hips before resting them together in front of my stomach—my admittedly flatter stomach. This body, this version of myself, looks better than I ever did on Earth.

She laughs lightly. "Absolutely not. I think it is perfect. King Silas may be offended if you do not wear it, but if you really do not like it, the whole closet is yours to choose from."

She's right; he did pick out this dress for me to wear. I should take it as a compliment that he thought I'd look nice in this, even if it's out of my comfort zone. I don't think Wyatt ever did that for me. He was the kind of guy who told me I looked good in whatever I wore. I don't think he paid attention to what I had on most of the time.

Something about knowing Silas selected this particular dress for me to wear gives me little butterflies and makes my heart skip. I push those feelings down. He's just being a good host. Nothing about this gesture means anything. Does it? No, it can't. He's a king and I'm just Daphne. It honestly doesn't matter either way... I won't be staying here very long.

"It's fine. I'll wear this. It does look nice, doesn't it?" I sit back on the bench, smoothing the creases out of the skirt as they form.

"Yes, ma'am." She puts blush on my cheeks from a small metal compact. She brushes my lips with a deep pink stain from a jar and removes the curlers from my hair. "All done."

I stand and walk back to the mirror. I look beautiful. When was the last time I thought that about myself?

"Wow." Silas's voice comes from the doorway. Blushing, I turn around. He's now dressed in a suit the same shade of green as my dress and wears a golden crown atop his head. "You clean up nice."

First I look "better," now this? I don't know if this is his attempt at flirting or what. "You're not very good at compliments, are you?"

He disguises a laugh as a cough. "I suppose not. Let me see you." He gestures for me to twirl and I oblige, turning back to find a wide grin across Silas's face.

"Thank you. The dress is beautiful."

"I do not think it is the dress."

I laugh awkwardly and run my fingers through my still tightly bound curls. If he is bad at giving compliments, I'm allowed to be bad at receiving them.

"I got you something." His smile brightens.

I tilt my head as he pulls a small black box out of his pocket and hands it to me. Inside the box, I find the dragon pendant from the shop. "What's this?"

His eyes glimmer with nervous excitement. "A gift."

"I can't accept this. It's too much." How did he even know I looked at it?

"Think of it as an 'I'm sorry I lied about being a king' gift. It'll give you something to remember this world by. Also, the jeweler said no refunds, so you have to keep it." He takes the pendant from its box. "Here, lift your hair."

I stand in front of the mirror and pull my hair out of the way. My pulse quickens as Silas's strong arms move over my neck, draping the necklace and clasping it into place. He smiles at me through the mirror. "Shall we go now?"

I hold the delicate pendant between my fingers and my lips pull in a tight smile. It's not the necklace Wyatt gave me, but the gesture is incredibly thoughtful. "Yes, I'm ready."

Amaleana nods then opens the door and Silas offers me his arm. At first, I hesitate, but then I link my hand around his strong bicep as he leads us down the staircase. He takes care to walk slowly so I don't trip over the flowing bottom of my gown.

Music and sounds of happy chatter emanate from behind the ballroom doors. "Relax and try to enjoy yourself." Silas adjusts the lapel of his jacket with his other hand before two guards in full suits of metal armor open the double doors for us to enter the party.

CHAPTER NINETEEN

The dim ballroom hums with the static energy of magic. Stars fill the skylight above and the two moons glow down on the party. White flowers are wrapped around every pillar. Extravagant centerpieces shaped like dragon eggs sit on the elegant linens that line the tables. A long table holds endless trays of decadent desserts.

Servants walk around with crystal flutes of champagne, glasses of wine, and plates of hors d'oeuvres. A small stage is set up in the corner of the ballroom where instruments float in the air, playing themselves. They must have some sort of enchantment on them.

Fae and other magical beings of all races are joyously dancing, drinking, and eating together. There must be over a hundred guests, all dressed in gorgeous dresses and suits. Most of the females' outfits are more revealing than mine, which makes me relax slightly.

The crowd splits, allowing their king to make his entrance. I feel every single pair of eyes land on me, the strange and unknown female on the arm of the king. This doesn't feel like something I should be doing. Slowly, I start to pull my hand away from Silas's arm. He puts his other hand firmly over mine and steps into the parted sea of fae.

Knox heads directly for us, clapping his arm over Silas's shoulder, and the crowd resumes their dancing and mingling. "It seems like every high-ranking member of the court and then some have shown up for your soirée, my friend."

"They are happy we retrieved another dragon egg. It's been a while since we have been able to. It's a cause for celebration," Silas remarks dismissively.

"I do not think that is the reason they have all shown up tonight." Knox winks at me.

"Oh god. Are they here because of me? How do they know who I am?" I say.

"Not a lot going on in the continent right now. I am sure the palace workers were quite excited for this tidbit of gossip." Knox shrugs and drinks from his cup, changing the subject by pointing out Ajax and Finch on the dance floor.

Finch's hand cups the back of Ajax's head as they gaze longingly at each other, dancing drunkenly to the rhythm of the music. They look happy and in love. If I wasn't so aware of both of their suspicions of me, I'd think maybe Ajax forgot about wanting to kill me, at least temporarily. It's unsettling to see him in such a different setting, but at the same time, it's relieving to know he isn't always an asshole.

"Oh gods, are they really already drunk?" Silas puts his hand to his forehead in disbelief.

"They showed up that way. Would you expect anything different?" Knox answers.

Silas lets out a low chuckle. "No, you're right. It's good for him to let loose. He cannot always act like he has a stick up his ass."

A short-statured male, whose arrogant presence tells me he's of some importance, escorts an equally petite female toward us. "King Silas, welcome home. Congratulations on finding another dragon egg for the kingdom. You remember my daughter, Meadow, don't you?" The beautiful female has rich mahogany hair and vibrant green eyes. Her tight-fitting golden gown compliments her tan skin and the plunging neckline shows off her ample cleavage. She dips into a small curtsy that further exposes her chest.

"Of course, Lord Dahl." He nods his head at her in greeting.

"She would love your first dance of the evening if you'd do us the kindness of obliging. Unless you're..." His eyes drop to my hand, still wrapped on Silas's arm, then up at me, and his lips twitch in a tight, challenging smile.

I pull my hand to myself, prompting a quick sidelong glare from Silas. "Oh no, no. Silas—King Silas is just being a polite host."

Silas lowers and raises his brows as if to say 'alright then,' and turns to smile at Meadow, who smiles back, her flirtatious smile making her already gorgeous face even more alluring. "Yes, I do not see why that would be a problem." Her hand takes the place of mine on his arm and they make their way to the dance floor.

A brief tinge of jealousy hits me as they begin an intricate ballroom-esque dance. Embryanna and Novalora make their way to me and Knox from somewhere on the dance floor. Embryanna wears a tight-fitting deep-red gown that shows off her curvy figure. Novalora's layered off-white gown sparkles like snow and flows as she moves. Knox's eyes brighten and his lips curve into a flirtatious smile as he takes in the pair.

"Well, don't you look gorgeous?" Knox winks at Novalora.

She smiles shyly in thanks and Knox grabs Novalora by the hand and spins her, causing her skirt to poof as she twirls. She giggles as they make their way to the dance floor.

"Just the two of us then." I smile in an attempt to befriend Embryanna.

"Yes, just the two of us," she responds cooly as she crosses her arms over her chest and scans the dance floor.

We stand in awkward silence. I need to find something, anything, to talk about with her. "So, you're all fae. But not everyone is, right?"

"Correct." Her response is blunt.

"Okay, what about him?" I tilt my head in the direction of a male who looks almost fae, but his eyes are more animal-like.

"Shifter."

A pale-skinned female with vibrant red eyes smiles at a fae male by a bowl of punch. "And her over there?"

"Half vampire," she answers quickly.

Hoping to get more than one word from her, I ask, "So you all live together in harmony?"

Her eyes narrow on me, suspiciously. "For the most part, yes."

I scan the crowd, desperate to keep the conversation going. "What about her?" From the dance floor, a petite female with fire-red cropped hair smiles at Embryanna, asking her to dance.

Her lips pull into a tight smile. "She is a witch."

And then, I'm alone.

I place a few hors d'oeuvres on a plate and make my way to a nice spot on the wall that's quiet and out of the way. The lively music plays and I watch as people dance. The guests get increasingly more drunk as the night goes on.

Brynne drapes over Syrrus's neck as they sway in place. Brynne looks at him like he's the only one in the room, and he looks the same way at her. I remember having that same look on my face when I looked at Wyatt. The way Wyatt made me feel is one of the only reasons I could get past the sneers and dirty looks of other women.

The dancing gets noticeably more risque as I nibble my food. Couples dancing transition from waltzing to something resembling a salsa at the turn of the music. This isn't exactly how I imagined the dancing at a royal ball, but I'm not on Earth, so how would I know what to expect? Across the room, I catch Finch and Ajax escaping out of a back door behind the instruments. Silas now dances with another beautiful female, who is pressing herself against him. She lifts her bare leg through the slip in her gown up on his hip, and he lowers her into a dip. I roll my eyes and stuff a bite of a spinach puff pastry into my mouth. From what I know about royalty on Earth, I assume these females want to be chosen as his queen. But that doesn't make it look any less desperate.

Silas catches my glance from across the crowd. I try to look anywhere else, but it's too late. He excuses himself from the dark-haired female he was dancing with, grabs two glasses of wine off the nearest servant's tray, and makes his way over to me. He hands me a nearly full, stemmed crystal glass and I take a sip of the sweet red wine. Its delicious notes incline me to continue sipping.

"You are really not having fun?" he asks before taking a long sip from his glass, the disappointment evident in his tone.

"No, no, I'm having fun. I told you, I'm not a party person. Your guests have been very entertaining to watch." I nervously drink more. It tastes almost like juice. I look down and realize I've almost finished my glass. "You look like you're having fun. Don't worry about me. I'm fine, I pinky promise."

"You do what with your pinky?" he asks, confused.

Right, I guess pinky swears is a foreign concept here. "It's just a saying. You link pinkies, say your promise, and it becomes unbreakable." I demonstrate by linking his pinky with mine. "See, I'm fine. Pinky promise."

"So it's like a bargain? Or a deal?" He takes my empty glass and sets it on a passing servant's tray.

Both of those sound much more serious than a pinky promise. "Uh, more like a deal."

His head tilts at the concept. "And you don't get any marks from making one?"

Definitely more serious. "Marks? Like a tattoo? No. It's not like a super serious thing."

He looks up, still trying to make sense of it. "Your world is strange. Come, dance with me." Before I have the chance to object, he slips my hand into his from its previous linked-pinkies position and drags me to the center of the dance floor. "Indulge me. Just one song."

"I don't know how to dance." I try taking my hand away, but his hold is firm.

"Nonsense." He smirks and a flicker of amusement sparks in his eyes as he pulls out a small vial from his coat pocket. "Drink this and follow my lead."

My eyes widen at the vial in his hand. "What is that?"

"A specially-brewed fairy liquor. It's enchanted. That is what I had to get at Farver's. Drink just enough and you can dance to any song. Drink too much and the effects will dwindle as the alcohol takes over, then you're drunk, like most of those around us."

"And you say my world is weird." My eyes move from the purple vial in his hand to his charming smile. If he's going to make me dance, I want to at least stand a chance of not looking like a complete idiot. "Fine." I take the bottle and drink half of the sweet, honey-tasting liquid.

The music slows as the song comes to an end. My head rotates around the room as the dancing bodies still and all eyes land on us. "Silas, everyone is looking at us," I whisper while nervously searching for an escape route. "I don't think this is the impression you want me to be making right now. People will talk."

"Let them. I do not care what they have to say unless it is regarding the good of my kingdom." The music starts again and Silas places one of my hands on his shoulder and the other in his hand before guiding me to the sound of the violins. And we dance.

My feet feel light as if I am no longer fully in control of them. They move in sync with Silas's. With the help of the enchantment, my body knows each step of this dance. We move gracefully and elegantly in smooth circles around the cleared floor. It's like we rehearsed the dance a thousand times.

Momentarily forgetting the dozens of eyes on me, I smile brightly as I enjoy dancing for the first time in my life. A strong hand presses on the small of my back, and I lean into a dip as the song comes to a melodic end. The following silence is filled with light applause from those still watching. My face flushes with embarrassment. Silas grabs two more glasses of wine and we leave the dance floor.

His lips brush my ear, sending a chill down my spine, as he whispers, "Are you having fun now?"

My breath catches, as I fumble my way through a response. "That was more fun than I've ever had dancing, but I still don't like parties."

He rolls his eyes and flashes me a flirty smile. "Fine. Let us get out of here then."

"This is your party. You can't leave," I say, trying to sound matter-of-fact.

"I'm the king. I can do whatever I want." He shrugs, already headed for the door Ajax and Finch left through. If we're going to leave, we aren't going that way. I have no desire to find out what's going on behind that door at this particular moment.

I quickly move in front of him, blocking his path. "Let's use a different exit."

He raises an eyebrow. "Why?"

"You have to just trust me on this," I answer with a laugh.

His face relaxes and he shrugs in acceptance, then brightens with excitement as he gestures smoothly to the main entrance.

CHAPTER TWENTY

Silas quietly opens the main doors just enough for his broad shoulders to slide through and holds it open for me. He raises a finger to his mouth and winks, telling me to remain quiet as we sneak through the palace. The remaining guests are too drunk to notice our absence by this point anyway, but it's exhilarating. My anxious heart flutters. It feels like we're teenagers trying to sneak around without getting caught.

He finishes his glass of wine and places it on top of the banister at the top of the staircase before opening the door to the terrace. His steps become clumsy; he's definitely drunk after that last glass. I shiver as the chill night air blows around us. Before I can rub my arms to warm myself, Silas removes his jacket and places it loosely over my shoulders. Its thick fabric smells of his fresh cologne. He retakes his place from earlier against the railing, overlooking the bright night sky full of stars. The two crescent moons shine high over the kingdom.

I put my elbows on the rail beside him and place my head in my hands. "I can't believe you have two moons here."

"The two moons have names, you know." He wraps one arm

around my shoulder and points up at the sky. "The one that rises in the east is called Iyla, and the one that rises in the west is Ojai. To our people, it is symbolic of the mating bond. The two moons spend their whole life circling Threa, searching for each other, but only when the timing is perfect and each moon is in the correct phase will their paths perfectly intersect and form a full moon. When that happens, the whole night sky fills with bright light. But only for a moment. If you are not paying attention, you miss it. Just like with finding your mate."

"How often does that happen?"

"The moons crossing? Every couple of decades or so. The beings of Threa find their mates much more often than that. But it is rare nonetheless."

The glow of moons seems to shine brighter for a moment. "It's saying to pay attention and not let opportunities pass you by."

He laughs quietly. "Yes, that is the jist of it."

"Thank you." I break my gaze from the stars to look at him.

"For what?" He tilts his head.

"For saving me, for taking care of me the last few days, the jacket. All of it."

"It's nothing." He smiles drunkenly at me. As if the wind were beckoned to repeat itself, a strand of curled hair is blown into my face and Silas pushes it behind my ear. Without Ajax to interrupt this time, his hand lingers, cradling the back of my head. He tilts my face up, his face and drunken smile only inches away from mine. "I know I have told you this before, but you are absolutely stunning in the moonlight." His mouth parts and the reflection of stars dance in his eyes. He leans closer and his warm lips land on mine.

The heat of his body, now pressed against mine, makes me melt and my heart skip in my chest. Silas's lips are soft and taste like the sweet wine we were drinking. He wraps his fingers in my hair and grabs my waist with his other hand. When I push up on my toes to kiss him back, an image of Wyatt flashes in my mind and my heart drops into my stomach. I lower my heels and pull away.

I can't do this yet. I'm not ready for this. No matter how right it feels, it's too soon. The railing behind steadies me as I step back, feeling like I'm going to vomit from the speed at which my mind is reeling. My fingertips brush my lips. "Silas, we can't do this."

He takes a step back. His cheeks flush with embarrassment and his eyes widen. "I am so sorry. I did not mean to. I thought... I must have read the situation wrong. I thought you wanted me to kiss you." He stumbles through the apology.

A primal instinct in me is raging and screaming for stopping him. Maybe I do want him to kiss me. Why am I having such conflicting feelings? "It's not that I didn't want you to kiss me... There's a lot going on right now. I just found out that you're a king... I have to go home to my own world. And anyway, you're drunk. You shouldn't be kissing anyone." I play nervously with the loose strands of my hair. I do want to be kissed by him. But the timing.

"You are right. I'm sorry. It will not happen again." He runs a nervous hand through his own hair. Part of me wishes it were back in mine.

My heart aches. I do want it to happen again. I think. Maybe if the timing were different and I weren't stuck in a world that isn't my own. If I didn't have to focus on getting back home. Maybe if I found it in me to allow myself to move on. Maybe if it wasn't so soon. "It's late. We should probably get some rest. Would you mind taking me back to my room?"

Sadness lingers in his eyes, but he nods and leads me off the terrace.

We walk down the hall in awkward silence. A sinking hole of regret forms in my stomach. This is the right decision. We don't need any distractions. I don't need any distractions. It's not like I can pack him up and take him home with me.

"Good night, Daphne." Silas holds open the door to my room.

As I slip past him into my room, I accidentally brush against his chest. My heart races at the brief contact. "Good night." I close the door behind me, pressing my back to it and leaning on it for support. My fingers find and hold the dragon pendant he gifted me.

Why did I do that? Why didn't I just let him kiss me? I should open the door back up and kiss him. That's exactly what Gabby would tell me to do if she were here with me. She would reprimand me for not letting him kiss me, for not letting it play out, for not allowing myself to move on... She would tell me it's been a year since I had any action, that I deserve this small sliver of happiness. Even if it's only for a few days, until I have to go home.

Twisting back around, I reach behind me, resting my hand on the door handle. This is a bad idea. A stupid reckless idea. But maybe, this could be how I get my feet wet in the dating pool again. It's zero commitment. Once I leave this place, I'll never ever see him again. A fling never hurt anyone.

The metal handle is cool in my hand as I twist it open—to find nothing. I look down the hallway, but Silas is gone. Before someone has the chance to walk by, I quickly shut the door and slump to the floor in defeat.

This is for the best.

I get back up with a heavy sigh. On the bed is a nightgown Amaleana laid out for me. It's lilac, with cream lace around the neckline. The fabric clings to me as I climb into bed to wallow in self-pity and regret. The memory of the last kiss I shared with Wyatt plays in my mind. It was quick. I was already running late to get the kids that night and he had a million things to do. I wish I had kissed him longer. Held him a second more. I can remember the feeling of his hand holding mine, the way he would kiss me in the middle of an argument and I'd forget why I was mad, laying in bed together talking until we fell asleep. How am I ever supposed to move on from a man who was so good to me, who made me so happy?

The memories remind me how badly I miss Wyatt. He was my first and only love. He came into my life and swept me off of my feet. When he died, my world was shattered irreparably. How could anyone fill his place? He was my soulmate, my prince charming, my other half. *He'd want me to be happy.* That's what I tell myself, but I never let myself fully believe it. I made myself believe I should be alone and grieving for the rest of my life.

But now... Silas's kiss awakened something in me—a need for the physical contact I'd been deprived of. Maybe once I get back home I'll finally let Gabby set me up with one of Tommy's friends. She'll be ecstatic.

CHAPTER TWENTY-ONE

Day Three

"Ma'am, you are being called to the stables." Amaleana's voice wakes me. I struggle to open my eyes, my head aching from last night's wine. She enters the room and places a tray of pancakes and fresh fruit next to me before hurrying into the closet. Next to a glass of fruit juice is a small vial of clear liquid. "What's this?"

"King Silas sent it. It is a tonic that helps with hangovers," she calls from the closet. That was kind of him. The chalky tonic is thick in my throat as I swallow. In an attempt to wash the taste from my mouth, I take a swig of juice. I gag. That was a mistake. It tastes like the equivalent of orange juice and toothpaste.

Amaleana is taking an awfully long time. How big is that closet anyway? I didn't get the chance to go in there yesterday. Both the pancakes and the bowl of fruit are gone before she returns. Today, she brings me a long white and green skirt and dark green corset top with embroidered daisies. I will say, I do love the clothes here. "Do you know why I have to go to the stables?" I ask as she tightens the lacing on the back of my top.

"No clue, ma'am. His majesty is in an odd mood this morning." One last pull of the lace pushes the air from my lungs, and then she ties it off.

My body stiffens at both her comment and the tightness of the corset. Am I to blame for his odd mood? Is he calling me to the stables to have a pegasus fly me out of the city? Was his ego that bruised by my rejection? Oh god. I truly am an idiot, aren't I?

"You look a bit pale, ma'am. Is the lacing too tight?" she asks with genuine concern.

"No, it's fine," I lie. Barely able to breathe, I carefully position myself on the bench to make sure I don't stab myself with the corset's boning.

"Hmm..." she clicks knowingly. Her fingers work a french braid into my hair. "Do you know why he is acting funny?"

I swallow. "Can't say that I do."

"I have never seen him act quite like that before. He seems quite... beside himself. But you did not hear it from me." She uses a delicate green ribbon to tie off the bottom of my hair. "I think you will be fetched shortly." She collects the food tray and leaves me.

Something else must have happened. There is no way he's upset over me. He could easily have had any one of the females who spent the evening throwing themselves at him. I'm just... me. Anxiety takes over and I pick at my cuticles as I walk over to the closet.

Time to see what's behind this door while I wait.

This is the biggest closet I have ever seen. It's the size of my master bedroom back home. I run my hands through the fine silks and cotton, organized by type of outfit. There's a wide variety of clothing: casual and formal dresses, coats, tops and skirts, several pairs of pants, shoes, and accessories. Anything I can think of that belongs in a closet is within these four walls. There are more choices in this single closet than in most stores on Earth.

When I leave the closet, I find Brynne waiting for me on the bench at the end of my bed, drinking a cup of tea. Her hair is disheveled and her face looks like she hasn't slept. She looks me up and down over the rim of her cup. She knows. Great, do they all know?

"Good morning!" I say chipperly, closing the closet door behind me.

"How did you sleep?" She runs a hand over her lap and places her teacup gently down beside her.

"Great, actually. This bed is so comfy. Much better than the bedrolls." I laugh at my own attempt at a joke.

"That is good to hear. Are you ready to go?" she asks impatiently.

Her tone is unexpected. Maybe they really are going to send me away. "Yes, but why are we going to the stables?"

"The egg we retrieved is hatching. Silas wants you to be there." She stands and walks toward the door, the expression on her face unreadable. I follow behind her, down the stairs and through the gardens to the stables. Syrrus and Ajax stand guard outside the stable doorway. Brynne pecks a quick kiss on Syrrus's cheek and he steps aside, letting us into the stable.

"Good morning," I say as I pass, only to be ignored. Wow. I guess they don't take lightly to their king not getting what he wants. Trying to calm my nerves as I enter the stable, I remind myself that Syrrus hasn't spoken at all since I arrived, so maybe only Ajax is mad at me, or maybe he's just being Ajax.

In the center of a stable, Knox hovers over the silver dragon egg that lays on a dense pile of hay. Silas sits close by with his yellow dragon, Kaida, resting her head in his lap. He strokes her long nose calmly as her eyes flutter closed. Cracking sounds come from inside the shell.

Brynne places her palm down on the egg and closes her eyes. "She will be here soon." The egg rattles slightly in response to her touch. "The magic was siphoned when we returned to the palace. She is good to come whenever she likes."

"How does that work? The siphoning?" I look at Silas, but his stare doesn't break from the egg.

"My healing magic allows me to move the excess magic from the dragon while it is still in its egg and into special vials that are enchanted to withstand immense power. This particular egg had more magic than I have ever worked with before. Many of our sickest people will be able to receive the cure they need," Brynne answers, without breaking her contact with the egg.

We spend the majority of the day in the barn, sitting around, waiting for the dragon to break through its shell. Syrrus brings us snacks and lunch every couple of hours. Knox, Silas, and Brynne discuss the other dragons. Aside from Silas's little pack, a few more dragons belonging to the Azurite Force live at the palace. The egg rocks occasionally and cracking sounds continue to come from inside.

Feeling like an alien spectator to a very intimate occasion, I remain quiet in the corner. Even though I was invited, I still feel like I'm intruding. Shortly after lunch, the cracking sound slowly grows louder and a small piece of the egg pops off.

Then nothing.

The air falls silent and everyone holds their breath for what seems like an eternity. Brynne takes an anxious step forward and the egg stills.

"Silas, it is taking too long." Brynne rushes to the counter along the wall.

"Is it going to be okay?" I ask quietly.

Silas finally looks up at me. "We do not know."

When I had Ariella, the doctors had to use a vacuum to get her out, because her birth was taking too long and it was dangerous. Does time apply to dragon's hatching in a similar fashion? "How long is it supposed to take?"

"Not this long." Knox mutters.

Brynne hurries to the egg with a bag of tools. She pulls out what looks like a chisel and chips away at the eggshell. With each strike, she appears to be exerting a lot of force. How strong is the exterior of a dragon egg? She frantically chips at the egg over and over again, only breaking small pieces of the shell off at a time. Looking up to the sky in what seems like prayer, she closes her eyes and lifts the chisel all the way behind her back, giving the egg one more strong, precise hit. A loud crack follows and the top of the shell shatters.

Brynne collapses from exhaustion and Syrrus rushes forward to hold her. He wipes her sweat and makes her drink from a cup of water.

A small, iridescent, white dragon lies curled up on the bottom half of the remaining shell, asleep. The baby dragon reminds me of an iguana in likeness and size, with the addition of little nubs of horns and glittering wings. While its mother was downright terrifying, it is the opposite. It's the cutest thing I've ever seen. Golden eyes flutter open and it yawns, revealing a mouthful of sharp teeth, before sticking its head out of its egg and peering around at us. Sighs of relief fill the room.

I kneel to get a better look at the dragon and its eyes meet mine. It attempts to leap out of the egg, stumbling over to me and laying across my lap. My eyes widen in shock. I don't know what I should do. Do I move it? Do I sit here until it moves? How dangerous are baby dragons? Everyone's eyes are on me.

Brynne walks over and crouches to me and the dragon. "You can pet her." Her voice is soft and kind, her earlier agitation gone. Warily, I stroke the dragon's back. Her spine curls at my touch. A noise hums from her chest that sounds somewhere between a growl and a purr. Brynne lets out a small, relieved laugh at the sound.

"She likes you." Knox cleans up the bits of silver shell scattered through the hay. I smile down at the dragon. A motherly instinct to protect her pulses through me.

"Do you want to name her?" Silas asks me. Brynne and Knox give sharp glares at this suggestion.

"Oh, no, I don't think I should," I murmur. The sleeping dragon in my lap reminds me of the stuffed dragon Ariella takes everywhere.

Wyatt bought it for her at the farmers' market we went to when I was pregnant with her. We were wandering aimlessly through the rows of vendors when I found this handmade stuffed dragon, crocheted with sparkly white yarn. It was so cute I insisted he get it for Ariella's princess-themed nursery. He reluctantly paid the hefty price tag when I begged, telling him, "Every princess needs a guard dragon."

Silas smiles. "I insist. Remember, dragons choose their caretaker and it seems like she chose you." He points to my left arm. Where bare skin had been, is a dragon inked in white, taking up the entire length of my forearm. How did that get there? The tattoo is an aerial view of its back with its wings spread, flying toward my hand.

A dragon bond.

How am I going to explain this to my family? I swore I'd never get another tattoo. That's a problem for later.

I pick the dragon off of my lap. Her yellow eyes open as I hold her up to my face. "What about Iri? That's the name of my daughter's toy dragon. It's short for Iridescent." The tiny dragon yawns, sticks her tongue out, and blinks at me.

"It is perfect." Silas takes Iri from me and scratches under her chin. "Brynne and Syrrus will take care of her and introduce her to the other members of our little dragon pack." He hands her off to Syrrus. She looks incredibly small against Syrrus's large frame. He smiles as he cradles her like a baby in his arms. Brynne leans on Syrrus and they carry Iri with them out of the stable. Kaida follows at their heels, sniffing Iri as they walk. The four of them look like a family leaving the hospital with their newborn.

"Do they have any children?" I ask aloud to no one in particular.

"No, not yet. Some fae are blessed with children easily, but not all are so lucky," Knox answers.

"They'll be good parents," I say, and mean it. Syrrus seems like a good male who dotes on his beautiful mate. And Brynne seems incredibly kind and caring. Despite her shortness with me earlier, I was incredibly impressed with how she helped Iri hatch.

"They will be. One day," Silas adds as he walks off farther into the stables.

"You know, he has never invited anyone outside of the Azurite Force to watch a dragon hatch before," Knox says teasingly, as he lifts the bottom of the empty egg in his arms. The shell is strikingly beautiful, like nothing I had ever seen before. The outside is several inches thick and looks like it's made from stone or rough metal. The interior is crystalized, like some sort of egg geode.

"Guess I'm special." I smile to myself.

"Looks like it." Knox laughs and carries the eggshell out of the barn as Silas returns.

"Where are they taking Iri? And the eggshell?"

"They are taking her to another building on the other side of the palace. This one isn't fireproof. We keep our dragons there, where they are tended to around the clock by the members of the Azurite Force when they are here, or palace workers when they are not. You are welcome to visit her whenever you please." Silas offers me a hand, helping me to my feet. "The shell will be used by the oracles and priestesses. Some pieces will be displayed for their beauty in their temples and other parts will be used in ceremonies and potions."

Hay drops out from my layers of skirt as I stand. "Seeing Iri hatch was an incredible experience. Thank you for inviting me."

"It was a once-in-a-lifetime opportunity for you. I want to make sure you experience all this world has to offer before you leave." The corner of his lip pulls up in a half-smile.

Watching his lips move reminds me of how they felt against mine. Which then reminds me of everyone's coldness toward me this morning. "I have to ask... do all of them know what happened between us last night?"

His grin turns to a confused scowl and his brows narrow. Did my question offend him? "No. Why would I ever tell them about that?"

"I don't know. They all seemed... angry." I play with my hands nervously.

"They are just hungover. I did not send everyone a tonic this morning; they are all old enough to handle the consequences of their actions. Plus, they were worried about how long the dragon was taking to hatch. Sure, they may be a little bitter that I invited you to this, but they will get over it." He rubs his face in disbelief and laughs. "I cannot believe you thought I would tell them. They would make fun of me for it indefinitely. I would never hear the end of it from Knox."

"They'd make fun of you for kissing me?" I know I'm not from here and all of the other females are way more beautiful than I am, but I didn't think that would be embarrassing for him.

He shakes his head. "No. They would make fun of me for being rejected by someone as beautiful as you." He pushes a piece of dark hair out of his face, leaving his hand resting on the top of his head. "Knox already told me I did not stand a chance with you on your first day here. It would only add fuel to his insult repertoire."

He talked about me with Knox on the first night I got here? I bite my lip as I think, looking at him through narrowed eyes. Maybe last night wasn't just a drunken mistake. Maybe one of the reasons he agreed to help me is because, for whatever reason, he actually likes me—or liked me, rather. How am I so stupid? Of course he didn't tell his friends about last night. But why would someone so inarguably handsome find someone like me attractive? So many questions. So many things I should say. So many things I *want* to say. Though the only word I can manage to get out is, "Oh..."

CHAPTER TWENTY-TWO

Two palace guards enter the stable to retrieve Silas for a meeting. He leaves with one and the other brings me to the library, where I decide to spend the remainder of my day. Luckily for me, Silas was called away before I could make an uncomfortable conversation worse.

I'm grateful Silas suggested spending some time here today. Being among books has always brought me a certain level of peace I've never found anywhere else. Amaleana arrived shortly after I did to help. She's currently searching the shelves for books on introductory magic wielding. If Stone is covering my physical training, it looks like it's up to me to learn how to control my magic to survive in this world. My stomach drops every single time *that* thought crosses my mind. The thought of not making it home.

While I wait for Amaleana to return, I station myself near the fireplace in the corner of the main floor of the library. A small stack of books is piled on a side table between two tan leather high-backed reading chairs. Their covers are well-loved, the spines worn in and flexible as if they've been read over and over again. Is this particular stack of books what Silas is currently reading? It's his library, after all. Picturing him in the chair reading one of the books by the light of the fireplace brings a smile to my face.

Curious as to which books have been read so many times, I lift the top book off of the pile to examine it. It's the same black leather-bound book Silas picked off the shelf yesterday. Two crescent moons and the title *Intertwined Fates* are embossed with silver foil on the cover. The title alone doesn't tell me if it's a history book or smut, so I flip to the first page. A single quote is written in script in the center of the page: "At birth, the gods gift us free will. Still, much is decided by the stars, far beyond our control. From the moment we are conceived our souls are connected to another."

Amaleana's footsteps come from the top of the stairs. I quickly close the book and place it carefully back on its pile, exactly how it was.

Three thick books are nestled in her arms. "I have collected *Finding Your Magic: A Beginner's Guide*, *Water Magic*, and *Magic: From the Heart*. That will be a good start."

I take the stack of books from her hands. "Thank you. I think I'll sit and read for a while."

She nods, heads for a nearby shelf, pulls a book from it, and sits at a table across the main level, flipping the book open about halfway. Reading about how to use my magic seems like the best use of my time. At this moment, there's nothing else for me to do anyway. We haven't heard back from Embryanna or Novalora yet. Silas is doing... whatever it is kings do. A meeting? Something like that, I suppose. Learning more about my magic will be good for me. Plus, I need a distraction from my other distraction.

Making myself comfortable on one of the high-backed reading chairs, I open to the first page of *Finding Your Magic: A Beginner's Guide* and squeeze my stack next to the other on the table. It's the thinnest of the three books, which is odd. I would think the foundation would cover the most. Perhaps magic will come more naturally than I think, once I begin practicing.

The first few chapters, which go over exactly what Silas taught me in the cave, are easy to skim through. The next few chapters are separated into magic types. I flip until I find the water section. It gives instructions on how to connect your mind with your magic so you can shape the element.

Closing my eyes to feel for my magic, I make a ball of water appear above my hand. Using all of my concentration, I imagine the ball of water in the shape of a small dragon, in the shape of Iri. To my delight, it works. A little water dragon floats above my hand.

"What are you doing!?" Amaleana shouts at me from across the room.

Startled, I drop my dragon and water lands on the pages in front of me. My eyes widen in horror at the soaked book. "I'm so sorry. I didn't mean to—"

"That is exactly why you cannot be doing that in here." She rushes over, grabs the book from me, and blasts the water away with a burst of air magic. "Water can be as damaging to books as fire. You are not skilled enough with your magic to be using it so freely. If I knew you wanted to actually practice, I would have brought you out to the garden, or a field—literally anywhere else besides the library."

Her reprimanding tone strikes me. It's so unlike the soft, timid girl who's been helping me since I arrived at the palace. I'm embarrassed that I didn't realize water is unacceptable in a library. I don't let anyone bring drinks into our shop for this exact reason. "It was an accident. You're right, I wasn't thinking. I just got excited. It won't happen again."

The anger on her face fades and is replaced with worry. "I'm sorry, ma'am. I lost my temper. I should not have said anything. These books are our history. They have to be preserved. I have grown protective over them. Without a guest to tend to, I have not had much to do. I spend the majority of my time among these shelves. I want to read everything here. It has become my personal duty to protect the books at all costs."

This poor girl thinks I'm going to tell Silas she yelled at me. I offer her a small smile. "I understand. In my world, my husband and I—

my late husband and I—own an antique shop and bookstore. Don't worry, I completely get why you got upset with me. Also, you don't have to treat me like royalty. I promise I'm nobody important."

She runs a hand nervously over her skirt. "Sorry, ma'am. I do not know very much about your world."

My smile widens and I place my hand on her shoulder. "Do you like stories, Amaleana?"

Her face lights up with a grin that reaches her green eyes. "Of course I do."

We sit on the floor of the library and I tell her about my life on Earth. She watches me with wonder in her eyes as I tell her the same bedtime story I've told my kids countless times about how I met Wyatt. I tell her about how he was ripped away from me—after explaining what cars are—and I tell her how I found the mirror and fell through it.

"Mirror? What did it look like?" Her tone is full of nervous curiosity.

The image of the mirror is etched firmly in my mind. "It was an arched mirror, huge and heavy. I'm surprised I was able to move it by myself, now that I think about it. The frame was made of real silver, it had tarnishing on its corners and crevices, and the frame looked like woven tree branches. At the top... there was a small silver dragon." A shudder runs through me and I look down at my hands, remembering the feeling of the glass transforming into liquid when I touched it, falling through, and the pulse of energy that went through my body before I landed in this world. When I look back up, Amaleana's face is pale. "Is everything okay?"

She gets to her feet. "Yes, ma'am. Everything is fine. I'm just feeling a little faint. Probably overtired. I think I am going to go home for the evening."

I get up to help her; she looks like she's going to fall over. "Are you okay?"

A small bead of sweat forms on her forehead, which she wipes away quickly. "Yes, ma'am. I forgot to eat today, and it has gotten quite late. I will return in the morning to get you ready to train with Stone."

The sky above us has turned the skylight to an inky black. "I hope you feel better. See you in the morning." I collect my stack of books, hoping no one minds if I take them with me.

At some point while we were talking, a servant left a tray of fruit and pastries on a table. It sat ignored until now, as I notice the gnawing hunger in my stomach. A folded note on the tray reads: "I was told you were reading. I did not want to disturb you. –S." I smile at his thoughtfulness and grab a peach from the tray.

As I make my way up the staircase, I notice a figure out on the terrace. The muscular body is just a silhouette of shadows in the darkness, but I know it's Silas. I hold my breath as I stand at the top of the staircase, watching him for a moment. My nails dig anxiously into the skin of the peach. He looks deep in thought.

I shouldn't disturb him.

He glances over his shoulder, his eyes meeting mine. He straightens his body and makes his way to the door. Frozen, I stand there. I can pretend I didn't notice him. I can make it back to my room if I turn now and keep walking.

Too late.

He opens the door and gestures for me to join him, then looks down at the peach in my hand. "There you are. I am glad you got the basket. When I went to fetch you for dinner, the guards told me you and Amaleana had not left the library. I know what it is like to get pulled in by a good story."

My heart skips as I pass him to walk onto the terrace. "Thank you. I got your note. That was kind of you. I was trying to learn more about my magic, and then Amaleana and I got talking. We lost track of time."

"I am glad the two of you get along. But did you say that you were practicing? Show me." He lies on one of the two metal chaises and smiles challengingly at me.

Nodding, I close my eyes and concentrate on my magic. A ball of water appears above my hands. I elongate it and make it swirl. The elegance of it surprises me. There hasn't been much time for practice and I wasn't sure if it would work the way I wanted it to. Silas's eyes light up at the water flowing in the air. A few more swirls and I send it over to fall over a planter.

He gives me a gentle round of applause. "Impressive."

I take an exaggerated bow before I sit down beside him. "Thank you, thank you."

"That is very good. It takes most a few days, if not weeks, to learn how to manifest their power. You are a quick learner. You picked that up from reading?"

My cheeks warm at the compliment. "Well, yes. I just did exactly what was instructed in the book Amaleana gave me. Maybe it's because I'm older than most fae who are learning magic for the first time. I can follow instructions better than a child, I suppose." I shrug.

"I can have Ajax teach you more, if you would like."

Oh god no, I don't want to spend more time with Ajax of all people. Doesn't Silas have water magic? "Why can't you teach me?"

"I assumed you would not want me to after last night. I figured Ajax would be a good option."

He's wrong for two reasons, but he doesn't need to know why I don't want to be alone with Ajax. "Oh... Don't worry, you were drunk. It's okay. I'd prefer you to teach me. If I get stuck here, we can work on it together. If you want to, anyway."

He looks at me for a moment, almost longingly, before looking away. "Of course. I'll teach you if that is what you wish. But, Daphne, I did not kiss you because I was drunk."

"Oh... I didn't mean..." My heart flutters and I nervously play with the fabric of my skirt. "Then why did you?"

"I kissed you because I wanted to. And, I thought you wanted me to. But don't worry, I will not do it again." He runs a hand through his hair as if *I* am somehow making *him* nervous. "Unless you tell me you want me to." The nervous flutter turns into a quick thud as I watch his arms flex as he stretches them behind his head, getting comfortable. "Let's pretend it never happened."

As if I could do that. I manage to force a smile. "Right, like it never happened. Pinky promise."

His smile turns coy and he raises his pinky. I link my pinky in his and he winks. "Pinky promise."

A blush crosses my cheeks and I tilt my head away shyly. My eyes catch a thick blanket lying on the empty chaise beside him. "Are you planning on sleeping out here?"

"Probably. Fresh air is good for you. Helps clear your mind." He yawns and his eyes flutter closed.

"Alright, well... I've got that training with Stone in the morning, so I should probably go get some rest."

He grabs the blanket and tosses it over himself. "I'll see you in the morning. Sleep well."

"See you in the morning."

Being alone with my thoughts as I make my way back to my room brings me nothing but questions and self-doubt. Should I have taken that empty chaise next to him and slept outside? Did he want me to tell him I wanted him to kiss me again? Probably not. Any chance I had at that was probably sabotaged when I accused him of telling his friends. Why am I so bad at flirting, or whatever this thing is?

Leaning onto my window, I stare out at the city beyond the gate. From what Silas showed me, it feels full of wonder and all sorts of new things to discover. For just a moment, I imagine what it must be like to live here.

CHAPTER TWENTY-THREE

Day Four

Darkness lingers outside when I'm woken by a new lady's maid, who doesn't introduce herself. She serves me a breakfast tray and hurries to the closet. My legs stretch out under the covers and I eat the sweet bread and maple sausage she brought. The full-figured brunette female reappears from the closet door. Her eyes narrow on her square, hard face. She places a long-sleeved white tunic and gray cotton pants on the bed.

She takes my breakfast from me before I can finish, placing it on the bench at the foot of the bed before pulling the covers off of me. "Best be hurrying now. Stone is not a male who cares for tardiness."

Still not fully awake, I shiver, surprised by the cold air. This female is not very pleasant and I am not a fan of her rude wake-up call. "Where is Amaleana?" I ask as I get out of the bed.

"I am not sure. She asked me last night as she was leaving if I would be able to fulfill her duties for a few hours this morning," she says, waving a hand toward the bed. The sheets tuck themselves in with the aid of her magic.

Amaleana looked really unwell last night. "Is she okay?"

"I am sure she is fine. Let us get you dressed. Now."

Happy to get into something more comfortable than the dresses and skirts I've been wearing, I change into the clothes she gave me. The shirt and pants outfit is much closer to my usual attire. It's a safe bet to say that I won't be able to keep these on for the remainder of my time here, though. Not that I mind the dresses and skirts—they're just taking some getting used to. I take my place on the bench, where the still-nameless female combs my hair roughly, jerking my head back before tying it up tightly at the top of my head in a sleek bun.

Now I'm awake. I didn't know my hair could be pulled so tight. I rub my temples to ease the pain from the tension of the bun. The skin on my face feels like it's being pulled back with it.

"Stone will meet you in the foyer. He is probably already waiting for you."

"Thank you..." I wrinkle my face in thought, trying to remember if she told me her name and I missed it before I fully woke up. "I'm sorry, I don't remember your name."

"Penelope."

"Thank you, Penelope." She grabs the plate of half-eaten food and walks out the door. I follow behind her quick steps. Stone and a small orange dragon are waiting for me right at the bottom of the stairs. Stone taps his foot impatiently.

"It's about time." His tone lands somewhere indistinguishable, either sarcastic or deadly serious. I don't know him well enough to determine which it is. Penelope throws a quick glance over her shoulder in lustful admiration of Stone's good looks as she continues on her way.

I look at him in disbelief. "I got ready as quickly as I could."

"Do not make a habit of being late." He laughs.

Okay, he's just teasing me, but I'm still not going to be late again. "I won't. If you don't mind me asking, what exactly is this training going to consist of?"

"Today we will run a lap around the palace, then—"

"Run? How far are we talking?" I haven't ran in ages. Gabby once insisted I do a half marathon with her a few years ago and I walked the whole thing. I came in dead last. Running isn't for me.

He looks me up and down, probably realizing how out of shape I am beneath the guise of my new fae body and regretting accepting me as his student. "I guess we will see how far you make it. Then, I will show you some basic defensive maneuvers. After seeing how well you do at that, we may have time to start a little weapons introduction."

Great. This is going to go great. "All right then." I smile weakly, reluctantly accepting the challenge. I have to at least try. "Who's this?" I gesture to the dragon at his feet.

"This is my dragon, Saffron," he says. The dragon peers up at me.

Saffron flies off in the direction of the dragon barn when we get outside the palace. We briefly stretch before we begin our lap. Stone starts the run at a slow pace and I'm almost immediately out of breath as I try to keep up with him. I refuse to give up. Sweat already drips down my back, despite the cool morning air. Meanwhile, Stone looks right out of a sports ad, effortlessly increasing his pace.

It's a good thing that Penelope didn't let me finish my breakfast earlier, or I surely would have puked it up. We make it halfway around the palace when my body decides it has had enough. Once we slow to a stop, I bend over and put my hands on my knees for support. The sun isn't even up yet. How am I going to make it through this whole lesson? It takes Stone a few strides to realize I'm no longer behind him. He turns and jogs back to me.

This is humiliating.

He stops in front of me. His taut muscles flex as he stretches his arms back over his head. "You do not run in your world?"

"No, not really," I mutter, still catching my breath.

"What do you do when you are attacked?" His defined brows draw together in confusion.

Between breaths, I manage a laugh. "We don't have that problem."

His lips purse. "I see. Tomorrow you can jog instead. But make no mistake, in a few days, you will be running. You just have to be consistent with your training."

We start the second part of today's lesson in an open field beyond the stables. He shows me a few ways to escape and disarm an attacker. He informs me we'll go over these moves each day until I have them perfected, and he won't go easy on me after today.

I barely catch the wooden practice sword Stone tosses at me from a weapons storage shed on the edge of the field. He teaches me how to properly handle the weapon: how to hold it, swing it, where to jab it, and how to spar with it. No matter how much effort I put in, I lose sparring matches over and over. Why would I expect something different? He's a god-knows-how-old fae trainer of warriors. And I'm a thirty-six-year old mom. Still, it's disappointing to not land a single blow.

"If I have magic now, why do I need to know how to use a sword? Why is there a need for weapons at all in this world?" I ask as I toss the sword in the air, catching it on the way down.

"Sometimes magic cannot kill your enemies. Most magic and weapons do not kill fae. Damage, disarm, sure. But you need a weapon made of iron and forged in dragon fire to kill one of us. Not to mention should you deplete your magical energy, you will need other ways to defend yourself so you do not burn your magic out entirely."

"What do you mean, 'burn out?'" I raise a brow and lift my wooden sword in front of me to study the intricately carved dragons on its wooden blade. It makes me realize how sore my arms are from the lesson.

"If you use too much power, you can lose your magic permanently. Or worse, your life. When wielding magic, you must be careful of how much energy you exert." He stands across from me, swinging his sword at his side. "It is lunchtime, so that will be it for our lesson today. We will pick up where we left off tomorrow. Do not be late."

"See you in the morning. I promise I'll be on time." I cross my arms in front of me and wink at him.

He chuckles at me. "Hopefully you will not be too tired from today's lessons." He waves a hand before walking off into the busy streets beyond the palace gate.

I most certainly am tired from today's lesson. Every muscle—which hasn't been exercised in quite some time—sings in agony. Hopefully, I'll be able to take a long soak in the bath later to relieve some of the soreness.

Once the top of Stone's head is no longer visible among the crowd of fae, I make my way back inside the palace. Brynne is heading up the entry stairs in a hurry with a dark green dragon trailing behind her. That must be her dragon. Quickening my pace as much as my sore body will allow, I try to catch up with her. "Everything okay?"

Worry is written all over her face. "It is the baby dragon, Iri... She is not getting along with the others in the pack. She is quite feisty. She even tried to bite Fern here, and she is the most docile of the bunch." She lets out a small, nervous laugh. Fern narrows her eyes defensively toward me, which gives me the impression she can sense my connection to Iri.

I bite my lip anxiously. "Is that normal?"

"It is not *not* normal. Dragons are, well, dragons. They all have their unique personalities."

"Then why do you look so worried?"

Brynne darts her eyes away from me, purses her lips, and scrunches her nose, deciding if she's going to tell me what is going on. "In the past, if a dragon showed this extra fire in them, we made sure the fae who became their caretaker only ever had one dragon. Which is normally fine—the dragon goes and lives a happy life with its chosen handler." She takes a deep breath before continuing. "But Iri chose you."

My heart sinks into my stomach. She chose me, who will leave this world, leave her. "Can't she choose someone else?"

Brynne smiles uncomfortably and shrugs. "We will not know until after you are gone. If a dragon's handler dies, they usually go on and choose another. But you are not dying. I do not know what she will do. I believe Silas planned on taking care of her for you if she allowed it. But if she is not getting along with the others... She is picking fights with them and she is strong, and will only grow stronger.... I do not know what her fate may be."

The two guards stationed outside the palace open the doors for us and we enter the foyer. There must be something they can do for her. Silas is the king. Surely he will have a solution. "Why don't you ask Silas?"

"Where do you think I am going?" The sarcasm in her tone makes me cringe at myself. Of course, that's what she's doing. And I interrupted her.

"I'll go with you." I say. If Iri chose me, I need to be her biggest advocate.

She turns to me, halting in the middle of the foyer. "That is okay. You do not have to."

"I want to. I finished training for the day already."

The look she gives me tells me that she isn't concerned whether I want to go or not. She doesn't want me going for another reason. "How about you go have some lunch, and I will let you know what he decides?"

My stomach growls at the mention of food. I'm hungry, but something doesn't seem right. Iri needs me to make sure she's taken care of. I narrow my eyes and tilt my head toward her. "Why don't you want me to go with you?"

Her eyes widen. "Daphne... I think it is best if you stay out of this."

Anger heats my cheeks and my hands tighten at my sides. Ever since I got here, things continue to be kept from me. "And why is that?"

She nods and offers polite smiles to some passing servants, who have arms full of linens, waiting for them to be out of earshot before continuing quietly, "Silas... He has not been making normal choices where you've been involved. It is nothing you did. I just think it is best that I talk to him alone about this, so he can make a rational decision."

"Oh..." My tone softens and I relax my hands. If I'm causing Silas to act out of character, I see why she doesn't want me there. Though I can't explain the maternal instincts I have for Iri. I didn't ask to be chosen, but from the moment she crawled into my lap, she became mine to protect. "Iri chose me. I want to know what is going to happen to her."

"Daphne, you are hoping to leave this world. I know a dragon's bond is strong and those are the emotions you are feeling right now, but this decision needs to be handled carefully. Silas needs a clear head to figure out a plan for her."

"What kind of plan does he have to figure out?" My mind goes to Earth, and what happens to a pet that fights others or causes too much trouble. My voice becomes a whisper as tears swell in my eyes. "Is he going to have to kill her?" My heart drops at the thought.

Brynne looks offended at my question. "Of course not. Why would he kill her? That would defeat the whole purpose of saving her in the first place. He needs to decide if he is going to send her off somewhere she would be better suited, like one of his brother's kingdoms, or have a separate structure built for her. My only fear is that he will wait to see if you can get home before deciding, and then the day will come, you will be gone, and arrangements will not have been made for her. That is not fair to Iri."

"Oh."

"Why would you think he would kill her? Has he given you any impression he is that sort of male? Have any of us given you the impression we would let that happen? Our goal is to *save* these dragons."

I sigh apologetically. "No, of course you haven't. On Earth, it's quite common for people to take the easy way out with animals. I guess that's why I thought that. I'm sorry for offending you." Poor Iri. She didn't know she was choosing the wrong person.

"That is repulsive. We are a bit more civilized than that. Daphne, dear, you are going to have to trust us at some point. Silas is a good king. He always does what is best. He will make the right choice."

Is she still talking about Iri, or something else? "I do trust you. I trust Silas. Can you let me know what he decides, please?"

"Yes. I will come to you once he has made a plan for her and let you know what he has decided."

"Where is Iri now? Can I go visit her?"

"She is in the dragon barn with the others. Syrrus is there. I think Iri would love to see you." She smiles and walks up the staircase in the direction of the palace's west wing.

Heading to the dragon barn, I turn around and walk back out of the palace. The weather in this city is perfect: sunny, not too hot and not too cold. Delicate aromas of blooming flowers grace my nose as I walk through the garden. The gardenias and roses are perfectly pruned. I stop and admire them for a few moments before I approach the large metal structure that houses the dragons. The structure is several stories tall and has large open windows the dragons can easily fly through.

The metal door is heavy against my palms as I push it open and enter. Syrrus is busy holding back a growling black dragon. Ash. Several other dragons, including Kaida and Hurik, are gathered watching the scene. Iri stands in front of Ash, baring her teeth and hissing.

"Is everything okay?"

Syrrus lifts his gaze to meet mine. His expression is akin to an overwhelmed mother trying to keep toddlers from killing each other. Except with dragons, I suppose that's a much more real possibility. Iri's golden eyes light up when she sees me. She forgets about Ash and happily pads over to me, tail and wings wagging. The sight brings a smile to my face. Syrrus visibly relaxes as Ash rejoins the pack.

I crouch down and scratch her head. "Iri, you can't pick fights. These are your friends."

She tilts her head and blinks at me, as if telling me she has no idea what I'm talking about. I run my hand down the cool scales of her back and she plops her body to the floor and shows me her stomach. She makes an adorable sound akin to purring as I rub her belly. She rolls back to her feet and puts her paws on my chest, licking the side of my cheek.

Picking her up under her front arms to bring her face to mine, I whisper, "I don't know why you chose me, but I will take care of you while I'm here." She blinks again, accepting my declaration. "Syrrus, can I take her with me?" He nods in relief and Iri seems to smile as I cradle her in my arms like a baby.

We head to the palace kitchen and find the staff busy preparing another meal. They're too occupied to notice me grabbing a chicken leg from a platter. Dragons can eat chicken, right? I'm sure it's fine.

Iri scarfs it down in a few quick bites, bone and all, on our way up the stairs. We enter my room, where Amaleana sits waiting with a smile that reaches from ear to ear. After we get inside, Amaleana closes and clicks the door locked behind us. Something's in her hand, hidden behind her back. "Good afternoon, Daphne. Are you busy?"

I place Iri down on my bed and she lies down in a ball on one of the fluffy pillows. My brows furrow in curiosity. Did she just call me Daphne? I guess she agrees we're friends now. "Yes, I'm alone. What do you have there, Amaleana?" I try to glimpse whatever she holds behind her.

She rocks up and down on the balls of her feet with nervous excitement and pulls a book forward. "It is a book. A children's book my parents used to read to me. It is very old and has been passed down in my family for centuries. It took me some time to find it. That is why I had Penelope help me this morning. I think you will like it." She clutches the faded book against her chest.

I take a seat on the bench at the end of my bed and unlace the boots I wore for training. "I'd love to see it." I stretch my toes forward, feeling the burning in my muscles, which ache to soak in the bath as soon as possible. Amaleana walks over and hands me the brown leather-bound book. Oil stains from tiny fingers line the worn edges. Flecks of gold paint lie in the letters of the embossed title: *The Travelers and the Five Mirrors*.

My eyes dart from Amaleana to the book a few times before flipping to the first page. The faded illustration was clearly once intricate and beautiful: five fae, three males and two females, standing with their hands joined, facing a mirror. The large arched silver frame was forged to look like twisted tree branches.

At the top of the mirror sits a small silver dragon curled around an egg-shaped crystal.

CHAPTER TWENTY-FOUR

My pulse races and hands tremble as I read *The Travelers and the Five Mirrors* aloud: "Once upon a time, there were five friends. They each hailed from one of the five great kingdoms: Ailse of Tswangohin, Evander of Fracilonia, Mairead of Schasumetsats, Olvir of Roladif, and Theodosius of Skaans. Each of them was blessed by the gods with the gift of traveling. Individually, they were incredibly powerful. When they worked together, they grew their gifts to strengths never before seen.

"Over the centuries, the friends began to wish for others to be able to travel throughout the five lands as freely as they did, without fear of the long and often dangerous journeys between them. They dreamed of seeing their kingdoms united after thousands of years of separation. Combining their magic, they forged five mirrors, through which others without traveling abilities could move between the kingdoms.

"Each kingdom received one as a gift from the Travelers. In return, the kings of each land granted protection to the Travelers to ensure their safety and the safety of the mirrors. The people of the kingdoms rejoiced, using the mirrors to see the other kingdoms, trade goods, and form the grand continent, Carimea, with the capital in Skaans City."

There are pages torn and missing. I pause and look up in confusion at Amaleana, who shrugs. I run my finger down the torn edges in the middle of the book and continue, "After the war, the use of the mirrors was banned." Another torn page. "The end."

"So is that it? Is that the mirror you fell through?" Amaleana turns back to the first page of the book, points at the haunting image of the mirror, and looks back at me.

It is. Undeniably. Disbelief washes over me as I stare blankly at the page. Why is it written in a children's book? Why are there pages missing? Why don't Novalora or Embryanna know about this book? How did the mirror end up on Earth?

I don't know enough about Carimea to know where to start. Surely, someone should have some memory of the Travelers. My head aches from all the questions. "Yes, it is. But what's on those other pages? Do you remember?"

Her eyes fill with slight sorrow. "No. They have never been there as long as I can remember. During the revolution, books were censored by the previous monarchy in an effort to keep things from the people. It is also a very old book, so the pages may have been torn by one of the children in my family. I always thought it was only a children's story, until you described the mirror. This story is not in any of the history books I have read. So, if it is real and was censored, it has been that way for a very long time. Before the revolution, possibly before the previous ruling family took the crown, many centuries ago."

I take her hands. "We need to show Silas. Can you bring me to him? I saw Brynne heading to him in the west wing. We need to go now."

She shakes her head. "I cannot. The west wing is warded. Only those with King Silas's permission may enter unless they are escorted."

"This can't wait. I have to show him this. Can I borrow this, Amaleana?" I say urgently, already getting to my feet.

"Of course. It is yours to keep. I would not have brought it had I expected it back." A small smile appears on her face.

"Can you get a message to Embryanna and Novalora to meet us as soon as they can?"

She nods affirmatively, as if accepting an order, and I cringe.

"Great. I'll meet you as soon as I find Silas. Thank you, again, for everything." I pull her into a hug. She stands frozen like she doesn't know what to do with her hands before she reaches up and hugs me back.

"Happy to help, Daph." Her smile widens and she leaves the room.

Once the door closes behind her, I grab my phone from where I had it stashed in the side table next to the mirror. My home screen lights up and I open a photo of Ariella, Ronan, and Ryan from two Christmases ago—our last Christmas with Wyatt—and smile. I'm one step closer to getting home to them. The right corner of my screen taunts me: only seventy percent battery remains. The screen fades to black as I hold the power button and toss it back in the drawer.

Iri snores from her spot on my pillow. I run my hand over her head and she opens one eye lazily. "Please don't burn the palace down. I think Silas would be really mad at me."

I swear she rolls her eyes before she goes back to snoring. Grasping the book to my chest, I rush to the other side of the palace. A magical energy radiates from beyond the threshold at the edge of the hallway, like there's an invisible barrier. I don't know where anything is in the west wing. Where will I go once I cross that threshold? *If* I can cross it. Maybe if I shout for Silas, he'll hear me with his heightened senses. I try this and wait a few moments before realizing no one is coming.

My body shakes with nervous energy. In my hands is possibly the key to figuring out my way back home. I only have ten more days to get back before anyone realizes I'm gone. What did Amaleana say about the west wing? Only those with King Silas's permission can enter. Maybe I have permission? What's the worst that can happen? The wards incinerate me?

There isn't time to waste. I inhale deeply, hold my breath, and step through the barrier into the hallway.

A slight tingle of static energy washes over my body as I walk through, but that's it. My eyes dart around, quickly scanning my surroundings before I turn back to make sure I've actually entered the West Wing. I'm still in one piece—not incinerated—and the book is still in my hands. I did it. I actually did it.

The long hallway is decorated the same as the rest of the palace: light neutral colors and stone tile flooring. Paintings of various fae in glamorous gowns and suits wearing crowns and jewels line the walls. Silas's family members, perhaps? It seems warm and inviting—a normal hallway, just like the east wing. But its length and countless number of wooden doors, all adorned with silver dragon eggs, is daunting.

This may have been a mistake.

There is no way for me to know which of these rooms Silas is in. Something draws me to a spiral staircase at the end of the long hall. My hand wraps around the wooden banister and I begin to climb the stairs. Looking up, I find it goes up more flights than any other area of the palace. This must be a staircase for one of the palace's towers.

My body throbs with soreness as I climb, but the adrenaline of being closer to finding my way home to my family fuels me up the six flights. The staircase ends at a single door. There's no response when I knock, but the door opens slightly with a squeak.

"Hello?" I call, but nothing. I push open the door and peek my head in. A long window wraps around the half-circle-shaped room; you can see the city below, past the gates, and all the way out to the ocean. A forest green flag hangs on the wall behind me. It's flecked with gold, reminiscent of stars against a dark sky. In the center of the flag, in embroidered metallic gold stitches is an aerial depiction of a dragon with an ornate crescent moon on either side of it.

A large table covered by a map sits dead center in the middle of the room. Small figures and little flags are stationed all over the map. My stomach turns. This is a war room. I shouldn't be here.

My curiosity gets the better of me and I walk over to the table. I find hundreds of tiny boats, soldiers, and dragons placed in various locations all over the map. Not terribly shocking. "Carimea" is written in bold letters at the top. I place the book down on the table and look at the names of the five kingdoms—not that I can pronounce any of them. The locations of their capital cities are all marked in script.

In the northwest is Tswangohin, the capital city, Tesalte. In the southwest is Fracilonia, capital city Sol Salnege. In the northeast is Schasumetsats, capital city Stobon. In the southeast is Roladif, capital city Dorolan. The largest kingdom sits in the center of the map, Skaans, capital city Pateko. To the west of Pateko, in black ink "Skaans City" is labeled. The lines and the curves of the map are all too familiar.

I stare at the map in disbelief as my heart pounds like it's about to beat out of my chest. Before me, drawn on thick parchment, is a rough map of most of America.

Carimea. America.

Tesalte, Tswangohin. Seattle, Washington.

Stobon, Schasumetsats. Boston, Massachusetts.

Sol Salnege, Fracilonia. Los Angeles, California.

Dorolan, Roladif. Orlando, Florida.

Pateko, Skaans. Topeka, Kansas.

I've heard the names of these places before, but I didn't put it together until I saw the names spelled out, lying on the map in their very particular locations.

My fingernails dig into the wood as I lean closer to the table to get a better look. Surely, my mind is playing a cruel trick on me.

It's not. There's a reason the dragon breeding grounds looked familiar: it's labeled the Izon region... It's Zion National Park. The park Wyatt spent countless hours talking about visiting with me one day. The borders of the five kingdoms are much larger than our states and expanded both north into what would be Canada and further south, including Mexico and most of Central America. The locations of the cities aren't exact, but they are too close to be a coincidence. This is definitely a map of America.

Where the fuck am I?

"Daphne?" Silas's deep voice comes from behind me. I spin, grabbing the table behind me. Figurines topple and go flying as my body weight shakes the table. I clutch my chest, as if my hand can stop my heart from lurching out. "What are you doing in here?" he asks. I follow his eyes. He looks directly toward my hand, which lays on top of the book perched on the edge of the table.

CHAPTER TWENTY-FIVE

Silas takes a step into the room. Embryanna, Novalora, and Amaleana file in behind him. My mind reels. I have no idea what any of this means and I've been caught snooping in the palace war room, where I definitely shouldn't be, by the king. "I was looking for you. Amaleana found something and…" I trail off, turning back to look at the map one last time, making sure I'm confident in what I say next. "Silas," I swallow back my fears before whispering, "this map… it doesn't make sense. This map is the same, well almost the same, as my country back on Earth."

Embryanna and Novalora exchange glances while shock and confusion wash over Silas and Amaleana's faces. Silas walks to my side, taking a spot so close to me that I feel his body moving as he breathes. He looks down at the map with me. "Are you certain?" His voice is barely a whisper.

"Yes. I'm certain. At least I think I am. The borders don't exactly line up with ours. You have five regions and we have fifty states and your borders go much further north and south… but yes. I am almost one-hundred percent certain." I turn my head to look at him; he's staring down at the map of his continent. "Your kingdoms and capital cities seem to be anagrams for states and cities in my world." I point out each city and tell him what we call it on Earth. "I didn't realize how large Carimea is. I know you're the King of Fracilonia, but who rules these other kingdoms?"

"My parents are the High King and Queen of Carimea. They rule from the city of Pateko in Skaans. Until we came of age, my father appointed lords to look after the kingdoms. Now, my oldest brother, Quinn, rules Tswangohin, my older sister, Zefarina, rules Schasumetsats, and my youngest brother, River, rules Roladif."

"Roladif." My hand hovers over the place it's marked on the map. "That's where I'm from. We call it Florida. My home is close to what you have labeled as the capital city." I turn my head to look at Silas, who stares intensely at the map.

"Florida. What a strange name." Silas scratches his beard.

"Why is this one, Skaans City, different from the others?"

"That is the old capital of Skaans. That is where King Ameldrick ruled from." He looks at me, eyes full of wary confusion, before turning to Embryanna and Novalora. "What does this mean?"

Embryanna looks down at Novalora, who still looks as weak as she did when she left the reading. Embryanna flips her braids off of her shoulder. "It means that our suspicions have been confirmed."

Silas's tone grows deadly quiet, his eyes narrowing at the pair. "What suspicions?"

"I believe she came from an alternative world. Not much is known about them, other than that they do exist," Novalora begins, her airy voice nearly depleted of energy. "But I believe her world is as she says. The same as ours, but without magic. We have spent the past few days looking for more information on these worlds. But King Ameldrick's followers burned almost all of the information we had on traveling during the war. And the travelers we have contacted have not ever heard of traveling between worlds. We have sent word to the other temples on what to look for, but so far we have not found anything."

"We may have found something," Amaleana's timid voice interrupts. "Ma'am," she quickly adds.

"And who are you, exactly?" Embryanna snarls. "Are you not just a lady's maid?"

"Embryanna!" Silas narrows his glare at her further. His tone and face soften when he turns to Amaleana. "Amaleana, what did you find?"

I pick up the book from under my hand and clutch it tightly to my chest. Looking to Amaleana, I wait for her to give me a sign of approval. Once she nods, I extend the book out in my trembling hands for everyone to see. "Amaleana brought me this. It's been in her family for a very long time. The mirror it talks about... it's the same as the one that I fell through."

Silas lifts the book from my hands and walks to the chair at the head of the table. His chair, I realize. The chair meant for the king to sit in to discuss armies and enemies—the chair that overlooks the map of his kingdom, of his family's continent. Embryanna and Novalora stand behind him to read over his shoulder. Embryanna's face goes blank for a split second from something I can't quite discern. She shakes her head and her normal expression returns. The three of them read the entire book before they look at Amaleana, wide-eyed.

"How do you have this book?" Embryanna barks.

"What do you mean?" Amaleana asks. "My family has kept it for centuries."

Embryanna's features harden and her voice grows into an impatient growl. "This book has not been seen in hundreds of years. Every single copy was burned or destroyed in the war. It was supposedly just a children's story and now it is believed to be a piece of missing history. How did you, a lady's maid, come upon it?"

Amaleana's eyes dart around the room nervously. "I, uh."

Novalora walks over to Amaleana, grabs her hands, and holds them comfortingly. "Amaleana, it is okay. We are glad you brought this to us. It will lead us on the right path to get Daphne home. You are safe. Pay her no mind."

Amaleana looks pleadingly at Silas. "My great grandmother was human. She worked in the palace in Skaans City for King Ameldrick a very long time ago..."

Silas looks at her with understanding in his eyes. "What did your grandmother do, Amaleana? How did she come to possess this book?"

Tears swim in Amaleana's eyes. "When they started destroying and censoring the books in the libraries, far before the revolution, she began sneaking books from the palace into her home to protect them. When my family fled for Sol Salnege, Lord Dahl offered her a position in the palace. My family has worked here ever since. I am sorry. I know she should not have stolen, but she was doing what she believed was right," she chokes out between sobs.

"She is telling the truth," Novalora says gently as she releases Amaleana's hands.

"Amaleana, it is okay. You will not be punished for something your grandmother did to a queen and king who no longer rule this continent and abandoned their people. Thanks to her, we may be able to send Daphne home. Thanks to you, Amaleana. You are free to go. We have much to discuss here amongst ourselves."

Relief washes over Amaleana's face as she curtseys to Silas and exits the war room.

The history of this world must be far longer and more complex than I initially believed. What did he mean they abandoned their people? Are the previous king and queen—the ones who believe there's something wrong with saving people using dragon magic—still alive somewhere? Is that why rebel groups are so ready to attack Silas and take back the kingdom?

My heart drops at the thought of them killing Silas to take his kingdom. But why do I care? This isn't any of my concern. I'm an outsider who doesn't belong here. And now, I'm one step closer to getting out of this world. One step closer to going home. But I do care—about him, and about this kingdom.

Silas brings his hands together, pointing his index fingers and placing them on his lips. He closes his eyes in thought. "What do you two suggest we do?"

"I have to let the other priestesses know what we have uncovered," Embryanna says. "Maybe one of them will have more answers. I am the youngest of the high priestesses. It is possible one of the others has a better memory of this book and knows what was on the pages that have been torn from this copy."

She takes the book from Silas, opening it to the section of missing pages. She stares longingly at the torn edges, where answers may have been, then clutches it to her chest. "According to this, there are four other mirrors. I think we need to find one of those to send her home. We will come back tomorrow afternoon. That should give me enough time to discuss our findings with the other priestesses and find out if anyone knows the location of the other mirrors."

"Do you think this will help me get home?" I bite my lip anxiously.

"I believe if we can find one of these other mirrors and get it to work... it would be your best shot." Embryanna's tone is soft and unsure, as if she doesn't fully believe what she's saying.

Novalora nods her head in agreement. "Before we head back to the temple, I would like a word with Daphne. Alone, please."

"You are still not recovered from the last time I left you alone with her," Embryanna snaps.

"In *my* war room?" Silas casts a sidelong glance at the oracle in disbelief of her request.

Novalora looks at them blankly and blinks once. Silas and Embryanna glance at each other before leaving us, muttering under their breaths.

"Is everything okay? Are you okay?" I am curious if this amount of strain is normal after she goes into someone's mind, or if this is a first—as it seems many things that concern me are.

"Yes, I am alright." She adjusts the cuff of her long-sleeved, sage-colored gown. "I can tell you are feeling very anxious about returning to your world. I wanted to give you some information that will hopefully ease your mind. I figured out what the two doorways mean." Novalora pauses.

What feels like an eternity passes, but she remains silent. My impatience gets the best of me and I blurt out, "Well? Are you going to tell me?"

"You have two distinct paths you can follow. Usually, there is one doorway. The choices everyone makes ultimately send them down the same path they are destined for. Their doorway. I believe two doorways mean you have two distinct futures. Perhaps, one on your Earth and one here, on Threa." For a split second, the glow she had during our reading returns to her eyes, but it's gone in a blink.

I laugh in surprise. A future here? That absolutely cannot happen. I need to get home to my family. Is it going to be hard to go back to a world without magic, dragons, and a handsome fae king to save me from danger? Sure. But there is no way I could stay here without my kids. "There is no future for me here without my children."

Novalora gives me an understanding but sad smile. "I am not here to tell you to stay. I am only saying that you are going to be okay. Everything that happens under the stars is for a reason. No matter which path you end up on, just know you are stronger than you believe."

"Why didn't you say that in front of everyone?" I whisper, conflicted emotions coursing through me.

She purses her lips and blinks slowly at me. "I think you know the answer to that." She studies me for a moment before continuing. "Our king has taken quite a liking to you. While he has historically made right and level-headed decisions, I am unable to tell which decisions he will make concerning you. If the universe has granted you two futures, I believe you are the one who should be in charge of which path you take."

"You think he wouldn't help me get home if he knew?"

"No, but I believe he may be less motivated should he learn of your second path's existence and it possibly being one here on Threa."

I suck in an agitated breath. "I don't understand. Why does he care so much? He barely knows me."

"The gods only know." She rolls her eyes and walks to the window, peering out to the stars. I didn't realize how late it was. "You may leave now. I need time alone with the stars to replenish my energy."

The glow from her eyes reflects against the darkened glass of the window. These fae are so strange. How can she drop such a huge bomb on me and expect me to go about business as normal? Frustration takes over and I nearly stomp down the stairs. Silas waits for me alone at the end of the hallway. He looks at me with concern in his eyes. "What did Novalora tell you that upset you?"

I peer up at him. I can't tell him. "Nothing. It's fine." It feels wrong lying to him, but if Novalora is right, which I assume she is because she is the goddamn oracle, I can't risk any delays in finding my way back to Earth. "How was your talk with Brynne? Have you decided what's going to happen to Iri when I leave?"

His eyes scrunch and he raises an eyebrow at me. I sense he can tell I'm not fine, but he doesn't press me. "Yes. We will get to work on a separate shelter for her immediately."

"That's good." I sigh with relief. That's the best place for her. I'm glad she will be well taken care of. Looking down at the floor, not wanting to make eye contact, I whisper, "Thank you. I won't have to worry about her once I'm gone if she's with you."

When I look back up, I find a warm, soft smile on his face. "She will be a very spoiled little dragon indeed." He takes a step closer to me, closing the gap I purposely left between us.

A smile pulls the corner of my lips up. I flutter my eyelashes and tilt my head to look up at him. God, why does he have to be so good-looking? So charming?

"That is a rather attractive quality you have."

"What?" Startled by the compliment, my voice comes out as barely a whisper.

"Your heart. You know almost nothing of this world, you've only been here a few days and yet, you care so deeply about one of our creatures. If you care so much about a dragon, I can only imagine how fiercely you care for the people in your life."

"Well, yes. She's just a baby. Someone needs to make sure she is taken care of since she doesn't have her mother. I can't explain it. Since she curled up on my lap, I've felt connected to her. Like I have no choice but to protect her."

"They will do that to you. Once a dragon chooses you, you are connected. You will feel that as long as you are both alive. And once she has grown, she will have the same need to protect you. But be warned: dragons protect their own ferociously." He winks.

I laugh nervously. "I can imagine." For a moment I let myself see it: staying here in this world, letting this play out. I stare up at him longingly. If we can't figure it out and I do get stuck here, it's not the worst place to be.

No. I will go home. I will get back to my family. My stomach turns with guilt that the thought even crossed my mind.

CHAPTER TWENTY-SIX

Day Five

This morning, I won't be late. Before Amaleana arrived, I got ready and picked out my own outfit from the expansive closet: pants similar to leggings and a loose, pale-blue tunic. Amaleana walks in as I'm heading out the door. I pluck a pastry off the plate she brought, waving to her as I leave. "We'll talk later!" I promise over my shoulder as the door closes behind me.

I'm never late; it gives me awful anxiety. So, instead, I'm always early. It's one of the few things my mother ingrained in me.

Stone isn't in the foyer when I arrive. I win! Smiling triumphantly to myself, I take a seat at the bottom of the stairs and take a bite of the strawberry-filled pastry.

A few servants pass me, carrying various items through the palace. I smile at them as they pass. They look at me strangely before smiling back and continuing about their business. They're probably not used to seeing a female sitting at the bottom of a grand staircase eating a pastry. I stand, brushing the crumbs off of my lap, cringing as they fall on the spotless floor. One of the maids notices me do this and rushes over with a broom to sweep up my mess.

"I'm sorry!" She gets to me so quickly. Was she watching me this whole time? Are they all watching me? I swallow the last bit of my pastry.

"Not a problem, ma'am," the female replies quietly.

"Daphne. You can call me Daphne."

She gives me the same confused, apprehensive look Amaleana did when I told her not to be so formal with me. "Not a problem, Daphne." She finishes sweeping up my crumbs with the dustpan.

"And your name?"

"Marjorie, ma'am."

"Nice to meet you, Marjorie."

She smiles and nods at me before she leaves to take the dustpan from the room. The palace doors open and Stone and Saffron walk in. "Look who made it to training on time," he mocks.

"I'm ready." I place my hands confidently on my hips.

"How sore are you from yesterday?" He laughs.

"Not very," I lie. "I took a long bath when I got to my room last night. I feel brand new." I did take a bath. However, the water grew cold quickly, so I got out and read more of *Finding Your Magic: A Beginner's Guide* and used the water to practice my magic for a few hours. I'm exhausted, but I'm not telling him that.

"We will see about that." He smirks.

Saffron leaves us to rest on the palace steps and we begin our lap around the palace. Yesterday's jog has been replaced with a full-on run. The pace is so fast that I'm certain it isn't natural. Or maybe it is for fae. By the time I make it to the halfway point, Stone passes from behind me. He full-on lapped me. I let out a cry of frustration and pick up my speed, running as fast as I can. Hopefully my fae body will catch up.

When we turn a corner, males are working on the ground near the dragon barn. Silas wasn't joking when he said he'd have them start on a structure for Iri immediately. Building things must be easier when you don't have to worry about permits or money.

I actually finish my lap today; I'm out of breath and tired, but I finished. My hands shoot up in victory. Stone comes from behind me once again, completing his second lap. Sunlight breaks over the palace, making his brown skin glow as he comes to a stop in front of me. "Well done. Maybe one day you will be able to keep up with me." He hands me a water skin.

I take a few sips and return it to him. "I doubt I'll ever be able to run that fast. Even if I do have fae speed or whatever it is that allows you to run so fast, I won't be here long enough to work up to that." I'm just impressed with myself for making it the entire way without vomiting.

"Right." Do I hear a hint of sadness in his voice?

We go over defensive moves again and he coaches me through some new strength training before we head to the weapons cabinet. He hands me a bow.

"No more swords?" I ask.

He shrugs. "You may not always have a sword. I want to make sure you are able to use whatever is at hand at least to some degree. We will work our way through all the basic weapons throughout your training."

"Fair enough."

He gathers several arrows and walks to the field, where Finch is already practicing shooting arrows at the targets lining the edge of the trimmed grass. Saffron runs to join a blue dragon basking in the sun near him. Finch is dressed in loose-fitting pants and a sleeveless tunic. The longer portion of his white-blonde hair is tied in a knot at the top of his head. His muscular, tattooed arms tighten as he pulls back the wooden arrow docked in his bow. He lights the tip of the arrow with a spark of fire from his hand and it whizzes through the air to land dead center in the middle of the target, which bursts into flames.

"You have still got it, I see," Stone remarks as he smiles proudly.

Finch lowers his bow and smiles back at Stone. "I learned from the best, even if it was centuries ago. Are you still teaching it the same way you did back then? Or do you have a few new tricks up your sleeve?" He takes a few strides to the edge of the field but doesn't leave. I guess I have an audience for this lesson.

Stone, unfazed by Finch's watchful gaze, lays three arrows on a ledge in front of me. "We have three different types of arrows. First, your training arrows: they don't do much damage, but can help you catch dinner in a pinch. Next, you have golden arrows, which we dip in sleeping potion. They will not kill anything unless your aim is perfect, but they will knock out your target for a few hours. And lastly, we have dragon iron arrows. They are lethal to almost every magical being."

A long wooden bow and the three arrows sit in front of me. At least I won't be as clueless as I was with the sword. I did archery once, at a Renaissance festival we took the kids to. That day, we watched Ronan and Ryan try desperately to hit their targets for the better half of an hour. The twins went through so many sets of arrows, only hitting the edges of the targets a few times before Wyatt stepped in and took a turn.

I can still see him. His sandy blonde hair was longer than usual; he was growing it out. His strong arms lifted the bow and pulled the string. The muscles in his back flexed as he shot bullseye after bullseye. A sizable audience formed from the crowd and a round of applause followed his final arrow. I watched him in awe with them, incredibly amazed by my husband.

He was always into hunting, but I had never seen him shoot a bow, or gun, or anything before. Hunting trips were sacred to him and his dad. He planned to eventually take the boys with them... hopefully, Mel will still take them when they're a little bit older. Once Wyatt finished his turn, I told him to teach me. And he did, right then and there. I can still feel the warmth of his strong arms wrapping around me, guiding my arms, and his breath on my neck as he whispered instructions before helping me hit the target.

I'm brought back to the present as Stone shows me how to avoid hitting the side of my arm when I draw the string back. Then he tells me how to aim: "You want to make sure your arrow is lined up directly with where you want it to land. Keep your shoulder straight, pull your elbow back to your ear, and release."

I take a deep breath, holding it in as I lift my bow, aim the arrow, and release the bowstring and my breath. My eyes follow the arrow as it lands right in the center of the target. Just like Wyatt taught me. A low clapping comes from behind me. When I turn, Finch's arm is draped over Novalora's shoulder. Silas and Embryanna stand next to them at the end of the training field.

Silas grins widely. "That was surprising."

"She does seem to be full of those, does she not?" Embryanna adds, her tone landing somewhere between annoyed and snarky.

"Where did you learn how to do that?" Silas walks over to me.

Lowering the bow, I push back a strand of brown hair that fell out of my braid. I'm not very good at braiding, so I did a simple three-strand braid down my back. Ariella is always disappointed that I can't recreate the same intricate braids her friends' moms can. "My husband taught me once. I wasn't sure if I'd remember it, though. Must be muscle memory." I shrug.

"He taught you well," Stone comments.

I look at Embryanna and Novalora. There's only one reason they'd be here right now. "Did you find something?" I hand the bow to Stone.

"We did," Embryanna answers, looking at her nails.

"And?" I urged her to continue.

Novalora looks to Embryanna, who folds her arms over her chest and looks off at the various stable hands and garden workers roaming the palace grounds. "We need to go somewhere more private for this discussion."

"Stone, how about you come with us?" Silas claps a hand on Stone's shoulder.

"I will be right in. Let me put away the equipment." Stone gathers the arrows he laid out.

"There is no time for that. Leave it," Silas says almost snappily.

Stone looks up with concern at this command.

"Do not worry. I have got it." Finch takes the bow from Stone.

Silas leads us through the palace to the war room. Brynne, Syrrus, Knox, and Ajax are all waiting for us, stationed in chairs around the map. They all seem unsettled. Looks of confusion and worry pass across their faces as they gaze up at us.

"I have filled them in on what we have figured out so far: how your world is in some way parallel to ours. I have told them about the book Amaleana gave you as well. It is shocking to learn. They are adjusting to the new information."

"Oh, that's fair." How do they think I felt when I got here? Finding out there's a magical world was mind-boggling. I completely understand how they're feeling: everything we know about both our worlds has changed. Embryanna and Novalora didn't seem nearly as shocked last night. Maybe they know more than they were letting on. It would make sense. They *are* the high priestess and the oracle.

Embryanna clears her throat. "I have spoken with the high priestesses of the other kingdoms. Stellamaris, the High Priestess of Tswangohin, the oldest of the five high priestesses, now faintly recalls the Travelers and the mirrors. The other three only have only gotten back vague memories of the children's book, and they all believed it to be just a story, not history. Stellamaris told me the last known location of one of the Travelers, Ailse, was the Pylocim Mountains. Right here." She places a manicured finger down on the map. "West of Tesalte. The other travelers, however, have not been seen or even talked of in centuries."

Knox runs a hand over his jaw and rests his face in his hands. "What do you mean, they have 'gotten back' memories? Why is Stellamaris the only one who remembers them? Would we not at least have some recollection of when people could travel through the kingdoms?"

Ajax's dagger eyes are for once not looking at me, but pointed right at Embryanna. "Right. Why have none of us heard of these mirrors?"

"This seems like essential history. It should not be a secret." Brynne bites anxiously at her nails.

Embryanna looks at the group nervously. "We are not sure. Our job as priestesses includes protecting the history of the continent. But this seems to have slipped from our memories until Daphne's appearance, somehow. It is as if her arrival triggered a rift and allowed some of us to recall things that were forgotten or hidden from us by a glamour. We are unsure. The only way we can get more answers about how the mirrors work and their history is by asking Ailse herself."

"We have to find her." I lean over the map to see where she's pointing.

"We *will* find her." Silas's voice is steady and reassuring. "We will leave right away."

Knox looks at Silas incredulously. "That region is too dangerous. It is full of Reclaimers who support Ameldrick."

"Silas, you cannot keep putting yourself in danger for this female. She is no one to us. We owe her nothing," Ajax bites, getting to his feet.

Silas clenches his jaw. "You do not speak of her like that. No one may speak of her like that." My eyes widen. I'm not used to someone coming to my defense so aggressively. It makes my heart do things it shouldn't during such a serious conversation.

"I will speak how I would like to." Ajax slams his hands on the table, leaning toward Silas, anger edging his voice. "I am your second. I am your friend. We are your friends." He gestures to Bryne, Syrrus, Knox, and Stone. "Not one of us understands what you are doing here, Silas. Are you really about to risk your life to maybe find an ancient traveler? What happens if you do not find her? What happens if Ailse is on the wrong side and hands us over to the Reclaimers? Hands *you* over to the Reclaimers."

Silas flinches.

Ajax continues: "There are plenty who would love to see you dead and put their Returned Prince right on your throne. And for what? A female who does not belong here." He glares at me. "And may I remind you, if you die, one of River's children will become the King of Sol Salnege. Silas, you are too important to this kingdom to not be thinking with your head. You cannot do this. Send Knox and me to search for Ailse. You cannot go."

Swallowing nervously, I look from Ajax to Silas. Everything he said is true. I am no one. The king should not be helping me personally. I shouldn't be causing issues like this in a world I'm not a part of. I play with my hands anxiously and wait for Silas to respond.

Silas growls so low, so threateningly quiet, it sends a chill down my spine and a prickling under my skin. "That is not your call to make. Sit down, Ajax," he grinds out through gritted teeth.

Ajax bares his teeth for a split second before he concedes with a scrunch of his face and huffed sigh. He returns to his seat, throwing up his hands in defeat.

Knox's eyes dart nervously between his king and the second-in-command. It's unnerving to see a male of such intimidating stature so on edge. "Ajax has a point."

Silas's irritation grows on his face. His brows come together and wrinkles form on his forehead and he grinds his teeth, waiting for the next person to speak up against his plan.

This is my fault. I need to fix this. "It's okay. You don't have to go. I'm sure Ajax and Knox will be able to take me to find Ailse."

"Not happening." The words come out like a protective snarl.

"You heard her. It's fine. We can take care of it. Let us do our jobs. Let us keep you safe for the good of the kingdom," Knox pleads.

Novalora raises her hands. "Stop it, all of you. He is your king. You will do as he says. He has never led you astray before. Do either of you recall a single mission Silas has sat out on?" She pauses, waiting for a response, but receives silence. "I did not think so. Not to mention, he is more powerful than both of you combined. The stars do not show an untimely demise for our king. He will be fine. He is going with Daphne, like it or not."

Knox's eye twitches with frustration. "Novalora, you cannot seriously be encouraging this."

She crosses her arms over her chest. "I have spoken."

Silas stands, leaning onto the table. "We leave tonight. Syrrus, can you ready the supplies and the pegasuses?" Syrrus nods in response. "We should be able to get a few hours of flight in before sunset." Silas looks at me, his lip curling in a half smile, like he's asking me if I'm okay with flying. Even though I'm nervous about flying again, my fear of the sky isn't nearly as bad as it was. I shake my head yes and his lips form an accepting smile. "Embryanna, can you get a message to Trinity? Tell her to let Quinn know we will be arriving at the palace in Tesalte tomorrow morning."

CHAPTER TWENTY-SEVEN

Lying on the bed petting Iri, I turn my phone on while Amaleana gathers a few days' worth of clothes for me. When I got back to my room, I filled her in on everything that had happened since last night and thanked her over and over for bringing me the book. Syrrus stopped by and brought me my own enchanted bag to pack my things in; it was such a simple, kind gesture. He probably didn't think anything of it, but it meant the world to me.

My battery is down to sixty percent. How is that possible? I've only had it on for a few minutes at a time over the past few days. I let out an annoyed sigh and snap a photo of Iri. When I get to my photo library, I scroll through my photos until the pictures of the Renaissance festival pop up.

There are dozens of photos of the kids and Wyatt. The only photo of all of us from that day was taken by a kind, drunk, twenty-something-year-old woman dressed like a fairy. She offered to take one with me in it after watching me take a few of the kids with their dad. Ryan is on Wyatt's shoulders, I'm holding Ronan horizontally in my arms, and Ariella is sitting in front of us, the bottom of her princess dress a sparkly pink poof around her.

Ariella insisted we all dress up and Wyatt did anything his princess requested. My outfit was a long medieval dress I'd bought at the party store one Halloween. The twins wore tiny tunics and had foam swords strapped across their backs. Wyatt went all out for Ariella: his outfit was all black, complete with leather armor, a sword, and all the accessories. He was so handsome, I could stare into his jade-green eyes all day and never get bored. I often did this, wondering how I'd gotten so lucky. I miss him so much. Now, my heart aches for all of them. They would all love to see this place.

The creak of the door signals that Amaleana is coming, so I power down my phone and slip it into the bag before she notices. I'm still not quite ready to explain technology to anyone. Frankly, I don't understand it well enough to explain it. I guess I could say it's Earth's version of magic, but they'd have more questions than I'd have answers. I'm an antique store owner who happens to have magic and be part fae, but I'm not a tech wizard.

She returns with a small pile of clothes: mostly pants and sweaters, a blue dress that I assume is for when we arrive at the palace at Tesalte, and a thick cloak. The exterior is a dense powder-blue fabric that glitters when the light catches it as I pull it off the stack. The interior is lined with soft white fur.

"You will be needing that. It gets quite cold up north this time of the year, especially near the tops of the Pylocim Mountains. There is snow this time of year."

"It's beautiful." I run my hand over the velvet. Little embroidered silver dragons decorate the edges.

Her face lights up at the compliment. "I thought so. I picked out the prettiest one in there for you to wear." She grabs the brush from the side table and untangles my poorly done braid.

My thoughts drift to the journey ahead and everything that led me to this point. I'm reminiscing on my first few days here when I remember the glowing figure from the forest. "If I ask you something, can you keep it between us?"

"I swear it." Her fingers gently pull apart a knot.

I pick at the beds of my nails, unsure if this is the time, but there may not be another opportunity. "Does this world have ghosts?"

She chuckles beneath a breath. "I do not think so. Why?"

I turn to face her and look into her kind green eyes. I can trust her. "I don't know if I hallucinated it or if it was real, but on my first night here, I saw a woman in the woods. She was glowing and translucent. Like a ghost. She told me not to tell anyone I saw her."

She cocks her head and her brows furrow with concern. "It sounds like an astral projection. But that is a very rare gift only those with extreme power possess. The priestesses and oracles can astral project, besides them, there only a few others can. "

"Maybe I imagined it." I look out the window, soaking in the view of Sol Salnege for the last time. I wish I could freeze time to learn more about this place.

"Maybe." She returns to brushing my hair. "I won't say anything. But I do think you ought to tell King Silas."

She's not wrong. I should tell him. But I can't shake the figure's words from my mind: "They will kill you if they find out about this." But I trust Silas with every fiber of my being. "Why do you think he is the way he is with me?"

"What do you mean?"

"Everyone says he acts differently around me."

"He does."

"I don't understand it."

"I think that is something for you and the king to discuss."

"But, Amaleana, I need your help. Normally my best friend, Gabby, would tell me to stop thinking about it and have fun. But she's not here to give me the courage. I need someone, a friend, to tell me what to do."

She pauses. "Well, how do you feel about him?"

"I don't know. He's handsome, kind, and thoughtful. But I'm leaving this world. He knows that; I know that."

She continues detangling my hair. "It is clear the two of you are attracted to one another and care for each other. If it were me, I would be using every second of time I had to my advantage."

She's right. Why haven't I thought of it that way? "It's hard, having these feelings again."

"I understand. Losing someone you love is hard. But you cannot allow yourself to be miserable the rest of your life. I think your husband would want you to be happy. As far as the king is concerned, the heart wants what it wants. You would be insane to let an opportunity like *that* pass you by. I mean, have you seen him?"

We both laugh. Once Amaleana finishes brushing out my hair, she pauses for a long moment. I turn back to her and memorize my friend's features. Her freckles, green eyes, and light copper hair. "Thank you for everything, Amaleana."

She smiles softly before she starts reworking my hair into a tight braid. "Happy to do it, Daphne."

"You may be the reason I get home." I choke out, becoming emotional in my gratitude to this female who has become my friend so quickly.

Her cheeks flush with warmth. "You're welcome." She pauses. "But do not be reminding Silas of that fact. I quite like my job here. Most days I get to read all day waiting for guests who never come." She laughs, adding a lace ribbon to the bottom of my hair, blue to match the cloak.

I laugh with her. "Don't worry. I won't. But in case I don't come back here, really, thank you for your help. And for being my friend the past few days."

"Until we meet again." Her eyes glisten and she pulls me into a tight hug. I squeeze her back, unable to return her sentiment because I don't think we'll ever see each other again and I can't lie to her. She picks the cloak off the bench and drapes it over my shoulders, tying it tightly at the hood. "That should be good. Would not want the wind taking it."

Iri climbs onto my shoulders and we make our way to the stable. Finch stands beside Ajax's pegasus with his hand on the small of his mate's back. Novalora and Embryanna stand patiently at the back of the stable. Syrrus, Brynne, Knox, and Stone wait on top of their pegasuses. They're all dressed in leather armor and have gleaming black weapons strapped to their backs and legs. Dragon iron weapons. This is an armed guard; they are here to protect their king. Those weapons are not just for defense. They're for killing. Another thing I don't think I'll ever get used to.

I smile as I walk over to pet Lucy. "You're coming too?" I ask Stone.

He raises an eyebrow and the side of his lip quirks up. "Did you think you would be able to miss training?"

I roll my eyes dramatically. "Of course not." As I stroke Lucy's mane, I realize we're missing someone. "Where's Silas?" Did he decide not to come after all and let the others take me to find Ailse? I would understand if he were convinced to stay, but it does make me the slightest bit sad thinking I may never see him again.

"Right here. Sorry for the delay." He trots up, wearing elegantly fashioned leather armor.

"Where were you?" I ask as Lucy kneels, allowing me to climb into the saddle.

"Had to say goodbye to my dragons." A flicker of sadness crosses his face.

"Why can't they come?" I tilt my head.

"They are too small to fly long distances, so we would have to stop more frequently, which would not be safe for anyone. Especially since I knew you would not let us leave Iri behind. We will already have a target on our back traveling with one dragon." He looks around at his friends. "While I have no doubt all of our dragons can defend themselves, I will not put them at risk."

"Oh, I'm sorry, Silas." The thought hadn't crossed my mind. I automatically brought Iri with me. Where I go, she goes. At least as long as I'm still here. I look around, noticing she's the only dragon with us. If I have such a strong need to protect and be with Iri, who only chose me a few days ago, I can only imagine the sadness leaving their dragons behind brings everyone. Iri tightens her grip around my neck like a scarf. I settle in on Lucy's saddle and she rises. Silas starts to climb on the saddle behind me.

This shouldn't have surprised me; there's no other pegasus to be seen and I don't really know how to ride one by myself. But I can't help but question him: "What are you doing?"

He pauses, his body half pushed up on Lucy's side. I'm impressed he's able to keep himself suspended there. The muscles in his arms and back flex as he looks over his shoulder, checking the surprised expressions of those around us. "Getting on my pegasus? What does it look like I am doing?"

"Can't I ride alone?" I straighten my back, reaching for Lucy's reins.

He laughs, as if that was the most ridiculous request he's ever heard. "Absolutely not."

"Why is that? I stayed on fine last time." I'm not sure why I am arguing with him. As if I don't want him to ride with me. Having him hold me, his strong chest pressed against my back in the saddle, is something I certainly wouldn't mind. Maybe I'm fighting him because if I make him believe I'm not attracted to him, he'll stop acting so damn charming around me. Stop caring so much about me. That would make everything easier.

Silas blinks slowly at me in disbelief. "You barely stayed on the last time and you screamed louder than the banshees."

"Banshees? They exist here?"

"Yes. Maybe we will get you some books on the different types of fae and magical beings who dwell here once we return to Sol Salnege. But no more changing the subject. It is not safe for you to ride alone. Not only are you not a strong enough rider, but you are not armed and have not been training long enough to wield a sword in battle, let alone hold onto one in flight should we be attacked. I will not force you to ride with me, but you do have to ride with someone." He shrugs, pushing himself off of Lucy's back and landing back on the ground with a heavy thud. "You ride with Ajax or you ride with me. Your choice."

Ajax focuses on the dragon iron dagger he's sharpening and nonchalantly resheaths the razor-sharp blade to his thigh, pretending he can't hear our conversation.

I look at him and his threat from my first night rings in my ears. Ajax shoving me off mid-flight or taking his dagger to my throat like he promised to do doesn't seem ideal. Riding with him would give him the perfect opportunity to take care of the problem plaguing their king and clouding his judgment. He's barely acknowledged me since we got back to the palace, and after what he said about me earlier, I'm certain he hasn't moved past his hatred of me. I frown and sigh in defeat. "Fine. You can ride with me."

Silas half grins in satisfaction as he pulls himself up into the saddle. He settles in behind me, leaving just a small gap between his chest and my shoulders for Iri. "Thank you for giving me your permission to ride my mount."

"Please, we both know she likes me better," I mutter under my breath.

Knox laughs. "She's got you there, Silas."

I hadn't realized he was paying attention to our conversation. Is he always listening? It makes sense that he is. His job is keeping Silas alive, after all.

Silas grabs Lucy's reins with his right hand and me with his left, ignoring Knox's comment. My heart races when his chest presses against my back, his body heat warming me. My heart skips as his grip tightens protectively.

Stupid heart. I swallow, trying to push away those thoughts, but fail. I can't believe I'm so close to finding my way out of this world and I continue to push him away. Why am I deliberately screwing up the chances of anything more happening between the two of us? I could be spending my time here having the best fantasy fling of my life, but instead, I've been training with Stone and teaching myself magic in my bedroom. There's no doubt I'll be kicking myself over this for the rest of my life. Maybe not the learning magic part. But the whole not-having-an-epic-romance-with-a-fae-king part? Definitely. Clearly, my countless hours spent reading about this exact situation did not prepare me well enough for it actually happening.

What's wrong with me? Why can't I let myself be swept off my feet? He obviously wants to do exactly that. Each time I push him away, I regret it, but I can't help myself. Maybe it's the guilt from moving on so soon after Wyatt. Maybe it's self-sabotage. Maybe I just don't want to fall for someone I can never be with.

Silas clears his throat, interrupting my winding thoughts. The others stiffen in their saddles, ready for instruction from their leader. "We will fly low along the coast for a few hours until we reach the Tswangohin border. We will make camp before sunset. Tomorrow morning, we fly to Tesalte to meet with Quinn and High Priestess Trinity to decide on the most probable locations of Ailse. Their spies are scouting the Pylocim Mountain Villages, trying to get a lead on her whereabouts. Remember, there have been more sightings of rebel activity over the past few weeks. Keep your eyes and ears open at all times."

The five others nod their heads in near unison, accepting the orders. The mention of increased rebel activity doesn't exactly ease my anxiety. If these rebels are part of the same group we narrowly escaped from on the way to Sol Salnege, what's going to stop them from attacking us again?

Ajax leans over the side of his pegasus, pulling Finch into a passionate kiss. It isn't the quick kind of kiss you give your significant other when you're running an errand. It's deep and full of unquestionable love. The kind of kiss you give someone when there's a chance you won't see them again.

The unspoken implication makes my stomach twist with anxiety.

Is this the right thing to do? How am I asking these people to put their lives in danger for me when there are people who love them so much?

Novalora and Embryanna wave to us. Before I can voice my doubts, the pegasuses run in formation, Lucy at the center, Syrrus and Brynne on our left, Knox and Ajax on our right, and Stone at the rear. Lucy's wings flap and her feet leave the ground—we're in the air.

My heart nearly stops and my stomach lurches. It reminds me of the feeling just before the launch of a roller coaster. The feeling of being in the sky is both terrifying and exhilarating. Instinctively, I tighten my grasp on the pommel. Silas's arm wraps more firmly around my waist in response to my fear.

We ride in silence, with nothing but the sound of the wind around us, for what feels like ages. I'm not sure if it's the anxiety from my fear of heights or not wanting to swallow a bug that's keeping me quiet. The world below passes quickly, dozens of quaint villages dotting the coast.

Not one of them is nearly as large or impressive as Sol Salnege. The towns are made of mostly older wooden homes and buildings. In front of some towns, boats bob up and down in the waves near the shorelines. I imagine them being sleepy little fishing villages full of magical beings and amazing stories. I look out to the ocean and watch the calm water for some time, wondering if it holds the same animals ours does, or if other creatures lurk below the surface.

Maybe the books Silas told me he'd find on this world's inhabitants hold that information. Not that I'll get the chance to read it... My chest aches slightly with confliction at knowing I'll be leaving soon. I'll miss this world and the people who have become my friends.

The cool wind gets stronger the farther north we travel. Iri moves from around my neck to my lap under my cloak for warmth. I tuck her in the fabric before wrapping myself in it tighter as well. I'm grateful that Amaleana gave me this cloak. I'd be freezing without it.

Silas adjusts his position in the saddle, filling the small gap Iri left when she moved, and sends a whirling shield of warm air around our party, silencing the loud winds around us. "Are you doing alright?"

"Never better," I chirp as I rub my free hand over my body. "I didn't expect it to be so cold."

He leans closer to me, somehow making even less space between us, allowing his body to warm mine more than it already was. "It is only this cold because of the winds at this height. We will land shortly, so we have enough time to set up camp before the sun sets. Once we do, it will not be as cold and Knox will get a fire going."

"Hopefully he's more proficient in starting one than you are," I say mockingly.

The joke flies over his head. "Yes. He has fire magic." His tone is serious and matter-of-fact.

"Oh, I remember."

"Then why did you…" He trails off.

"Do you not remember how long it took you to get a fire going on our way to Sol Salnege?" I laugh.

He scoffs as the joke finally clicks. "You are an asshole. I did my best. My magic is air and water. The complete opposites of fire. It is not exactly the most natural thing for me to do, you know."

I suck in an exaggerated breath and click my tongue. "Sounds like an excuse."

"Alright, if that is how you're going to be, then you best be prepared," he replies playfully.

A smile grows on my face. "Oh, I will be, your highness."

His bearded chin brushes the top of my head as shakes his head behind me. "Remember who is flying the pegasus you are on, Daphne." My name sounds like a taunt on his lips.

"I won't, King Silas," I tease.

He sighs, letting me know he's given up for now. He lifts his hand from the reins and points in front of us at a cliff overlooking the ocean. "Look, right there. That is where we are landing."

The six pegasuses begin their descent. The muffled sound of wind is replaced by that of lapping waves hitting the wall of the cliff below as we land on a cliff. Silas drops the air shield and I inhale the crisp salt air. Iri jumps from my lap, stretches her body out like a cat, and jumps playfully into a pile of leaves. She spins her body a few times before curling up into a cozy ball.

We dismount from the pegasuses and survey the area. I walk to the edge of the cliff to look down at the water. Rocks jut out of the ocean, the waves spraying over them. The fall from this height over the edge would be perilous. Maybe my fear of heights isn't gone entirely. I back up and face away from the cliff. Opposite the water is an endless forest of towering redwood trees. Everyone is already setting up the camp as I stare in awe of the scenery.

We took a family trip to northern California a few years back. Wyatt and I spent the majority of the time arguing about what we wanted to do. He wanted to go hunting and fishing early in the morning with his dad. The kids wanted to see the redwoods. After a huge fight about priorities, I took the kids by myself. The tainted memory forms a knot in my stomach. I should have waited for him to get back before we went. For some reason, I had decided to be stubborn on that trip. I wish I'd been a better wife when I had the chance.

The clearing is just big enough for the tents Syrrus is setting up and the small fire Knox is starting. I count the tents Syrrus set up almost instantly, thanks to his magic. Five tents form a semi-circle around the fire. One for Syrrus and Brynne, one for Stone, one for Ajax, one for Knox, and one for—oh, hell no. He is not seriously pulling this again.

"There's a tent missing," I point out to Syrrus. Syrrus gives me a confused shrug before looking to Silas for his response. Syrrus clearly does not want any part of this.

"There is no room for another tent. It is fine. Do we really have to do this again today? I will offer you the same deal: you share a tent with me or with Ajax. I am not leaving you unprotected out here. Even with the wards up, I want to make sure you are safe."

"What about Knox?" I suggest, folding my arms over my chest. He must know I'm not the biggest fan of his second, otherwise why would he keep making himself the obvious choice?

Knox looks up at us from where he sits warming himself by the fire. "He would not allow that one in a thousand years, Daph. He knows how persuasive I can be with females. He would not want me to be the one warming your bed." He winks. "Maybe some other time, though."

Silas makes water appear over the fire. He drops it, extinguishing the flames and sending a cloud of smoke into the air. "You're right. Not in a thousand years."

Knox throws his hand up. "Seriously? Come on now, you know I was joking. We all know how you are about this one."

"You must be sick of me by now. Don't you want your own space?" I ask.

He cocks his head and smiles. "Quite the opposite, actually."

My cheeks flush with embarrassment. It seems that he has an answer to everything.

He runs a hand through his hair. "It will be fine. Do it as a favor to me for bringing you to find Ailse. I know you will be safe, so I will be able to sleep."

"Yeah, sure, 'sleeping' is what you will be doing," Knox calls as his fire roars back to life, lighting up the campsite with a warm glow.

I roll my eyes and gesture to Knox. "See. This is why we can't sleep in the same tent. That's what they'll all think. And the last time you promised to stay on your side, I woke up with you... you cuddling me!"

"I promise I will not cuddle you again—unless you ask me to." Silas steps closer to me, his voice a low whisper. "Why does it matter to you what they think? Is your problem with this sleeping arrangement that they will think we slept together? Or is it that you will be wishing that is what we are doing? Because you are leaving this world. Why would you care what they think of you?"

My eyes widen. I should smack him for that. What's gotten into him? I stand up a bit taller and brush sand from my cloak. "Like everyone keeps telling me, I may not get home, so I don't want to get any sort of reputation."

"So you do not want to sleep with me?"

The heat returns to my cheeks. "What?" How is he going to ask me that right now? This really is a different side of Silas. I guess I really don't know him that well.

"In the tent. You do not want to sleep with me in the tent?" He smirks.

"No! I do not want to sleep with you!" I nearly shout, covering my mouth quickly, but it's too late. All heads turn in our direction.

Silas glares at them and they return to their tasks. "I think we both know that's not true."

"And why's that?" I whisper.

"I can feel your heart race when I touch you, so either you are incredibly afraid of me or—"

"That's not true. That's not possible." My voice wavers as I object to the insinuation. Is it possible, though? There's so much about being fae I don't know. My senses have been growing stronger the longer I'm in this body, but I can't hear heartbeats... I should have been spending my evenings reading about what it meant to be fae instead of practicing magic.

"Fae senses." He shrugs. "And by your smell, I am almost certain you are not afraid of me." He winks.

My mouth parts slightly in mortification. "Oh my god."

CHAPTER TWENTY-EIGHT

My whole face heats up as embarrassment fills my cheeks. The idea briefly crossed my mind, but I forgot to ask Amaleana about it. My body tenses. There's nothing I want more than to become invisible right now. Apparently, that power isn't going to manifest itself no matter how much I wish for it.

Do they all know, then? Why hasn't anyone said anything to me before this moment? Maybe they're all so used to hearing and smelling each other that they ignored it. And surely it isn't uncommon to be attracted to Silas. He's undeniably one of the most handsome people I've ever seen. Not to mention he's thoughtful, funny, and caring. *This is normal and nothing to be embarrassed about*, I try and fail to assure myself.

I haven't heard anyone else's heart. Maybe more skilled fae can control these things. Or, maybe my fae senses have yet to develop that particular ability.

I shift my body uncomfortably, as if the small movements can shake the embarrassment out of me. Silas's sudden shift in behavior has me caught off guard. He's being much more... direct than before.

What's gotten into him? How do I continue this conversation without making it awkward?

As if she can hear my mental pleas, Brynne stands from her spot unpacking the cushions for around the fire. I'm sure with her fae senses, she heard every single thing we said.

She walks right up to Silas; the top of her head barely reaches his shoulder. "Why would you tell her that?" she scolds. She turns to me and grabs my hands. "Do not worry. It is completely normal. No one really notices those things unless they are actively trying to. Almost every female has the same reaction to him." Silas smiles at that and she rolls her eyes. "Then they get to know him and realize he is incredibly annoying." She sticks her tongue out at him.

I laugh, trying to come to terms with all of this. "Well, that is... good to know."

"You haven't noticed any differences in your senses since arriving?" she asks me, releasing my hands.

I look down at my hands. My heart rate is now calm and my cheeks cool; she literally healed the embarrassment from me.

"I've noticed they're all a little stronger, but not how you two are describing. Maybe they need more time." I run a finger over the point of my ear. "Do you all just... sense each other's feelings? All of the time? That must be overwhelming."

"Oh gods, no. Most of the time we ignore them. Everyone smells of some emotion or another almost all of the time. It can give you a nasty headache if you do not learn to block them out. However, none of us have been able to ignore the effect you have on Silas. It is a good thing your senses are not fully there yet. He reeks." She flashes Silas a wicked smile that tells him he better leave me alone if he doesn't want her to continue.

"Is that so?" I tilt my head and smirk. At least I'm not the only one who smells of... whatever it is they're all smelling around here.

A faint tinge of red creeps under Silas's tan skin—only for a second, but I catch it. "Brynne, should you not be helping your husband?" he says. "Or doing literally anything else besides sticking your nose in my business."

"Actually, I think Knox requires your attention." She bats her eyelashes tauntingly at him.

He blinks cooly at her. "Does he now?" He stalks off to where Knox stands over a roaring fire.

"You have to ignore him, Daph. Males can be quite insufferable when they are in this state."

"What state is that?" I ask.

"When they want something and they restrain themselves from getting it. They go nearly feral. You will have to forgive him. This is not him; it is his instincts."

Before I have a chance to ask her what she means by that, Silas walks back to us. "Knox did not need me."

"Oh?" Brynne asks in a mock confused tone.

"No," he answers bluntly.

"My mistake, your highness." Knowing she'd gotten under his skin just enough, Brynne smiles sweetly and throws her unbound blonde hair over her shoulder and walks with a triumphant bounce in her step to rejoin Syrrus. She looks back, throwing one last taunting smile at Silas before linking arms with her husband.

"I like her." I grin.

He scratches the side of his neck as he watches Brynne kiss Syrrus's cheek. "Of course you do. She is like an annoying older sister; I love her but she knows exactly how and when to irritate me."

Brynne and Syrrus walk arm and arm off into the forest. Maybe they're going to look for herbs or berries. Or maybe they are off to... I stop my thoughts while they're ahead. Once Brynne and Syrrus are out of earshot, Silas runs a hand through his dark hair. "They are going to do exactly what you are thinking they are going to do."

"Oh my god. What is wrong with you?" I put my hand on my temple in irritation. What has gotten into him?

"Why do you keep saying that?"

"Saying what?"

His brows furrow together. "'God.' Is there a specific one you are referring to?"

"What? No." Thank god we're changing the subject. "I mean, yes, technically. On Earth there are different religions, and some have more than one god. But I've never been religious. It's just a saying."

"Do people on Earth not have contact with their gods?"

"Uh... No." I tilt my head curiously. "Do you talk with the ones here?"

"Yes. Well, not me. The priestesses have contact with the gods and goddesses. Part of their job is keeping their legacies protected and spreading their wisdom. Each of the five high priestesses runs a temple for one of our five gods. The five gods watch over our world: our five kingdoms, five temples, and five high priestesses. Each of the five gods powers specific types of magic. Those who exhibit those powers are proof of their gifts to us. In Sol Salnege, our temple is dedicated to Ciela, goddess of the air and skies. You are telling me there is no contact with them in your world? How do you know what they want or what you should do to please them?"

That is an excellent point, but religion isn't my thing. If they have actual contact with their gods here on Threa... What does that mean for Earth? I don't want to think about it right now, or ever, frankly. Some things are left best unknown. I shift uncomfortably at the weight of his question. "I'm not sure. People follow many religions. But there isn't one everyone agrees on, so most of us try to respect each other's beliefs. There isn't really any proof that one is more valid than the next. They must have come from somewhere, I suppose. Maybe a long time ago, humans did talk to one, or several."

"That is odd. Not knowing how your world's religions truly came to be." Silas reaches his arms behind his back and stretches his neck from side to side. "Let us go find a river. I can help you work on your magic while Stone, Knox, and Ajax catch us something for dinner."

I look around the campsite and notice we're now alone, aside from Iri, who is snuggled in her pile of leaves. "What about Iri?"

"She will be okay. Syrrus warded the camp and Ajax put up a

light shield the moment we landed. We will not be far. There is a stream only a hundred yards or so from here," Silas assures me.

I hesitate, looking at Iri, who snores peacefully, leaves moving around her with each exhale. It would be fun to learn more about wielding my magic from another fae rather than a book. I'll give myself some credit: I've taught myself quite a bit the past few nights from the books Amaleana gave me from the palace library. Water magic, I learned, is easier and uses less energy when you're first learning if you are using a source, like a stream or a lake, or in my case a tub, rather than manifesting it.

I tried using the water from my bath last night to practice and completely soaked the floor. Luckily, I got the majority of the water back into the tub before having to throw a dozen of the plush towels I found in the closet down to absorb the rest. Practicing with more water and in the presence of someone who can instruct me on what I'm doing right or wrong is the best way for me to improve. "Okay, let's go."

His face brightens unexpectedly. He probably assumed I would say no. We make our way through the redwood trees to the nearby stream. I look back every couple of yards while I still can to make sure Iri doesn't wake up. Once we pass the wards and light shield, the camp disappears. The fire and tents are replaced with trees and dirt. Knowing I truly can't see into the camp eases some of my anxiety. At least I know Iri will be safe while we're gone.

It takes less than five minutes to reach a small stream. The magnificent trees around us are various shades of vibrant green. Fallen needles float gently on top of the crystal-clear water. The golden light of the sun setting filters through the branches, shimmering and making the whole area glow. I spin slowly to admire each inch of this enchanting forest. "Everything here is so beautiful."

Silas's eyes are bright and full of wonder as he too takes in the scene around us. "We believe our worlds are the same. Does your world not look like this?"

"No, not exactly. There are beautiful places, don't get me wrong. But everything I've seen here is much more breathtaking. A lot of Earth has been overdeveloped by humans. And they keep building more, destroying what little nature we have left on our planet. These trees in particular are rare on Earth. I saw them once, but they weren't nearly as impressive."

A displeased frown forms on his face. "That sounds like an awful place to live. It makes sense. Humans reproduce more quickly than fae, so you need more places to live. Remind me why you want to go back?"

I shrug. "If I didn't have my kids... I don't know." I bite my lip as the confession slips. I pause for a moment before shaking my head. "I couldn't stay here. My life is back on Earth."

"You could though, you know. Start a new life here," he offers.

The sheer ridiculousness of what he's implying startles me and I laugh. "And then what? What would I do here? Where would I stay? I don't think you'd want some random person and her children held up in your palace for the rest of... How long do fae live for?"

"We're immortal, so forever." His head cocks to the side. "Unless we are killed. But you and your family can stay at the palace as long as you wish. I assumed you understood that."

I sigh. Part of me doesn't want to give up this world, my magic... but I can't abandon my kids. Not only will they be orphans if I don't get back, but my heart would ache constantly for them. They're my whole world. "No, Silas. Thank you, but no. I have to go home."

"It was worth a shot. Okay, show me what you have learned and I will show you how to use the river to your advantage."

I'm glad we're going to work on my magic; it'll be a good change of pace. I don't understand why he wants me to stay. Sure, he finds me attractive, but he just met me. It's an awfully big leap: meet a strange female from another world in a cave; oh, let's invite her to move in for a happily ever after a few days of knowing her.

I shake the thoughts out of my head, calming my breathing and feeling for my magic. Once I find it, I show Silas the ways I had learned to bend and shape water. The water moves smoother and I wield it more confidently than the last time I showed him.

"Very good. You have been practicing." He smirks.

"I've been using the bath water," I say, moving water through the air in spirals.

"Rather resourceful." He takes a step closer to me at the edge of the river. "Now watch this." He lifts a single hand and the river turns into millions of water droplets suspended in the air. He moves them around the forest, making them spin and dance in the beams of light that cut through the trees. Rainbow prisms appear through the droplets as they move through the light. My mouth parts slightly as I watch Silas create art with the water he controls.

He steps closer to me. The water droplets surround us and they still. It feels like we're in a rain shower that is frozen in time. I turn to face him, my mouth parting slightly in awe. We stand chest to chest as hundreds of millions of small rainbows are reflected on and around us. My breath becomes shallow and my heart races. "This is..." I look up at him, losing my words when my eyes meet his. His smile is soft, but it makes the corner of his eyes crinkle, gleaming with delight at my astonishment.

I try steadying my breath. If he can hear my heartbeat, I'm sure he can sense how rapidly my chest is moving. Probably, everyone with water magic can do this; it's only special because I've never seen anything like it before. My lashes flutter as I look down, breaking our eye contact.

He uses a finger to lift my chin to look back into his eyes. The details of his face become clear in this light: the strong lines of his jaw under his trim beard, his sharp cheekbones, even his nose is perfectly straight. Why does he have to be so incredibly good-looking? The longer I stare, the more I want him to kiss me. I do want him to kiss me, I realize. I don't care how heartbroken it leaves me. Let it break me. Our eyes remain locked. And then I hear it. *A second heartbeat.* Silas's heartbeat is moving as rapidly as mine. But he doesn't make any motion to kiss me.

He glides his hand from my face to the back of my head. *Kiss me.* "I told you, I won't kiss you again unless you tell me you want me to."

I swallow. I place my palm on his chest, feeling his muscles beneath my hand. Standing before me is the man every girl dreams of, and he wants *me*. But why? I have to know. Oh god, what am I about to do? "Silas, why are you acting so differently?"

A slight sadness washes over his face and he brushes his thumb along my cheek. Why did I have to say that? I'm excellent at ruining moments. Why don't I let this tall handsome fae king have his way with me? He leans his head in closer, placing his forehead on mine. A half-sad smile appears on his face as he looks down at me. "We are going to get you home." His voice is low. The combination of his voice and the way he is still holding my head possessively sends a chill down my back. "I only have a short time with you. I decided I should stop wasting it."

My eyes grow wide at his confession. "Oh." I whisper. I pause, deciding. Is this what I want? There is no going back. "Then... yes."

His eyes light up. "Yes?"

"I want you to kiss—" His lips are on mine. His gentle kiss sends a rush through my entire body. I kiss him back feverishly, wanting more, needing more. His other hand finds the small of my back, drawing my body closer to his, kissing me slowly. I lift my hands from his chest, wrapping them around his neck. I push up on my toes, begging him. *Kiss me. Harder.* He moves his hands down my body. Once he reaches my thighs, he lifts me off of the ground. I wrap my legs around his torso. I haven't been kissed so thoroughly in so long. A small moan escapes my lips between breaths and suddenly the water droplets find gravity, soaking us both with the freezing water.

The temperature shocks me and I shriek from the chill. Silas looks at me, embarrassment washing over his face. "I meant to do that."

I cover my mouth, trying to stifle the giggle that I can't hold back.

I look down at our sopping wet bodies, his shirt clinging to the muscles underneath. "You sure know how to make a woman wet."

CHAPTER TWENTY-NINE

Silas throws his head back, laughing, and kisses me softly on the forehead. "I knew there was a reason I liked you."

"Is it because I'm exceptionally beautiful, even when I'm soaked in freezing cold river water?" I mock. I know very well I am far from beautiful, especially compared to the fae standards. Memories of the gorgeous females who threw themselves at Silas the night of the party make me feel a bit self-conscious.

His flirtatious smirk reaches his eyes. "Especially when you are soaked in freezing river water. You are quite possibly the most exquisite creature I have ever seen."

I smile at the compliment. He pauses looking longingly into my eyes. "You are not like any female I have ever met before. They are always so desperate to impress me, so insistent on following all of these societal rules. But you—you never cared what I thought of you. You are unashamedly yourself. I think that is what I find most appealing about you." His fingers run through my wet hair that has escaped its braid.

Shyly looking away from him, I unwrap my legs from his waist and he places me back down on the soft ground. The sky turns orange and red as the sun lowers.

"We do not have very long. Ajax will have my head if we are not back before dark," he warns, sending a blast of air magic over us, drying our clothes and hair instantly.

"Or mine." I roll my eyes, running my hands over the dry fabric of my clothes.

He raises an eyebrow. "What do you mean?"

I should not have said that. I should not bring any drama to a place I'm not truly a part of. Sure, I'll let whatever this thing with Silas is pan out, but only for as long as I stay here. I really need to learn to keep my mouth shut. "Nothing. I didn't mean anything by it. I just said it. Sometimes I just say things. I can't help it." I shrug.

He lowers his brows and his jaw slackens. "Daphne, you need to tell me what you meant."

I swallow uncomfortably and open my mouth to speak, but words don't come out. My fingers get caught in the tangles the blast of air caused as I run my fingers through my hair. What's a good way to tell him his second-in-command is a psychopath who threatened me on my first night here and very obviously hates me? Nope, there isn't a single good way to say that. Saying something isn't worth the drama that would ensue. Especially after what happened between us. *It's not my place*, I remind myself.

This is going to be a few nights of fun; that's all. Nothing worth causing internal issues within a magical kingdom's court. But I can't lie to him, either. He'll know if I am. "I don't think he likes me very much, is all." Not a lie, but not the full truth either.

He accepts this response. "Ah, well, Ajax does not really like anyone besides Finch. He has a very hard time trusting anyone. His past is complicated, to say the least. My parents assigned him to me as my personal guard when I was a teenager, and he eventually became my second-in-command when I took my place on the throne. He is loyal to me, so he will have to come around eventually. Or, rather, he would have to, if you were not leaving."

Knowing that as long as Silas wants me alive Ajax won't kill me in my sleep is a relief. "You say that as if you don't want me to."

"To what?"

"To leave," I whisper.

He remains silent, his blue-hazel eyes flickering with desire as they roam up and down my body. He takes my hands in his. "I think I have made it very clear. I absolutely do not want you to leave."

We arrive back at the camp, hand in hand, as the final bit of the sunlight disappears behind the horizon. I'm unable to mask my gleeful smile as we join the others gathered around the fire. Each of them gives us a quick, knowing glance before exchanging similar looks with each other. The only one who can't be bothered to look at us is Syrrus, who tends to the fish roasting above the flames.

My body hums with the pure bliss and excitement of this new romance. Hell, I feel downright giddy. I haven't felt this way since I first met Wyatt. God, I'm in trouble. The attraction I feel toward him is definitely more intense than that of a fling. I think we both know it. This is going to ruin me. If not now, then when I have to leave.

Silas sits down on a cushion and I go to take the one next to him when he grabs my hand and pulls me down, sitting me on his lap. A few hours ago I would have objected, but I let it happen. My choice has been made. I'm going to have fun with this while it lasts. He was right after all: why does it matter what anyone thinks? I've already spotted three of them sneaking away to share intimate moments with their lovers, and I'm certain they did much more than kiss each other. It's fair to assume that sexuality isn't nearly as taboo here as it is on Earth.

Stone coughs, breaking the silence. "This is unexpected."

"You owe me ten silver pieces." Knox chuckles, playfully punching Ajax on the arm. Ajax rolls his eyes, shelling coins out of a leather pouch strapped to his belt.

"You were taking bets? On what, exactly?" Silas groans.

"How long Daph would be able to resist your charm, sir." Knox winks and laughs. "Ajax thought it would never happen, Brynne gave her two days, and I gave her a week. Brynne, you too." He holds out his hand and waits for her to place the small silver coins in his palm. She instead throws them one by one, each pegging him before landing in front of him with small thuds. "Thank you!" he says as he picks them out of the dirt.

I turn my head back to Silas, unsure of what to make of this.

"Here I was thinking we were being discrete." His lips form a tight smile and his eyes narrow sharply at Knox. "You are awful. You know that?"

"Discrete my ass. And I may be awful, but I am now twenty silver pieces richer thanks to the two of you." Knox blows him a mocking kiss. "It was only a matter of time before the fair maiden here fell for our handsome king. Cannot blame me for capitalizing on it."

"I have not fallen for anyone!" I say defensively—admittedly perhaps a bit too defensively.

Knox rolls his eyes and purses his lips before giving me a wicked half grin. "You keep telling yourself that."

Brynne gets up to hand out plates of bread and vegetables. Syrrus takes the fish off the fire and walks the rod they're skewered on around to each of us. He serves Silas first, then places a whole fish on my plate. The blackened fish stares back at me. I've never eaten a whole fish like this before. It makes me squirm a little. How do I even go about eating something like this?

"Thank you," I tell him as he moves on to continue distributing everyone's dinner.

Everyone holds their fish with their bare hands, eating it like a piece of fried chicken. This is totally normal. People eat fish like this on Earth too. I've never been an adventurous eater; my diet consists mainly of coffee, chicken nuggets, and pizza. Fish is usually not my first choice at all, but I'm not going to risk offending Syrrus, who kindly spent his time making this meal for us. I force a smile and bite into the fish.

I'm pleasantly surprised by how good it tastes. The skin is crisp and the inside is unbelievably buttery. None of the fish I ate on Earth tasted quite this good. Threa's fish must taste so much better due to the lack of pollutants in the water. My forced smile turns into a real one as I continue to eat, leaving a clean plate.

Once we all finish our meals, Knox takes a flask out of his bag. "I brought us a little something." He shakes the flask in the air before removing the cap and taking a swig. "Might as well have a little fun while we are out here."

He hands the flask to Brynne, who follows suit. It's then passed to Syrrus, then Stone, who takes two long swings. Once Silas takes his turn, he hands it to me. I examine the silver flask, smelling the strong scent of alcohol before taking a mouthful of the liquid. It burns my mouth and down my throat as I swallow it. The taste reminds me of cheap vodka: pure alcohol, no flavor. My face scrunches up in disgust and I cough. "How did you all drink that?"

They all laugh.

"Centuries of practice," Brynne says.

I laugh and wipe the remaining alcohol off of my mouth and hand the flask to Ajax. His body tenses slightly as he makes eye contact with me. I offer him a smile of truce, reaching the flask out a bit farther toward him. He smiles back at me and takes the flask, finishing the contents, earning a round of applause from his friends. His body relaxes as he hands the empty flask back to Knox.

As the night goes on, Silas, Ajax, Stone, and Knox remember and exchange tales of their previous battles, conquests, and failures over the fire. Just old friends having a great time together, not a king and his most trusted companions. I lean my head back to rest it on Silas's broad shoulders. It feels so natural, me sitting here with them, listening quietly as they talk, enjoying their stories and learning more about them.

Ajax offers to take the first watch of the night. He gets up from his seat, grabbing a sword before he walks off into the woods around the camp. Knox is first to head to bed, saying he'll take the second watch. Brynne drunkenly leans on Syrrus, who helps her stumble back to their tent.

"That is real love right there," Stone remarks, his words slurred together.

"It really is." Silas's strong fingers trace lazy circles along my collarbone.

"How does that work between them?" I ask without thinking.

"What do you mean? They are mates," Stone answers, as if I have lived here my whole life and should know what all that entails.

"I know. But I've never heard Syrrus talk. Does he only talk to Brynne?" I link Silas's fingers between mine, pulling his hand against my chest, still feeling the buzzing euphoric effects of whatever was in that single shot of magical liquor.

Silas's hand tightens around mine gently. "Through their bond. You said when you were with Novalora in your mind you saw a mating tether, right? When the bond is complete, the pair can communicate through it."

"Oh, okay. Got it. That makes sense." I nod and my eyes flutter half closed. It must be well past midnight by now. Silas strokes my cheek sweetly, almost lulling me to sleep.

Stone stretches his hands behind his head and pushes himself off the ground. "Alright, Daphne, I will see you before the sun rises. We will train for a bit before we head out to Tesalte."

"I'll see you in the morning." I wave to him as he makes his way into his tent.

"I do not think you will be training in the morning," Silas whispers over my shoulder, causing the hair on the back of my neck to rise.

"Why's that?" I ask sleepily.

"You probably will not be able to walk by the time the night ends," he purrs into my ear.

I smack his chest lightly. "Silas!"

He grins and leaves a trail of kisses up my neck, erasing any trace of drowsiness from me. He stands abruptly, holding me in his arms.

Startled, I let out a small shriek. "What are you doing?" I laugh.

He extinguishes the fire with a small gust of wind. The only remaining light comes from the moons and stars high above us. He carries me into our tent. "Hopefully, you."

My pulse quickens watching as he pulls his shirt over his head and throws it to the floor. The dim light of the lantern casts shadows across his toned, tattooed chest. My lips pull at the corners as I watch him. He cups my face in his hands, bringing my mouth to his. His lips part slightly as he pulls away. The flame of the lantern flickers in his eyes as they meet mine. "Do you want this?"

My lashes flutter quickly and I swallow. Running my hand down the side of his face, I pause. Thinking. I didn't think it would be possible for me to desire someone this much. Maybe it's the liquor talking. Who am I kidding? This is something I think we've both wanted since the night of the ball.

He smiles, pushing the hair out of my face. "It is okay if you do not."

"No. I definitely do. It's just different. And it's been a while." I can't remember the last time Wyatt and I had sex. Probably a few months before the accident. How out of practice am I? How experienced is he? Does it matter?

"We will take it slow. You tell me if you want me to stop."

Bringing my hands to his chest, I look up at him. Words would do no justice in describing exactly how badly I want this, so instead, I kiss him in answer. He picks me back up and carries me onto the bedroll.

CHAPTER THIRTY

Day Six

A smile grows on my face as I open my eyes to the soft sounds of birds chirping. Our still naked bodies are twisted in a tangle of blankets, and Silas's bare, tattooed arm is wrapped snugly over my waist. I turn my body over to face him. When I inhale, I become suddenly aware of his scent. The smell of sage and lemongrass that surrounds me grows stronger as I breathe.

My sense of smell must be strengthening. Slightly overgrown facial hair prickles my fingertips as I run my hand delicately over his face. I press my mouth lightly to his, careful not to wake him, before getting off the bedroll. I tiptoe around the tent as quietly as I can, searching for my clothes in the darkness. I trip over Silas's boots and nearly fall right back into the bed, before I catch myself and stumble forward.

"Where are you going?" Silas asks groggily. He sits up with a lazy smile forming on his face. The blanket slips down to reveal his muscular body, inked with thick-lined tattoos I memorized last night as I fell asleep pressed against him. A moon on each of his shoulders, a dragon wrapped around his arm, and tribal designs across his chest. Maybe one day I'll ask him what they're for. "Slipping out in the cover of darkness? That bad?" He smirks, knowing that is not what is going through my mind.

I pick up the boot I tripped on and throw it at him. He easily dodges it and it lands on the floor beside the bed with a thud. "No, you idiot. Last night was whatever the opposite of bad is. I have to meet Stone for training before we fly to Tesalte, remember? Help me find my clothes."

The corners of his eyes crinkle as he grins. "*Idiot*. Don't think I've ever been called that one. I like it." His eyes drift from my face, making their way down my body. "I do not think I want to help you find those."

"Oh my god. Don't make me throw the other boot at you. This time I won't miss," I whisper angrily as I kick around the piles of fabrics on the floor, attempting to discern which are mine. "Never mind, I found them. No thanks to you." I pull on my riding pants and long-sleeved tunic.

Silas tosses my cloak at me. "You're going to want this." He lays back down, pulling the blanket over his head to go back to sleep.

Lucky him. The journey here and what we did in this tent last night left me exhausted. But, I'm an adult who has to live with her choice to stay up and not rest before training. I lace up my boots and tie the cloak around my neck. Iri wakes from her spot in the corner of the tent and pads over, following me. We step out of the tent, into the chill morning air. It's eerily quiet, the only sound coming from the waves hitting the cliff wall below.

Stone sits cross-legged near the edge of the cliff, overlooking the ocean. The wind grows stronger the closer I get to the water. I pull my cloak in around myself, tucking it tightly around me as I sit. Iri climbs under my cloak and onto my lap. The endless dark sea in front of us is unsettling. Stone has his eyes closed and takes long, slow breaths.

Does he even realize I'm here? He remains silent with his eyes closed for a few moments longer before he acknowledges me. "Good morning, Daphne. By the sounds heard coming from your tent last night, I trust you slept well?"

It's too early for this conversation. "I have no idea what you're talking about."

He half opens one eye. "Right. Anyway, today we will be working on training your mind."

"Like yoga?"

"What's yoga?" He casts a sidelong glare in my direction.

I'm barely awake. I don't have the energy for a lengthy description of an Earth exercise. "Never mind. So what are we going to be doing?"

"Calming your mind, focusing. It is essential to sense and be aware of every part of your mind and body in both physical and magical combat."

Great. Focusing has never really been my strong suit. My ADHD mind moves at a thousand miles per minute and there is always a minimum of ten things happening there simultaneously. Though it's been almost a week without my medication. And I haven't been anything like that. Sure, my personality is the same, but my mind has been calmer, I've been able to think things through, I don't feel restless... "Hey, Stone?"

"Daphne, this is supposed to be a quiet training." He exhales slowly.

I tap my hands nervously on my knees. "I know. I'm sorry. I have to ask you something."

He opens his eyes and turns his head to face me. "Can it not wait until later?"

My eyes meet his, pleading for him not to make me keep the thought inside. If I don't say it now, it will be gone forever. I shake my head no.

He sighs. "Alright. Go ahead."

"On Threa, does anyone have this... issue with their brain? Where they have a lot of energy, they can't focus, they think too fast, sometimes they're super fidgety and can't stop moving?"

He tilts his head curiously. "Can't say that I've heard of someone suffering from such an ailment. Why do you ask? Does it exist on Earth?"

I look out at the ocean and pause for a moment to gather my thoughts. "Yes. It's pretty common. I have it. Usually, I take medication to help me focus and go about my day like a normal person. Since I got here... I haven't needed to take anything. I feel fine. I feel more normal here than I do on Earth even with my medicine. It's strange. I don't understand it."

Stone focuses on me. "You said this ailment comes about when a person has little control of the energy in their body and how it affects them. And they usually have an excess amount compared to the other humans on Earth? Does it come from your parents?"

"My mom doesn't have it, but I don't know who my dad is. But usually, yes, it runs in families. My kids all have it. Sometimes I swear theirs is worse than mine." I shrug and let out a small laugh.

He rubs his jaw between his fingers and moves his mouth to the side. "Here is what I think. You, Daphne darling, have an exceptional amount of magic within you. You may not have accessed it or felt it yet, but as someone who has spent nearly five centuries training the children of the most powerful fae in Carimea, I can tell. I am pretty sure your magic has lived in you your whole life. In your world, it had nowhere to go, so it manifested as this ailment you speak of. But I do not think it is really an ailment after all."

My eyes widen and my mouth opens slightly. "You think that my ADHD is just... my magic? Like, it's been trapped inside of me and didn't have a way out?"

"That is precisely what I believe. But what do I know?" He rolls his neck, stretching side to side before straightening his back to return to his meditation pose.

I lean toward him, needing to know more. "What about everyone else on Earth with ADHD? Do you think they might also be fae? How are there so many of us on Earth?"

"Possibly. But there are so many different races of magical beings. There are the fae, the shifters, vampires, witches and warlocks, and many, many more. Magic presents differently for each race, and there are even variants of the magic within the races. Take your water magic and Knox's fire magic: complete opposites. Yet they both stem from the same type of magic. As far as how so many people would have magic on your Earth, I do not know.

"I have been thinking about the humans. They are the only non-magical beings that dwell on Threa. How did they get here? There is no record of when they first appeared, either. I am hoping that this quest leads us to answers not only for you, but to the missing bits of our history." Stone looks out over the water as the first rays of light emerge from behind us, changing the sky from deepest black to hazy lavenders and oranges.

He stands, reaching his hands above his head and stretching out his lean, athletic body. His amber eyes look down toward me. "That is it for today's training. We have to get ready to fly to Tesalte. King Quinn and Queen Rosa are expecting us shortly. If there is someone on this continent who hates tardiness more than I do, it's Quinn. He is the biggest royal pain in the ass." He laughs and heads back to his tent to pack his things, leaving me by myself on the cliff.

I stay seated by the water a bit longer, watching birds dive into the waves and the rest of the world wake up. Alone with my thoughts, I go over the theories Stone threw at me. What he said makes complete sense, but I really don't like how this epiphany is making me feel.

On one hand, I'm grateful to have been given this chance to learn about and explore magic and what it means to me. But on the other hand, I've struggled my whole life, thinking I have something wrong with me, only to fall into this magical world and find out it may have been magic trying to find its way out of my body.

If living with ADHD means I can wield magical water, it's worth it. Though it will be incredibly frustrating when I go back to Earth, for my mind and body to go right back where it was before. My heart aches at the idea of losing this newfound piece of me. Look at me: the sun is barely up and I'm having an existential crisis. My laugh echoes into the silence around me.

What if it's not only ADHD that's caused by trapped magical energy? What if other mental illnesses signify the different races of magic? Who knows what other things on Earth are affected by the lack of our world's magic? I shake my head, huffing a sigh of frustration. I may simply never know what the truth actually is. After all, these are just theories a six-foot-four fae combat trainer and I discussed before the sunrise. No one on Earth will ever know this conversation happened.

I briefly imagine myself telling other people on Earth there is nothing wrong with them and that all of their issues exist because they are magical beings trapped in the wrong world... Put that on a t-shirt: "It's not ADHD; it's my magic." How fast would that earn me a trip to a mental rehabilitation facility?

If this theory is correct, how do so many people on Earth have magic... and what does it mean? I close my eyes and focus on my breathing. Iri squirms and jumps out of my cloak, growling.

"Daphne, can you control your *pet*?" The hiss of a familiar airy whisper startles me. My eyes shoot open. Crouched in front of me is the translucent glowing female from days ago. I grab Iri and fall back on my hands. My mouth parts open to scream, but she covers my mouth, her transparent hand surprisingly weighted. "Shh. Do not be afraid. I am here to check in on you. I am going to remove my hand, but I need you to promise me that you will be quiet."

My eyes widen in terror. Who is this female who keeps showing up? *What* is she? How does a translucent hand muffle my voice? I nod, she moves her hand, and Iri attempts to snap a bite at her. "Who are you? Why do you keep showing up?"

She smiles. "I am a friend. We have not been able to find you for the past few days. We thought something horrible happened, but we sensed you last night and luckily tracked you down. Do not worry. We are coming to help."

"Can you stop being so vague? I do not need saving. I am perfectly fine, thank you."

Her smile turns to a frown and her eyes fill with pity as she rises from her crouch. "You will understand soon enough."

I straighten my back and muster as much of a threatening tone as I can. "I'm going to tell them about you."

Her brows furrow and her nostrils flare. She takes a deep breath, calming her expression to a tight smile. "That would be most unwise. Should you wish to live and see your family again, Princess, my visits remain between us." She turns her back to me and walks toward the cliff. Her form disappears into nothing but a faint glow over the water.

CHAPTER THIRTY-ONE

A million thoughts flood my mind. My breathing becomes labored and my heart races as a panic attack settles in. *Calm down. She's gone.* I take long breaths. In through my nose, out through my mouth. Whatever that thing is has to be lying. Silas is trustworthy. They're all trustworthy. I don't understand why she thinks I would trust her when she hasn't even told me her name.

What could she want from me? And how does she keep finding me? Why does she think I'd be in danger if I told my friends about her? How does she know I have a family? How can I keep this from Silas?

She knows *something*. She knows who I am. She knows I have a family. Maybe she's an oracle like Novalora... Did other oracles have visions of me arriving like Novalora did? My body shudders as a chill races up my spine. I pull my knees close to my chest and rock in place.

In through my nose, out through my mouth.

Repeat.

Repeat.

Repeat.

Exhale.

Breathe.

I look around. No one has left their tent yet. Suddenly aware of how alone I am, I get off the ground and head back to our tent.

Silas is lacing his boots when I walk through the door. "Are you alright? You look like you have seen a ghost."

I laugh and shake my head nervously. "I'm fine. Tired is all. It's far too early to be awake after the night we had."

His eyes narrow on me. He walks over and wraps his arms around me. He kisses the top of my forehead as he pulls my body into his. "If you say so."

I rest my head on his chest, inhaling his sage and lemongrass scent. Memorizing it. The smell comforts and calms me in a way I've never felt before. What else will I be able to smell now that my fae senses are growing stronger?

"Are you excited to see your brother?" I bury my face deeper into his chest.

He pulls away slightly so he can see my face. "Quinn? Yes." He pauses. "Well, sort of."

I tilt my head up to meet his gaze. "Do the two of you not get along or something?"

He lifts one arm behind his head and runs a hand through his hair. The tousling dishelves it. Somehow, he looks even sexier with his hair like that. He breathes a heavy sigh. "We do not not get along. With him and I... it's complicated. Quinn's my older brother. My overbearing older brother. He grew up thinking he was in charge of all of us since my parents were occupied with ruling the continent."

The simplicity of sibling conflicts in this magical world makes me release a small breath of a laugh. "Typical older sibling."

"Exactly. He was always harder on me than my siblings. Zefarina was the princess and River was sick until his magic came in, so Quinn protected him. I was the one who got all of his tough love. To this day, he treats me like the younger brother he has to keep out of trouble." He looks up, shaking his head.

The look on his face tells me there's more to his relationship with his brother. "Are you sure that's all?"

He looks back down at me and smiles solemnly. He tucks the loose hair behind my ear and caresses my face. "Quinn is next in line for my father's title. He is to be the next High King of Carimea. However, he and his mate, Rosa, have not been able to produce any living children in the century they have been married."

"That's terrible," I whisper. It must be awful trying to have a baby for a century. I had a hard time getting pregnant with the twins, but it only lasted a few years before we got pregnant with IVF. To go through such a difficult time for so long and with the added pressure of producing an heir for the kingdom... I can't imagine how hard it must be for Rosa.

"It truly is. The healers cannot figure out a reason for it, either. And Rosa would be a lovely mom, really. She is one of the most caring females I have ever had the fortune of knowing." He frowns. "My father is not very understanding of their situation. He is not exactly sensitive about the subject, either. He is a good man, but he wants to make sure our family's rule does not end so soon after it started. He told Quinn that if he does not produce an heir, by the time he steps down, the throne will go to me. It has put some strain between the two of us over the past few decades."

Talk about intense sibling rivalry. I offer him a sympathetic smile. "I'm not exactly close with my siblings. They're all much younger than I am and I never got to know them very well, but I can see why that would make things with your brother... complicated. Does Quinn hold it against you?"

He shakes his head. "Quinn doesn't blame me for our father's choices, but it certainly didn't help our relationship. I have more empathy for his mate, though. My father wasn't very kind to her at our last family gathering."

"Poor Rosa." I pause as a wave of sadness for a couple I've never met washes over me. "You don't have any children, though. Why does your father want you to take the crown? Do your other siblings not have any children either?"

A small, startled laugh escapes his mouth. "My father banks on me finding my mate faster than any of my siblings producing an acceptable heir. My sister's mate is another female, so they cannot have children. They are happier that way, though. They fill their time with their studies. Their kingdom, Stobon, is the most advanced of our kingdoms thanks to their work.

"My younger brother, River, has children. However, Estelle, his mate, is half shifter. During the revolution that brought my father to the throne, most of the shifters allied with King Ameldrick. A good portion of them still support him, due to their bonds. The group of shifters that attacked us in the valley are his supporters. Ever since my father became high king, there have been whispers of an uprising—to take the throne back from my family."

"Do you think that will happen?" What would that mean for Silas? For Sol Salnege?

"It seems like a waste of their energy. No one knows where he is. But, over the past five years, the whispers have grown, saying that two of his sons have come back and are ready to lead a rebellion."

"What would you do if they were to try? And why does your father take their actions out on Estelle?"

"Our armies are prepared and the majority of Carimea's people do support us... My father has always been wary of Estelle. I do not think his concerns are warranted. Not every shifter in the continent supports King Ameldrick. Plenty of shifters are bonded to those in our own armies, or civilians. Regardless, Estelle adores my brother and she is his mate. She literally could not betray him. Their bond would not allow it.

"That should be enough for my father to accept my nieces and nephews as true heirs to the throne. But he is a stubborn old man. He will not let River take the throne. If you ask me, out of the four of us, he is the one who should be on that thing. He is the best of us. And I sure as hell don't want it."

My face scrunches in confusion. "You don't? Why not? Isn't that what anyone here would want? To be the high king of the entire continent sounds like an honor."

He throws his head back and laughs. "Oh gods, no. I mean yes, it is an honor, but I did not even want to be King of Fracilonia. I would much rather not have the responsibility. Do not get me wrong, I love my kingdom, but sometimes I long for a simpler life. I was not born into royalty. I had eight years before my father became king. Before that, he was King Ameldrick's second-in-command..."

Well, that's unexpected. Perhaps I should have squeezed in some reading about the history of Carimea while I had access to the palace library in Sol Salnege. I try to hide my shock. "Your father was second-in-command to the last king? And he didn't understand what your father was going through with your mother's illness when he used the power from the dragon eggs?"

"My father did try to reason with him, get him to understand why it would be beneficial to everyone. But King Ameldrick was a strict ruler who believed it was best to stick to the way things were always done. But most of our people were ready for change and wanted to heal their sick friends and family. Especially when they heard about the miracles the dragon eggs could grant. That is why so many supported my father in becoming king.

"I am sure if King Ameldrick's mate or children were as sick as my mother was, he would have done the same thing."

"What happened to them? Did your father..." I pause. This is a magical world with swords, dragons, and royalty. The past few days, I've been training with weapons so I can defend myself. "Did he kill them?"

He cocks his head, carefully considering his response. "My father has killed before. We all have, in battle and defense, but never without just cause. While King Ameldrick's death would have been warranted for the amount of people he killed during the revolution, he was not killed. At least not to our knowledge. Right before Ameldrick's forces burned their own capital city to keep my father from claiming it, he and his family escaped off the continent and overseas."

"And he what? Lives there happily with his family after being dethroned and causing a war over such a trivial matter?"

"No one knows for sure. I wouldn't put it past some of my father's more aggressive supporters to have killed them at some point, though. The things King Ameldrick did in an attempt to keep his rule over the continent were truly horrendous." His face drains of color, and a distant look glazes over his eyes, like he's remembering the things he witnessed as a child. "Many people would love revenge."

I take his face in my hands and tilt it toward mine. Pain swims in his beautiful eyes. "I'm sorry that you had to live through that."

"It is okay. It was a long time ago. My father has created happy kingdoms and a peaceful continent. But it was not easy. I do not know if I would be able to do what my father has had to do to keep our continent safe. I do not think I am fit to rule an entire continent."

I want to comfort him more, but I'm not sure how. My childhood trauma is nothing compared to growing up in the heart of a revolution. The most I've ever had to worry about is if I'm doing a good job raising my children and keeping them alive, which I now feel is a drop in a bucket of water in comparison. I can't imagine having to bear the weight of an entire continent of magical beings. I squeeze him a little tighter. "I think you'd make an excellent high king."

He squeezes me back and lifts a hand to cradle my head, pressing it firmly to his chest. He runs his fingers through my hair. "It is time to go now." He kisses the side of my head. I nod in understanding, even though I don't want to leave yet. I've never seen such honesty and vulnerability in a man. It makes me want to wrap our bodies back in the sheets.

We gather our satchels and Syrrus comes to fold our tent, placing it neatly in his bag. He hands us each a blueberry muffin and stalks off to meet the others. Silas kisses me one more time, then takes my hand in his and we walk to where the others are gathered, ready to begin the flight to Tesalte.

CHAPTER THIRTY-TWO

The shadow of a city forms in the distance between the mountains. "Welcome to Tesalte." Silas's lips brush against my ear. The flight was short. It took just over an hour from where we camped last night.

Strong gusts of wind push against the air shield. Above us, four enormous dragons glide in the air. Silas has panic in his eyes when I turn my head over my shoulder to look at him. His hand moves from the reins to grasp the hilt of the sword strapped to his side. His eyes move to Ajax, who nods his head. I assume that's confirmation that he has light shields in place camouflaging us. And then to Syrrus, another nod. He must have an enchantment in place, too.

I hold my breath as the four dragons lower in the sky, almost at eye level with us. Each of the dragons has a rider dressed in all-black leather armor saddled to its back. I can only make out vague details. On a red dragon sits a female with long black hair. A male with short dark hair sits on a smaller blue dragon. A large framed dark blonde male rides a green dragon. At the front of the pack is a silver-scaled dragon, which is easily twice the size of the others. A strong-looking male with shoulder-length blonde hair sits on its back. The dragons tilt their bodies in unison and shift left, out over the ocean.

Once they're out of sight, I release my breath.

"Was that?" Knox calls from his pegasus.

"Yeah, I think so," is all Silas replies.

Moving into a tighter formation, the pegasuses head inland. The four massive dragons become nothing but specks on the horizon. "Silas, why are all dragon riders Reclaimers?"

"What? Who told you that? They most certainly are not."

"Then why do you all ride pegasuses? Those were the first full-sized dragons I've seen besides the one that tried to eat me."

"During the war, the dragons took sides as well. It was bloody and brutal. The dragons who sided with us lost a lot of lives in the battle. After the war, most of them went into hiding to protect and regrow their numbers. Some do still live with their riders, but most of them reside in remote areas far from the kingdoms. My sister, Zefarina, is bonded with a full-sized dragon named Nyssa. That is how we find most of the eggs we siphon."

"What do you mean?"

"All dragons within the larger den are connected. They communicate over vast distances. When an egg within the den is too powerful, they let Nyssa know, who in turn tells my sister."

"Oh." That's right—he mentioned full-sized dragons could speak mind-to-mind with their riders. I look down at Iri, nuzzled in my cloak, and the dragon tattoo on my left arm. *I wish I could know what you're thinking, Iri. Talk to you. Apologize for having to leave you so soon.* I scratch her head and she purrs. "So why pegasuses?"

"They can fly and are powerful and easy to train. Even if some of them have a bit of an attitude."

Lucy huffs a neigh and shakes her head.

Soon, Tesalte comes into clear view, settled in a valley between snow-capped mountains. In the center of the city is a striking cylindrical palace. The tall, impressive structure is made entirely out of curved panels of opalized wood, set so seamlessly the palace looks like it was carved out of a single massive tree trunk.

As we fly closer, the vibrant city buzzes to life. Magical beings move quickly through the streets, popping in and out of the intricate buildings below. Every shop and home looks a little different, as if they were each custom made. Most of them have stained glass windows that reflect rainbows down on the polished black stone street. It reminds me of a busy city on Earth.

We approach the palace gates and Silas's grasp on me tightens, bracing for landing. Six sets of hooves hit the stone heavily. I nearly slip from the saddle at the impact.

Iri jumps to the ground from her spot on my lap to stretch out her legs once the pegasuses have come to a complete stop. She flexes her long body like a cat, iridescent scales shimmering in the morning light, and yawns. A dozen or so palace workers greet us immediately. The pegasuses are taken through the gates to the stables as soon as we dismount. One of the workers offers a tray of fruit, which I politely decline; I'm far too nervous to eat. Knox and Ajax take a few pieces each. A muscular female with a blonde pixie cut begins collecting our belongings.

She approaches me to collect my bag. I hesitate; my phone is in there. If they went through my bag's contents, what would they make of it? She holds out her hand in a silent nudge to comply and I begrudgingly give it to her. A female with light brown skin and a pretty, angular face makes her way to us from the palace. She has a dark chin-length bob with bangs across her forehead. Her long, shimmering, topaz-blue dress compliments the inlay details of the palace walls behind her.

As she gets closer, I notice the silver crown with opal stones on the top of her head. A grin widens on Silas's face as he embraces the female. "Rosa! It has been too long." He kisses both of her cheeks before he turns to me, one arm still wrapped around his sister-in-law's shoulders. "This is Daphne."

I quickly attempt a curtsy. "Queen Rosa. The pleasure is mine." I have no idea if these are the correct formalities. It's not like they teach royal social etiquette in American public schools.

She smiles softly, taking my hands to raise me from my bowed position. "Rosa is perfectly fine. Anyone that Silas claims is considered family here."

I'm not exactly sure what to make of that, so I politely smile back.

"Come, everyone. Quinn and Stellamaris have been in the kitchen bickering over where to find this Ailse female since the sun came up. And honestly, I would like to go back to bed to recover the hours of sleep I have lost." She turns and walks back toward the palace.

Several armed guards flank our group, dressed from head to toe in uniforms of the deepest navy, which could easily be mistaken for black when not in the sun. A thin fabric is pulled over their faces like a mask, making them indistinguishable from one another. Iri pushes her body against my leg for me to pick her up. She climbs from my hands to up around my neck. The guards walk us past the palace gates and two others close it behind us with a heavy thud. I hear a lock click into place.

The security measures in place here are much heavier than those in Sol Salnege. I whisper as quietly as I can to Silas, "Why are there so many guards? Is everything okay?"

Apparently, I didn't whisper quietly enough. Rosa turns her head over her shoulder without stopping walking. "Reclaimer activity around our capital has been at a high as of late. Just a few pub fights here and there, but due to certain circumstances, we are handling the situation with the highest level of caution." She casually pushes the fabric of her dress to her belly, cradling the bottom of a small bump.

"Rosa! Are you..." Shock turns to beaming happiness in Silas's eyes and he grins widely.

Rosa's eyes brighten. "Yes. We are not very far, but so far this babe has survived longer in my womb than any of the previous."

Silas hugs her warmly. "Congratulations."

"Not yet. It is too soon for that. You can congratulate us when the babe makes it Threaside." She quickly blinks away the trace of silver lining from her eyes.

"Of course. How is Quinn doing with the news?"

"He is nervous as he always is. But Katya foresees a successful pregnancy in our future. I am hoping this is the one." She smiles as she rubs her rounded belly. "We were planning on telling everyone when we gather for the Solstice in a few months. We were not expecting to see you beforehand."

"Do not worry. Your secret is safe with me." Silas hugs her again.

The guards usher us into the palace and lock the door once we're inside. Blue and purple lights flow into the castle through the opal in the petrified wood walls, splaying onto the dark-grained floorboards. The guards dissipate, taking positions around the main level of the palace. Rosa leads us through the eerily quiet palace to the dining hall. A male and female hover over a paper map at the end of a long black table, their brows furrowed with scrutiny as they speak to each other in hushed tones. The table is decorated with fine plates and decorative vases filled with blue and purple flowers.

I can tell the male seated at the head of the table is Quinn from his striking resemblance to Silas alone. The only noticeable differences are his hair, which is a shade lighter, and his build, which is a bit rounder than Silas's. Otherwise, I could have easily mistaken them for twins. I guess the fair-skinned, petite female next to him is Stellamaris, the high priestess. She wears her lavender hair braided in a crown around her head. When she looks up at us, her long face is riddled with wary exhaustion. Her eyes, the same shade of purple as her hair, soften as she smiles at me. Quinn doesn't look up from the map as we walk over.

Silas claps his arm over his brother's shoulder, startling him. "Hello, Quinn. This is Daphne." He gestures to me, standing behind them. I wave. Quinn does not acknowledge any of us. It seems like Quinn and Rosa are on opposite sides of the spectrum of personality. "What have you found, brother?" Silas asks.

Quinn finally looks up from the map, glancing over me before replying, "We have reason to believe that Ailse has taken up residency here." His commanding tone is edged with irritation. He lands a finger on the map. "Near the summit of Mount Pylosum. No one has heard of her, and we believe if she is hiding in this mountain range, the only place she could remain unseen for so long is on the highest peak. There is no village there, as it snows nearly year-round and is home to creatures of nightmares. But if you are hiding from the world and are an incredibly powerful traveler who can escape danger at a moment's notice, it is the perfect spot."

Silas leans over the table to see where Quinn is indicating. "Are you certain?"

"It is our best guess based on the information we have gathered, or rather not been able to gather," Stellamaris answers, her voice soft but confident, wise but youthful.

Silas nods and turns to face us. "Are you all ready for this?"

All five of his companions nod without hesitating, ready to follow their king. I pause for a moment. If this place is so treacherous, is it really a good idea for us to go there in search of Ailse?

It's too late to change my mind now. We've already come all this way, and this is the only way to find the answers I need to get home. To get to my children. I nod. "Yes."

Silas straightens and smoothes out the leather of his riding jacket. "Alright, we will go now then. Thank—"

"You cannot go now. It is not safe. There have been reports of heavy snowfall and strong winds in the area," Quinn cuts him off. "I am not letting my little brother travel into certain death over a hunch."

"Really? Is the weather that bad this time of year? It is still fall. Is that normal?" Silas asks.

"No, not really. But the weather on Mount Pylosum has always been unpredictable. I suggest waiting until tomorrow. Katya predicts clear skies in the region," Stellamaris answers.

"Who is Katya?" I whisper to Brynne, who's standing beside me.

"She's the Oracle of Tswangohin," she says quickly and quietly beneath a breath. I can't help but notice that not one member of the Azurite Force has spoken a word since entering this room. All four of them, plus Stone, stand with straight bodies, hands behind their backs at attention. Something about being in Quinn's presence has them all on edge. This isn't the group of friends I've come to know. This is a king's guard. A king's inner circle. The elite Azurite Force.

It keeps slipping my mind that the charming male who swept me off of my feet is also the ruler of a kingdom. Then, I recall what Silas told me earlier: he's second in line to rule the entire continent after King Quinn. And now, his queen is pregnant. The tension makes total sense. But Silas seems so happy, so pleased for Rosa. Does Quinn not believe that Silas doesn't want the throne? If he thinks that Silas wants the throne... God, this sibling relationship is complicated. Does Quinn want to get rid of his competition? Of course not. Silas is still his brother. Not that I hadn't heard of such things happening...

I shake my head to clear the thoughts from my mind and refocus. I catch the end of the conversation Silas and Quinn are having on strategies for locating Ailse. Silas clears his throat. "We will leave first thing tomorrow to search for her there. Would you be kind enough to host us for the night?"

Quinn rolls the map up tightly, tying it with a gold woven string. "Of course. You are always guests of the kingdom. I will have your rooms prepared. Six, yes?"

"Five will do," Silas replies.

Quinn glances over at me, then gives Silas a disapproving look before handing him the map. "Okay, five. Rosa will have the cooks prepare a feast for us to enjoy this evening. I have many matters to attend to this morning, but feel free to enjoy the city."

Silas takes the map and hands it to Ajax, the only one of us who managed to keep his satchel. "Thank you, Quinn."

Quinn walks from his place at the head of the table to exit the dining hall, followed by the two guards who were stationed by the doorway. Stellamaris gathers the books stacked on the table. "It was good to see you, Silas."

"You as well, Stellamaris." He nods to her as she leaves the room.

"I wish the two of you the most luck in finding the things you seek." She smiles over her shoulder before following Quinn.

Silas makes his way back to me. "Well, Daph, it looks like we have some time on our hands. Would you like to see Tesalte?"

A wide smile spreads across my face. "I'd love to." I didn't get to see much of Sol Salnege, and I regretted it as I watched it disappear from view as we flew away from the city.

"Great. You lot can take the afternoon off. We will be around for dinner."

"You are so gracious," Brynne says sarcastically, arm already linked with Syrrus's, pulling him toward the exit. "We will be at the nearest pub if you need us."

"Same here." Knox grins and gestures to himself and Stone as they rush to tag along behind Brynne and Syrrus, as happy and carefree as teenagers.

Ajax stares disapprovingly at Silas. "You cannot actually be planning on going out into the city. Did you not hear what Rosa just said? There have been increased reports of Reclaimers in the city. It is not safe for one of the kings of the five kingdoms to be out wandering unguarded."

Silas sighs in annoyance. "Fine, you can come if you must, but I am not responsible for what you may see." He pulls my body to his. A mischievous flicker sparks in his eyes as he brings his face close to mine, saying, *Play along.* I smile back coyly and he places his lips on mine. Normally public displays of affection are not my thing, but for some reason with Silas, in this world, it doesn't make me nearly as uncomfortable. So I kiss him back.

A roaming hand makes its way up my thigh and squeezes my ass. I should tell him to stop. This is too much. But if this will make Ajax less inclined to tag along, so be it.

Ajax clears his throat, saving me the trouble of stopping Silas. "You have made your point."

A wicked grin crosses Silas's face. "Are you sure? I can continue my demonstration."

He turns to leave. "That is alright, Sir. I will see you at dinner."

"Wait. You are on dragon duty, my friend." Silas picks up Iri and hands her over to Ajax. Iri bares her teeth at him.

Ajax holds Iri under her front legs at a distance from himself. "Yes, sir." He sighs as he exits. I can't believe Silas put his second-in-command on babysitting duty. Though, if his dragon is back at the palace in Sol Salnege, I don't know why Iri makes him so nervous. Can she really be as vicious as Brynne described her? A moment later I hear Iri growl at him from down the hall and a small shriek that I can only presume is Ajax.

I giggle, picturing what's going on out there. "Well, that was—"

"Amazing?" His grin grows.

I roll my eyes. "I was going to say a little ridiculous."

"Oh? You do not like when I kiss you?" He laughs. I'm sure his fae senses tell him that isn't the case.

"I didn't say that! I've never been nearly as open with such things back on Earth." I take a step toward the door. "Anyway, I think you were about to show me the city."

"The city will still be there when I am done showing you around the palace of Tesalte." He makes a wide gesture around the room. "This is the grand dining hall." He pulls the chair from the head of the table and shoves it across the room. "This is Tesalte's grand dining chair." With a burst of air magic, he clears the long, black wooden table of the dining ware and floral arrangements. A satisfied petty smile grows on his face as plates and vases shatter loudly on the floor.

My eyes widen and my mouth drops in disbelief. "Your brother is going to kill you."

Ignoring my comment, he kisses me as he lifts me and sets me on top of the table. I kiss him back.

CHAPTER THIRTY-THREE

Piles of broken glass and flowers are strewn across the dining room floor. "How are we going to clean up this mess?" I ask as I lie breathless on the edge of the wooden table.

Silas grins as he tucks his shirt back into his pants. "Magic, obviously." He helps me to the ground. With a swish of his wrist, all of the items move back to the table, undamaged as if they hadn't been in pieces mere seconds ago.

I watch in astonishment as I shimmy my pants back on. "That will never get old."

A teasing grin flashes across his face. "The magic, or…"

I roll my eyes. "Both. But the number of times I could have used magic like that to unbreak the thousands of things my kids have destroyed over the years… I wish I could just take you home with me." The words slip from my mouth quickly, before I think to stop myself.

Silas's smile vanishes and his eyes flicker with a hint of sadness. "Me too." His lip quirks back up in a forced, one-sided smile. "Let us go get changed into some proper clothes so I can take you out into the city. There are loads of shops and bakeries within walking distance of the palace."

My stomach rumbles at the mention of food. "A bakery sounds like a lovely place to start."

We exit the dining hall and find two guards waiting for us. No words are exchanged as they follow behind us as we walk through the palace. What did they hear from behind the doors? A blush crosses my cheeks. "Do they not speak?" I whisper.

"No, they do not. The Tswangohin guard is an elite force who swear a vow of silence upon entering into service. They can only speak to each other and their king. They are my brother's prized possession," he replies snarkily. I get the clear impression he does not agree with this concept. He and Quinn seem to have very different approaches to ruling.

The two guards are a lingering, silent presence behind us, like shadows, as we make our way to the room I assume is ours. They take up position on either side of the ornate copper door as we enter. The room is smaller than my room in Sol Salnege, but it's still larger than any bedroom I've been in on Earth.

A bouquet of lilies is arranged in a purple crystal vase on the table in the middle of the room. I can't tell if it's my new fae sense of smell or if the flowers are overly potent, but their fragrance fills the entire space. Behind the table is a large bed fitted with a violet silk comforter with eggplant paisley stitching. Two fluffy pale-blue accent chairs sit between the bed and the table. On the far end of the room, a stunning swirl of blue opal decorates the petrified wood wall.

Silas heads into the bathroom and I take a seat on one of the chairs. The cushion is hard under me despite its plush appearance, like no one's sat in it before. On the table near the vase of lilies sit a few books on the plants and sights of Tesalte. I giggle at the mundaneness of coffee table books existing in this world, especially since they don't have coffee.

I pick up one of the paper-bound books. Its lightness is

surprising as I turn it over in my hands to inspect all of its sides. The more I hold it, the more it reminds me of a fancy magazine. *Tastes of Tesalte* is printed on the cover. I rifle through the pages, flipping through some drawn images of pastries and seafood and some harsh reviews of local restaurants. As I turn page after page, I come across a page with a drawing of a steaming cup of—

I pick up the book and run into the bathroom. "Silas! Look!" I point at the image on the page.

He looks up at me in shock from his seat on the toilet, grabbing a nearby towel to cover himself. "A little privacy?"

I roll my eyes, ignoring him. "Look!!!" I urge him again, pushing the book into his face.

His eyebrows furrow in confusion. "It is a cup of tea?" Silas lowers the book with a single finger. He raises a concerned eyebrow at me, as if I lost my mind when I barged in here.

I let out an exaggerated sigh of frustration and turn the book back around to myself and read the page aloud: "Aurora Bakery in Tesalte is the first of its kind, debuting a one-of-a-kind beverage. This delicious concoction is an energy-containing drink made with roasted beans found south of the Carimean border. You can enjoy this tasty treat hot or iced. Its naturally bitter flavor can be made more pleasant by adding flavors, milk, or creams. It is the perfect morning pick me up."

Silas narrows his brows again. How is he still not understanding? "Whatever this is, could it not wait until I finished using the bathroom?"

Excited energy hums through me. I nearly jump up and down as I show him the pages again, pointing repeatedly at the image on the page. "It's coffee!"

He takes a moment to remember what coffee is. "Your drug from Earth?" A single breath of a laugh escapes him and he purses his lips together in a tight smile.

"You are such an asshole. Yes. The drug from Earth. We have to go! Please tell me you'll take me," I beg.

He smiles at my excitement. "I guess we can. Let me just—"

Unable to help myself, I bend over and throw my arms around his neck squealing, "Thank you! Thank you! Thank you!"

He nods and clears his throat. "Of course. Anything for you. Now can you please give me a few moments?"

For the first time, I realize how uncomfortable he looks. My eyes dart around the room and my cheeks heat with embarrassment. I cover my eyes with my free hand. "Oh my god, yes. Yes." I feel behind me for the door handle. Once my hand finds the cool metal knob I turn it until I feel it click and make a quick exit.

I get back to the seating area and throw myself on the hard chair, mortified. All I can do is laugh at myself. I must look incredibly insane right now. Silas isn't the man I was with for seventeen years; he's not Wyatt. I can't just charge into the bathroom like I own the place while he's using it. God, what is wrong with me? Clearly, my sense of boundaries is nonexistent. Having three kids will do that to you, I suppose.

I quickly forget my embarrassment when I remember how excited I am for my first cup of coffee in a week.

Silas emerges from the bathroom what feels like an eternity later. I guess being fae doesn't change the male habit of spending much longer than is possibly necessary in the bathroom. He wears navy pants and a pale-blue long-sleeve tunic.

"We will blend in better in these." He hands me a long navy-blue skirt with silver stars along the bottom, a long-sleeve top the same shade of pale blue as his, and a corset made of shimmering fabric. The colors of the corset shift between blue and green in the light, reminding me of an aurora.

My hand grazes over the heavy fabric of the skirt. This outfit definitely fits in better with what I've seen so far in Tesalte than the clothes I'm currently wearing. The fashion here starkly contrasts the light, airy outfits the females wear in Sol Salnege.

Silas takes the chair next to me. He leans his head back and reaches both hands over the armrests. As he gets comfortable, his muscular legs open, *manspreading,* to take up the whole chair. I get up to walk back to the bathroom to change. "What, do you need a little privacy?" Silas teases.

I pivot to face him. A spark of challenge lights in his eyes. My lips curl into a tight smile. "No." I pause. My heart flutters. Am I actually about to do this? There's a first time for everything, right? "Nothing you haven't seen before."

Slowly, I begin taking off my clothes. I prop my foot up on the table, unlacing my boot. I throw it to the corner of the room. It lands with a clunky thud that makes me wince. The corner of Silas's lip quirks in a half grin.

Nice. Real smooth.

What am I doing? I'm not sexy. I should stop. I need to stop. But it's too late; I can't back down. I have to commit to this. Breathe. It's fine. Everything is fine. I wiggle out of the tight leather riding pants and slide them across the floor toward the boots. How in the world are you supposed to be sexy while taking off pants? Strippers do not get enough credit. The sweaty, long-sleeved knit top gets stuck halfway up over my head. I finally wrestle it off and look up through the disheveled pieces of hair that have fallen in front of my face. Silas stares at me, amusement dancing across his face, in his smile and eyes.

I freeze. Then I hurriedly move my hands to cover my nearly naked body. My chest tightens and my pulse races. My eyes dart around the room, searching for anything to look at except Silas, but end up landing exactly where I don't want them to. Our eyes lock for a moment.

His eyes move up and down my body, taking in each and every inch of my bare skin. "Do not stop now."

Panic races through me. I grab the clothes off the chair and run into the bathroom, closing the door behind me. Attempting to breathe slowly to calm myself, I lean against the cool metal door, making sure Silas can't follow me. I slump to the floor in defeat. What on Earth, what on Threa, what in the worlds am I doing right now? I'm a thirty-six-year-old widowed mom of three. I'm not this person. I'm way out of my league here. For god, gods, whatever sake, he is a king. He is surely used to far more beautiful and more experienced partners. Why am I trying so hard to be someone I'm not in a world I don't belong in?

"Daphne?" Silas calls from the other side of the door. "Daphne. I'm confused... What happened? I thought we were having fun. Is everything okay? Are you okay?"

I don't answer. I hope he goes away and leaves me alone.

The door I'm leaning on moves from behind me. Silas looks down at me on the floor. "Daphne, you know this door opens outward, right?" He crouches down next to me and tries to look me in the eyes, but I turn my head. He gently takes my face in his hand and turns it back toward him. His blue-hazel eyes are full of concern. "Are you okay?"

I force a smile as a single tear slides down my cheek. "I'm fine. Why does it matter to you anyway? You're a fae king and I'm just... I'm just me. I'm not meant for this." I gesture behind me.

"You are not meant for the bathroom?" His brows knit together in mock confusion.

I take a heavy breath, ignoring his attempt at a joke. "I'm not meant to be around royalty or any of this world. I'm supposed to be getting back to my kids, not doing..." I sigh and push the fallen hair out of my face. "Whatever this is. I don't understand why you're interested in me. If you're interested in me. I don't know. I just don't get it. I'm not graceful, or beautiful, or sexy. And I know this was always meant to be just fun. Temporary."

I sniffle. "I've never done anything like this before. I don't know how this is supposed to work. I know it shouldn't, but it hurts knowing that at the end of this thing, you get to go on, live forever, find your mate or whatever you call it, and forget about me. I get to go home and live another fifty years, if I'm lucky, but how am I supposed to move on from this world? Move on from you?"

Silas takes a handkerchief from his pocket. Of course, he has a handkerchief; he's perfect. He runs it over my cheek and wipes the tears streaming down my face. "Daphne, I am not sure what is going on or how you got that impression. Of course, I am interested, whether it be for the time you are in this world or the rest of our lives. I never had any intention of this to be *just* fun. I promise as long as I live I will never be able to forget you."

Stupid perfect response. I exhale sharply through my nose. "How can you say that? You barely know me."

He folds up the handkerchief and places it in my hand. "I know plenty. I know you are stubborn, a tad awkward, and unique. And I told you as soon as I met you that I think you are beautiful."

My face scrunches. "Is that supposed to make me feel better?"

He chuckles softly and smiles. "I know we do not know each other very well. But I want to get to know you. All of you. In the week I have known you, I have learned you are by far the most interesting person I have ever met. You are smart, and you take care of the ones you love fiercely." He pauses, as if searching through his recent memory. "You own an antique shop, you have three children, and you can shoot an arrow frighteningly well. You love a drink called coffee. You have water magic powered from your heart and you are at least part fae, so I know you do in fact belong here, despite how desperately you want to leave."

I wipe the remaining tears from my face, finally meeting his gaze, "It's not that I *want* to leave. I *have* to. I can't stay here living in a fantasy world and leave my children on Earth."

"Why do you not... bring them here?"

"But how?"

"I assume once we find out how to get you back to Earth, you can return with your children the same way you came." He shrugs. "Seems simple enough."

"You would let my children stay with me at the palace? You actually meant that when you said it?"

"Of course. They are a part of you. And kids love me." His soft smile is so genuine I know he's telling the truth.

The idea is incredibly tempting. The kids would love it here. And if they're fae too... We'd all live much longer here. I picture the three of them discovering they had magic, meeting Iri, seeing the pegasuses fly, and the delight they'd have.

But I'm a planner. I can't spontaneously pick up my kids and move to another world. More logical thoughts roll in, ruining the perfect world I was building in my head. "You have no idea how long that might take. What if it takes me too long to get back, and you've met someone else? What if time doesn't work the same? What would I do then? Me and my children would we be stuck on the streets of Sol Salnege?"

He closes his eyes, rubs his temples, and takes a deep breath. "You are rather dramatic." He reopens his eyes and stares into mine. His expression grows serious. "I would wait an entire life time for you."

"And I'm the dramatic one?" I smile as I look up at him, blinking through wet eyelashes. "I'll think about it."

He rolls his eyes and kisses me on the forehead. "Alright then. What do you know about me?"

My eyes widen. I don't like being put on the spot. I spurt out facts: "You're the King of Fracilonia, you have two brothers and a sister, you have air magic that comes from your head, you have a small pack of adorable puppy dragons, you like helping people, saving damsels, all the good stuff a king should do."

He laughs. "Is that it?"

I smile, biting my lip. I have never been good at compliments, at flirting, any of it. "You are kind, smart, and brave. You would do anything for your people. Your friends adore and respect you, and would—and probably have—killed for you. You're the most attractive male I've ever seen." I regret my words when I remember Wyatt and look away.

An uneasy half smile appears on Silas's face. "It is okay—to move on. I am certain he would want you to be happy."

I shrug. "I know. It's just hard. Moving on, letting myself move on."

"If you want to talk about him, you can."

"He was my first love, my first, well, everything. When we met, I was only eighteen. He showed me the world; he taught me how to be. He really was an incredible husband and father..." I swallow. "Now he's gone. I haven't figured out how to fully accept that he won't walk through the door to our house one day." I look down. Silas holds my hands in his.

He pulls me into his chest. "Take it one day at a time. How about we get you dressed and go for that cup of drugs you were so excited about?"

I laugh and nod into his chest. He helps me to my feet and I put on the outfit he handed me earlier. Amaleana isn't here to help me. I frown at the memory of the friend I probably won't see again. Luckily, the corset is laced in the front and I can get it on by myself. Silas probably doesn't have much experience in lacing up corsets. Undoing them, sure.

"You look beautiful."

I twirl and watch the stars on the skirt move around my ankles. "Thank you."

He takes my hand and leads me out the door.

CHAPTER THIRTY-FOUR

We pass through the copper door of our room and the two guards trail us again. Silas and I enter the bustling city streets right outside the palace gates. The cold air smells of the pine trees that surround the city. While the fae and other magical beings in Sol Salnege recognized Silas and were excited to see him, the people in Tesalte are far too engrossed in their own lives to notice the others around them. As the street grows more crowded, Silas grabs me by my waist, tugging me close to him as we walk.

Dozens of vendors are set up along the streets selling different wares. Some have crystals and herbs, some have baked goods and loaves of bread, and others have jewelry. It almost reminds me of Camden Market, with the colorful tents, brick storefronts, and huge crowds of people.

One of the very first trips I took with Wyatt abroad was to London. We strolled under an umbrella and shared a pretzel around the market one rainy afternoon. He told me on that trip he knew he was going to marry me, even though we'd only been dating for a few months. At the time, I thought it was crazy. We were so young. But he was right. Wyatt was always right.

We find the brick facade of the Aurora Bakery. The air inside is warm and cozy and the smell of fresh coffee fills the room as we walk through the doors. I inhale deeply; the familiar scent brings a wide smile to my face. We add ourselves to the long line in front of a display case of bread and delicate pastries.

It's a pleasant surprise that Silas gets in line. He doesn't just walk up to the counter like I'd expect a king to do. It's both impressive and refreshing to see how much of a down to Earth—down to Threa? Whatever—ruler he is, especially now that I've met his brother. And have seen how he's... well, not.

It takes no time to glance over the menu written in chalk above the display case and decide on my order. They only have two options: hot bean juice or iced bean juice. Underneath there's a list of additions: cream, sugar, vanilla, caramel, and cinnamon. It would be such an interesting experience to come back to this shop and teach them all I learned about coffee from my years working at The Coffee Bean. I'm unreasonably giddy to get my hands on a cup of the nectar I thought didn't exist in this world.

It's finally our turn to order. The female at the counter is tall and slim. Her blue-black hair is shaved on one side and the rest falls at a sharp angle down her face. Her arms are covered in black swirls of ink and her pointed ears have an uncountable amount of piercings. Her hauntingly beautiful gray eyes look Silas up and down like he's a piece of candy. "What can I get you?" She asks him sweetly, fluttering her thick, coal-lined lashes at him.

Silas looks at me. "Whatever she is having, I suppose."

When she realizes I am also standing in front of her, she rolls her eyes, glares at me, and purses her lips. "Name?" she asks sharply. Her change in tone and facial expression tells me all I need to know. She thinks he's way out of my league, or she thinks she can steal him from me. It's a look I grew way too familiar with when Wyatt and I started dating. I shudder, remembering how many women back home tried throwing themselves at Wyatt before *and* after we got married. Wyatt never intentionally flirted with them, but he always had that super charming, flirtatious personality that made women believe they had a chance.

Gabby was right when she said I would make enemies if I dated Wyatt, but I made a valiant effort to make friends. I started the Hot Moms Book Club, and Wyatt seemed more than happy to put in a little extra work the night before to make sure the shop looked its best. It kept him late on Tuesdays.

The all-too-familiar feeling of guilt flickers through me. Maybe if I hadn't had book club the next day, he would have left earlier. Maybe he wouldn't have gotten into his car at that moment. Maybe he would still be here.

"Name?" The barista clicks her pen impatiently.

I furrow my brows and clench my jaw as I'm brought back to reality. Am I jealous? No.

"It's Daphne. We'll have two hot bean juices with cream and cinnamon. Thank you!" I grab Silas's hand and pull him to the end of the counter where the drinks come out.

A smirk appears on Silas's face. "Is that jealousy I smell on you?"

"What? No." I shake my head. "She was basically throwing herself at you is all. It was kind of embarrassing."

The male behind the counter sets out two cups and calls out my name.

He laughs softly. "She just asked me what I wanted to drink. Remember, I can indeed smell the jealousy on you." He takes the drinks off the counter and hands me one.

Stupid fae senses. I wish mine would hurry up and get stronger already. The only thing I can smell is Silas's sage and lemongrass scent, and normal smells are a little more enhanced. But I haven't been able to smell feelings like jealousy or desire or anything on Silas, or anyone for that matter.

I glare at him before we exit the busy shop and re-enter the street. "Whatever. You saw how she looked at you."

"Awfully strong reaction to have about a male you're 'just having fun' with." He shrugs and takes a sip of his coffee. His lips tighten and his nose scrunches in disgust. "This is the beverage you covet so highly? It tastes like bitter dirt water."

He doesn't know what coffee is supposed to taste like. It does take some getting used to. I take a sip of mine and nearly gag. He's right. "Oh god, this is not coffee. Well, it is, technically, I guess. It's just not good coffee."

We walk to a nearby trash can and toss the full cups in the bin. "I'll bring real coffee with me if I decide to come back here. Maybe I'll open up my own coffee shop in Sol Salnege."

"If that is what you wish. We will find you the perfect place to bring your drugs into my city." He chuckles. "But you know you will not have to work when you come back."

"What do you mean?" I've worked my entire adult life. I started at The Coffee Bean the day after I turned eighteen. Wyatt had plenty of money from his trust, but we both always worked. Even when I was pregnant and after we had kids, I still worked. I have never not worked. It keeps me sane and gives me a sense of purpose.

He looks around, seeing if anyone near us is paying attention, before he leans in and whispers into my ear, "In case you haven't noticed, I am the king."

I narrow my eyes at him and smirk, trying to contain my laughter. "That doesn't mean anything! How else am I supposed to make sure that if I move my family here I'm not without coffee for the rest of my life?"

His facial expression softens. "I want you to know I will take care of you and your children. You will never want for anything. If it is the lack of coffee you are worried about, we can pay to have our farmers grow the beans and you can instruct them on what to do with them to make your 'coffee' taste how you would like. Hopefully it is better than whatever that nasty concoction was. But if you truly wish to open a coffee shop, who am I to stop you?"

Does he really mean that? Why is he offering me so much? I know he's interested in me, but part of me still doesn't understand why he's so willing to take care of me and let me into his life so quickly. Maybe I did hit my head and I'll wake up from this dream tomorrow.

We stop in a bakery and Silas picks up a box of what he tells me are his favorite pastries before we continue through the city. Silas enthusiastically tells me about the importance of local goods and explains how trading works between the kingdoms as we go into each store. Both the goods and economic system remarkably similar to those on Earth.

The time slips away from us as we explore the shops. Our casual conversation is interrupted when one of the guards who has been following us taps Silas's shoulder and points to the sun. Silas looks at the sky, which is full with shades of orange and purple. "Ah, looks like we have been out longer than I thought. It is time we head back to the palace for dinner with Quinn."

To say dinner at the palace in Tesalte is tense is an understatement. Silas tries to make conversation with his brother, who only replies with one or two words at a time.

Members of Quinn's inner circle are also present. Ajax and the bulky male I assume to be Quinn's second spend the entire meal watching each other unnervingly. Brynne, Stone, and Knox make pleasant exchanges with the other members of Quinn's inner circle, joking about their respective kings and how needy they are. Quinn looks annoyed at the jokes made at his expense while Silas laughs along. After dessert— slices of a lovely, crisp apple pie—the members of the two inner circles excuse themselves, leaving Silas, Quinn, Rosa, and I.

Silas clears his throat and wipes crumbs of apple pie crust from his beard. "I hear congratulations are in order, brother."

Startled by this comment, Quinn looks to Rosa, who smiles sweetly and nods encouragingly at him. "I told him when they arrived. I was just excited to share it with someone. Please do not be mad, my love."

Quinn wipes crumbs from his beard with a napkin and places his hand on Rosa's thigh. "Thank you, Silas. We are very happy about the news."

Silas's eyes gleam with joy for his brother. "I am happy for you, Quinn. Truly."

For the first time since our arrival, a small smile creeps onto Quinn's face. "I think it is time we call it a night. You lot have an important journey tomorrow."

Rosa rubs her growing bump. "Agreed. I am exhausted. And it is so rare I get a full night's rest these days. It was so nice meeting you, Daphne. I hope you have a successful mission tomorrow."

"Thank you for having us. The food was fantastic." I take the last bite of pie from my plate.

Quinn helps Rosa to her feet and they make their way to their wing of the castle, followed by their four guards.

"That was... nice," I tell Silas.

A flicker of a smile appears on Silas's face. "That was the most pleasant my brother has been with me in a very long time." He wraps his arm around my shoulders, kissing the top of my forehead. "We really should get to bed."

Yawning, I stretch my hands up over my head. "You're right." I am tired. Riding into Telsalte this morning and walking around the city wore me out. My legs ache when I stand. The thought of the long walk back up the stairs to our room at the very end of the hall makes me frown.

"Everything okay?" Silas asks, concerned.

"I'm tired and don't want to walk up the stairs." I laugh at the ridiculousness of this complaint. Here I am in a magical world, complaining about being tired.

Silas nods in understanding. "I think I have a solution for that problem." He bends to wrap his strong arms under me. With a swoop, he lifts me off of my feet and holds me against his chest. I shriek gleefully. We giggle the whole way through the palace, up the stairs to our bed. My smile grows wildly. This is the happiest I've felt in a long time. I can tell in my heart this is right. Wyatt would want this for me.

CHAPTER THIRTY-FIVE

Day Seven

Silas's heavy arm is draped over my waist and the bare skin of his chest is pressed cozily to my back as we lay under the silk of the purple paisley blanket. His sage and lemongrass scent mingles with the room's strong lily aroma.

Stone mentioned skipping training at dinner last night, since today's journey would be enough of a training exercise. I think he and Knox had too much to drink at the pub and he didn't want to wake up earlier. Whatever the reason, I'm grateful for the few extra minutes I get to snuggle in Silas's warmth before we set out for the snow-capped Pylocim mountains.

I've never been a cold weather person. Being born and raised in Florida means anything under sixty degrees requires a puffer jacket and my favorite pair of worn Uggs. After fall, I do my very best to stay indoors.

Blue and purple light filters over us through the swirling opal on the wall as the sun comes up. This is probably the latest I've slept in since arriving on Threa. Quinn suggested we wait for daylight to start our journey, as it isn't safe to travel the Pyolcim Mountains in the dark.

I intertwine my fingers with Silas's and pull his arm tightly against me. His hand swallows mine. My eyelids flutter closed and I take a deep breath of his comforting sage and lemongrass scent. *Just five more minutes of this.*

As I begin to drift back to sleep, a jarring pounding comes from the other side of the door. Startled and half asleep, I sit upright. Silas shoots out of the bed, completely naked, and walks across the room to open the door.

Standing on the other side of the door, leaning smugly against the frame, is a bright-eyed and bushy-tailed Knox. With how drunk he was at dinner, I have no idea how he looks so awake. Seemingly unphased by our nakedness, he pushes past Silas and enters our room. Looking down, I realize I too am still naked. I pull the blanket up to cover my bare breasts. There better be a good explanation for this.

"Good morning, you two. I would inquire about how your night was, but I think that goes without asking." He gives Silas a teasing smile, winks, then claps once. "Alright, lovebirds, get your clothes on. Time to get going." Knox takes his job as resident alarm clock seriously.

"We will be down soon. Get the pegasuses ready." Silas takes a pair of black leather pants from his bag and pulls them on.

"What, do you not want me to stay?" Knox makes kissy faces at Silas.

Silas throws a decorative pillow at his face. "Get out."

Knox gives Silas a mock salute, laughing as he leaves the room. Silas groans and heads into the bathroom, meaning I probably have a good amount of time by myself. My feet hit the cold floor as I roll out of the bed. I wrap the blanket around myself like a robe for warmth and make my way to my bag. I will my phone into my hand and turn it on. The number in the corner of the screen makes me huff in frustration—the battery has dropped to fifty percent.

"Stupid thing," I mutter under my breath. My phone needed to be replaced months ago, but it was one of those things I kept putting off. I'm kicking myself for it now. God forbid we don't figure out how to get me back home, this is the only thing I have to remind me of my children and my life on Earth.

I pull up the last video I took of the kids. We were at a big playground close to the house a few days before I fell through the mirror. Ariella was running between the two swings her brothers sat on, pushing them as they screamed, "Higher, Ari, higher!" All three of their grins were so wide across their faces that their cheeks pushed their eyes nearly shut. Their laughs and screams were loud and full of pure glee. I can see the big gaps in the twins' smiles from lost teeth. My heart aches as the video ends. I power off my phone to conserve what little battery I have left. I'm one step closer to getting home to them. And then if I can figure it all out, if I decide I want to and if they want to, too... I'll bring them back here.

The stack of clothes Amaleana packed me is impressive. I sift through the different pieces before choosing the thickest items: a gray wool long-sleeve shirt, thick white cotton pants, and a dark blue velvet jacket. It seems like the warmest combination. My current priority is not freezing to death, not fashion.

Once on, the outfit choice is interesting, to say the least. At least it's hidden when I drape my cloak over my shoulders. When Silas returns, he's dressed in a warm-looking black leather ensemble. A thick black cloak lined with black fur flows behind him on what seems to be a current of air. I'm not sure if he's using magic to make that happen or if it's happening naturally. I didn't think he could look better, but I was wrong. On the other hand, 1 look like I ransacked someone's donation pile. Oh, well. At least I won't be cold.

"Are you ready to go find Ailse?" He pulls a glove over his hand.

I grab my satchel from the bed and search for the white gloves I knew Amaleana packed for me. Where are they? Oh right. Magic bag. I will them to my hand and pull the tight fur-lined gloves down my fingers, then secure my satchel strap over my body. "As ready as I'm going to be, I suppose."

"Love the confidence." He takes my gloved hand in his and leads me to the courtyard in front of the palace. Knox and the others sit on top of their pegasuses, ready for the day's mission.

Ajax leads his pegasus to me, holding Iri out in his arms. "You forgot someone with me last night." Iri squirms her way out of Ajax's hands and runs over to me, wings flapping and tail wagging.

"I'm sure she helped keep you warm." I pick her up under one arm, covering her with my cloak, and climb into Lucy's saddle.

Silas pulls himself up behind me and clears his throat as he readies to address everyone. Before he can begin, he is interrupted by the creak of the palace gates swinging open abruptly. A cloaked female strides toward us, a rich purple cloak concealing her features except for the tips of her blonde hair. As she approaches us, I catch a small glimpse of her tan arm. "Silas, wait," her low, raspy voice calls. "I must tell you something before you embark on this journey."

The female pulls back the hood of her cloak, revealing a slightly aged round face. She still looks young, but somehow a little older than everyone else I've met. Fine lines frame the corners of her eyes and lips. If the others still look so young and are centuries old... How old must she be to have signs of aging? Her startling deep-blue eyes meet mine. "To find the answers you seek, you must not fly once you reach the mountain. You must hike from the base up."

"Care to elaborate on that, Katya?" Silas asks, annoyed at her vagueness. Katya. I remember the name. This female before us is the Oracle of Tswangohin.

She shakes her head before pulling her hood back over her face. "That is all I can share. The rest of your fate is up to you to form. You know I cannot interfere with your path any further." She doesn't leave room for a response. Her cloak blows behind her as she twirls and exits through the still-open gate.

Knox lets out a heavy sigh of frustration. "Fucking oracles. Why do they have to be so unclear? They are so annoying. Why can they not be like, 'Oh, you are looking for this Ailse lady? She will be at the pub at 7:45. Good luck!' Instead, they are always like, 'Go on this treacherous journey where you may or may not survive. Have a nice life.' It is bullshit if you ask me."

Brynne snickers. "Are you saying you do not like the oracles?"

"No. I am just saying they're annoying," Knox replies.

"How would a certain oracle feel if she found out her lover was saying such traitorous things about her sisters?" Brynne places a dramatic hand over her heart. I thought I sensed something between Novalora and Knox the first night in Sol Salnege. Good to know I was right about that.

Knox glares at Brynne. "Oh, shut up. You know that is not what I was saying. And it is not like Novalora can accept the mating bond while being the oracle anyway, so what difference does it make if I speak my mind?"

Novalora is Knox's mate? And she can't accept it because of her position as the Oracle? That is... that's not fair. An ache forms in my heart for my new friends. Poor Knox. It must be awful knowing you can't be with the person you were destined by the gods to be with. What a cruel fate for Novalora, having such an incredible gift, helping the kingdom, having the ability to go into someone's mind and search for the presence of a mating bond, but never being able to complete her own.

Silas claps his hands together to call everyone's attention. "As much as I love hearing the two of you bicker, we do really have to head out now. You heard the old hag—as obscure as she was, we will heed her words. We will fly to the base of Mount Pylosum, which should be quick, and then hike our way to the summit, where Quinn and I believe we have the best chance of finding Ailse.

"It is a big mountain. It is going to be a long journey to the top. One or two days." He pauses and looks at each of his friends. "We all know whose dragons we saw yesterday. I want us all to fly close together and remain as silent as possible. We do not want to attract any unwanted attention. Be on high alert. Ajax, keep the light shields up at all times." Everyone nods in unison. "Let us go."

With that, the pegasuses run through the gates onto the empty black street. It must be too early for the city to be awake yet. We're in the air within a few strides.

Tesalte fades from view as we head west for Mount Pylosum. Dozens of small boats, a handful of merchant ships, and three larger ships are docked in the harbor. The larger ships all fly a familiar green flag, flecked with gold. In the center of the flag, in embroidered metallic gold stitches, is an aerial depiction of a dragon with an ornate crescent moon on either side of it. Those must be warships flying the flag of Carimea.

Is Quinn preparing for a war? Or is it normal for a kingdom to always be at the ready? I suppose both make sense.

My chest tightens at the idea. Kingdoms and continents at war isn't something I'd thought about. On Earth, I'm fortunate enough to be far away from such things. Choosing to be with a king will come with the risk of being thrown into the middle of whatever conflicts may arise. And with the way everyone speaks of these Reclaimers... Is this something I should risk bringing my kids back to? On Earth, I do anything to avoid danger. Is it worth it?

I reach for the dragon pendant on my neck. I haven't taken off since the night of the ball. The stone and metal are cool against my skin as I spin it nervously between my fingers. I don't know if I can bring them here. I haven't told Silas if I'm coming back or not yet, but I assume he will want an answer before I leave this world. There is still time. I'll decide later.

A significant drop in temperature alerts me that Mount Pylosum is now in front of us, covered in a thick blanket of white glittering snow. The pegasuses begin their descent. The snow absorbs the impact, making for a soft landing. Shivering from the cold, I tug my cloak closed and hold Iri tightly to my body.

Silas wraps his arm around me and rubs my arm over the cloak. "Knox, do you think you can lend a flame?"

"On it." Knox dismounts from his pegasus and heads to the treeline. He rips a low-hanging branch from a tree and sends a spark from his hand, lighting the top of it and creating a torch. He hands it to Silas as we dismount from Lucy.

"Thank you, Knox." I say gratefully. Silas hands me the torch and Iri peaks her head out from beneath the cover of the cloak. Her yellow eyes glow in the light of the flame. She looks around at the snow in front of us, decides it's too cold for her, and returns to the warmth of the cloak. Are dragons cold-blooded like reptiles, or does their magic keep them warm? They do breathe fire. I'd think they'd be able to keep themselves warm, but Iri's cool shivering scales tell me otherwise.

There is so much more I have to learn about this world.

My boots fight me as I try to pull them out of the snow. It's much thicker than I expected. I thought there would be a light dusting of snow on the ground, not an entirely white mountain.

Despite the intimidatingly steep mountain before us, the seven of us begin the hike and our search for Ailse. Ajax takes the lead, Silas and I walk side by side with Brynne and Syrrus, and Stone and Knox follow behind. Brynne asks me to tell her more about Earth, so I entertain her by telling her about electricity and technology. Somehow, I end up talking about cell phones.

"With cell phones, when we connect to the internet, we have access to almost all of the information in the entire world. Right at our fingertips. They can take and store thousands of pictures at any given time. We take them everywhere with us."

She gasps. "Do you have one on you?"

"I do. The thing never leaves my side."

She squeals and her smile pushes at her cold, reddened cheeks. "You have to show me pictures of your kids. You do have some of them, right? I bet you have the most beautiful babies. I mean, look at you."

"Okay, okay." I laugh and hand the torch over to Silas, who also seems curious about what my family looks like. I reach my hand in and dig through my bag. Magical bag. Why do I keep forgetting that? I will my phone to my hand, hold the power button, and wait—but the screen doesn't light up. "Come on." I try again. And again. "Stupid thing. The battery must have died. I'm sorry. I'll make sure it's fully charged when I come back."

Ajax stops abruptly in front of me and I almost bump into him. "When you come back?"

Brynne's eyes glow with excitement. "You're going to come back?"

Looking nervously at Ajax, then Brynne, then into Silas's hopeful eyes, I swallow. "Maybe. I haven't decided. I don't know if it will be a real possibility. But if I do, I will bring a phone with plenty of battery life."

Ajax continues forward. I catch the remnants of a small frown on Silas's face as it quickly disappears and we keep walking. Why did I have to say that?

The winds around us howl loudly and snow falls rapidly.

"I thought Katya said the weather was going to be fine today," Knox calls from behind us.

"She did!" Silas answers.

A low growl comes from the tree line.

CHAPTER THIRTY-SIX

An unworldly screech follows the growl, then the loud crack of a tree snapping in half. Through the breaks in trees, something is crouched and stalks back and forth. I squint, trying to get a better look. White fur. No, feathers. No, fur. Both? More snapping; trees begin falling rapidly. The members of the Azurite Force surround Silas, Iri, and I, forming a barrier. A hum of energy grows in the air as they ready their magic. We collectively hold our breath as the great white beast emerges, slowly making its way toward us.

My eyes widen as I take in the creature. It's the size of an elephant, with the body and printed coat of a leopard. It has the head, wings, and sharp beak of an owl. The beast's large golden eyes narrow on us as it throws its head back in a screech-like roar. Its claws dig into the snow as it advances toward us—its prey.

"Do not move," Silas whispers to me.

Terrified, I ask, "What is that thing?" I continue to hold my breath, waiting for my imminent death to come. I hope it's fast. We only made it a quarter of the way up the mountain, and we're going to die before we get answers from Ailse. I am not making it home.

"A snow griffon," Ajax mutters beneath a breath. Everyone strips themselves of their bags and cloaks, throwing them in a pile behind us.

"I thought they had gone extinct." Brynne looks up at Syrrus with fear in her eyes.

"I did too." Silas lets go of my hand. He walks up behind Ajax and steps into the circle his friends formed.

"It can't see us with your light shields, though, right?" I whisper through clenched teeth.

"It does not need to see us," Knox answers, his hands growing a flame in front of him.

"Daphne, you need to stay back," Silas tells me.

There is no point in me arguing, I know that. I've only had two days of training and no formal magic instruction. I'm a sitting duck, a liability. The six of them form a defensive line and I stand behind them, holding Iri tightly to my chest. Behind the snow griffon, a group of armed fae dressed in all black stalk out, swords and shields drawn.

"Are those?" I shout.

"Reclaimers, yes," Brynne calls back.

Knox hurls the powerful ball of fire he grew at the snow griffin, starting the battle for our lives. The griffin roars in response, rearing on its hind legs in the snow. The fireball does nothing to the beast aside from irritate it. It moves at us faster, snow flying behind it. One of the Reclaimers throws blades of ice through the air, which Silas expertly melts, refreezes, and sends hurdling back, faster, sharper.

A Reclaimer hurls a boulder toward me and I narrowly dodge it. Silas yells, "Daphne, I need you to be careful."

Like I didn't think of that.

Another boulder knocks Syrrus off his feet. Brynne roars in anger. She lifts her hands, sending vines to ensnare the beast. The vines tighten and tighten, pulling it down, down, down until the snow griffin is flat against the ground. Her arms strain, holding the vines from this distance, as the beast thrashes.

As the Reclaimers draw near us, Silas, Knox, Ajax, and Stone unsheathe their swords. A Reclaimer makes a beeline for me and Iri. Silas takes him by the shoulders and runs a hand over his face, knocking him out before throwing him stumbling toward Stone. His abdomen lands directly on Stone's ready dragon-iron sword. Silas and Stone smile triumphantly at each other as Stone shoves the Reclaimer's body down on the snow and removes the blood soaked blade. It's a whirl of sharp, calculated movements. They've done this before.

Twisting to shield Iri from the sight, I meet the dark eyes of a Reclaimer, who sneaked up behind me. In one swift motion, Ajax takes a sharpened dragon-iron sword from his back and slices clean through the fae's neck, sending bright red blood splattering over the snow and the edges of my cloak. I scream as his body lands inches from my feet. Dragon-iron arrows fall from the quiver on his back into the pool of blood seeping from where his head should be.

I am going to vomit.

My gaze breaks away from his body just in time to see Knox bang two the Reclaimers' heads together, disorienting them, before shoving two blades deep into their chests.

For a moment, I think we've won.

That thought vanishes when the last Reclaimer cuts the vines that tethered the snow griffon. Knox sends a burst of flames rushing at him as he attempts to retreat. The male screams as his body bursts into flames. Stone uses his magic to hurl boulders at the griffon as it charges at us, aiming for its head. The massive beast paws them away as if they're nothing but flies. Ajax and Silas use the snow around them as a source to create rows of ice walls between the griffin and us, but it smashes through them, sending shards of sharp ice through the air. I jump back and throw a hand up, successfully melting pieces that flung toward me.

No one's magic is affecting this monster. The six powerful, trained fae send attack after attack on the beast to no avail. The

Azurite Force grows visibly weaker with each intense burst of magic they hurl toward it.

This is the end for us.

No.

I need to get back home. I need to get back to my kids. I can't die like this. I *will not* die like this.

I place Iri on the snow and cover her with my blood-splattered cloak. She cowers into the fabric and looks up at me with fear in her eyes. Crouching down to her, I whisper, "I'll be back. It's going to be okay." Bitter wind bites at my cheeks and blows my hair in every direction. I set my eyes on the bloodied bow and dragon-iron arrow that lie with the Reclaimer's body. Unnerving warmth radiates from his fresh corpse, sending a shudder through my body as I retrieve the weapon.

Breathe, Daphne. You've got nothing to lose. Even if you miss, you're dead anyway. I hurl a rock at the beast to get its attention.

Silas's eyes land on me. "Daphne, no!" he screams as the beast charges forward.

I dock the arrow on the bow and stare my target in the eye. Slowly, I pull my arm back as I walk through my friends, past Silas, as they put every ounce of their magic into this fight. Bursts of fire, whips of vines, boulders, frozen water, and blasts of air surround me, yet none of them touch me.

Elbow back, shoulder straight. I inhale deeply and aim the dragon iron arrow right between the eyes of the beast. Exhale and release. Everything around me grows silent as the arrow flies through the air.

The beast lets out a blood-curdling roar as my arrow hits its mark. Its body goes rigid as it falls with a thud, shaking the ground beneath it.

Silas clears his throat, breaking the tension in the air. "Uh, well done, Daph. Much better weapon choice than a rock."

"That was brilliant!" Brynne exclaims. Her eyes gleam with something like pride and she laughs wildly in delight.

Knox and Stone pat me on the back and Ajax gives me an approving nod.

I did it.

I'm alive.

I'm safe.

We are safe.

Ajax's hand lands on my shoulder and my body stiffens. "I will take that as your initiation into the Azurite Force." I start crying and laughing all at once. Silas picks me off the ground, lifts me above his head, and spins me around, looking at me with pride in his eyes. He lowers me into a kiss and everyone cheers loudly. My smile reaches my eyes as I look at each of the faces surrounding me. I realize only six of us are here.

Syrrus stands frozen near the snow griffon's body, looking up the mountain.

"Syrrus!" Brynne calls as she runs to her mate, planting a kiss on his cheek. "Come over with us, my love!"

Syrrus audibly swallows as he looks back at us with horror in his eyes. "Avalanche."

CHAPTER THIRTY-SEVEN

When the shock of hearing Syrrus's gruff voice wears off, our new impending doom settles in. There is nowhere for us to go. We're too far up the mountain. We'll never make it down in time.

Silas puts me down and looks at each member of the Azurite Force, his closest friends. "I can try to hold an air shield around us. But I do not know how long it will last… The battle depleted my magic."

Realization slowly pours over each of their faces. I pick Iri out of the snow and stroke her head as calmly as I can. Her big, innocent yellow eyes look up at me. Silas wraps his arms around me. Brynne supports Syrrus as they walk over to us. He's limping. That boulder must have done more damage than I thought. They wrap their arms around Silas to share one last embrace with their king. Knox and Stone join next. Seconds later Ajax walks over, completing the circle around Silas and I. All of us stand linked together as the snow hurdles ferociously toward us. Silas's face is pale with exhaustion and defeat pale as he throws a dome of circling air around us.

My chest tightens as the panic sets in. *This is it.* There have been so many times I've thought I was going to die since landing in this world. But this is truly it. There's no escaping this fate. The sound of the rushing snow grows louder. I look over Silas's shoulders just in time to see the snow hit the air shield. Within seconds, we're surrounded by a cover of white.

A tear rolls down Silas's cheek. "Thank you all, for every single thing you have ever done for me. I could not have asked for a better group of people to call my friends—my family." His voice and strength waver, and skin grows warm to the touch, as he begins struggling to hold the shield up around us.

"It has been our honor to serve you," Ajax says with a stoic face and teary eyes.

The shield tightens as Silas's power fades, growing smaller and smaller until the swirling air nearly touches us.

Tightening my grasp on Iri, I brace for impact.

A glimmering thread of foreign magical energy trickles through my body, combining with my own magic when it reaches my heart. The intertwined magics move through my being and pour into Iri, then Silas, then Brynne, then Stone, then Knox, then Ajax, and it reaches for Syrrus. But he bends over in pain, grasping his leg, breaking the chain. The magic surges and there is a flash of light so blinding it forces my eyes shut.

The ground beneath me hardens and the air warms. Smoke, cinnamon, and dust fill the air. I open my eyes and look down. My feet are on the hardwood floor of a log cabin. It looks to be a single room with a lit fireplace against the far wall. The shelves of the cabin are full of knick knacks, random piles of yarn, and half-finished knit blankets.

Where are we? Why am I so tired?

I walk to the window. Snow is falling outside. All eyes are on me when I turn back around, looks of confusion and surprise painted on each of my friends' faces. What? Why are they looking at me like that? Do they think I brought us here? Did I?

"Did you know she could do that?" Knox asks bluntly, his jaw gaping in shock.

Yep, they definitely think I did this.

Silas raises his brows in confusion and shakes his head. "No. No, I did not."

Across the room, Brynne stumbles forward, clutching her heart. She lets out a blood-curdling scream as she drops to her knees. What's wrong? I go to move toward her, but my body feels weak and I can't catch my breath. My head spins and my vision grows blurry. As I reach my arm back to lean onto the window sill for support, my body collapses out from underneath me. Silas rushes toward me. The last thing I hear is him screaming my name as I hit the hard floor and the world goes black.

DAY EIGHT

DAY NINE

DAY TEN

DAY ELEVEN

CHAPTER THIRTY-EIGHT

Day Twelve

Something warm and slick moves up my cheek. My head pounds as the stark scent of smoke fills my nose. My body throbs on the stiff surface beneath me. When I blink my eyes open, my vision is still blurry. Iri is a fuzzy blob on my chest, licking my face. I try to move my hand to stroke her scales, but can't. Silas is sitting on the floor beside me, holding my hand as he sleeps. Searching the unfamiliar room for anything recognizable, I find Brynne, Ajax, Stone, and Knox's faces across the room. Iri plops off of me onto the floor. Putting my arm behind me, I force myself up on the old, hardened flannel couch. The movement makes me wince in pain.

The jostling wakes Silas. "Daphne, you are awake. Are you feeling alright?"

"Where are we?" My voice comes out rough. I am so thirsty.

"That is not important right now." Silas cradles my head in his hand, bringing my face to his and our foreheads together. "All that matters is we are safe."

Ajax hands me a glass of water. The cool liquid hitting the back of my throat is more refreshing than I could have imagined. When was the last time I had anything to drink? I finish the entire glass in a few gulps and my vision starts to return. We are still in the same cabin from before I collapsed. Snow falls gently outside the window. The piles of yarn and blankets have been moved and the air smells of dust and stale alcohol. What is this place? Then I notice her.

A heavy-set female wearing a tan fur-lined cloak and snow boots sits poised in the corner of the room on a rocking chair, knitting white and red yarn into... something. Her jet black hair nearly brushes the floor, and her warm tan skin looks like it's long shown signs of aging.

"Who are you?" I ask.

Her nearly black eyes look up at me above her knitting needles. "You're the one who has been lying asleep on my couch for the past four days. Shouldn't I be the one asking you questions?" Her voice is low and raspy.

No, no, no. "Four days?" I whisper. Four days? I count the days in my head... That means I only have three days left to find my way back to Earth before anyone notices I'm gone. My breathing becomes rapid and uneven. When I try to stand, I find my body is too weak to hold me.

Silas catches me as my knees buckle. "It is okay, love. We have a plan. But you need to rest. You almost burned out saving us."

"I've been asleep for four days. I don't have any more time to rest. We need to leave and find Ailse so she can tell me how to get home."

The female in the corner cackles. I glare at her. What's her problem? Silas helps me ease back onto the couch and kneels in front of me, taking one of my hands. "Daphne, meet Ailse." He gestures to the female, who is fussing over a dropped stitch.

My eyes dart to each of the others in disbelief. "This is the powerful traveler who is supposed to have the answers to get me home? She's... she's just been hiding here this whole time... knitting?!"

"I am retired," Ailse scoffs. "I can do whatever I want with my time. And right now, what I want to do is figure out why I cannot get this yarn to do what I want it to. I can wield the elements and travel through the worlds, but I cannot figure out how to make a blanket," she says under her breath as she continues to fight with the long wooden needles.

I look around the room again, trying to figure out if this is a joke, and realize a face is missing from the crowd. "Where's Syrrus?"

Brynne drags her feet as she joins me on the couch. Her eyes are red and tired. She looks like she hasn't slept in days. She lays a hand on my knee. "He did not make it here, Daph."

No. No. Not sweet Syrrus. Not Syrrus who did nothing but treat me with kindness. Not Brynne's mate. The image of her dropping to the floor in agony replays in my head. I grab Brynne's hand tightly. "Brynne... I'm so... I'm so sorry."

Quickly wiping a tear from her face, she manages a faint smile through the pain. "It is not your fault. We would all be dead if you did not bring us here."

"Brynne... I..." I stare down at my hands, angry at them for doing this. Having been in her position less than a year ago, I know there is nothing I can say or do that will ease her pain at this moment. "I don't know what to say. I don't know what I did to get us here."

Her eyes look up at the ceiling in an attempt to keep more tears from falling. "We have learned a lot from Ailse over the past four days."

I let her take the time she needs to compose herself before I ask, "What did you learn?"

"I am not sure you are ready for us to tell you everything yet," Silas answers for her.

I glare at Silas. "I'm ready. Tell me." There is no more time to waste.

"She needs to know. She is up now. She will be fine. She is stronger than you think," Ailse says from her corner.

Brynne places her hand back on my knee. The energy of her

healing magic pours through me. "She is not ready. I have done all I can to heal her, but she was too close to the edge. She needs more time."

"You do not know her, Ailse. She almost died saving us. The only reason she is alive right now is because Brynne spent the last four days healing her. Can we not let her rest? It is too much for her to process right now," Silas argues.

Brynne spent all that time healing me? While she was mourning the loss of her mate? Why would she do that for me? What have I done to deserve her kindness?

Ailse raises an eyebrow in challenge. "This is my house and you, Silas, are not the king here. I will tell her all she needs to know. The rest of you, leave. Go make yourselves useful and find something for me to eat. You lot have nearly eaten me out of house and home."

"I'm not leaving her," Silas says firmly. Ailse lowers her brows begrudgingly before nodding her acceptance.

Knox, Ajax, Stone, and Brynne excuse themselves, muttering complaints under their breaths as they grab weapons out of the pile on the table and head out into the snow. The wind pushes several snowflakes inside as the door opens, which quickly melt into a puddle on the floor. Ailse moves her hand and the log door slams behind them, the lock clicking into place.

The couch cushion shifts under me as Ailse sits beside me on the couch. What does she know that Silas doesn't think I'm ready for? Is there not a way for me to get home?

She smooths the tan fabric of her cloak and looks me directly in the eye. "I am not going to repeat myself, understood?"

I nod in silent response as I study her facial features. Her skin is a deep tan and a broad nose sits between her large, black almond-shaped eyes.

"There is a reason we tried to hide this history from both of our worlds. Clearly one of my old friends did not stick to our agreement, or you would not be here."

"What do you mean? What agreement?" I ask.

She blinks slowly at me before continuing. "The five of us agreed we would never go back to Earth under any circumstances. But here you are. And you, my dear, have the gift of traveling. And not just regular traveling abilities. Ancient traveling magic runs in your veins. Magic that powerful can only be passed through the blood of the descendants of the gods. Meaning that, if what your mate here says is true, your father is either Theodosius or Evander."

"My father? You know who my father is?" How did my mom not know? I guess if he could leave the world whenever he wanted, that would explain why she doesn't know who he is. A descendant of the gods? Would that make me a... There is no way.

"Yes. Well, what the book you found doesn't mention is that Theodosius and Evander are brothers, so I can't tell you which one of the bastards sired you. But you do look just like them. There is no way you could be Olvir's. He stopped traveling to Earth after one of his friends tried to poison him at a dinner party. He ended up marrying a vampire and settling down near Dorolan. His wife was kind enough to write to me about his passing a few centuries ago. Meaning that either Theodosius or Evander must have gone to Earth after we lost contact, long after our decision to never go back." She shrugs casually, like she's discussing the weather, not dropping a bomb on me.

She knows who my father is. Or, at least, she narrowed it down to two possibilities. That's closer than I've ever been to knowing who my dad is and where I came from. It explains the ears and the magic.

I'm a traveler? I brought us here. I saved us.

"You've been to Earth before?" I ask.

"Yes. Now no more questions. You will distract me and I will not get through what I have to tell you. There will be no coming back to this cabin for more information. I am old and like being alone. My cabin is much too small to host freeloaders."

"I told you I would have the palace send gold to compensate you for your hospitality when we get back to Sol Salnege," Silas interjects.

She glares at him and rolls her eyes. "As I was saying. Close to 10,000 years ago, the five of us granted the mirrors to the rulers of each kingdom, who joined forces to create the grand continent of Carimea. They named the first high king, who was eventually overthrown by King Ameldrick's great-grandfather. The kings of the five kingdoms built the original capital city in Skaans City. Your book got that right.

"As time went on, the five of us explored and pushed our traveling abilities. We discovered we could travel between worlds. Most of them were empty and desolate. But we kept searching. Eventually, we found a world akin to ours: Earth. This world was built exactly like ours, but without magic. We did not find a receptive host on the first continent we landed on, so we traveled across the seas and met the humans on the other side of the world. Their language was so different from ours, it was difficult to communicate, but after some time we developed a common tongue so we could communicate with each other. After some time on Earth, we returned back to Threa.

"The efforts of many years of research paid off when Mairead discovered that when there is an eclipse anywhere in either world, the combined energy from the sun and moon is enough to power the mirrors to allow non-travelers to travel between the two worlds. We decided to share this magic with the humans of Earth, and traveled back to show them. But when we returned, we found an entirely different world. Generations had passed, and the people we met had conquered the lands we know here as Carimea, naming it America in homage to us. As the details of their actions came to light, we were left mortified. Despite this, we chose to give their descendants a chance."

There was an eclipse on Earth the day I fell through the mirror. Ariella wouldn't stop talking about it. That must be how I fell through the mirror.

"For a few decades, fae, witches, vampires, shifters, and all sorts of magical beings moved freely between the worlds using the mirrors. Sometimes they brought humans back with them, and sometimes they stayed on Earth. For the most part, we lived in harmony. Ideas, technologies, stories, and cultures were all shared between the peoples of the two worlds. Both worlds thrived.

"Until about 1,700 years ago. Word spread that magical beings living on Earth were being persecuted, burned alive even. When we heard of this, all travel to Earth was halted. A group of greedy humans found the mirror and entered Threa. They set out to conquer our lands like they did to America on Earth and take every last dragon egg, whether it was on the edge of burnout or not. They destroyed cities throughout our kingdoms along the way. They brought human weapons that our magic could not compete with. When we finally defeated them, we decided humans of Earth could no longer be trusted.

"At the time, we allowed magical beings with families in both worlds to choose which to stay in. Some of them did return home to Threa, but many stayed on Earth. With the help of powerful witches, we placed a glamour over every magical being on Earth to look human. Many witches stayed on Earth and to this day protect people of magical descent from being exposed.

"We decided the best thing for Threa was to end communication with Earth. Theodosius and Evander were tasked with finding and destroying the mirror on your planet, and we erased all memories of the mirrors and travel between worlds from everyone's minds. Glamours do not work perfectly on such a large scale, so there are slips from time to time. Some older beings in this world have started to remember things. On Earth, humans have written all sorts of stories about us. Good ones, bad ones. They call them fairytales. And in both worlds, things like that book of yours have sneaked by unnoticed for centuries."

"It all makes sense…" My mind reels at these revelations. How connected things on Earth are to Threa. "But if the mirror on Earth is gone, how did I get here…"

"I do not know how you found a mirror on Earth. The five of us agreed to destroy the mirrors here on Threa and we did. Or, at least I thought we all did. Then you show up in *my* cabin on the brink of burnout from traveling with a group of six plus a dragon. Utterly reckless behavior. Impressive. But reckless." She shakes her head disapprovingly. "That is how I could tell you were one of us. Normally, travelers can only transport themselves to places they have been. You brought all of them and you have never once been to or seen this place."

I remember Silas saying other travelers could only visit places they've been before. "How did I get here?"

"Your magic is powered by your heart, which is rare in itself. I am willing to bet you wanted to find me so badly your magic brought you here, right past my wards. I still have not pieced together how you did that."

"You said eclipses are what powers the magic of the mirror to allow me to travel to Earth. When is the next eclipse?"

Silas grabs my leg. "In two days. Here on Carimea, we have eclipses often, because of the two moons."

"Is that all you heard? From everything I said?" Ailse stands and the couch sinks back beneath me. "You tell them everything they need to know to not leave this world, and they still want to go." Irritation grows in her voice and across her face.

Completely ignoring her, I grab Silas by the shoulders, nearly shaking him with excitement. "We need a mirror. Do you know where we can find one, Ailse?"

"They were supposed to have been destroyed, but I guess blood pacts don't mean anything these days. I could not tell you. You should not use the mirrors at all. You belong on this world, not on Earth," she grumbles.

Silas takes my hands from his shoulders and holds them in his. "I know. The only mirror we know for a fact is destroyed is Ailse's. If Theodosius or Evander is your father, it is a safe bet one of their mirrors is the one back on Earth. That leaves Olvir and Mairead's mirrors."

Ailse sighs. "This is what you get, Ailse. You try to help but they only hear the things they want to hear. This is why you live here so you do not have to deal with ungrateful idiots," she mutters under her breath as she walks back to her stool to resume knitting. "She is awake, so you can all leave my mountain now. I like it better alone. And do not tell anyone you saw me." With a wave of her hand, the door swings open. She makes another gesture and a gust of wind shoves us out the door. Iri chases behind us. The lock clicks once she bounces over the threshold.

I grab my bag from the steps of the cabin and pull out *The Travelers and the Five Mirrors*. "It says Mairead is from Schasumetsats and Olvir is from Roladif." My legs feel weak under me, causing me to sway.

Silas wraps a steading arm around my waist and helps me down the stairs. "There is no way one exists in Schasumetsats without Zefarina knowing. She has more spies than the rest of us combined. Nothing exists in her kingdom without her knowledge. And if she knew where one was, she would have been trying to replicate it for decades, or, at the very least, she would have bragged about it at family gatherings."

"We have to find Olvir's mirror then. Ailse mentioned that he had a wife. Do you think she'll know where his mirror is?" Sharp pains move up my legs as I step across the snow.

"If she is a vampire, she may be difficult to find. There is only one way to find out."

My knees buckle and I nearly slip off the last step. A small scream escapes from my mouth.

"Here. Let me carry you," he offers.

"I'm fine," I insist.

He lowers his brows. "You are not fine. Trust me, I can tell when something is not fine with you. Stop being stubborn and just let me help you."

I want to fight him; I want to show that I am strong enough to walk out of here by myself. But I don't have it in me. My mind and body are too weak to continue arguing. Silas gathers me in his arms and carries me to where Lucy waits alongside the five other pegasuses. Only four of them now carry riders.

"How did they get here?" Exhaustion creeps back over me and beads of sweat drip down my face. I don't even have my cloak on. How am I not cold?

I pick Iri up into my arms and run my hand lazily down her back. She makes the sound that reminds me of purring. She feels so much heavier than she did three days ago. How fast do dragons grow? Lucy kneels and Silas climbs on while continuing to cradle my body against his. "The weather calmed down a bit the day after we arrived. Stone, Ajax, and Knox went to retrieve them."

"Would have been easier with more hands, but Silas refused to leave your side," Ajax remarks cheekily.

I turn my head up at him. "You sat with me for four days? Why?"

"It is not important right now. What is important is getting us to Dorolan as quickly as possible. Normally it takes two full days. But we have to make it by tomorrow. We will stop in Pateko to have their priestess send a message to their sisters in Dorolan to let them know we are coming."

My eyes struggle to stay open as we take off. The few steps I took from the cabin completely drained me of whatever energy I had left. With a breath that takes far more effort than it should, I nestle my head against Silas's warm chest, inhale his sage and lemongrass scent, and close my eyes. A few more minutes of rest is all I need.

CHAPTER THIRTY-NINE

The impact of hooves on the ground jostles my body enough to startle me awake. My eyelids feel heavy as I try to open my eyes. My vision is hazy again, but I can tell whatever is in front of us is a large gold... something... palace, maybe? Two figures rush toward us from the building. Their faces are nothing but blurs, but I can tell the male has tan skin and the same dark hair as Silas. Squinting in an attempt to focus my vision to make out the details of the blonde female beside him makes my eyes fall shut instead.

A wise and powerful male voice that I don't recognize says, "This is her, Silas? What in the gods' names have you let happen to her?"

"How could you have let her do this, Silas?" The female's voice is soft and calm despite the urgency in her tone.

"I did not know. She did not know. It just happened. I should have made sure she had time to focus on learning her magic. I know," Silas whispers solemnly.

Silas slides us gently off of Lucy's back and he walks toward them. Are they talking about me? Their hushed voices become too quiet to understand.

A cool, delicate hand brushes my face. "Get her to Apolynea's Pool," the female says.

There's worry in Silas's voice when he speaks. "But it is forbidden."

"You must do whatever you can to save her. If what the oracles say about her is true, there will be no issue taking her there," she tells him.

Silas's grasp tightens around me. "But—"

"Do not argue with your mother further. That is an order, son," the male voice barks. Mother? Son? Are these Silas's parents? I try to open my eyes again, but instead I drift back to sleep.

CHAPTER FORTY

Day Thirteen

The pungent smell of sulfur fills the air and the sound of chimes swinging in the wind reverberates around me. I open my eyes and make out the shadows of Silas's face as he holds me in darkness. Where are my shoes? Where are my clothes? The only light comes from the blue glow of the water he's standing in. Silas walks further into the pool until he's waist-deep in glowing water. My toes are the first thing to touch the warm water. He presses his soft lips against my forehead as he lowers my body. Water covers me as he releases me. Soft splashing echoes off the walls as he exits the pool.

Why is my body so warm? Where am I?

The weightlessness of floating envelops me, relaxing all of my senses and clearing my mind until I'm completely calm. An invisible force pulls me to the middle of the water. I take a long breath and my face slips beneath the surface.

When I open my eyes, I'm surrounded by nothing. Am I dead? I didn't make it back home. I failed.

The floor beneath my feet grows uncomfortably warm with each step, like I'm walking on hot coals. In the distance, I see a familiar shape. My memory reservoir. I'm in my mind. Not dead. I breathe slowly to calm my nerves as I approach the bowl. The liquid is bubbling. No. Boiling. I go to lean on the edge but quickly recoil my hand. It's scalding. Beads of sweat drip down my forehead, evaporating as they hit the floor.

A gentle female voice comes from behind me. "That was brave of you, Traveler of Heart." A faceless figure made of pure light appears near the fountain. "That combination of ability and source was surprising, even to me. I do not think we have ever seen it before." One of her glowing fingers dips into the boiling liquid. It hisses and steam rolls over the bowl as the liquid freezes, replaying the moment the snow hit Silas's air shield. The figure watches intently as light flashes and we arrive in Ailse's cabin. "I am sorry about your friend, granddaughter." She touches the liquid again and it ripples gently as it had when I was here with Novalora.

Did she just say granddaughter?

"Who are you?" I whisper.

"I am Apolynea, Goddess of the Sun and Healing. Your grandmother."

A goddess? What is a goddess doing in my mind? My grandmother? "Apolynea, Grandmother... What should I call you? How are you my grandmother?"

"Apolynea is fine. Evander and Theodosius are my children."

"Do you know which one of them is my father?" She's a goddess; how could she not know?

"I cannot say. It would interfere with your fate too much."

That nonsense again? Why are all of these mystical beings so frustrating? "What are you doing here? What am I doing here?"

She tilts her head up and I follow her gaze to the bright, glowing golden thread above us. It's shining more brilliantly than the last time I saw it and the once frayed ends seem to be in a state of repair. Beside it now runs a white iridescent thread. The energy coming from it is the same power I felt before I traveled us to Ailse's house. Is that the dragon bond—my connection to Iri? Did she power my magic?

"I am here to decide if you are worthy of the grace of the gods, to spare your life. You used a lot of magic to save your friends. Too much. Your body is at war within itself." She walks toward the two doorways. "Your soul has held on to your physical being quite fiercely. But it continues to slowly fade."

Traveling must require a lot of energy, or at least when you travel so many people. What would have happened to me had I brought Syrrus as well? If she can save me... "Can you save Syrrus too?"

She pauses. "No. He resides in the city of the gods now. But find some comfort in knowing a piece of your friend's soul now lives on within another."

Brynne. His mate. He lives on within her. Why did my power fail him? Fail me?

Apolynea's voice shakes me from my thoughts. "Because if you had succeeded in bringing all of your friends, not one of you would be alive now. Exerting that much energy all at once should have already pushed you far beyond the edge. Adding another soul would have been catastrophic."

Did she just? I follow behind her, minding my thoughts. The ground grows hotter on my bare feet as we walk, the pain almost unbearable. "How do I prove that I'm worthy?" I need to convince her that I am. If she saves me, I can still get home. I need to get home. I need to see my kids again.

"You cannot do anything. I will be able to see what I need in order to make my decision." She halts in front of the two doors of light, then reaches both hands up, placing a palm on each one. Her light glows a little brighter and energy radiates from her body. Her hands pull away from the doors abruptly. "That is enough."

That's it? That's what will determine if I live or die? "What do you mean? What did you see?"

"Like I said, I saw enough." Turning quickly, she walks back to the memory reservoir.

The floor begins to cool, sending a chill up my back. My body temperature drops. Sweat stops falling.

She saw enough to save me.

I exhale in relief. "Thank you." Without thinking, I wrap my arms around her.

"You're welcome." Instead of embracing me back, she gently pushes me away, awkwardly patting me on the shoulder.

"Apolynea, while I'm here, can I ask you something?"

She nods.

"Why don't we have contact with god, or any gods for that matter, on Earth?"

She stiffens, then shrugs. "I cannot answer for your god or gods. We each rule our worlds differently. Some of us choose to make ourselves known to all, and some choose to only make themselves known to those who believe in them. Some do not make their presence known at all, they just watch. Each god has their reasons."

"Got it..." It's vague enough that I'm still not certain of what or who I should be believing in, but I find comfort in knowing there's at least someone watching over Earth.

"Before I wake you up, I will tell you this: Not everything was as it seemed. Your life is now entangled with the fate of this world. I believe when it is time to decide which path will be yours, you will make the right choice. That is why I chose to save you. Do not disappoint me, Traveler of Heart." She puts her palms together in front of her and bows her head.

CHAPTER FORTY-ONE

My lungs gasp for air as I resurface from underneath the sulfurous water. My body flails in all directions as the weightlessness I felt before disappears. I orient myself enough to tread water, my feet not reaching the floor of the pool. When I look up, the sun is directly above me. Angelic beams filter down through a hole in the rocks, lighting up the water surrounding me; everything past that is hidden in darkness. The water has lost the glow it had when we arrived. Was it glowing before, or did I imagine it? Silas quickly wades through the water from the edge of the spring to me.

"Silas." I breathe and begin swimming.

When we reach each other, he is still able to stand, holding his head just above the water. The rims of his eyes are red and streaks of dried tears stain his cheeks.

"Silas... Apolynea... she..." Before I can finish, Silas has me in his arms, holding me tightly against him. His strong hand cradles my head, pressing it to his chest as he supports me above the water. He presses a kiss to the top of my head and carries me out of the pool.

Water drips from our bodies as we stand on the rocks that

overlook the perfectly formed circular body of water in the ground. Apolynea's pool is an underground hot spring. As my vision clears I can make out the delicate vines hanging down from the opening at the top of the cavern. Moss grows on the damp, jagged walls and a lingering hum of magical energy radiates through the air like static.

Silas takes my hand in his. Without saying anything, he leads me to a path of tan cave rocks that make a staircase up out of the cavern. The stones of the stairs are uneven and slick with water, making the climb a challenge. How did Silas manage to carry me down here? His hand wraps around my waist to steady me. His silence is starting to make me uneasy.

Reflexively, my hand moves over my face to cover my eyes, shielding them from the burning light as we exit the cavern. Chill air hits my wet skin, sending goosebumps over my entire body. Iri is asleep on a rock nearby, basking in the sun, and Lucy is tied to one of the surrounding forest's trees. As soon as we're fully out of the cave, Silas turns me to face him and presses his lips against mine. I pull away, confused. He hasn't spoken to me since I woke up and now he's kissing me? "Silas, what happened? What is going on?"

"Apolynea granted you the grace of the gods," he states in an attempt to be matter-of-fact about the situation, but his voice is shaky and hoarse and falters at the end of the swallowed sentence. Was he that upset over me? Did he think I wasn't going to make it? He hands me my bag from where it was thrown near the entrance.

"I know that. She explained that to me."

His eyes widen. "You met Apolynea?"

"Well, yes." I lower my brows. "Did you not know what was going to happen when you put me into that spring?"

"No, not really. It has been forbidden to enter Apolynea's Pool for centuries. But it was the only thing left we could think of doing to save you. Beg the gods for their grace on your life."

The blurred image of the golden castle and the two people I could barely make out flashes across my mind. "We as in you and your parents?"

"You were awake for that?"

"Kind of. Why am I naked?" I gesture down at my body.

His lips purse as he looks for an answer. "It's a sacred pool."

Part of me wants to be mad at him for just hoping bringing me here would save me, but it worked. I'm alive, so how can I be mad? I pull clothes out of the bag, settling on a pair of thick cotton pants and a long-sleeve shirt. When I find my cloak, I'm startled. Blood stains speckle the edges. It looks like someone attempted to scrub them, to no avail. Flashes of the Reclaimer's attack trigger a sense of panic. *Breathe, Daphne. You are safe.*

I tie my cloak around my neck. All I can do now is push forward. "Why haven't you said anything to me until now?"

"Out of respect for the gods, we remain silent in these types of places." He shrugs.

That makes sense. It also explains why he waited until we were out of the cavern to kiss me. "Oh."

He reaches to pull something out of his pocket. Between his fingers he dangles my dragon necklace. "Do not forget this."

My fingers brush the spot where it should be. I smile. He didn't let me lose this one, too. Turning around, I let him clasp it around my neck. "Thank you."

"What was she like? What did she say?"

"Who, Apolynea?"

"No, the other goddess you met."

We laugh and I playfully smack his arm. "She was kind... She didn't really look like anything. She was like pure light, shaped like a human, or a fae, I suppose. She told me that my life is linked to this world, and that she would let me live because she thinks I will make the right choice when I choose my fate."

"I think she's right. Is that all she said?"

I frown. Should I tell him? "She told me Syrrus lives in the city of the gods now. Is that good?"

A sad smile tugs the corner of his lip and he tugs me in close, until there's no space between our bodies. "Yeah, it is good." We linger there in each other's arms for a moment.

"She also told me that she's my grandmother."

A look of pure disbelief crosses his face. "I am sorry, what?"

"She wouldn't tell me who my dad was, though."

"Are we going to skim over you being Apolynea's granddaughter? Do you know what that makes you?"

"It doesn't make me anything. I'm still just Daphne."

"You were never just Daphne. But really, this is important news. Are you okay?"

"Honestly, I don't want to talk about it right now. I want to focus on getting home."

His brows furrow with concern and the look in his eyes tells me we aren't done with this conversation. "Alright. How much do you remember from Ailse's cabin?"

"Not a lot... I remember that we have to go to Roladif to find Olvir's mirror. Why?"

"Just curious." He kisses my brow and I inhale his comforting sage and lemongrass scent. Something presses against my shoulder. Startled, I push away from Silas. I look down to find Iri's happy face right at my arm, eyes bright, tail wagging, and wings flapping.

A wide smile makes its way across my face. "Iri! You're flying! When did you learn how to do that?" I reach my arms out to grab her and she lands, snuggling into my arms.

"The day before you woke up for the first time. She can't go long distances. None of them can. It's a side-effect of the siphoning. But she can fly for short periods."

A sadness equivalent to missing my child's first steps nearly overwhelms me. "Oh... I can't believe I missed her first flight..."

"It is okay. There will be plenty more firsts for you to see."

My eyes move from Iri to Lucy and then I try locating the others, but it doesn't seem like anyone else is with us. "Where is everyone?"

"Stone went back to look after Sol Salnege for the time being. Ajax, Brynne, and Knox have gone ahead to Roladif. They flew straight from Ailse's cabin, non stop. They are searching for Olvir's mirror. They will meet us in Dorolan later today."

"Today?" Did I miss another day?

Silas looks away and frowns, then gives me a sad smile. "Yes, today."

If I slept another day, I only have two more days to get home. "How far are we from Dorolan?" I walk quickly to Lucy and untie her reins from the tree.

"Only a few hours flight. It's still early in the day, only a little past noon. We will make it there before the eclipse."

"We need to go. Now." Lucy kneels and I climb into the saddle. Iri makes her way to my shoulders. She's getting heavy, and I'm not sure how much longer I'll be able to carry her like this. "When is the eclipse?"

"Tonight." Silas lifts himself into the saddle behind me. "We just have to hope one of the others finds the mirror in time."

With a flick of the reins, Lucy is airborne over the sea of warm-colored fall trees that decorate the endless mountain landscape. If I weren't so anxious about getting to Dorolan in time, I would appreciate how magnificent it looks.

CHAPTER FORTY-TWO

The mountains, maple trees, and beautiful weather are replaced by vast wetlands, palms, and balmy air that smells of the swamps below. The sky is overcast and it feels like it's about to storm. We must be getting close to Dorolan.

The kids hate storms. Whenever the thunder got bad, all three of them would try curling between Wyatt and me in bed. He always sent them back to their rooms. He was never a fan of the middle of the night kicks. He would always tell them they needed to be brave, that the lightning couldn't hurt them inside of the house. It always made me a little sad when they whimpered back to their rooms. The memory brings a heavy ache to my chest. I would give anything to feel those tiny toes pressed into my spine right now.

Iri lands softly back on my lap and cozies into the cloak I still wear, despite the heat. She's moved from my lap to the sky intermittently the whole trip.

The sun shines down on the horizon, and I imagine what it looks like back on Earth, the wetlands drained, buildings everywhere. "I was born and raised here. Well, not *here* here. In Orlando, on Earth.

It's so different in this world... So much more beautiful, like everything else on Threa."

"What is it like in your world?" Silas asks, adjusting his position in the saddle. It's getting uncomfortable for me too. This is the longest I've flown at one time. I'm sure Lucy is getting tired too, with the extra weight of me and Iri.

"It's, well... a lot of streets, lots of buildings, lots of people. People visit from all around the world to visit the mouse that rules the city."

"A mouse?" The shock in Silas's voice sounds so sincere I can't help but burst out laughing. "I do not get the joke. Does a mouse truly rule your city on Earth?"

"No, no..." I think of how to explain theme parks, television, and most of the things we have on Earth. "It was a bad joke. I pinky promise. We are governed by other humans. At least I think they're human. But I also thought I was until I came here. So who knows? Maybe they're aliens."

"I'm not sure I like the sound of your Earth. I can't imagine why you'd want to stay there."

And there it is. The question I've been avoiding. I still don't know what I'm going to do. I think I want to... I don't know. I just...

In the distance, a huge off-white wall surrounding a city with buildings all built from the same material comes into view. "Is that Dorolan?"

"It is." He sounds disappointed that I didn't respond to his implied question. "Hold on. Landing on the limestone can be a bit rougher than what you have grown used to, and you definitely do not want to fall onto it."

Rougher? Oh gods. Without hesitation, I adjust my grasp so I'm firmly holding the pommel with both hands.

Lucy's hooves hit the jagged limestone below. The roughness makes me feel like I'm going to be thrown off the side of the saddle. The city and buildings around are made of the same rock as the road.

No one greets us when we land. Instead, we dismount from the saddle and Silas leads us to the wall surrounding the palace. I don't see any grand gate like at the palaces in Sol Salnege and Tesalte. "How do we get inside?"

He walks up to a set of carved moons on the wall. "There is a peculiar entrance to my brother's fortress." He presses a single finger to the massive piece of limestone right between the two crescent moons, and it spins like a revolving door, revealing the palace courtyard. Inside, nearly a dozen sculptures of the moon, sun, and planets, all carved out of limestone, surround a fountain.

It looks eerily similar to a landmark I visited once in Miami. What was it called again? The coral... Coral Castle? Something along those lines. I'm pretty sure I remember them saying they didn't know how it was built on the tour. Could the man who built it have been from here? There are so many things on Earth I can link to Threa and the time when the worlds were open to one another. Nothing could surprise me at this point.

The palace in front of me is shorter than the palaces in Sol Salnege and Tesalte, but what it lacks in height, it makes up for in length and width. The single-story structure expands both backward and to the sides, the equivalent length of several city blocks. It truly is a fortress. It was probably built short to withstand storms like the ones we have back at home. If they have the same weather here, that is. I don't know why they wouldn't if everything else about our worlds is so parallel.

A slim male, slightly shorter than Silas, wearing an extravagant forest-green linen outfit makes his way from the entrance of the palace. His face is clean-shaven and short hair is nearly white blonde, but I can tell from his strong jawline and blue-hazel eyes that this is Silas's younger brother. King River of Roladif.

Following behind him is a beautiful female nearly the same height as River. She has light olive-toned skin, brilliant pale-green eyes, and dark-brown hair that's pulled behind her face in a long braid down her back. Her face is slim and her jaw is pointed. The dress she wears is the same shade of green as her king's. A crown made of braided gold and adorned with small emeralds lays across her forehead. This must be his queen, his mate, Estelle.

"Brother!" River reaches his hand out to Silas and Silas pulls him into a hug.

"Good to see you are well. Thank you for having us on such short notice. River, Estelle," Silas gestures to me, "this is Daphne."

I smile and curtsey. "Thank you for having us."

"So nice to meet you." River pulls me into a hug that leaves me frozen. What do I do? This greeting is vastly different from the one I received from Quinn. *Hug him back, Daphne. Don't be weird.* I raise my hands and awkwardly hug him back. Silas hugs Estelle.

"Nice to meet you as well," I say and he releases me. I make my way to hug Estelle, which I assume is what's expected of me here.

Five children accompanied by five small dragons bolt through the palace doors, leaving them wide open behind them. The dragons take off flying through the courtyard. Iri runs from my side to join them.

I keep a cautious eye on Iri. She didn't get along with the other dragons in Sol Salnege. Maybe now that she can fly, she will feel more relaxed around other dragons. I hope.

The children run up to Silas and the smaller ones grab at his pant legs. The three girls and two boys vary in height. They each look like a different combination of River and Estelle, but all of them inherited their mother's striking eyes. They shout loudly and with excitement different updates and questions for their uncle.

"Uncle Silas! Look, I lost a tooth!" the middle female child says. She looks the most like River, with white-blonde hair and strong features.

The younger of the male children asks, "Uncle Silas, how long are you staying?" This one is the most blended combination of the two of them; he has Estelle's triangular face and eyes and River's hair and skin tone.

The tallest one of the bunch, the oldest male, maybe fifteen, asks in a cracking voice, evident of puberty, "Uncle Silas, who is that female with you?" He has his father's face but his mother's eyes and hair.

The smallest female child is the spitting image of her mother, a gorgeous little princess. "Uncle Silas, is she your girlfriend?" she pipes.

Looking nervously at Silas, I swallow. Good question. We haven't really had time for such a discussion. But now isn't the time for it.

The oldest female looks about the same age as Ariella, maybe a little younger. She has light-brown hair and all of River's features. She saves us both from answering when she interrupts, "Uncle Silas, my magic has started coming in! Watch this!" She makes vines with little white flowers move across the ground like snakes.

Silas picks the girl up and spins her in the air in excitement. "Princess Evolet, that is amazing. Now tell me, where do you feel it?" He asks as he places her back among her siblings.

She points to her head. "Right here. Just like you and father."

"Excellent." He pats the top of her head and her eyes beam with happiness at his pride. "This is Daphne. She is a very good friend of mine." He smiles back at me over his shoulder. "Daphne, these are my nieces and nephews. The princes and princesses of Roladif." Giddy laughs follow from the children at the mention of their formal titles.

"Nice to meet you, Daphne," they squeal in unison before running off into the courtyard.

"Uncle Silas, bet you cannot catch us!" The younger boy says. Silas smirks and bolts after them.

"You have beautiful children," I tell Estelle.

"Thank you. They are royal pains in my ass. Literally." A laugh escapes her as her watchful eyes follow the children chasing each other. "You kids need to learn to close the door behind you. You are not a bunch of animals!" she shouts at them.

But are they part animal? Silas did mention the reason his father won't let River inherit the kingdom is that Estelle is half shifter. Does that mean their children are part shifter too? This isn't the time or place to ask such questions, so I keep my thoughts to myself. Instead, I ask, "What are their names?"

"The oldest is Harlow. The second is Evolet. She is the one who just came into her magic. Her brother is a bit jealous, as he has not manifested yet. Magic appears later in males, generally. Then there's Decla, Archer, and Noreida. They love it when their Uncle Silas visits. It's been a while since the last time he made it over here."

A smile curls at my lips at that. If I bring Ariella, Ronan, and Ryan here, would they like him? If not, could they grow to like him? Estelle and I watch the children run. Laughs and playful screams fill the air as Silas gets closer to them, just out of reach, pretending not to be able to catch them.

"They make me miss my own children," I say.

"Your own?" River asks. I forgot he was standing here with us.

"Pardon my husband. He may be a king, but sometimes he forgets his manners. I think he may find them somewhere else." Estelle glares at him and tilts her head toward the courtyard.

"Yes, dear." His eyes widen and he rushes off to join Silas in chasing the children.

I like her.

"What we've heard from High Priestess Genevieve is that you fell into our world through a mirror. We have learned of the hidden history of the Travelers, and have been focusing on piecing it together. It is, after all, the story of our continent, if not our entire world. The priestess did not disclose any of your personal details other than that you are important to Silas. Therefore, you are important to us." She offers me an apologetic smile.

"Oh, thank you." I'm not exactly sure what I'm supposed to say to that. Even though I'm happy to hear that I'm important to Silas, isn't it a bit fast to declare such things to his family? "I have three kids back on Earth. My husband died almost a year ago."

She places her hand on mine. "I am sorry to hear that."

"It's okay. I'm okay now." I'm not, but the longer I'm here, the more okay I begin to feel.

"No need to hide your feelings. I too lost someone. Before River, there was another. His life was also cut short." Silver lines her eyes as she looks out at her husband.

"I'm so sorry." I can't believe she's revealing such an intimate detail to a stranger. Her attempt to find common ground with me does make me feel somewhat at ease. It's strange being around these new people who happen to be royalty and the family of the male I've very recently become entangled with.

"Oh, it is alright. I have been with River for over 160 years now."

If she's been with River for over 160 years... how did she get over her first love? They're mates, so perhaps it's different than it is for me. Wyatt still consumes so much of my mind that I'm having a hard time fully committing to coming back here. I have no idea how long it will take for me to stop feeling guilty for moving on from him. "Do you think of him often?" I whisper.

She closes her eyes and smiles softly. "I do think of him at times, but the heart knows how to heal when you let it." River scoops Noreida in his arms and throws her in the air, a belly laugh echoing from her as he catches her. The sight brings a wide grin to Estelle's face.

Silas lifts the two other small ones, Decla and Archer, under his arms. They wiggle and scream as they try to escape. "Hopefully mine will." I smile.

She turns to face me. "You know, I have known Silas for a very long time. He is a good male. I knew him before I knew River."

"Oh?" I say, surprised. I can't imagine any male meeting someone as beautiful as Estelle and not being interested in pursuing her.

"Yes. He introduced me to River. He did not know that he had found his brother's mate. I was playing the piano in a pub in Pateko after my first husband died in order to make ends meet. Silas and I were so young..." She pauses, smiling at the memory. "We were in our thirties and River was only twenty-four. Silas heard me pouring the sorrowful sounds of my soul out on the keys. He approached me and said he wanted to help get me out of the pub. He said I was too talented to be there and that he could get me an audition at the palace to play at their parties."

Oh. That definitely sounds like he was interested in her when they met. For some reason that makes me... jealous? Why? I have no reason to be. That was one 160-something years ago. And Silas, well... he's not fully mine to be jealous of. Clearly, my thoughts are written all over my face, because Estelle blushes before she chuckles under her breath.

"Oh gods, no. It was not like that. I will admit at first I thought he was flirting with me, but I soon realized he was genuinely offering. He has always looked out for every single person he has ever met as long as I have known him. Like I said, he is a good male. Anyway, it sounded like a big step up for me if I could land the gig. I was not sure if they would let me audition, being a wolf shifter and all, but that same day, Silas had me playing piano for the High King and Queen of Carimea. That is where I met River.

"I did not know he was my mate for a long time. But I had never met a more persistent male in my life. Every single party I played at, he would sit and watch me play, ignoring all of the court females begging him for a dance. It really pissed off his parents, Hearst and Cassia. They held these grand balls to find brides for their sons and River could only watch the shifter pianist. I think he knew we were destined for each other far longer than I did. I will always be grateful to Silas for bringing us together. It is funny how the stars work sometimes."

"It is funny, isn't it?"

"It is. You know, Silas has never once brought a female home with him. Sure, he has had lovers, but never once has he let them meet his family. Especially not his nieces and nephews."

My heart skips, but I shrug off the smile forming on my lips.

"Maybe it's just because he's helping me get back to Earth. You said it yourself: he can't stop himself from helping people."

"Maybe," she says, giving me a knowing glare. "But I do not believe that to be all it is."

A single drop of rain lands on my cheek as I look up at the darkening sky.

CHAPTER FORTY-THREE

Rain pours from the sky as it turns black, the looming clouds roll in, and the wind picks up around us. Drenching us.

"Everyone! Quickly, inside." River shouts at the children. We enter the palace right as a bolt of lightning cracks behind us. Servants rush up to us with towels. I push the plush green fabric against my face. A gust of wind brushes over my skin, drying me.

The children laugh.

"That tickled!" Decla says.

"Thank you. That was much quicker than using a towel." River laughs and rolls his eyes.

Silas winks. "You are welcome."

"Sorry about the weather. It is a tad unpredictable here," Estelle says, collecting the towels from the children to hand back to one of the servants.

"Oh, it's okay. I'm used to it," I say.

"Really?" River asks.

"In her world, she lives here. They call it Orlando, though. Such a funny name for a city." Silas laughs as he puts an arm around me. An intimate gesture around family, in my opinion, but neither River or Estelle give a second look at his lingering arm on my shoulders.

"Well, I don't live *here*. I live near here. It's a town called Mount Dora. It's a little further north," I tell them.

River's brows knit together in confusion. "There are no mountains near Dorolan."

I sigh. He's not wrong. I've had this conversation a million times on Earth. When we traveled, people asked where we're from, so my response is well prepared. "I know. There are a few hills, though."

River crosses his arms and purses his lips. "Your world is strange." The similarity of the two brothers makes me laugh.

Outside the wind grows louder as we enter the dimly lit palace. If it weren't raining, the small windows in the main room would still barely let in any natural light. It's safe to say this palace was built for safety from storms rather than for aesthetics.

River moves his hand and light floods the room. One of his powers must be light magic. The main entrance of the palace is magnificent. Ornate paintings of the ocean hung in golden frames decorate the foyer. The depictions of the green and blue waters contrast the limestone walls beautifully. I can almost make out tiny seashells in the limestone tiles under my feet. In each corner, the main room narrows to a hallway.

"Silas, I am worried the others will not make it back in time if the weather keeps up like this. Even if they do find this mirror, how will their pegasuses fly in this rain?" River asks as he takes a torch from a guard.

Silas narrows his gaze seriously at his brother. "The Azurite Force has flown in much worse conditions than this. They will make it. I have faith they will find the mirror."

With a crash the palace door swings open. Lightning bolts dance in the dark sky, lighting up a shadow in the doorway. The children scream, hiding behind their parents for protection. Dark hair covers the drenched figure's face as he enters the palace and closes the doors. It's only Ajax, alone, no mirror to be seen.

"No luck then?" Silas asks disappointedly.

Ajax shakes his head, drops of water falling from his long dark hair. "Negative. Before we left Pateko, Trinity gave us each a list of possible locations of Olvir's widow she and the other priestesses had narrowed down. She was not in the northern cities of the kingdom. Brynne and Knox went to the southern cities together."

Silas frowns and claps his hand on Ajax's shoulder. "It is okay. You did what you could."

My fate lies in either Brynne or Knox walking through that door with a mirror in time for the eclipse to power it, meaning there's only one more chance for me to get home. While that means that I'm possibly only a few hours away from seeing my kids again, that also means I only have a few hours left in this world. Only a few hours left with Silas.

I have to decide whether I will come back here. He said he'd wait a lifetime for me. But what if I can't get back? What if the mirror we had at the shop only worked that one time? When is the next eclipse on Earth? Does time work the same here? What if I get back to Earth and 1,000 years pass?

I shake my head of the thoughts. That can't be the case. It has to work. When I get home, I'll try to find my way back here. That's what I want to do. It's what I will do.

Estelle looks at a large wooden clock by the door. "How about we all go get ready for dinner? It is getting late and I am sure you three are starving."

"Absolutely," Silas agrees.

River, Estelle, and the children head for the hall at the back-left corner of the room. Silas leads Ajax and me through the hallway on the opposite side, first stopping at one room to let Ajax in, then leading us a little further down the hallway to another room.

He places his palm on the door and energy pulses through it, like he's lifting a magical lock. "It is warded so only I can enter. Similar to the enchantments I have on the hall to the west wing in my palace."

I never did ask him how I got into the west wing the other day.

The door swings open, revealing a large room with a fluffy bed with sage-colored linens with forest green stripes in the center. It's like a five-star hotel room. Luxurious, light-colored wood furniture fills the walls.

"My private suite." Silas holds the door open and gestures for me to enter the room. Without removing his muddy shoes, he walks inside and throws his body on the perfectly made bed. The cloud-like mattress sinks under him. I, on the other hand, unlace my boots, which are now badly worn from the snow and dirt of the campsites, and put them by the door, not wanting to make a mess on the pristine stone floor. I'm certain it wouldn't matter, though.

I carefully place my cloak on top of a long oak dresser before I sit on the edge of the bed next to him and run my hand over the cotton comforter. "Your own private suite? You must come here often."

Silas stretches his arms above his head. "I do. As often as I can, anyway, being a king of one of the five kingdoms and all."

I lie down and look up at the exposed wooden beams that support the ceiling. "You really love your nieces and nephews, don't you?"

"Like they are my own." He turns his head and I look back at him, our faces inches apart. We smile longingly at one another.

"Do you think that you'd be that way with my children? Their happiness is a factor, after all. If I come back." My breath catches at the end of my words. I can't believe I asked that. I've known this man for two weeks and I'm talking about bringing my kids to live with him. Why don't I feel more bothered by this?

"If they are anything like their mother?" He looks back up to the ceiling. "Definitely. That should not even be a question."

"You never know." Following his gaze up to the ceiling, I search for patterns in the limestone to calm my racing mind. "They aren't your children. I'm not entirely certain what your plan is."

His head snaps back toward me. "What do you mean?"

I continue looking up, not wanting to meet his gaze. "If I come back, what exactly is the plan? What are we doing? It isn't like we're dating. And it's not like I'm moving a few cities away. I would be uprooting my whole life for another world. I'm sorry—it's just a lot to think about and wrap my head around. What do you have planned for us when I get back? And what happens if it doesn't work out? Do I pack my kids up and head back to Earth? I'm not sure it will be that simple, Silas."

The air goes still. We sit in the silence for only a few heartbeats, but it feels like an eternity.

"Daphne, look at me."

Slowly, I turn my head to face him. He's going to tell me not to come back. That I'm crazy. That this was all indeed a wild fantastical dream that's coming to an end.

"This is my plan: If you choose to come back, which I am praying to the gods you will, I will court you in a more traditional sense, make you fall madly in love with me—" He pauses, chuckling. His handsome face stills to stoic seriousness. His heart thuds loudly, accelerating in the silence. "And make you my queen."

My heart skips and my palms sweat as shock washes through me. I'm not sure what I was expecting. But it wasn't that. I guess I haven't thought about it very much. And it seems like he's spent an awfully great amount of time thinking about it. He is a king, so that would be the normal course of things. But *me*? A queen? I'm just... I'm just Daphne. I'm not meant to be a queen. "And if it doesn't work out?"

"I think it will." He cups the side of my face and strokes my cheek with his thumb. "But if the moons don't align," he shrugs, "that is up to you. You will always have a home in my palace and you will be a guest of the five kingdoms. You and your children may go wherever you please. Or if you want to go back to your magicless Earth," he teases, "then we will send you back. But I do want to know if I will see you again once we send you through a mirror."

My lips form an anxious, tight smile. Think, Daphne. He deserves an answer. There is so much to think about. I've never made an impulsive decision in my life. I'm a planner. Every single thing I do is planned. But I don't have time to sit and plan or weigh the pros and cons right now. I need to make a choice. "Okay." I pause. I have to be absolutely certain of what I am about to say next. "I will *try* to come back."

A bright smile appears on Silas's face. "You will try?" he whispers.

"Yes. As long as I can figure it out by myself when I get back. We will come back. I think I can do it. I'll need to wait for an eclipse. And, hopefully, time works the same in our worlds and it's not a thousand years in the future when I get back. And I still have to figure out why Whitney has the mirror in the first place."

"What did you say her name was?"

"Whitney. Why?"

"No reason. Just curious. But you will come back to me?"

I smile and nod. Pure excitement and happiness radiate from Silas's entire being. Magic sings within my body. It's a strange tingling feeling that I've never experienced. The look across his face makes me believe he feels the same sensation. He leans over, his lips meeting mine with passion and what feels like a spark of static. We laugh and he kisses me again, strong hands pulling me closer until my body is tight against his. I reach toward the waistband of his pants when there's a knock at the door.

CHAPTER FORTY-FOUR

Silas answers the door while I remain lying on the plush bed. What we discussed has my mind racing. I can't believe it. Silas intends to make me his queen. My heart flutters and I can't help the smile that's plastered across my face. I'm really going to do this. I'm going to come back here, for good.

Every single one of the moms in my book club will be so jealous. Gabby will be so... Gabby... I forgot about Gabby. I can't believe I'm going to leave Gabby. Surely she will want this for me. She would be mad if I didn't come back here. Maybe I can get this traveling thing down and visit her.

Ajax stands outside our door, dressed in fresh clothes. I look down at my dirty shirt and pants. We got lost in conversation and changing slipped our minds.

"This better be important, Ajax," Silas says impatiently.

Ajax spots me on the bed and clears his throat uncomfortably. "The guards told me they've spotted three pegasuses descending toward the palace."

I push myself up on my elbows. It has to be Brynne and Knox. "Did they find the mirror?"

"We do not know yet. They are about to land."

"Only one way to find out." Silas looks back at me.

I get off the bed and start to put on my boots.

"No time for that. Let's go. Ajax, let River know we may be missing dinner," Silas says. My eyes widen at the command in his voice. It's startling and yet attractive. Though, I'm pretty sure I'd find anything he does attractive. His tone says I shouldn't question him, so I follow behind him back to the courtyard, barefoot.

Ajax looks at Silas incredulously as we approach the door to the courtyard. "Silas, you cannot seriously be thinking of going out there. This storm is angry. We can wait inside."

"It's only water." Silas pulls the door open.

Outside is completely black, lit only by the rapid flashes of lightning strikes across the sky. The racing winds are so harsh the rain falls sideways.

"Silas!" I shout, covering my face from the rain as I follow him out into the storm. Why doesn't he put up an air shield or something? Is his magic still too depleted to use?

Ignoring me, he pushes the hidden door in the wall open again with a single finger. I look up, squinting, trying to find them in the dark sky. The shadows of the pegasuses are only visible to my eyes once they're mere feet from us. Brynne sits tall in her saddle; Knox is... hunched over. He's probably exhausted from so much flying. I can't help but realize neither of their pegasuses carries a mirror.

"They didn't find it," I whisper.

My heart breaks knowing my chances of going home are gone. Every single drop of rain feels like it's pelting my skin, like a thousand needles. The defeat makes me begin mentally shutting down.

Knox's pegasus lets out a loud cry as she lands. Brynne jumps from her mount and races to Knox's, catching him as he nearly falls out of the saddle. That's when I see the black arrow protruding from his shoulder. *Dragon iron.* My self-pity swiftly turns into panic at the sight of blood spilling from Knox's back.

"Brynne, what happened!?" Silas shouts, rushing to support Knox's other side. Instinctively, I grab the reins of their pegasuses and lead them toward the palace. I touch the wall exactly as Silas did and the door revolves, opening to the courtyard. The rain comes down harder, colder. I wave for a guard to meet me. He grabs the reins from my hands and takes pegasuses toward the palace stables.

"On the way here we were attacked by a group of Reclaimers. I do not know how they found us. We barely got away. We did not find the mirror. I am sorry Daphne," she says as she and Silas work to move Knox inside, carefully helping him walk, making sure to not push the arrow deeper.

"Don't worry about that. Focus on Knox." The palace door is heavy against my back as I hold it open for them to get inside. Brynne and Silas lay Knox on the ornate rug in the entryway, turning him on his side. Blood pools under him, a bright crimson contrast on the pale-green rug. Brynne and Silas kneel beside him and examine the wound.

Without an ounce of hesitation, Silas pulls the arrow from Knox's shoulder and Knox groans in pain. "Stay with us, Knox," Silas shouts desperately as Knox drifts in and out of consciousness.

Brynne presses her hands to the spot over his leather jacket where blood gushes. "He is losing too much blood. Call for River's healer. My magic is too weak, still."

What she doesn't say, but I know, is that her magic is too weak from spending four days healing me. Guilt gnaws in my stomach as I watch Knox lying there on the ground, bleeding out. His eyes flutter open and closed with each labored breath.

Silas's teary eyes meet mine. "Stop that right now."

"Stop what?" I ask.

"Stop thinking what you're thinking. This is not your fault." He applies pressure on Knox's wound.

I swallow. But it is. None of them would be here right now if it wasn't for me. How did he know where my mind went?

Four guards led by a small female with fiery red hair make their way to us from the front right halls of the palace. Her round face looks somewhat familiar. She must be River's healer. Her eyes widen as she crouches down over Knox. She presses her hands to his shoulder and closes her eyes, letting her magic pulse through him.

"Get him to a bed." She pauses, waiting for the guards to move. "Go. Now. I will be right there." Her voice is surprisingly low and authoritative for her small stature. Four guards carefully lift Knox and carry him down the hallway they came from. She looks up at Silas as she wipes Knox's blood on her white apron. "I am not going to lie, it doesn't look good. But I promise I will do everything in my power for him."

Silas's face drops and his mouth forms a tight line across his face. "Thank you, Emerson."

Emerson follows the guards down the hall.

Silas looks to Brynne. "Could you tell who it was?"

Worry fills her face. "It is like they have been claiming. Prince Sterling was there." She takes a long pause. "Along with his brother. At least that is what it looked like. It was pouring and I could only see his eyes through those garments they wear. But, Silas, they were his eyes. I know I have not seen him since he was a boy, but I am sure he is the one who shot the arrow at Knox."

Silas nods, his nose and mouth twitching as he tries to conceal his anger. "I know you are right."

Feeling lost, I ask, "Who are you guys talking about?"

"The Reclaimer's Returned Prince. Five years ago, the rumors of his return started... we have not been able to confirm them. We thought we saw his father's silver dragon on the way into Tesalte, but I didn't get a good enough look to tell whether the rider was truly him. King Ameldrick had three children. Prince Sterling remained after the war and has led the Reclaimers' efforts. But his other son, the heir to the kingdom, who was chosen for his immense power from a young age... He disappeared along with his father, mother, and sister."

"It explains the storms," Brynne adds.

"What do you mean?" I ask. There is so much about this world I don't understand.

"We did not get to see his power grow, since he has not been seen since he was four years old," Silas says. "But when we were children, we were friends. The princes, princess, my siblings, and I. Remember, my father was King Ameldrick's second-in-command, so our family lived in their palace in Skaans City for a long time. We grew up together during the first seven years of my life, before my mother got sick. Sterling is the same age as Quinn. The other two are younger than I am.

"The prince exhibited powers of weather manipulation at age three, and his sister could control shadows. Together, they were expected to become an incredible force to rule over the continent, with the prince as king and the princess as his second-in-command. If this is truly him, and his power has grown..."

"Do you think with his return the Reclaimers stand a chance of taking the kingdom back from your family?" A pile of towels sits neatly folded by the door; the servants must have left them. I gather a few in my arms.

"No, I do not think so. Our forces are strong. But they will definitely try." Silas runs a bloody hand over his pants.

"If he is causing these storms, how do the Reclaimers keep finding you? What do they want?" I try to clean the blood from the floor. The cost of this rug must be astronomical. It probably cost the equivalent of my car back on Earth. They're going to have to buy a new rug. Or maybe someone can magic the blood away. That must be a thing.

"My best guess is they want me as some sort of pawn or ransom to get my father to give up the crown. I have no clue how they keep finding us. Perhaps their oracle has found a way to trace my location."

Brynne stares with bleary eyes down the hallway Emerson and Knox went through. "Cordelia was always powerful...I'm going to go help my sister." She hurries after them.

"Is Emerson really Brynne's sister?" I'm not sure if she means that literally or if all healers call each other sisters in the same way the priestesses do.

"Yes. Emerson is Brynne's half-sister. They share a mother. She was married before she found Brynne's father. They are mates, so she could not deny the bond, even though she loved Emerson's father deeply. Emerson never forgave their mother for it, so she and Brynne are not very close. That is why Brynne does not speak of her family often."

"That is so sad..." A small, ugly part of me ignored my siblings for similar reasons, so I understand why Emerson feels the way she does. Maybe Emerson will find it in herself to be there for Brynne. She needs someone after losing Syrrus... And if Knox doesn't make it —*no*.

CHAPTER FORTY-FIVE

Emerson kicked us out of the infirmary while she worked on Knox. She told us hovering wouldn't do anything. We skipped dinner. Neither of us could eat, not even if we wanted to. Not wanting to go to our room yet, Silas and I find ourselves sitting in silence in the palace library. The library is an expansive room with bookshelves carved into the interior limestone walls. The exterior walls are lined with massive, arched stained-glass windows with emerald-cushioned bench seats beneath them.

Each of the impressive works of art depict something different. Iri snores in a curled ball near my feet as I sit with my knees pressed to my chest on one of the benches, watching the rain drip down the panels of the ornate stained-glass window. Blue, purple, and yellow shards depict Threa's two moons, Iyla and Ojai. Through the thick glass, the statues in the courtyard are a blur of white masses.

Silas distracts himself by plucking a familiar, black leather-bound book off a shelf. It's too dim in the library to tell if it's the book he was reading in Sol Salnege, *Intertwined Fates*. He sits on the floor and flips to a page like he knows what he's looking for. Water from the rain drips from the strands of his dark hair. Neither of us has bothered to dry ourselves. Amaleana's words about the destruction of water echo in my mind, so I don't dare touch a book.

Normally among books is where I feel the most at ease. But with so much for me to process right now, I don't think any setting would grant me peace. I'm not getting home. I'm never going to see my kids again. I rock nervously back and forth. A few days ago, I was finally beginning to feel happy again. Everything was right on track to finding a way home. And I decided to come back here with my kids. Now, I'm trapped here and I'll never see my kids again. Not only that, Syrrus is gone and Knox is sitting on death's doorstep. And it's all my fault.

Tomorrow night when my family goes to pick me up from the airport, they'll know I'm missing. What are they going to think? What is going to happen to them? I swallow and don't allow the tears to come. Silas is going through a lot right now too. It's not fair to let him worry about me.

I need to be strong. Even if I don't make it back to today, I will make it back to them one day. Sure, I'll have some explaining to do, but nothing will stop me from seeing my children again.

Distracting myself by watching Silas for a while, I notice that his entire body is tense with worry as he flips the pages in his book. The words won't come to my mouth to ask him what he's reading. Not that I deserve to know anyway. I did this to him. I shouldn't have ever gone into Whitney's office. If I minded my business, I would be on a retreat, Syrrus would still be alive, and Knox wouldn't be in critical condition... but I also wouldn't have ever found this world. I would have never met Silas.

Stupid lose-lose situation.

He looks up at me over his pages. "Daphne, are you alright?"

I smile sadly but say nothing.

He puts the book back in its place and sits next to me. "I am sorry we did not find Olvir's mirror. We will keep trying to figure out a way to get you home. I pinky promise."

His thoughtfulness brings a smile to my face. My bare toes are cold as I curl them beneath me and switch to a cross-legged position. "But how can we?"

"What do you mean?"

"How can we keep trying to send me home when people keep getting hurt? This shouldn't have ever happened, Silas. If it wasn't for me, you all would be back in Sol Salnege doing whatever you liked, as it was before I arrived. Syrrus would be alive and Knox wouldn't be fighting for his life. You would all be happy and safe."

His eyes soften and his lips tug in a sad half smile. "Happy and safe seems boring." He takes my face in his hands. "Everything that has happened since you came here was supposed to happen, Daphne. Good and bad events are inevitable. How we handle them and how we grow from them is the fabric necessary to weave a beautiful life. A life worth living. I know you do not understand, or you do not want to. But Daphne, you are not here by accident. The stars do not make mistakes." His blue-hazel eyes meet mine. It feels like he's looking directly into my soul. His thick lashes flutter closed and he rests his forehead on mine.

A loud crack of thunder echoes through the library, rattling the walls, startling us from the moment. It's followed by dozens of lightning strikes that illuminate the courtyard, reflecting off of something into the library. With my still-damp sleeve, I wipe condensation off the window. In the courtyard, a cloaked figure pulls a cart. I squint to make out the large object that's being pulled.

A mirror.

Without saying a word to Silas, I jump to my feet, accidentally knocking Iri off the bench. She looks up at me like she's about to growl. I give her an apologetic smile before I turn and race through the palace, out into the courtyard. Limestone scrapes the bottoms of my feet as I run faster than I ever have before. Maybe my fae speed is making an appearance. Or, I'm fueled by pure adrenaline. One of the two. Probably the latter.

The deep puddles splash as I run through them to the ominous figure. Her stature tells me she's female, but all her other features are covered by her cloak. The mirror in her cart appears to be made of silver, its frame is shaped like tree branches, and on top sits a small silver dragon, holding an emerald egg.

"Are you going to invite me in?" A flash of lightning glints off a shockingly white smile from under the figure's hood.

At the palace door, Silas, Ajax, River, and Estelle stand behind me. River nods his approval.

I look back nervously to the female awaiting my invitation. "Come on in."

CHAPTER FORTY-SIX

Silas and Ajax drag the cart inside the palace. Once we're inside the main entry, the female removes her hood, revealing long tendrils of silver hair that glow like moonlight, pale wrinkled skin, and glowing red eyes.

She curves her full lips, which are painted a deep red, into an unsettling smile as she looks me up and down. Her mouth parts, revealing two razor-sharp canines, much longer than Silas's or my own. "My my, what do we have here?" She sniffs the air, her eyes turning ravenous as she exhales. "I heard the kings were looking for my husband's mirror, but I didn't realize they had found another traveler. A powerful traveler. It's been far too long since I've had the pleasure." She licks her lips.

Turning to face my friends, I catch the remnants of glares directed toward her from River and Estelle. They're both visibly uncomfortable with her presence.

She can tell I'm a traveler by the smell in the air? Trying to ignore the fact she's insinuating she wants to drink my blood, I ask, "You're Olvir's wife?"

"Indeed. My name is Myrtia."

"Okay... Myrtia... And you're a..." I look to Silas for the correct word.

"Vampire," she says bluntly. "It's okay to say it. It isn't a dirty word. We embrace the title proudly."

"I'm sorry. I've only been in this world for thirteen days. I'm not certain of all of your, um... customs. How can you tell that I'm a traveler?"

Silas and Ajax's bodies tense and they stare apprehensively at Myrtia as she shifts her body. She smiles and takes a step closer to me. "We can tell nearly everything about someone by the smell of their blood. Our senses are much sharper than our fae friends'." She looks down at the carpet beneath us, still stained with Knox's blood. "What a waste. This blood was powerful, too. Before it dried up." Something in her demeanor shifts. I can't exactly place it, but she looks... hungry.

Silas positions himself between Myrtia and me. "How did you hear we were looking for the mirror?"

"When you live as long as I have, you meet lots of people, and they tell you lots of things."

"What do you want for it?" River asks sharply.

I didn't stop to think that whoever had the mirror might want something for it, that there would be a price tag attached to it. It seems obvious now. Why would she just give something so valuable to us?

"Who said I want anything for it?" she cackles.

"Your kind does not give things away freely," Estelle snaps.

Her tone catches me off guard. The words were sharpened daggers aimed at Myrtia. Estelle herself has faced discrimination for being part shifter; to hear her be so... judgmental based on Myrtia's race is shocking. Are vampires really that bad?

"And your kind likes to assume," she spits back and her red eyes meet mine. "How badly do you want this mirror?" She twirls the ends of her silver hair between her long spindly fingers.

"Do not say anything, Daphne." Ajax places his hand on the hilt of his sword. I guess he meant it when he welcomed me to the Azurite Force.

I need this mirror. But what if I trade her something and it doesn't work? My next words have to be chosen carefully. "Before we talk about the price, what can you tell us about how to use it?"

Her eyebrows lower and a wicked grin pulls her lips tightly across her face. "Clever. I do not know very much. Olvir and I met after the five of them agreed to stop letting others use the mirrors to travel the lands and the worlds. He meant to destroy it, but I convinced him it may come in handy one day. It looks like I was right." She winks.

"They used them to travel between the kingdoms. I don't understand why a traveler would need it... unless." Her eyes flicker with excitement. She flashes another fanged smile. "Unless you don't know how to channel your power and you need to get to another world... That makes sense..." She clicks her tongue on her sharp fangs. "It explains why no one has heard of you. We vampires keep tabs on all of the travelers in this world. Your blood is oh so..." She pauses as her lips curve up tightly. "Unique. Like a fine wine. All I know is we used to be able to travel between our world and another during an eclipse."

A shudder runs through me. Did she just compare my blood to wine? "Do you know if it works?"

"I do not. I've never cared enough to try. Why would I want to go to a world without magic? And from what Olvir told me, that other world isn't too receptive of my kind."

Images of how vampires have been portrayed on Earth flash through my mind. She isn't wrong.

"Do you want my mirror or not?" She taps her foot impatiently.

Without hesitating, I step forward and answer, "Yes."

Silas grabs my hand protectively. "Daphne, wait. Name your price, Myrtia."

Myrtia begins licking the tips of her sharp fangs. "Just a drop."

"No," Silas answers firmly.

"Uh-uh-uh. Not yours. Hers." She points one long finger at me.

One drop of my blood for the mirror? What's the worst that can happen? I try to step forward. The pressure of Silas's hand tightening around mine almost hurts my wrist. "I know who you are asking about. The answer remains the same. There is no way that you would trade such a valuable item for a single drop of blood. There has to be more to it. It must be some sort of trick."

"Have you ever tasted a traveler's blood? Nothing tastes quite as... exquisite." Her hungry grin grows and a wildness creeps behind her eyes. "A single drop will keep my magic well fed for months—a very fair trade for me. Plus, the mirror is of very little use to me."

"I'm only half traveler," I admit in a whisper.

"Doesn't matter. The smell coming from you is," she inhales deeply, "fascinating. Downright delectable. Powerful. Dare I say, god-like."

My face scrunches in disgust. I wish she would stop talking about my blood like a plate of food. This is it though, my only option. My only way home. "Fine. I'll do it."

Silas snaps his head back at me. "Daphne, no. You do not know what it means. She will want to come back for more when the power runs out, especially if your blood is as potent as she says."

"Silas, it's fine. When she comes back I won't be here." I pull my hand from his grasp.

"What if you are? You are coming back still, are you not?" Silas asks.

"What?" River and Ajax ask in unison. We ignore them.

"Yes. I am. We will deal with it then if it comes to it." I meet Myrtia's hungry gaze. "One drop, we get the mirror, and then you leave."

Her smile tightens and her eyebrows raise as she licks her lips. She reaches her hand out and I take it, her hand like ice against my warm skin. "It's a deal."

A slight burning sensation singes my ankle, then suddenly red hot pain. I wince and reach for my ankle, nearly dropping to the floor. Looking for the cause, I bend and find a droplet etched into my skin in what looks like red ink. Another tattoo?

Silas steadies me as I straighten myself out. "It is a deal mark. They hurt a little more than other marks," he whispers.

"You didn't think to tell me that would happen?" I whisper scream at him.

He shrugs. "Would it have changed your mind?"

No. I lower my brows in annoyance and shake my head.

"Deal is a deal. Pay up." Her red eyes glow with anticipation.

Silas pulls a dagger from a sheath on his hip. "Ajax, River, hold her back so she does not get any ideas." Each of them holds one of Myrtia's arms back. Her face grows nearly feral. Her eyes widen and her mouth gapes. Silas takes my hand and lifts it carefully to the blade. "Hold your breath."

With the tip of the dagger, he makes a sharp poke on my fingertip. Crimson pools from the puncture and Silas brings my hand to dangle over Myrtia's wide mouth. He squeezes until a single drop of my blood falls into her mouth. She closes her mouth and moans in ecstasy.

I stumble back, my eyes widening at the sight in front of me. The signs of Myrtia's age begin to fade. Wrinkles disappear into smooth taught skin, her silver hair fills with rich auburn, and when she opens her eyes, they've turned a deep shade of brown. That's not what I was expecting. A drop of my blood did that?

A satisfied smile grows on her face. "Good luck. I hope you find your way to whatever it is you seek." She laughs maniacally as River and Ajax pull her through the palace.

Estelle and Silas watch closely until Myrtia is outside the palace doors. To break the silence that follows her piercing laughter, I clear my throat. "That was really fucking weird."

Estelle laughs. "That is the understatement of the century. If you ever bring another vampire into my palace, I am afraid I will have to kill you, my friend."

"Noted." I laugh uneasily, not sure if she's joking or not.

Silas wraps his arms around my waist and kisses my temple. "What a night."

"Do you think she killed Olvir? Drank all of his blood and…" I whisper, terrified, as I continue to stare at the closed door.

"I do not think so. He was worth far more to her alive than dead." Silas pretends to bite my neck and I shove him off of me.

My heart races at the sound of the clock by the door striking ten, playing a bright melody. After such a strange experience, it's eerily out-of-place. "What time is the eclipse?"

A frown appears on Silas's face and a glimmer of sadness hides behind his eyes. "It should start at 10:05."

My stomach twists. It's now. I have to leave now. "But I haven't said goodbye to anyone. Where's Iri?" My eyes dart in the direction of the library and then to the hallway that houses the infirmary that Brynne and Knox are in.

"Do not worry. You will be back soon enough. I will make sure Iri is taken care of." It doesn't feel right leaving without saying goodbye to her, but maybe it'll be easier for her this way.

Estelle hugs me. "It was a pleasure meeting you, Daphne. Until we meet again."

I smile and hug her back. She and I will be fast friends once I return. "Until we meet again."

"I will give you two some privacy." She gives me a soft parting smile before excusing herself to her wing of the palace.

I take Silas's hand and he squeezes mine. We walk up to the mirror, leaning against a limestone pillar. My chest tightens and tears form in my eyes. I'm not supposed to be sad leaving this place. This is what I have to do.

Silas pulls me against his chest and holds me, curling his fingers in my hair as he presses my head into his muscular shoulder. Taking a deep breath in, I let his sage and lemongrass scent fill my lungs one last time. He tilts my chin up to meet my gaze. Staring into his bright blue-hazel eyes, I try to memorize all the flecks of gold and green in them. "I will come back."

"I know you will." He kisses me deeply. The kind of kiss you give someone when you don't know when or if you'll see them again. A vibration hums through the air, almost like a cell phone. The mirror.

I pull my lips from Silas's and look at the mirror. "That's the sound I heard on Earth."

The mirror begins to glow. I take one last look at myself in this body. The body that's mine but somehow isn't entirely, not yet. I look at my pointed ears and sharp teeth, memorizing this magical version of myself. There's still so much more to learn about who I am here. How to use my magic, figuring out if I truly can travel, unlocking my fae senses. I have to find a way back to Silas. Before I landed here, I wasn't sure if I would ever be able to fall for someone again.

With one last kiss, he lets go of my hand. One more step completes the gap between myself and the mirror. "I'll see you soon." I hold my dragon pendant in my left hand.

"See you soon." A sad smile pulls at the corners of his lips.

I raise my right hand in front of me. Right as I'm about to press it to the mirror, I hear Silas's voice, so soft I almost don't hear it: "I love you, Daphne."

My head whips over my shoulder. "You what?" The vibration stops. My balance falters and my hand lands on the mirror, steading my fall.

It doesn't turn into a pool of liquid beneath my palm. It doesn't suck me through and pull me back to Earth. It's completely solid. I turn back to face the mirror. No energy pulses through the room.

No.

A scream rips through my lungs as my knees buckle out from under me. Kneeling in front of the mirror, I bang my first on the mirror. "No!" Bang. "No!" Bang. "No!"

CHAPTER FORTY-SEVEN

Strong arms lift me from the ground and hold me upright as I sob heavily. Tears stream down my face like a waterfall. As they hit the ground, they disappear, absorbing into the limestone. When I look up, we're surrounded by a dozen palace workers in their night clothes, guards with readied swords, River, Estelle, Ajax, Brynne, and all five children. My scream must have been loud enough to reach the far end of the palace.

My eyes widen at my unexpected audience. Great, just what I need: everyone to see me in utter hysterics. I have to compose myself. I wipe my face on the end of my filthy soaking-wet sleeve. I sniffle and inhale deeply as I straighten my back. My lips pull in a tight smile. I continue to blink away the tears, which won't stop no matter how much I beg them to. "Looks like I'll be staying after all."

Silas squeezes my shoulder in an attempt to comfort me. "I am so sorry, Daphne."

Estelle glares around at the gathered workers. "Get out, all of you. This is a family matter. Go busy yourself doing something else. Children, back to your rooms." They all glance around at each other before taking off in various directions. She comes up to me. "Are you sure it is not too early into the eclipse?"

I shake my head. "No, it wasn't the peak of the eclipse when I fell through. At least, I don't think so... I have no idea. None of these stupid old and wise magical beings know how to be anything but vague. I need clear instructions on how to get home and it's not like they gave me a manual."

"That would have been helpful," Ajax says with a click of his tongue. Silas glares at him.

"What about the weather?" Brynne whispers. Her face is swollen and her eyes are bloodshot from crying, her under-eyes tinted purple from exhaustion.

"What do you mean, Brynne?" Silas asks.

"Daphne, what was the weather like when you left your world?" she asks.

"It was warm..." I blink. "It was warm and sunny. There was a solar eclipse that day. Do you think the storm is affecting the mirror?"

She shrugs. "I'm not sure. Perhaps." She crosses her arms. "It is just a guess."

River rubs his chin and brings his brows together as he looks up in thought. "What she is saying makes sense. This storm is full of so much electricity, maybe the magical energy from the eclipse cannot make it through to power the mirror."

I run my tongue against the inside of my teeth and look at Silas. "What if we take the mirror out of the storm?"

His eyes widen and his eyes dart around the room. "It could work, I suppose. I am not sure."

"It is worth a shot." River suggests.

How long do eclipses last? Ariella shared so many facts about them with me over the past few weeks, I have to know something about them. Her little words echo in my mind as I picture her reading a book Whitney gave her at the kitchen table: "Mommy, did you know that the eclipse next week will only last a few minutes, but lunar eclipses last a few hours?"

I look at Silas pleadingly. "We have to go. Now."

Silas motions to the lone guard still in the room. "Go, ready the pegasuses."

Ajax looks at Silas dubiously. "Are you fucking mad?"

"Not entirely," Silas says.

Ajax's jaw drops. "You are going to ride through this storm? With Knox lying on a bed down the hall, possibly dying, after being attacked by Reclaimers a few hours ago? Not to mention we narrowly escaped a group of them on Mount Pylosum."

"Well, I am not going alone." Silas claps a hand on Ajax's shoulder. "You are coming with us."

There goes any hope of Ajax finally starting to like me.

Ajax inhales sharply and clenches his jaw. "Yes, sir."

River calls for four more guards. They appear and lift the mirror carefully out of the palace door. Knox's unsaddled pegasus pulls a small carriage behind it, just large enough for the mirror. The guards work quickly through the pelting rain, tying the mirror down tightly with rope. Iri trips over her feet as she races through the courtyard to catch up with us. I pick her up, give her a tight squeeze, and look into her big yellow eyes. "You can't come with us."

Iri tilts her head, asking me why.

"It's too dangerous." I hand her to Brynne. "Please take care of her for me."

She smiles and strokes Iri's nose. "I will make sure she is well taken care of."

Iri nips at Brynne's fingers and wrestles her way free. Silas looks over at us. "I do not think that is your call, Daph."

I look down at her shimmering white scales and innocent face. "Okay, but if anything happens, you need to fly back here. Understand?"

She nods her head as if she really does understand.

"I cannot believe you are making us do this, Silas," Ajax mumbles as he sheaths a dragon-iron sword to his back and mounts his pegasus.

Iri cradled in my arms, I turn to Lucy, who she kneels for me to climb into the saddle. "Thank you for coming, Ajax."

He nods. "Of course. Anything for you, I suppose." He rolls his eyes.

Does he hate me again, or is this the sarcasm shared between friends? He'll learn to like me when I get back, I will make sure of it. Silas settles behind me. He waves to his brother and Brynne, then puts an air shield around us. I turn back and look at him. He looks tired. Putting the shield up is taking more of his energy than it should be. The pegasuses start to run before I can tell him to take it down if it's depleting him that much, and we're airborne.

Raindrops ricochet off the opposite side of airshield's swirls of wind into the complete darkness surrounding us. Lightning flashes and I realize how incredibly reckless this is. But it's too late. We're doing this. I'm doing this. There is no fear in me—not of the lightning, not of the height. The only emotion coursing through my veins is the incomparable determination of a mother who will stop at nothing to get back to her children. Whatever it takes to get back to them, I will do it. And once I'm reunited with them, I will do everything in my power to bring us back here, to fill every single one of their days with magic.

"About what you heard," Silas says nervously behind me, pulling me from my thoughts.

"What?" I try to remember what he's talking about. So much is happening so quickly and my emotions are running high. Everything that's happened since we arrived in Dorolan feels like a blur. Then I remember what I heard. Or, at least what I thought I heard him whisper before I tried to go through the mirror. *I love you, Daphne.* That's what he said, right? A mixture of confusion and happiness fills my heart. My lips purse and half a smirk forms. "Oh, that you loveee me," I tease.

He clears his throat and I feel the rumble in his chest and his heart beating quickly against me. "Yes... um, that."

"What about it? Do you?"

"I, um, well. I did not know if I was going to see you again," he says uncomfortably.

My heart aches at the implication and my lips pull tight across my face. "So you don't."

"No, no. That's not what I'm saying," he claims defensively.

I pause, collecting my feelings. I'm not mad at him. How can I be mad that someone I've known less than two weeks isn't professing his love to me? That he isn't in love with me? He shouldn't love me. I certainly don't love him, or at least I don't think that I do. I think I will... one day... but it's only been... maybe I do love him. Or at least I think I'm falling in love with him. Whatever it is my stupid heart feels toward him, I am definitely not confident enough to go around declaring it. It makes me a little sad to think he can say something like that and take it back so easily. If he could do it with this, what else would he take back?

"Then tell me, what is it that you're trying to say?"

"Daphne." His voice is so soft and apologetic it makes my heart ache even more.

"Tell me you don't love me. It's okay. You shouldn't love me." My voice comes out a little angrier than I intended.

"I should not?" He laughs.

"No. You can't love someone you just met."

"I cannot or you do not want me to?" he presses.

"I never said that."

"Daphne, the only reason I waited until I did to tell you was to make sure my feelings didn't alter your decision to leave. I do not think you would have changed your mind, but I could not give you another thing to worry about. Or gods forbid it has any influence on you choosing to not come back. I want that to be entirely your choice.

"I was going to wait until you returned, but it did not feel right letting you leave without telling you. If you cannot figure out how to get back, I needed you to hear it at least once. I was not going to tell you that it was not true. I was simply going to explain myself and make sure you knew."

My heart skips a beat. It still doesn't make sense. "How?"

"How?"

"How can you possibly love me?"

"Do I really have to spell it out for you?"

My jaw tightens. I need to know. "Please do."

"You cannot tell me you do not feel anything toward me."

"I didn't say that. Love is so... complicated. It isn't a word I use lightly. Life isn't a fairytale where you meet a prince who sweeps you off your feet and you live happily ever after. Love takes time to grow, and is messy. It has ups and downs."

"You are right."

"I'm right?" I turn my head around in surprise.

"You are right, I am not a prince." A playful smirk meets his eyes.

"Oh gods, shut up." I smack his leg playfully and look forward.

He leans in close to my neck to whisper in my ear, "You are right, love takes time, but that does not change how I feel about you. You cannot sit here and tell me you have not felt it. The draw of you to me. And me to you."

A chill runs up my spine and there's a tug in my chest. My magic screams at me, sending a strange warm pulse of energy through me. Of course, I'm drawn to him. He saved my life and is a gods damn king, but that doesn't mean anything. My fingers tighten around the pommel anxiously. I need to control whatever my magic is doing. I don't want to accidentally travel us somewhere.

"Daphne, look at me."

I hesitate. Then slowly turn my neck as much as I can to face him.

"Do you understand what I am saying? What I have known since the moment I found you in that cave Novalora sent me to?"

A flicker of movement over Silas's shoulder catches my eye. I swallow, my breathing becomes short and quick, my eyes widen, and my jaw drops in horror. "Silas."

"Daphne? What is it?" Silas follows my gaze. "Oh gods. Ajax!"

The four dragons we saw on the way into Teslate glide closer to us. Each carries a rider in a massive iron saddle. This time, the riders' entire bodies are covered in gray fabric and chainmail, and the only skin exposed is around their eyes. Eyes that are all set on us.

"The shields are up! I do not know how they can see us!" Ajax calls.

"Fuck. Fuck," Silas mutters as he drops the air shield, reaching for his sword. Water begins pelting us. His magic must be weak.

Ajax readies a bow and pulls his arm back, firing a golden arrow through the sky, hitting the blue dragon. It lets out a roar as it falls from the sky.

"Will that kill it?" I scream. Why am I worrying about the people attacking us?

"The dragon? No." Silas answers. He made no mention of the rider on top of it. He's a Reclaimer. He's the enemy, I remind myself.

Ajax readies another bow as the red dragon sweeps in close to us, hitting Knox's pegasus with her tail, sending the mirror falling down out of the sky. I scream as I watch the mirror move rapidly closer to the ground.

"Ajax, go," Silas commands.

Ajax's nostrils flare and eyebrows narrow in frustration, but he follows the order. He presses his body flat against his pegasus as he dives at a wicked speed toward the falling mirror. Faster than I knew pegasuses were capable of flying.

"Silas. I'm so sorry," I shout as the remaining two dragons close in on either side.

"It is okay. We will be fine."

In that moment I realize no matter how reckless, impossible, and stupid this is, I do love him. I need to tell him before it's too late. "Silas, I—"

The male on the silver dragon walks effortlessly on the still wing of his dragon toward us. The rain parts as he walks, keeping him perfectly dry. My eyes don't move from him as I watch him take step after graceful step. This is the Reclaimer's Returned Prince. There is nowhere for us to go. Silas groans in pain behind me. Turning to him, I see a silver arrow sticking out of his back. Silver? What does silver do? To my right, I see the male on the green dragon with his bow still out and in position. I shriek as Silas's chest pushes forward, his body weight crushing me into me, into Iri.

"Iri, you need to fly. Go find help," I scream.

She looks up at me and I know she understands. She jumps from my lap and flies back toward Dorolan. Silas's chest moves up and down against my back. He's still breathing.

"Silas! Wake up!" I cry. "Oh gods. Oh gods."

He doesn't move. I wrap the reins around him and say a prayer to Apolynea. *Please, keep him safe.*

The male rips me from the saddle. I scream and kick, but when I look down, I realize how high up we are and my body freezes, my fear of heights returning with a vengeance. Silas slumps over the saddle, his body draped over Lucy's neck. A cry rips from my lungs as I watch Lucy look back at me before she makes a rapid but steady descent to the ground. The Returned Prince carries me across the wing of his silver dragon and shoves me into the saddle.

"Please! Don't do this. You don't want me," I plead. The male says nothing. "Silas!" I scream down toward the ground, as if somehow it would awaken him to come and save me one more time. "Silas!"

No.

I am not going down without a fight. I thrust my elbow back into the male's ribs and he groans, releasing one of his arms from around me. Taking the moment, I reach around to try to grab one of his daggers, kicking myself for not arming myself. He looks down at my hand and realizes what I'm doing. He grabs me by the shoulders and sharply twists my body. I close my eyes and clench my jaw as I cry out in pain. My shoulder throbs where he grabbed me.

I breathe deeply through the pain and open my eyes, looking for any way to escape. The male's face is inches from mine and through the slit, I'm met with a pair of familiar jade-green eyes. He moves his hand quickly over my face and the world goes dark.

CHAPTER FORTY-EIGHT

Where are you? A small voice I never heard rings through my mind. A dream. It's just a dream. Sleep calls me to return to it.

I pull the cover over my face and inhale the scent of lemon and lavender—the scent of home. The comforter feels smooth against my skin as I stretch beneath it. I blink my eyes open, expecting to see my fluffy white comforter above me. I'm startled by the velvet blanket that envelops me. When I emerge from beneath the covers, I see the black comforter has a silver dragon embroidered in the center. Where am I? My eyes widen as I look around the dimly lit room. The curved brick walls are painted a deep shade of gray. A small dark wood wardrobe sits next to a single large arched window framed with black metal.

As my vision adjusts, my eyes land on a black flag hung across the room. On it, two silver arrows are crossed in an 'X' behind a dragon's head. A small-framed female with long onyx hair sits on a chair in the corner of the room. *The glowing female.* Except now she isn't glowing and her body is not translucent. "Welcome home,

Princess." She walks over to the bed, her full hips swaying as she moves. "He will be most pleased you have finally awoken."

"Who is he? Who are you?"

She smiles, revealing sharp teeth. "My name is Cordelia. Prince Awyatheon will answer the rest of your questions." She walks out through the metal door. It locks behind her with a click.

The Prince? The Returned Prince of the Reclaimers? What could he possibly want with me? Sitting up further, I look around the room for something, anything I can use as a weapon. But the most dangerous object I can find is a pillow. If I had the strength, I guess I could smother him to death. Who am I kidding? It's not like I could ever kill anyone anyway, regardless of the method. I sigh.

The door clicks again and in walks the male who took me from Silas: the Returned Prince. He now wears all black leather and his face is free of any covering.

"No," I whisper beneath a breath. I push my back against the headboard and dig my fingers into the blanket as if it can protect me.

He looks so different here. His hair is a little longer, his body looks stronger and taller, and his face is more beautiful than I remembered. Then there are his ears. His pointed ears. But his eyes are the same.

He walks toward me wearing a devilish smile that reveals his sharp canines. He definitely didn't have those on Earth. "Hey, Daph. Miss me?"

"Wyatt?"

ACKNOWLEDGMENTS

I would like to personally extend my gratitude to every single person who listened to me talk about this book from the inklings of its conception and stuck with me to see my ideas become words printed on pages. Honestly, I have no idea how you all put up with me for so long.

Thank you to my editor, Julia Harmsworth, for working so hard on this with me and falling in love with the world as much as I have.

Thank you to my husband and children for allowing me to fully delve into this book with every fiber of my being. And my family for supporting me in this latest hyper fixation. I promise guys, I'm sticking with this one.

Shelby, thanks for holding my hand. Also, fireball.

And thank you to you, the reader, for picking up the book with the cool cover and giving me a chance. I can't wait to see you again for book two.

Made in United States
North Haven, CT
12 March 2025